SIX SAGAS OF ADVENTURE

SIX SAGAS OF ADVENTURE

translated by Ben Waggoner

Troth Publications
2014

A portion of an earlier version of *The Saga of King Gautrek* was previously published in *The Sagas of Fridthjof the Bold* (Troth Publications, 2009; ISBN 978-0557240203). An earlier version of *The Saga of Sturlaug the Hard-Working* was previously published privately by Troth Publications.
An earlier version of *The Saga of Hromund Gripsson* was previously published in e-book editions by Troth Publications.

Published by The Troth
24 Dixwell Avenue, Suite 124
New Haven, Connecticut 06511
http://www.thetroth.org/

ISBN-13: 978-1-941136-04-1

Cover emblem: A cynocephalus from the Arnstein Bible (British Library BL Harley 2799), written ca. 1172.
http://www.bl.uk/catalogues/illuminatedmanuscripts/record.asp?MSID=7862&CollID=8&NStart=2799

Troth logo designed by Kveldulf Gundarsson, drawn by 13 Labs, Chicago, Illinois

Cover design: Ben Waggoner

Typeset in Garamond 18/14/12/10/9

To my sister,
teller of sagas and tales
með alls konar strengleika

And in memory of my grandmother,
kvenna vitrust ok vænust

CONTENTS

INTRODUCTION   iv

    The Saga of King Gautrek   x

    The Saga of Hrolf Gautreksson   xiii

    The Saga of Bosi and Herraud   xvi

    The Saga of Sturlaug the Hard-Working   xx

    The Saga of Hrolf the Walker   xxiii

    The Saga of Hromund Gripsson   xxv

    Notes on Translation   xxix

THE SAGA OF KING GAUTREK   1

THE SAGA OF HROLF GAUTREKSSON   35

THE SAGA OF BOSI AND HERRAUD   109

THE SAGA OF STURLAUG THE HARD-WORKING   135

THE SAGA OF HROLF THE WALKER   169

THE SAGA OF HROMUND GRIPSSON   241

**APPENDIX: THE TALE OF GIFT-REF
    AND THE FOOLS OF THE VALLEY**   253

BIBLIOGRAPHY   268

ENDNOTES   284

INTRODUCTION

There was once a tendency for outsiders to view Iceland as a sort of cold-storage facility, where the ancient lore of the pre-Christian Germanic peoples had been perfectly preserved. Jacob Grimm had written in *Teutonic Mythology* that "we find a purer authority for the Norse religion preserved for us in the remotest corner of the North, whither it had fled as it were for more perfect safety, — namely, in Iceland."[1] The idea was taken up by others: the Victorian authority Alexander Stuart Murray wrote that, "unmeddled with by Christian priests, and disdaining the continental kings who were aping the customs of the new times, the Icelandic Norsemen preserved, for five centuries more, the pure faith of their forefathers."[2] Jessie MacGregor informed the Literary and Philosophical Society of Liverpool in 1884 that "fortunately, a pure stream of Scandinavian Mythology has welled up for us from a most unlooked-for source. . . . in Iceland—that sterile isle of the northern sea, buried as it were between lava bed and volcanic rock—the mythical poems and heroic Sagas of our forefathers have been preserved as securely as ever were the cities of the Italian plains beneath the ashes of Vesuvius."[3] And in a lecture given in 1887, William Morris described Iceland: "the rugged volcanic mass has become the casket which has preserved the records of the traditions and religion of the Gothic tribes, and collaterally of the Teutonic also."[4]

It's quite true that the written Icelandic language has changed relatively little in the past millennium. Modern Icelanders can read their sagas, at least with the spelling normalized, far more easily than most English speakers can read English texts of about the same age, such as *Sir Gawain and the Green Knight* or *Aȝenbite of Inwyt*. It's also true that by far the largest corpus of myths and legends of any Germanic-speaking people has been preserved in Iceland. For a number of reasons, generations of Icelanders wrote, copied, and studied prose and poetry containing myths, legends, and history, even into the early 20th century[5]—and some of what they copied almost certainly does go back to pre-Christian times. But to call that literary record "pure" is completely wrong.

By tradition, Iceland adopted Christianity as its official religion in the year 1000. At the time, variants of the rune writing system had been in use for centuries, and would continue to be used for centuries afterwards—but the rune alphabet had never been used to record lengthy texts. Christianity brought the Latin language and literature, the church's educational system, and manuscript culture to Iceland. In turn, literacy in Latin and exchange with the European continent gave educated Icelanders access to medieval literary culture, both Christian and secular. By the mid-13th century, the earlier "sagas of Icelanders" and "king's sagas" were being written to recount the histories of the Scandinavian royal families and the early settlers of Iceland. At the same time, clergymen at the Norwegian royal court were translating romances of Tristan and Charlemagne and King Arthur's knights. Foreign missionaries came to teach and preach in Iceland; Icelanders traveled to the Norwegian court, or went on pilgrimages to Rome or Jerusalem or other holy sites; and Icelandic priests studied in continental monasteries and universities. All of these travelers brought books of sermons, moral tales, learned treatises, classical texts, and chivalric romances with them. Presumably, they heard and told oral stories as well, whether their own adventures or tales that they had picked up. All of these influences can be traced in the sagas composed in Iceland, mingling with what must have been a strong native tradition of stories and poems.[6]

The six sagas in this book are traditionally considered *fornaldarsögur*, "legendary sagas" or "sagas of ancient times." This is not a name that medieval Icelanders used: the group was named and defined when Carl Christian Rafn published a collection of sagas under that name in 1829-30. Several others were later added to what has become a traditional *fornaldarsögur* canon of thirty-three sagas and tales. The *fornaldarsögur* are primarily set in Scandinavia (although with frequent excursions to the British Isles, continental Europe, Africa, Arabia, India, or realms not found on modern maps). Most are set in a rather nebulous past, and they deal with larger-than-life kings and heroes. Aside from that, they are a very diverse group, and there has been some controversy over whether the *fornaldarsögur* can be called a "genre", and if so, how best to define it.[7] Stephen Mitchell has proposed a working definition, which excludes some sagas in the traditional canon: *fornaldarsögur* are "Old Icelandic prose narratives based on traditional heroic themes, whose numerous fabulous episodes and motifs create an atmosphere of unreality."[8] Yet this definition still encompasses sagas in multiple literary modes. Even a single saga may switch from, say, the heroic mode to a wonder-tale, or from tragedy to comedy, or from archaic legends to the world of medieval chivalry.

It's common to divide the *fornaldarsögur* into three main types—with the caveat that many sagas blur the distinctions between types, or contain elements of more than one.[9] "Heroic legends" or *Heldensagas* contain very old material, often attested in texts in other Germanic languages; the plot encompasses several generations; the heroes are high-born and noble; and the ending is frequently tragic. *Völsunga saga*, *Hrólfs saga kraka*, and *Heiðreks saga* are clear examples: variants of the material of *Völsunga saga*, for example, appear in both *Beowulf* and the *Nibelungenlied*, as well as in other Norse sagas, Norse poems, and Viking-era art. A heroic *fornaldarsaga* often contains a sizable amount of poetry in Eddic meters, usually older than the prose; such sagas may have "grown up around" the poems.[10] "Viking sagas" or *Wikingersagas* often contain old poetry as well, but they generally lack the tragic sense of the "heroic sagas". They are generally set in or just before the historical "Viking age", and the milieu is typically "Viking", with plenty of battles on sea and land, quests for marvelous treasures, and assorted adventures leading up to a triumphant climax. *Ragnars saga loðbrókar* is perhaps the best-known "Viking saga"; the "Hrafnista saga" cycle, whose best-known member is *Örvar-Odds saga*, is also typical of the type.

The third class of *fornaldarsögur*, the "adventure tales" or *Abenteuersagas*, have neither deep legendary roots nor an especially historical setting. An "adventure tale" might have characters who are the very models of "Viking heroes", and plenty of Viking color such as dragons, dragon ships, hoards of gold, and so on—but these sagas were created after the Viking Age was a distant memory. There is generally no poetry in these sagas, or at most a few isolated stanzas (*lausavísur*), and the action spans a single generation, although the hero's father and/or sons may have supporting roles. On the other hand, there is a great proliferation of motifs from folk and fairy tales. The "adventure tale" hero may or may not be of noble birth, but he is generally either a splendid paragon of all manly virtues, or a "coal-biter" who does nothing but lounge by the fire. In either case, some danger or villainy forces the hero to set out on a quest, where he will face many foes and perils, but also get help from uncanny beings such as giants, dwarves, and/or witchy old crones. He will also make human allies (whom he often has to fight before they end up allying with him). The hero may win his first great conflict—the "first pivot"—but then have to rest and be healed, go off on a side adventure, or discover that his victory was not complete: there is still a greater deed that must be done or a greater prize to be won. These will lead him by various narrative twists and turns to the "second pivot," usually a colossal battle. The happy ending has the hero winning great wealth, a kingdom to rule, a friendly reconciliation with any surviving enemies, and a long-awaited marriage to a beautiful and wise princess.[11] The happy couple's descendants may be enumerated at length; some of these may figure in other legendary sagas, or else their lineage may be traced to a royal house of Norway or to a prominent Icelandic family. Or the saga may simply state that "many famous men are descended from them."

"Adventure tale" sagas overlap with the indigenous *riddarasögur*, "sagas of knights," composed in Iceland but inspired by Norse translations of continental chivalric romances ("translated *riddarsögur*"). In fact, a number of "adventure tale" sagas could be classified as either *fornaldarsögur* or *riddarasögur*. Such hybrid sagas, sometimes referred to simply as "romance" or "legendary fiction," may be set in ancient Scandinavia peopled with giants, dwarves, and even the pagan gods—and also feature knightly heroes, jousting and tournaments, and a generally chivalric atmosphere. Alternately, it may be set in ancient Greece or Babylon or France, and yet feature heroes with Viking names, sailing off in dragon-ships to battle giants and dragons right out of the *Eddas*. The most eclectic legendary fiction sagas draw on still more sources: medieval scholarly works, secular histories, and saints' lives.[12]

Despite the diverse materials that these "adventure tale" sagas draw on, a relatively small number of narrative patterns and themes tend to recur. The unpromising "coal-biter" who is roused to great deeds; the lady who outshines all other maidens of the Earth; the "maiden-king" who casts off the trappings of femininity and spurns all suitors; the monster who can only be killed by one magic weapon (and the fortunate appearance of said weapon in the nick of time); the helpful dwarf and the lascivious female giant; and at the end of it all, a wedding feast of roast fowl, washed down with spiced claret to the music of viols and harps—these appear in saga after saga. What Finnur Jónsson said about the indigenous *riddarasögur* could be said about most of the "adventure tale" *fornaldarsögur* as well: they are "like a kaleidoscope; every time it is shaken new configurations and patterns appear, but the component parts are the same."[13]

And yet. . . .

More than one scholar has pointed out similarities between *fornaldarsögur* and modern genres such as Bollywood films, murder mysteries, and Westerns.[14] For example, classic Western movies and television shows are set in a limited region and time period, and use a limited store of characters and scenes—the gang of masked outlaws robbing the stagecoach; the wisecracking brothel madam with a heart of gold; the lonesome cowboy with his code of honor and trusty steed; the U.S. Cavalry appearing over the hill just in time to fight off the Indians in warpaint—these have played their assigned parts in hundreds of movies and television series. Westerns do have a historical basis—the 19th-century American frontier did exist, as did Western heroes and villains from Kit Carson to Jesse James to Crazy Horse—and Westerns range from historically accurate depictions of the past to sheer fantasies. Yet despite its limitations, the Western genre was enormously popular at one time, and is still drawn on by modern filmmakers. Some patterns of the kaleidoscope simply "work better" than others. Even when turning the kaleidoscope yields lackluster results, good cinematography and strong acting can make up for less-than-novel or even less-than-coherent plots. A number of movies hybridize the Western genre with others; *Star Wars*, *Wild Wild West*, the *Road Warrior* films, and the television series *Firefly*, for example, blend Western themes and motifs with science fiction. All of these observations—the limited setting, the constant reuse of character types and motifs, the easy blending with other genres—could be said of the *fornaldarsögur*.

A final point of comparison is that some Western films and series operate within the conventions of the genre, while at the same time commenting on the genre itself, or on contemporary society. Some of these are "serious" commentaries on American militarism, racism, and ecological devastation, from *The Wild Bunch* to *Dances With Wolves* and *Django Unchained*. Other Westerns, such as *Blazing Saddles* and *Cat Ballou*, parody the Western genre itself; such parody Westerns may be quite funny, but at the same time may have serious points to make. In much the same way, the *fornaldarsögur* may be entertaining, but they were not written as purely "escapist" entertainment. Many of them comment directly on issues that were very much on the minds of their medieval Icelandic writers and listeners.[15] They provided a space in which issues and problems could be discussed and solutions envisioned. Finally, many of these sagas have humorous moments—and more than one makes a point of parodying scenes and characters from more "serious" sagas.

The six sagas in this volume form two sets connected by genealogy. *Gautreks saga* and *Hrólfs saga Gautrekssonar* cover three generations of a kingly family in Gautland, while *Bósa saga* deals with another branch of the family, although the main hero is not descended from it. The heroes of *Sturlaugs saga* and *Göngu-Hrólfs saga* are father and son, while key characters in *Hrómundar saga Gripssonar* (although, again, not the hero) are said to be descended from Gongu-Hrolf. These six sagas include some of the best *Abenteuersagas*, and some of the most popular sagas in any genre: there are currently 74 known manuscripts of *Göngu-Hrólfs saga*, while *Hrólfs saga Gautrekssonar* is preserved in 69 manuscripts at last count, squeaking past its prequel *Gautreks saga* which appears in 63 copies. Assuming that the number of surviving manuscripts accurately reflects the number that were once written and circulated, these three are among the most popular sagas of any kind. *Gautreks saga* and *Hrólfs saga Gautrekssonar* were the first sagas of any kind to be printed, at Uppsala in 1664; *Bósa saga* followed in 1666, and *Sturlaugs saga* in 1694. *Bósa saga* may well be in line for a Lifetime Achievement Award; known in a respectable forty-six manuscript copies at last count, it also has appeared in eight print editions between 1666 and 1996, and has been translated into nine languages.[16]

We have to be cautious in interpreting a saga scene as a parody, or indeed as being intended to be funny; medieval criteria for literary truth and fiction were different from our own. Medieval people saw no reason to doubt the existence of giants, dwarves, monsters, and sorcerors, and an episode that seems bizarre and comical to us might not have seemed outlandish at all to the saga's composers, copyists and readers. For example, the gradiose genealogies that open *Bósa saga*, proclaiming King Hring's descent from Odin himself, have been read as a joke that the audience would have taken as such,[17] but there is no real indication that the author or the audience would have taken them to be funny.[18] Still, I think we can safely say that a particular episode or motif is being used parodically when it subverts the meaning that it has the majority of times that it appears. Saga audiences would have known very well how a particular type of scene was "supposed to go", and a saga author could elicit shock and laughter by "yanking the rug out from under" his audience's expectations. The motif of going after one's death to Valhall, the hall of the god Odin, is found in many texts—but in almost all of them, it is a destiny meant only for warriors and kings who die in battle. When a family of stingy farmers attempts to reach Valhall by leaping off a cliff for foolish reasons, the shocking humor is clear. It's fairly common for saga manuscripts to end with a pious wish for God's blessing on the teller and the listeners, or even a short prayer[19]—but when a saga ends with a wish for blessing from a "saint" who is in fact a sorcerous, shape-shifting old crone, there's no question of the writer's intent. One useful feature of the set of sagas in this book is that readers can contrast the same motif or episode in different sagas—the "straight" stag-hunt in *Göngu-Hrólfs saga* versus the parody in *Gautreks saga*, the typical "Gravemound Battle" in *Hrómunds saga Gripssonar* versus Hrolf's visit to Hreggvid's mound in *Göngu-Hrólfs saga*, and so on.

The Saga of King Gautrek

Gautreks saga illustrates how an adventure tale might be assembled. The saga exists in two main recensions, shorter and longer; it is usually thought that the shorter version is older. The shorter version consists of the story of King Gauti and his sojourn with an outlandishly stingy family, variously called *Gauta þáttr* ("The Tale of Gauti") and/or *Dalafífla þáttr* ("The Tale of the Valley-Fools"). In some manuscripts this tale stands alone, but it is usually followed by *Gjafa-Refs þáttr* ("The Tale of Gift-Ref"), the story of how Ref won wealth, fame, and eventually marriage with the daughter of King Gauti's son Gautrek.

Both *Gauta þáttr* and *Gjafa-Refs þáttr* are light-hearted. *Gauta þáttr* in particular is probably meant to be humorous—even if the story's sense of humor is rather rough. The opening scene, in which King Gauti gets lost while hunting a stag, is a burlesque of the well-known "Guiding Beast" motif: the stag (or sometimes boar) that leads the hero to a supernatural encounter, sometimes in the Otherworld, and often with a *fée* or similar enchanted lady.[20] Several romances with episodes like this were translated into Norse,[21] and several sagas include scenes of this type that are played more or less seriously.[22] Here, King Gauti is drawn deep into the forest by the stag that he cannot catch, and in a romance, the hunt would lead him to a long adventure in the Otherworld, from which he would return reborn and transformed. In the saga, however, the hunt leads him to a strange but hardly supernatural family, and he impregnates the farmer's daughter and leaves, completely unchanged and playing almost no further part in the story.[23] Unlike the tales of Graelent, Peredur, or Lancelot, the saga's focus shifts from the male hero to the disastrous effects on his unwilling hosts. The self-sacrifices of Skafnortung's family, once interpreted as a plausible remnant of pagan practice,[24] are not considered authentic today, partly because the shorter and probably older version of the saga does not portray the suicides as religious actions.[25] Odin is the patron of kings and giver of wisdom: the idea that a family of stingy farmers could get to Valhalla by peevishly killing themselves off for foolish reasons would have been incongruous (and funny) to an Icelandic audience who knew the old myths.[26]

Gjafa-Refs þáttr is closely related to folktales in content and structure. The hero's unpromising beginnings as an "ashlad", his repetitive quest as he "trades up" each gift for something even better, and his glorious fate all are typical of folktales.[27] A version of the tale was known to Saxo Grammaticus, who mentions a King Gøtrik identified with the historical 9th-century Danish king Godefrid; his Gøtrik handsomely rewards an Icelander named Refo, after Refo plays on his desire to be more generous than other rulers.[28] There is also a family resemblance to the tale of the Icelander Audun, who buys a polar bear in Greenland, transports it to Denmark to sell it to King Svein, receives great wealth from King Svein, and then gives some of it to King Harald of Norway for an even larger reward. All three multiforms seem to draw on animal fables that had diffused into Europe from the Middle East, ultimately from the Indian collection *Pañcatantra*.[29]

Gauta þáttr and *Gjafa-Refs þáttr* are polar opposites, and were presumably written or selected in order to draw the sharpest contrast possible. *Gauta þáttr* shows how the backwoods family's miserliness, passivity, and unwillingness to engage with the wider world destroys them. In *Gjafa-Refs þáttr*, Jarl Neri's generosity with advice and diplomatic skill (if not with his personal possessions), coupled with Ref's pluck and determination, benefit them both. While the backwoods family values maintaining their stock of possessions above all else, Ref keeps giving his away, but always to gain something even greater. In fact, the shorter saga has been called, not a *fornaldarsaga*, but a *dæmisaga*—an exemplum, a tale that demonstrates a moral lesson.[30]

The later version of the saga—the basis for most editions and translations—has a very different section, sometimes called *Vikars þáttr* ("The Tale of [King] Vikar"), sandwiched between the two tales. While *Gauta þáttr* and *Gjafa-Refs þáttr* have little poetry, *Vikars þáttr* is constructed around a long autobiographical poem by the legendary hero Starkad. Such a poem, in which a hero reflects on his own life and noteworthy deeds, is called an *ævikviða*, "lifespan poem"; similar poems appear in a number of "heroic" and "Viking" *fornaldarsögur*.[31] And in sharp contrast to *Gauta þáttr* and *Gjafa-Refs þáttr*, *Vikars þáttr* is violent and tragic. Starkad is a firm friend to his liege lord King Vikar, from the day that Vikar rouses Starkad and gives him his first weapons, on through the many battles they fight—until the gods force him to sacrifice Vikar, a deed that not only costs him his foster-kinsman and greatest friend, but ruins his reputation. The only direct connection between *Vikars þáttr* and the rest of the saga is that *Vikars þáttr* introduces Jarl Neri.

Whatever its origin, *Vikars þáttr* is the only part of *Gautreks saga* that really looks like a "classic" *fornaldarsaga*. Starkad's story is told or alluded to in a number of other sagas,[32] and Starkad's sacrifice of Vikar appears in Saxo Grammaticus's *History of the Danes*, as does his monstrous birth with multiple arms (although in *Vikars þáttr*, it is a grandfather of the same name who bears the extra arms).[33] He may even make an uncredited cameo appearance in *Beowulf* as the old warrior whose speech breaks the peace between King

Ingeld's Danes and their adversaries, since he does exactly this, under his own name, in Saxo's *History*.[34] Furthermore, the description of Vikar's sacrifice matches historical accounts of pagan sacrifice by stabbing and/or hanging, from Adam of Bremen's description of hanged victims at Uppsala to the scene on the Stora Hammars I stone from Götland, Sweden, which shows a sacrificer wounding a man with a spear while another man hangs by the neck from a tree. Odin himself was said to have sacrificed himself by hanging on a tree, stabbed with a spear;[35] not only is a spear said to be his weapon and emblem, but his names in poetry include *Hangi*, "hanged one", as well as *Hangatýr* and *Hangaguð* "god of the hanged", among others.[36] Here we really do seem to have an account that is based on pre-Christian myth and practice.

What is *Víkars þáttr* doing in *Gautreks saga* in the first place? Earlier editors considered this "a pure caprice" perpetrated by a "bungler."[37] But *Víkars þáttr* actually shares themes with the other two tales, and has probably been shaped to emphasize these themes.[38] Paul Durrenberger suggested that the entire saga reflected a seismic shift in 13th-century Iceland, from a social order held together by reciprocal gift-giving among chieftains and their supporters, to one based on to the legal authority wielded by Church and State.[39] While he missed the fact that *Víkars þáttr* was probably added well after these changes had come and gone, he does show how the theme of exchange and gift-giving links all three parts of the longer saga. The backwoods family cheerfully sacrifices itself to Odin while giving nothing willingly to outsiders. Ref, their polar opposite, has nothing to do with the pagan gods, but exchanges gifts with all the kings he meets. As Odin's foster-son and Vikar's sworn brother, Starkad tries to give to both. He and Vikar maintain a warm friendship, but when Odin demands Vikar's life as repayment for his own gifts to Starkad, Starkad cannot escape the dilemma.[40] The author of the younger saga thus takes a dim view of sacrifice to the pagan gods; sacrificing to Odin is useless. On the other hand, giving to humans who will reciprocate, engaging in networks of exchange—that brings good fortune.[41]

The three parts of the younger *Gautreks saga* are linked further by recurring character types. Starkad and Ref both begin as unpromising *kolbítar*. Ref and the young Gautrek both give up a prize ox. Skafnortung and Neri are misers. Skafnortung's family and Vikar are sacrificed to Odin.[42] Jarl Neri becomes the linchpin that connects all three parts: like Starkad, he is a royal advisor who deceives his king; like the Valley-Fools, he is a miser who cannot bear to see his possessions diminish; and like Odin, he is a foster-father who cunningly advises his foster-son.[43] In fact, the author of the younger saga strengthened these links by adding themes that are not in the older saga. The younger saga emphasizes the backwoods family's stinginess, and adds that their suicide is meant as a sacrifice to Odin in hopes of reward in Valhalla—neither is found in the older saga. The younger *Gjafa-Refs þáttr* adds the scene in which Neri attempts to repay Ref by giving him a shield, but its loss makes him so miserable that Ref returns it. Ref's double generosity is then repaid with Neri's advice, which will bring him far greater reward. All in all, it seems that the younger saga was deliberately crafted as a meditation on the moral rightness of generosity and open-handed exchange with one's neighbors and peers in the wider world.

Gautreks saga has survived in 55 manuscripts ranging from the 14th to the 19th centuries.[44] The longer version is translated from the text in *Fornaldarsögur Norðurlanda*, edited by Guðni Jónsson and Bjarni Vilhjálmsson.[45] Their text is based on Rafn's original edition but was also collated with Wilhelm Ranisch's critical edition from 1900. Ranisch in turn based his text essentially on the 17th-century paper manuscript AM 590b-c 4to (Ranisch's manuscript A) but with emendations from two other manuscripts: the paper Codex Holm. 11 and the vellum AM 152 fol.[46] AM 152 is the oldest surviving manuscript of the younger redaction, dating to the first quarter of the 16th century. However, AM 590b-c has the most poetry; it contains 39 verses, including 32 verses of *Víkarsbálkr*. The other two are missing verses: Codex Holm. 11 contains only five verses of *Víkarsbálkr*, and AM 152 contains eighteen. The texts in these last two manuscripts have also been somewhat shortened.[47]

The oldest surviving manuscript of the shorter saga is AM 567 XIV g 4to, dated to around 1400; unfortunately, it is only a single page. The manuscripts that Ranisch used for the shorter saga are different enough from each other that he did not establish a single critical text.[48] I translated Ranisch's manuscript L, which he based on two nearly identical paper manuscripts, AM 194c fol. and AM 203 fol. Ranisch corrected errors in L using the allied Manuscript M (Holm. 1 fol. and ÍB 165 4to).

The Saga of Hrolf Gautreksson

Manuscript L of *Gautreks saga* concludes the saga with what is usually considered the opening of a separate saga, *Hrólfs saga Gautrekssonar*. *Hrólfs saga* might be the most eclectic of all the legendary sagas, bringing together details and motifs from other *fornaldarsögur*, chivalric romances, folktales, and learned medieval texts. Yet these disparate materials have been woven together skillfully, with vivid descriptive passages and a long and winding plot that hold the reader's interest.

Hrólfs saga is the oldest "bridal-quest romance" in Icelandic literature—
one whose entire plot is driven by a man's quest for a suitable wife. The
multilayered "bridal quest" plot of *Hrólfs saga* appears in other European
romances of the same age, and was probably inspired originally by the
legend of Tristan and Isolde, which was translated into Norse in 1226.[49]
However, even if the basic plot was borrowed, the Icelandic author used it to
create a richly developed, vivid saga. The basic bridal quest is repeated four
times: King Gautrek, his son King Hrolf, his other son Ketil, and Hrolf's
sworn brother Asmund each strive to win suitable brides for themselves.
Each quest is more difficult: King Gautrek has to fight off a jilted rival, but
King Hrolf has to fight his own would-be bride before she will submit to
him. Hrolf and Ketil have to invade Russia with an army and defeat twelve
ferocious berserks—and the bride's father's armies—before winning Ketil's
bride. Finally, Hrolf, Ketil, Asmund, Hrolf's ally and former enemy Thorir,
and Hrolf's own wife must all join forces in order to defeat the sorcerous
King of Ireland and win a bride for Asmund. This sort of plot development
wouldn't feel out of place in a video game, in which a player must defeat a
series of ever more difficult "bosses" in order to keep advancing.

Common themes link the various quests together into a very satisfying
narrative. Marianne Kalinké has pointed out that Gautrek's bridal quest sets
the tone for the rest of the saga. Ingibjorg makes a careful and reasoned
decision to marry Gautrek—thus avoiding the usual disastrous ending of
"May-December" marriages in medieval literature. Their son Hrolf will
inherit not only Gautrek's generosity, but Ingibjorg's reason and moderation,
as seen when Hrolf is given the throne ahead of his impetuous older
brother Ketil, and again when he holds back from pursuing Thornbjorg
until he feels the time is right. The slander that divides Gautrek and Hring
and almost brings them to blows foreshadows the slander that threatens
to divide Hrolf and King Ælle of England—in both cases, good sense
ultimately prevails.[50] Finally, in many episodes throughout the saga, a
woman acts as a wise counsellor, either urging caution and prudence, or else
encouraging a man to honor his ties of loyalty. Gautrek's queen Ingibjörg
and Hring's queen talk sense into their husbands when slander has brought
them almost to blows. King Eirek's queen Ingigerd has significant dreams,
interprets them correctly, and urges her husband to act honorably towards
Hrolf. Hrolf's queen Thornbjörg often counsels her husband, and is not
above reproaching him when he refuses to help his sworn brothers, while
King Halfdan's daughter reproaches her foster-father Thorir for refusing
to fight King Hrolf. Such a role may have been widespread in pre-Christian
Germanic culture; Tacitus famously states that German men respected their

women's foresight and prophetic abilities, "so they neither scorn to consult them nor slight their answers"[51]; and Old English poetry depicts queens as advising their menfolk.[52] Old Norse poems such as *Sigrdrífumál* depict women as giving wise counsel; while women in the "sagas of Icelanders" are noted for inciting their menfolk to deeds of violence, *Hrólfs saga* depicts women urging their men to make peace and act with gentleness, much more often than they urge their men to fight.[53]

The second of the bridal quests is one of the first appearances in Norse-Icelandic literature of the *meykongr* or "maiden-king." A maiden-king is a woman who rules a land and wields power in her own right, and who is not interested in marriage, primarily because it would mean giving up power. Would-be suitors are humiliated and sent packing, if not injured or killed. The hero must use all his wits and skills in order to win the hand of the maiden-king, and he may fail more than once before he succeeds. He may have to humiliate the maiden-king, sometimes raping her or otherwise treating her cruelly, before she will finally submit to marrying him. There are *meykongr* figures in a number of the *riddarasögur* and romances, and it's been suggested that the *meykongr* was imported into Icelandic literature from Continental romance. But older Norse sources are also not short of women who fight like men and reject marriage and womanly roles, usually because there is no male in the family: the goddess Skaði in the myths, Brynhild in the Völsung legend, Hervör in *Hervarar saga*, and valkyries and shieldmaidens in a variety of texts.[54] Thornbjorg in *Hrólfs saga Gautrekssonar* is very probably a composite figure, drawing on imported romances and folk tales, but also based on native traditions of shieldmaidens and woman warriors.[55]

In many sagas, the *meykongr* probably serves to express social anxiety about gender roles, a real concern in medieval Iceland. At a time when the Icelandic aristocracy was trying to consolidate power, marriage was a crucial way for families to form alliances and strengthen their political position. Men depended on women's willingness to be married off; any woman who tried to "buck the system" could have destroyed her family's position. By showing the independent, haughty *meykongr* outwitted, humiliated, and forced to agree to marriage, these sagas affirm a patriarchal social order, encouraging women to follow traditional roles.[56] That said, *Hrólfs saga Gautrekssonar* is one of a few *meykongr* sagas that subverts this purpose. Unlike most of the *meykongar*, Thorbjorg actively adopts a male social role, training with weapons, fighting quite capably, and forcing her followers to treat her as a man, even though they must know that she is biologically female. Whereas some of the *meykongar* suffer torture and rape from their suitors, Hrolf is careful to respect Thorbjorg, stopping Ketil when he has mocked her with an obscene joke. Although Thorbjorg turns to womanly pursuits such as embroidery after her defeat, she has no qualms about taking up arms once again when her husband faces danger in Ireland. This makes Thorbjorg a unique character in the sagas. By shifting readily between male and female roles, and "performing" both with skill, she demonstrates the artificial nature of the gender roles that the sagas supposedly uphold.[57]

Through all the tests that he faces, King Hrolf is consistently portrayed as an ideal ruler. Unlike his brother Ketil, he refuses to act impulsively, but he moves quickly and decisively once he has decided that the time is right, and he is careful to learn from his own and others' mistakes. At the same time, he always takes good care of his close companions, and uses his generosity and calm temper to turn enemies into friends.[58] Even the stories of Hrolf's adventures in England, which at first seem to slow the plot down, reinforce our sense of Hrolf's bravery, loyalty, and wisdom; in this, they resemble the various *þættir* inserted into the "kings' sagas", which use individual encounters and incidents to demonstrate the kings' personal qualities.[59] Torfi Tulinius points out similarities between the description of King Hrolf and descriptions of several prominent 13th-century Icelandic chieftains in *Sturlunga saga*, which were written at about the same time as *Hrólfs saga*. Even before Iceland's submission to the Norwegian crown in 1262, Icelandic chieftains had begun to internalize the values and attitudes of medieval kingship. The saga's portrayal of King Hrolf is thus a comment on a very real concern at the time it was composed: what would be an ideal king?[60]

A fragment of *Hrólfs saga Gautrekssonar* (AM 567 XIV β 4to) has been dated to the year 1300, the oldest known manuscript of a *fornaldarsaga*. Sixty-six manuscripts in all are known to have survived, the youngest dated 1898.[61] The text translated here appeared in Guðni Jónsson and Bjarni Vilhjálmsson's *Fornaldarsögur Norðurlanda*[62], which in turn was derived from Rafn and ultimately based on the 17th-century paper manuscript AM 590b-c 4to, also the source for the longer *Gautreks saga*. Lee Hollander has pointed out that many personal names and several incidents seem to be shared between this saga and the "saga of Icelanders" *Vatnsdæla saga*, and suggests that *Hrólfs saga* might have been written at the monastery of Þingeyrar, close to Vatnsdal, not long after *Vatnsdælasaga* was written in the same location.[63]

The Saga of Bosi and Herraud

Compared to the first two sagas, *Bósa saga ok Herrauðs* signals a shift in the development of "adventure tales." The hero Bosi is not of royal descent, and his vigor and sexual appetite contrast humorously with the royal, handsome, popular, but rather drab Herraud. Many sagas of all genres begin with the genealogy of the protagonists, but the grand and improbable genealogies that open the saga have been interpreted as a joke which the saga's audience would have understood right away.[64] The most obvious joke appears when Bosi briefly breaks the fourth wall, when he tells his foster-mother that he doesn't want it written in his saga that he'd accomplished anything by trickery that should be considered a sign of manhood.

The saga's view of kingship and chivalry is rather less respectful than in the preceding sagas; instead of the generous King Gautrek or the paragon King Hrolf, we get the rather irascible and small-minded King Hring. It's quite plausible that this is a wry comment on Iceland's political situation: Iceland had submitted to Norwegian rule in 1262, but by the mid-1300s, Iceland had became a nearly powerless backwater. The royal governorship of Iceland was freely auctioned off to the highest bidders, who were free to earn their investment back by imposing heavy taxes. It's not surprising that *fornaldarsögur* and *riddarasögur* from this time portray kings and heroes failing to live up to ideals of wise and honorable behavior.[65] King Hring's beloved bastard son Sjod ("Purse"), who collects the royal taxes and extorts extra money for his own profit, sounds rather like a royal official in medieval Iceland.

What's attracted the most attention are the three scenes in which Bosi seduces young women. While the *fornaldarsögur* and *riddarasögur* show concern that well-born ladies maintain their virginity until contracting a "proper" marriage, reflecting the concerns of the Icelandic aristocracy, Bosi's three paramours are of lower social standing and thus are free not only to have sex, but to enjoy it immensely.[66] Their sexual encounters are described in unusually explicit detail: the Icelandic sagas as a rule are reticent about sexual intercourse; if they mentioned it at all, they use euphemisms like "he lay down next to her" or "he turned towards her," or perhaps if the saga author was feeling especially daring, "he enjoyed himself with her" or "he laid his arm over her."[67] Anything more explicit than that is usually presented in verse, in which references to intercourse are camouflaged in complex figures of speech.[68] What saves *Bósa saga*'s sex scenes from being pornographic are the funny metaphors that Bósi and his partners use to describe what is going on—unlike the complex puns and metaphors of skaldic poetry, which obscure what is going on to all but a few, *Bósa saga*'s transparently obvious metaphors let everyone in on the joke. They seem to be derived from foreign literature: Bósi's second encounter borrows the erotic metaphor of watering a "foal" at a "well" from a French fabliau called

"*La damoisele qui ne pooit oïr parler de foutre*" ("The girl who could not bear to hear talk of fucking").[69] The other two sex scenes in *Bósa saga* use similar erotic metaphors that probably also derive from the fabliaux, although specific sources for these episodes have not been identified.[70]

Aside from the sex scenes, *Bósa saga* shows several other influences. The first part of the saga may have been influenced by traditional Russian *byliny* of Vasilij Buslajevich. Vasilij's patronymic is close to the name of Bosi's foster-mother Busla, and his wranglings with the citizens of Novgorod bear a resemblance to Bosi's conflict with King Hring and his men.[71] On the other hand, the saga, or at least its first episode, may also have drawn on the French *chanson de geste* of *Huon de Bordeaux*, or the German tale *Herzog Ernst*. In both of these, the hero is slandered to his king by a jealous counselor; after a series of hostilities, he is exiled along with a trusty companion and loyal retainers. The hero then sets out on a dangerous quest to exotic lands from which he eventually returns with great treasures won, eventually finding reconciliation with the king.[72] The French *Romance of Fergus*, which may have been a source for *Huon de Bordeaux*, is perhaps even closer: here the hero Fergus is a peasant at King Arthur's court who is sent on a quest to a Black Chapel, where he must defeat the guardian and take a magical horn and veil. On the way, Fergus stays with a woman who falls in love with him. After completing his first quest, Fergus goes out again to take a magic shield from a castle where it is guarded by a hag and a dragon; he slays the hag by cutting her hands off, causing her to lose her strength, and then kills the dragon. Later, he must kill the hag's husband and son, before finally winning his wife and her lands.[73]

Bósa saga also uses a plot device found in other sagas, the "Voyage to the North." The temple and idol of the god Jómali[74] are located in Bjarmaland; the likeliest location for Bjarmaland is on the shores of the White Sea. There is plausible documentation in several sources that Norwegians did sail around the northern tip of Norway and into the White Sea; the earliest, a late 9th-century account in Old English by a Norseman whose name is given as Ohthere, mentions hunting walruses for their ivory tusks and dealing with the *Beormas*, the same people as the *Bjarmar* in Norse sources.[75] There are other voyages to Bjarmaland described in the "king's sagas" and historical annals.[76] That said, in the world of the legendary sagas—which began to be written at roughly the time that actual voyages to the White Sea were coming to an end—Bjarmaland is the home of powerful magicians, giants, and monsters.[77] A substantial account of a Bjarmaland voyage in *Óláfs saga helga* probably inspired the "Voyage to the North" found *Bósa saga* and three other *fornaldarsögur*. A hero of humble origins is ordered to collect a valuable item from a temple in the far north. A foster-parent provides advice and aid. After various adventures, the hero finds the temple, kills its priestess and/ or other guardians, seizes the precious artifact, and destroys the temple.[78]

Finally, *Bósa saga* draws on several narrative types that are widespread in legendary sagas and that can also be seen in pagan myths. The saga's first episode, for all that it may have been influenced by Russian *byliny* or French *chansons de geste*, fits a pattern called "The Unjust Patriarch" by John McKinnell. A king or other patriarchal figure commits an injustice that brings him into conflict with his sons, but a seeress takes the sons' side against him and threatens him with a prophecy or curse. This pattern appears in episodes of *Ynglinga saga* and in *Hrólfs saga kraka*, and related stories frame the Eddic poems *Völuspá* and *Baldrs draumar*.[79] Bosi and Herraud's great fight with the monsters and ogre-priestess in the temple draws on McKinnell's "Thor pattern", with some variations. Like the god Thor in a number of his encounters with giants, Bosi has a companion, wins the help and sexual favors of a female partner on his journey, crosses a body of water to reach the lair of the ogres, and battles a strong female giant along with a male figure (the male giant in the Thor myths has presumably been replaced with the bull and vulture in *Bósa saga*). Several details of Bosi and Herraud's battle in the temple seem to draw on the related "Bear's Son" pattern, and also appear in sources as far-flung as *Grettis saga* and *Beowulf*.[80] In this case, there has probably been no direct borrowing, but widespread diffusion of a number of motifs.

The saga was popular, judging from the 43 manuscripts of it that have survived, ranging from the 15th century to 1903.[81] The version translated here is that printed in *Fornaldarsögur Norðurlanda*,[82] which in turn follows Otto Jiriczek's 1893 edition, whose text is primarily based on AM 586 4to but with corrections supplied from other parchment manuscripts.[83] In particular, the three sex scenes have been erased in AM 586, and Jiriczek restored them based on a different manuscript, AM 510 4to.[84] I have also checked the text against Sverrir Tómasson's edition of 1996, substantially the same but with a few variant readings from other manuscripts, as well as useful notes and commentary.[85] Jiriczek also published a younger recension of this saga based on paper manuscripts, the oldest of which dates from 1663. Hermann Pálsson and Paul Edwards's English translation first appeared in 1968; a slightly revised edition is currently still in print.[86] The only other English translation to date is George L. Hardiman's on-line translation (http:// tinyurl.com/bosasaga).

The Saga of Sturlaug the Hard-Working

Sturlaugs saga rivals *Hrólfs saga Gautrekssonar* in its "kaleidoscopic" eclecticism: almost every event and device in it appears elsewhere. Some characters and episodes are paralleled in other legendary sagas, or in other types of sagas. Others are drawn from myths, perhaps only half-remembered by the time the saga was composed. Still others come from chivalric tales, folk tales, or learned medieval lore. *Sturlaugs saga* has such diverse contents that it rather freely switches genres, passing from heroic romance to bridal-quest tale to slapstick comedy and back.[87]

Sturlaugs saga's quality becomes clearer when one realizes that much of the saga is parody, even more so than *Bósa saga*. The compiler of the saga took ample advantage of opportunities to spoof the conventions of heroic legend. Kings in the legendary sagas are supposed to be bold, daring, and always attentive to their honor and repute—but here we get the chicken-hearted King Harald Goldmouth. Female giants are often depicted as ugly, immodest, and none too bright, but Hornnefja takes the stereotype to one of the most ludicrous extremes in the *fornaldarsögur*. *Sturlaugs saga* also borrows motifs from better-known sagas, altering them in ways that strongly suggest a deliberate spoof: where *Völsunga saga* and *Tristrams saga* present two young and beautiful lovers who sleep together with a sword between them to preserve their chastity, *Sturlaugs saga* gives us a lascivious old crone who heads off her own lust for the young hero by putting a log between them in bed. The dialogue abounds in dry wit, often in counterpoint to the grotesque action. There's even a breaking of the fourth wall, when Sturlaug reminds his stay-at-home father that if they don't get out and about, their saga will be a short one.[88]

Sturlaugs saga is not a "bridal-quest" saga as such, but three episodes in it resemble bridal quests. In the first episode, which is reminiscent of King Gautrek's courtship in *Hrólfs saga Gautrekssonar*, King Harald Goldmouth is getting on in years when his wife dies and his counselors advise him to remarry. Unlike the wise Gautrek, who allows Ingibjorg to choose her husband, Harald acts like a berserk suitor, threatening his would-be father-in-law with death and refusing to ask Asa's consent. When a real berserk suitor turns up and demands Asa's hand, Harald is humiliated, and his attempts to get out of dueling with the berserk only put Asa out of his reach forever.[89]

The second and third bridal-quest episodes are part of a section that seems to have been added to the saga later. The second is very brief and almost an afterthought: Sighvat comes to King Dag of Russia to ask for his daughter Ingibjorg's hand on behalf of his sworn brother Aki. Dag refuses, Sturlaug invades, and the matter is resolved. The third bridal-quest-like episode is much more elaborate: Sturlaug's man Framar has sworn to marry Ingigerd, the daughter of King Ingvar of Ladoga. Ingigerd has the right to choose her own husband, and although she is not said to hate the idea of marriage, she has rejected every suitor. Framar fares no better; his attempt to press his suit is courteously turned down, apparently because he is presumptuous to think that she would marry a man of lesser rank. His attempts at subterfuge, playing on the princess's compassion, fail completely as well; it takes armed intervention by Sturlaug to finally win the princess's hand. The entire episode is strongly reminiscent of *Nítíða saga*, whose heroine is also beautiful, wise, and especially skilled at healing. Unlike Ingigerd, Nitida rules a realm in her own right, and is thus a "maiden king" figure. However, Ingigerd and Nitida both refuse all offers of marriage from men whom they judge to be of lesser stature—and, quite unusually for "maiden kings", both of them refuse courteously, without attacking or humiliating their suitors, except in response to a suitor's attack or trick.[90] More specifically, both Ingigerd and Nitida foil a suitor's attempt to disguise himself by means of a sorceror's magic,[91] and both allow a suitor to live in their household in disguise for some time, before revealing that they know perfectly well who he is.[92] The presence of all these motifs in *Sturlaugs saga* and *Nítíða saga* suggests direct influence, if not outright parody. Certainly the rather jarring ending of *Sturlaugs saga* subverts the plot of *Nítíða saga* by reverting to something much more typical of a maiden-king saga: while Nitida freely chooses a man who has won her respect, Ingigerd is forced into marriage when Sturlaug's hosts conquer her land and kill her father. (How Ingigerd feels about all this is not a subject the saga author chose to examine too closely.)[93]

The episode of the raid on the temple in Bjarmaland is descended from the more historical account in *Ólafs saga helga*, as is the account in *Bósa saga* mentioned above. This time, however, the monsters and traps in the temple have grown so egregiously monstrous that they become parodic. (To modern readers, this part may resemble an Indiana Jones movie). In *Sturlaugs saga*, the "Voyage to the North" has cross-fertilized with learned medieval lore about the monstrous races to be found at the ends of the earth. Ancient Greek authors had compiled accounts of strange peoples at the far edges of the known world: giants, cannibals, pygmies, headless men with faces on their chests, and so on. Drawing on their accounts, Pliny the Elder located a race of dog-headed men in India,[94] known as the Cynocephali. Later authorities adopted, modified, and embellished his accounts, and lists and depictions of the monstrous "Plinian races" are fairly common in medieval maps and learned texts, some of which were translated into Norse.[95] That said, the Norse lists have seemingly duplicated the dog-men; they mention the dog-headed *Cenocephali*, but also list the Hundings (*Hundingjar*, "dog-people" or "dog-descendants") as men whose chins have grown down to their chests, and who are as savage as dogs, but who are not actually said to be dog-headed.[96] The tradition that dog-headed or otherwise doglike people lived on the Baltic coast or in Russia goes back at least to the 7th or 8th century.[97] Adam of Bremen, whose work was well known in Scandinavia, mentions that Cynocephali live on the Baltic coast, adding that they speak by barking.[98] It's possible that the Hundings were ultimately borrowed from his work;[99] the fact that the Hundings' chins grow down to their chests (*var haka þeira gróin í bringuna*) might be a translator's interpretation of Adam of Bremen's statement that they "have their heads on their breasts".

Not all the pieces of *Sturlaugs saga* are put together skillfully. A few loose plotlines are left dangling (did the giantesses of Austrvík ever resolve their inheritance dispute?). Some episodes seem a little gratuitously macabre, such as the killing of Hornnefja and the death of Frosti and Mjoll. And the ending may leave us somewhat cold; even though it's fairly common for saga heroes to win an unwilling bride by force of arms, we might have been hoping for Framar to win Ingigerd's love by his wits and cleverness, not by wholesale slaughter. Perhaps for these reasons, *Sturlaugs saga* has not been the most highly esteemed saga; it was not translated into English until 1969, and has attracted relatively little critical attention. Yet it was popular enough in Iceland—forty-nine manuscripts have survived, written between about 1400 and 1896, a fairly typical number for a *fornaldarsaga*.[100]

The saga was probably composed after 1300, but the oldest surviving manuscript is dated to about 1400. This oldest manuscript, AM 335 4to, is so badly faded that Rafn's edition and most later ones have been based on AM 173 fol., a paper manuscript copied down about 1700. Guðni Jónsson and Bjarni Vilhjálmsson's text in *Fornaldarsögur Norðurlanda* is essentially a reprint of Rafn's text.[101] However, Otto Zitzelberger was able to restore the text of AM 335 from photographs made under ultraviolet light. I have based my translation on AM 173 but have checked and emended my translation using Zitzelberger's text of AM 335, which is very close to AM 173.[102] AM 335 and AM 173 both belong to the older recension of the saga, known as the A recension; this text is more loosely organized and makes frequent use of folktale and fairy tale motifs, often in triads (three suitors, three giantesses). A separate, later version, the B recension, is more tightly knit, with fewer characters, but stronger and more vivid characterization and somewhat greater literary sophistication. The B recension omits some minor characters and reduces the roles of others.[103] Zitzelberger translated both recensions into English; the only other English translation is Peter Tunstall's 2008 translation online (http://tinyurl.com/sturlaug).

The Saga of Hrolf the Walker

Göngu-Hrólfr, "Walking-Hrolf," so huge that no horse can carry him, shares his name and size with Rolf or Rollo, the Viking leader who conquered Normandy in 918. But a name is all they share: the hero of *Göngu-Hrólfs saga* is quite non-historical.[104] His saga incorporates a familiar range of borrowed motifs. The horse Dulcifal ultimately derives from Alexander's horse Bucephalus; the swallow bringing the golden hair of the maiden comes from the Tristan legend; the Otherworldly stag-hunt makes another appearance, although not parodied as in *Gautreks saga*; and plenty of motifs are shared with folktales and other legendary sagas. All of these are put together with undeniable spirit and good humor, nowhere more than in the digressions in which the author appears to step out of the story to defend his work to his audience against claims of exaggeration and unreliability. Yes, he says, the story tells of incredible events, but only fools would assume that their own limited experience is a trustworthy guide to the entire realm of possibility. If wise men of old have recorded such things, it's not nice to question their authority. And anyway, the story is only meant as simple entertainment! Such *apologiae*, as they have been called, are found in other sagas, including at the beginning of *Bósa saga* and at the end of *Hrólfs saga Gautrekssonar*, but *Göngu-Hrólfs saga* has no fewer than three: at the beginning, at the end, and in the middle of chapter 25.

Perhaps the most fun aspect of this saga is watching the character of Hrolf grow and develop. Hrolf begins as an inept and unambitious figure, rather similar to the *kólbítr* ("coal-biter") of many a saga, or the *askeladden* ("ash-lad") of Scandinavian folk tales. Passing through a series of harder and harder challenges and reversals of fate, and growing in strength, capability, and ambition, he ends up marrying a king's beautiful daughter and ruling a kingdom in his own right. Audiences must have "loved to hate" his opponent Vilhjalm, one of the most devious characters in the sagas, who switches from fawning servility to outrageous self-promotion at the drop of a hat—with just enough genuine cruelty in his makeup that we're glad to see him hanged in the end.

If the legendary sagas comment on contemporary social issues, it may not be out of line to see Vilhjalm as another satire of the royal officers that exercised authority in the 14th century and onward. Whereas the chieftains of the Icelandic Commonwealth had depended on support "from below", from their supporters, Iceland's union with the crown of Norway and later of Denmark marked a radical change in the purpose and function of the aristocracy. All power now came "from above"—from God by way of the king—and would-be nobles no longer needed the support of those who ranked below them. To maintain and advance their status, they needed to cultivate the favor of their superiors, while exploiting and punishing those on whom they once mutually depended.[105] And as was discussed for *Hrólfs saga Gautrekssonar*, Icelandic aristocrats in the 14th century were keen to consolidate their power by contracting advantageous marriages. Whether or not any specific royal official in Iceland was a model for Vilhjalm, surely there must have been officials who were servile towards their superiors, cruel towards their inferiors, and frantically eager to climb the social ladder by marrying upwards.

That said, the conflict between these two principals is mostly stage-managed by opposing supernatural forces. Without their constant presence, Hrolf and Vilhjalm would probably never have met, nor done anything worth telling a story about. As an undead mound-dweller, King Hreggvid sets the rescue of his daughter into motion by shapeshifting into a bird and dropping one of her hairs into Thorgnyr's lap. Grim Aegir, as we later find out, appears to Vilhjalm in a dream and gets him to deceive Hrolf and try to win a princess of his own. The elf-woman with the stag, and then King Hreggvid himself, counter Grim Aegir by getting Hrolf into situations where they can give him the magic items that he will need to survive and triumph.[106] Mondul the dwarf first appears as an antagonist, but once Hrolf has beaten him but spared his life, he provides magical help without which King Eirek and Grim Aegir could never be conquered. For much of the saga, Hrolf seems almost passive, accepting what happens to him, but unable or unwilling to control his destiny.

The supernatural parts of this saga can be read fairly literally, and were probably received that way by many listeners. Although the *apologiae* in this saga look like attempts to defuse skepticism of the more outlandish events in the saga, the simple existence of elves, dwarves, and sorcery was not in doubt in medieval Iceland (and has not faded away completely even in modern Iceland). But the supernatural can also be read as an allegory for the unpredictable nature of a person's fate. Every person sometimes receives strokes of luck, and at other times suffers setbacks, without necessarily doing anything to deserve either one. While these strokes of good and bad luck may not be "supernatural" in the sense of being caused magically by elves and sorcerors, they certainly may seem to appear out of nowhere. The fickleness of fate—the *Rota Fortunæ*—is of course a common theme in medieval literature in general, but it is also a common theme in old Germanic texts, from Anglo-Saxon poems like *The Fortunes of Men*, to Beowulf's reminder that *Gǣð á wyrd swá hío scel*. The question is: Given that good or bad luck can strike at any time, what should a person do about it?

Hrolf provides the right answer: Persevere, and hold to your oaths. All through his forced servitude, he never forgets his mission. After his servitude is over, when it would be easy to kill Vilhjalm, he nonetheless keeps his oath, even though he swore it under duress. Of course, this in turn sets up Vilhjalm's second betrayal, but without that, Hrolf would never get Mondul's indispensable help.[107] His generosity to Hrafn and Krak, although it seems odd at the time, will eventually bring him crucial help in his hardest fight. Even after suffering the loss of his feet and the seeming collapse of his mission, he perseveres in doing the right thing as he tries to rescue Bjorn. King Eirek, on the other hand, consciously tries to exploit the supernatural forces to gain lasting wealth and power; in the end, these are insufficient and he fails. Vilhjalm is too greedy and foolish to be anything but a pawn of the forces that are using him, and this also brings about his doom. By the time that Hreggvid and Eirek and Grim Aegir and Mondul are finished with him, however, Hrolf has fully come into manhood: he has earned worldly success, and he is able to leads a victorious army in his own right, no longer because supernatural powers are manipulating him, but because of his personal loyalty to his friend. It's a lesson that could have come from the *Hávamál*: You cannot control your fate, but it is foolish to abandon yourself to it. The best you can do is to keep your oaths and promises, to help those who have helped you, and to choose to live as long as there is any chance of living, because "many things may happen that you would think impossible."

Sixty-nine manuscripts survive of this saga, from the fifteenth century to 1883. I have translated the text published by Guðni Jónsson and Bjarni Vilhjálmsson in *Fornaldarsögur Norðurlanda*, based on the 15th-century vellum manuscript AM 152 fol. (the same text that contains the oldest surviving example of the younger recension of *Gautreks saga*). Guðni Jónsson and Bjarni Vilhjálmsson added the preface to the saga as it appears in a different manuscript, AM 589f 4to.

The Saga of Hromund Gripsson

The genealogical link between *Göngu-Hrólfs saga* and *Hrómundar saga Gripssonar* is slight. *Göngu-Hrólfs saga* claims that King Olaf (called Olaf

Liðsmannakonungr, "King of Warriors" or "King of Sailors" in other texts) is the son of Göngu-Hrólfr. *Hrómundar saga* itself makes Olaf the son of Asmund, one of the heroes of *Egils saga einhenda ok Ásmundar berserkjabani*. In any case, the hero of this saga resembles Bosi in *Bósa saga* in that he is descended from warriors, but is not a king himself. Persevering through adventures and adversity, he ends up with a royal wife and splendid descendants.

The opening episodes of *Hrómundar saga Gripssonar* are among the oldest documented saga material. *Þorgils saga ok Hafliða*, part of the great compilation known as *Sturlunga saga*, includes a famous description of a wedding feast at Reykjahólar, Iceland, in the year 1119. Guests were entertained with *dansleikar, glímur ok sagnaskemmtan*—"dancing, wrestling, and saga-entertainment":

> *Hrólfr frá Skálmarnesi sagði sögu frá Hröngviði víkíngi ok frá Ólafi Liðsmannakonungi ok haugbroti Þráins berserks ok Hrómundi Gripssyni— ok margar vísur með. En þessari sögu var skemmt Sverri konungi, ok kallaði hann slíkar lygisögur skemmtiligstar. Ok þó kunna menn at telja ættir sínar til Hrómundar Gripssonar. Þessa sögu hafði Hrólfr sjálfr saman setta.*

> Hrolf of Skalmarnes told a saga about Hrongvid the Viking and about Olaf King of Warriors, and breaking into Thrain's burial mound, and Hromund Gripsson—and many verses along with it. King Sverrir found this saga amusing, and he called such "lying sagas" the most entertaining.[108] And yet men are able to reckon their ancestry from Hromund Gripsson. Hrolf himself had put this saga together.[109]

This often-discussed passage is one of the earliest pieces of evidence for any sort of saga in Iceland. Even if the wedding account is fictionalized, a story corresponding to at least the first four chapters of the present saga must have been known when *Þorgils saga* was written in the mid-13th century.[110] Other sources confirm that Hromund Gripsson was considered an ancestor of Icelandic families; according to *Landnámabók*, he was the great-grandfather of Ingolf Arnarson, the first permanent settler in Iceland.[111] Thus, his identity and family history were part of the stock of common knowledge that saga-composers could draw on. In fact, Ingolf's sworn brother Leif, also a descendant of Hromund Gripsson, was said to have entered an underground chamber while raiding in Ireland, seized a sword from a man inside it, killed the man, and won much treasure—after which he became known as Hjörleifr, "Sword-Leif." Motifs in the legendary sagas tend to pass along genealogical lines and be repeated in the lives of successive descendants,[112] and the story of a *haugbrot* or "gravemound-breaking" may have become attached to more than one ancestor, as Ingolf's descendants passed it down.

The *Hrómundar saga Grípssonar* that we have now isn't the one described in *Þorgils saga*, which has not survived; the most obvious difference is that the wedding saga had many verses, and the existing saga has none. Instead, the story was retold in a set of *rímur* (long narrative poems) known as *Griplur*, probably in the first half of the 1400s. *Griplur* itself contains several references to characters speaking in verses; in all likelihood, its source contained verses as well, and was probably similar to whatever the *Þorgils saga* author had in mind.[113] The extant *Hrómundar saga* is similar enough to *Griplur* in its vocabulary, phrasing, and even alliteration to leave no doubt that it is a prose paraphrase. It even contains some probable errors caused by misreading a manuscript of the *rímur*.[114] This is not unusual; almost all *fornaldarsögur* in the standard corpus were turned into *rímur*, as were a number of *fornaldarsaga*-like narratives that now only survive as *rímur*. In turn, several *rímur* were retold as prose sagas.[115]

The first four chapters feature the *haugbrot*, "mound-breaking," mentioned in *Þorgils saga*. There are ancient Greek and Chinese variants of this tale type, but it flourished in medieval Iceland: aside from several canonical *fornaldarsögur* and post-classical romances, *Grettis saga Ásmundarsonar* and three other "sagas of Icelanders" contain variations on the *haugbrot*, as does *Orkneyinga saga*.[116] In a typical "Gravemound Battle" saga episode, the hero digs his way into a hollow burial mound, filled with darkness and a vile stench. He lets himself down into the mound on a rope and discovers fabulous treasures, but must wrestle the undead occupant. In the end, he cuts off the undead man's head with a sword. In several sagas, although not in *Hrómundar saga*, the hero discovers that his companions above ground have heard the noise of the fight, decided that he is dead, and abandoned him; he must then escape the mound himself. Such stories have drawn attention for their similarity with the fight between Beowulf and Grendel's mother: Beowulf also wrestles his enemy, he finds an ancient sword that he must use to deliver the coup de grâce, and his companions abandon him when they believe he's been killed. There may also have been Celtic influence on the "Gravemound Battle" tradition; an episode from the Irish *Voyage of Maelduin* is too close for coincidence.[117]

The main source for the second half of *Hrómundar saga Grípssonar* was the cycle of poems about the hero Helgi, partially preserved in the *Poetic Edda*. Helgi is loved by a valkyrie who protects him, and the couple is said to be reborn in three successive incarnations. First, he is Helgi Hjorvarðsson and she is Svava, as told in *Helgakviða Hjörvarðssonar*. Later they are reborn as Helgi Hundingsbani and Sigrún, whose lives are related in two poems, both known as *Helgakviða Hundingsbana*.[118] At the end of the poem *Helgakviða Hundingsbana II* there is this note:

> Þat var trúa í forneskju, at menn væri endrbornir, en þat er nú kölluð kerlingavilla. Helgi ok Sigrún, er kallat, at væri endrborin. Hét hann þá Helgi Haddingjaskati, en hon Kára Hálfdanardóttir, svá sem kveðit er í Káruljóðum, ok var hon valkyrja.

It was a belief in the old days that people were reborn, but that is now called old wives' tales. Helgi and Sigrun, it is said, were reborn. He was then named Helgi Haddingjaskati ["the Haddings' mighty man"], and she was called Kara Halfdan's daughter, as is told in the *Káruljóð*, and she was a valkyrie.

The *Káruljóð* or "Lay of Kara" has been lost—but Helgi Haddingjaskati's and Kara's fates are told in the second half of *Hrómundar saga*.[119]

Other aspects of the "Helgi lays" also appear in *Hrómundar saga*. Most notably, the episode in which Hagal conceals Hromund from the wicked Blind is borrowed from an episode in *Helgakviða Hundingsbana II*, in which Helgi is the one who is hidden from Blind. Since the connection between Hromund's story and Helgi Haddingjaskati's legend is made at the end of *Göngu-Hrólfs saga*, the connection must have been made before *Göngu-Hrólfs saga* was written in its present form, and after 1119 if *Þorgils saga* is accurate, or after the mid-13th century if it isn't.

Hrómundar saga Gripssonar lacks the wit and humor of the other sagas in this book. The process of transcription from the *rímur*—probably a defective manuscript of the *rímur*, at that—has added some rather perplexing errors and created a rather unevenly paced text. Nonetheless, the saga deserves better than to be dismissed as "a wretched paraphrase."[120] It is important for Icelandic literary history, as its assembly can be traced in several stages from the 12th century through the 17th. The fact that the story was retold in prose, in *rímur*, and in various ballads and other poems[121] attests to its interest for Icelandic audiences, as does the fact that 37 manuscripts have survived from the 17th to the early 20th centuries.[122] Though perhaps not the finest literature, the saga still tells a rip-snorting tale of a stalwart Viking hero battling plenty of bad guys, both human and non-human. Its undeniable brio must have entertained many generations of Icelanders on long winter nights.

The text that I used is based on the 17ᵗʰ-century paper manuscript AM 587b, and was published by Guðni Jónsson and Bjarni Vilhjálmsson in *Fornaldarsögur Norðurlanda*. Their text is fundamentally the same as Rafn's edition; no critical edition of the Norse text has been published to date. Other English translations of this saga appear in Nora Kershaw's *Stories and Ballads of the Far Past* (1921) and Bachmann and Erlingsson's *Six Old Icelandic Sagas* (1993), with another partial translation in Stitt's *Beowulf and the Bear's Son* (1992). A fourth translation by Gavin Chappell is available online at http://tinyurl.com/gripsson.

Notes on Translation

There has been a long and famous debate over to what extent the Icelandic sagas can be considered literary creations as opposed to transcripts of an oral tradition—the "bookprose versus freeprose" controversy. The question does not have a simple answer. However the sagas originated, the forms that we have today have been transmitted through writing, by people who were steeped in literary culture. That said, medieval copying was rarely intended to reproduce a text exactly, except in the case of Biblical and other sacred texts. Copyists could and did rework the stories that they copied, even adding or abridging material, giving the written texts something of the flavor of oral transmission.

Furthermore, the sagas were almost always received orally: most people received them by listening to them being recited. The collection known as *Sturlunga saga* cites several instances of *sagnaskemmtun*, "saga entertainment," in the 12ᵗʰ and 13ᵗʰ centuries, while *Íslendings þáttr sögufróða* depicts an Icelander who wins a place in King Harald's household by telling sagas. Churchmen fulminated against the reading of sagas and poems as early as the 16ᵗʰ century, joined in the 18ᵗʰ century by Enlightenment-inspired critics outraged at the common folk's low tastes—seemingly with little effect.[123] From at least the 18ᵗʰ century to the turn of the 20ᵗʰ century, the *kvöldvaka* or "evening wake" was common on Icelandic farmsteads during the winter months, featuring readings of sagas, *rímur*, and poems. The reader usually had a book at hand, but might improvise details every time, and the audience was quite free to chime in with questions and comments on the characters and the plot.[124]

The sagas in this book were copied and recopied so that they could be read aloud, and passages that seem awkward on the page could have come alive when told by a good storyteller.[125] This has guided my own attempts at translation. I have read these translations aloud several times, and have tried to create something that will work as an oral text. These sagas in particular, as befitting their hybrid origins, sometimes switch from straightforward "saga style" to a more ornate style derived from chivalric romance. I've tried to mirror this in my translation, switching between fairly plain English and a "loftier" style as needed. I've mosty maintained the paratactic syntax of saga prose, with parallel independent clauses instead of dependent clauses, but have sometimes modified the native syntax when the alternative seemed just too clunky in English.

I've usually translated names of fairly well-known places to their modern English equivalents, but transliterated more obscure names; thus *Sjóland* is Zealand and *Suðreyjar* are the Hebrides, but the lesser-known island *Þruma* is rendered *Thruma* instead of its modern name *Tromøy*. Even here I've made some exceptions that seemed like a good idea at the time. Personal names have usually been transliterated, but with a few exceptions: since *Ella* is a feminine name to most English speakers, I have turned King Ella into King Ælle, the Old English spelling of the name. For a similar reason, King Játgeirr seemed baffling, and I chose to render him by his Old English name Edgar.

My thanks go out to Sara Axtell, Thomas DeMayo, and Beth Patterson, who proofread the translations and made many helpful comments that much improved them. Any errors that remain are entirely mine. I thank Zoe Borovsky, Sean Crist, Matthew Driscoll, Silvia Hufnagel, P. S. Langeslag, Stefan Langeslag, Andy Lemons, Carsten Lyngdrup Madsen, and Jon Julius Sandal, who have created freely available electronic resources that were absolutely crucial for my work. The contributions of Dietrich Mateschitz has also proved indispensible to completing this book. The redoubtable and long-suffering Tim Purkiss was always able to hunt down sources I needed, no matter how obscure, and Chris Baty has provided inspiration and incentive for my work for years; I am deeply indebted to both. Last but not least, I thank Amanda Waggoner for her love and support, as always.

Svo gengur það til í heiminum,
að sumir hjálpa erroribus á gáng
og aðrir leitast síðan við að útryðja aftur þeim sömu erroribus.
Hafa svo hverir tveggja nokkuð að iðja.

THE SAGA OF KING GAUTREK

Gautreks saga

CHAPTER I

Here we begin a jolly tale of a king named Gauti. He was a wise and well-mannered man, generous and outspoken. He ruled over West Gautland. That country lies between Norway and Sweden, east of the Kjolen Mountains, and the Gota Alv River divides Gautland from Uppland. There are great forests there, and traveling through them is hard when the ground has thawed. This king whom we have mentioned often went to the forests with his hawks and hounds, for he was the keenest hunter and found that the best sport.

At that time, there were widely scattered settlements with vast forests standing all around, because many men had cleared the forest and built homesteads far away from the settled lands—men who had gone off the beaten path on account of some misdeed of theirs. Some left because of some quirk, or went off on a sort of escapade, thinking that they would be less mocked or scorned if they were far away from the ridicule of others. They lived out all their lives without ever meeting other people, except for those who lived nearby. Many had sought out places for themselves far from the roads, and so no one came to visit them—except it occasionally happened that people who got lost in the forest stumbled on their households, although they would never have come there willingly.

This King Gauti, whom we have just mentioned, had gone with his household and his best hounds to hunt wild animals in the forest. The king managed to spot a beautiful stag, and he was eager to hunt that very beast. He turned his hounds loose and pursued that animal hotly, as day turned to night. By that time he was all alone, and had gone so far into the forest that he knew he couldn't reach his own men, because of the dark night and the long distance which he had traveled all that day. What's more, he had thrown his spear at the stag, and it had stuck fast in the wound. The king by no means wanted to leave that behind, if he could get it; he felt it would be shameful if he failed to recover his own weapon. He had rushed forward so eagerly that he had flung off all his clothes except for his linen underwear;

he was barefoot and missing his shoes, and stones and brush had torn his legs and the soles of his feet. He hadn't caught the stag. Darkness was coming on, so that he couldn't tell what direction was going in. He held still and listened, in hopes of hearing something. He had been still for only a little while before he heard a dog barking, and he headed in that direction, because he reckoned that people would most probably be there.[1]

Then the king saw a small farm. He saw a man standing outside, holding a timber axe. As soon as the man saw that the king was making for the farm, he rushed at the dog and killed it and said, "You won't show guests the way to our home any longer, for I can clearly see that that man is so huge that he'll eat up everything the farmer owns, if he comes within these walls here. That will never happen, if I have anything to say about it."

The king heard his words and smiled at them. He thought to himself that he was hardly prepared to sleep outdoors, but he wasn't sure he'd be welcomed if he were to wait for an invitation. Boldly, he walked towards the doors. The other man got in front of the doors and didn't want to let him in. The king let the man who was blocking him feel his superior strength and shoved him away from the doors.

The king went into the living room. There were four men and four women before him. There was no greeting for King Gauti, but he sat down, all the same. The man who looked most likely to be the head of the household spoke up, and he said, "Why did you let this man come inside?"

The slave who had stood in the doorway answered, "This man was so strong that I didn't have the strength to resist him."

"And what did you do when the dog barked?"

The slave answered, "I killed the dog, because I didn't want him showing any more ruffians like this the way to the farm."

The farmer said, "You're a faithful servant, and even though these awkward things have happened, you can't be blamed. It's hard to reward you as you deserve for your thoughtfulness. I will give you your reward in the morning, and you shall go with me."

The buildings were well built, and the people were handsome and tall in proportion. The king found that they were afraid of him. The farmer had the table set, and food was brought in. When the king saw that food wasn't being offered to him, he sat down at the table next to the farmer, picked up food and brazenly fell to eating. When the farmer saw that, he stopped eating and pulled his hat down over his eyes. Neither one spoke to the other. When the king had eaten, the farmer raised his hat and ordered the dishes to be taken away from the table—"since there's no food to keep now." Then the people went off to bed.

The king lay down to sleep as well. And when he had lain down for a little while, a woman came to him and said, "Wouldn't it be a better idea for you to accept a favor from me?"

The king answered, "Things are looking up, now that you want to talk with me, because this household's a gloomy one."

"There's no need to be surprised at that, because we've never had a guest in all our lives, and I suppose that the farmer doesn't find you a welcome guest."

The king said, "When I return home, I can reward the farmer well, for all the trouble he's taken on my behalf."

She replied, "I think this accident will bring us more than honors from you."

The king said, "I'd like you to tell me what your family's names are."

She answered, "My father is named Skafnortung. He's called that because he is so stingy with his resources that he can't bear to watch his food disappear, or anything else that he owns.[2] My mother's name is Totra. She has that name because she never wants to own any clothes except those which have already been ripped and made into rags. She feels that this is remarkably good sense."[3]

The king asked, "What are your brothers' names?"

She answered, "One is named Fjolmod,[4] the second is Imsigull,[5] and the third is Gilling.[6]"

The king said, "What are your and your sisters' names?"

She answered, "My name is Snotra. I have that name because I'm the wisest of us all.[7] My sisters are called Hjotra and Fjotra.[8] There's a rock crag here, next to our farm, called Gilling's Crag.[9] Right there on one side is a cliff that we call Family Cliff. It's such a high, sheer cliff that any living thing loses its life if it falls off. It's called Family Cliff because we reduce our family size with it, as soon as anything dreadful happens to us. All our kinfolk die there, without suffering from any illness, and then they go to Odin. Our elders don't have to be a burden or an obstacle to us, because this blissful place is equally free to all our kin. We don't need to live in poverty or hunger, nor to put up with any other strange occurrences or disasters that may happen. You should know that my father finds it the strangest thing that you've come to our house. It would be a great wonder if a commoner had eaten food here, but it's unbelievable that a king, frozen and without clothes, should come to our house, because nothing like this has ever happened before. That's why my father and mother have decided to divide the inheritance among us brothers and sisters in the morning, but they want to take the slave with them and go over Family Cliff, and so go to

Valhalla.[10] Since our slave tried to drive you from the doors, my father wants to reward him for his good will with nothing less than enjoying this blessing along with him. He's certain that Odin would never receive the slave unless he were in my father's retinue."[11]

The king said, "I see that you're the most well-spoken one here, and I'll place my trust in you. I know that you must be a virgin, and you must sleep with me tonight."

She said that it was up to the king.

In the morning, when the king was awake, he said, "I have to ask you for a favor, Skafnortung. I came to your farm barefoot, so I'd like to get shoes from you."

He didn't answer, but he gave him shoes and pulled out the laces.[12] The king said,

> A set of shoes
> Skafnortung gave me,
> but then he took the thongs.
> You won't get gifts
> without guile, I say,
> from any man so mean.

Then the king left, and Snotra showed him the road. The king said, "I'd like to invite you to come with me, because I suspect that something will come of our encounter. If you're pregnant with a boy, have him named Gautrek. Take his name from my name, plus the wreck I've made of your household."[13]

She answered, "I do believe you've guessed right. But I can't come with you right now. Today my brothers and sisters have to divide up the inheritance from our father and mother, who intend to go over Family Cliff."

The king wished her a happy life, and invited her to come meet him whenever she felt the time was right. Then the king traveled until he reached his own men, and he rested quietly.

CHAPTER II

Now it's time to tell how Snotra's father was sitting over his wealth when she entered the house. He said, "A terrible calamity has befallen us: that king has come to our homestead and eaten up many of our belongings right before our eyes—and the ones that we were least willing to give up. I can't see how we can maintain all our family, thanks to this ruination. So

I've put together everything I own, and I intend to divide the inheritance with you my sons, but for me and my wife and slave to go to Valhalla. I can't reward the slave any better for his trustiness than to have him go with me. Gilling and his sister Snotra shall have my fine ox. Fjolmod and his sister Hjotra shall have my bars of gold. Imsigull and his sister Fjotra shall have all the grain and fields. But I beg you, my children, not to increase your numbers, because you won't be able to hold onto my inheritance that way."

When Skafnortung had said what he wanted to say, they all went up onto Gilling's Crag. The children led their father and mother over Family Cliff, and they went gladly and cheerfully to Odin.

Now that the brothers and sisters were in charge of the farm, they thought they needed to set their affairs right. They took sticks and pinned homespun cloth around themselves, so that none of them could touch another's bare skin. They thought this would be the trustiest way to ensure that their numbers wouldn't increase.[14]

Snotra found that she was pregnant. She shifted the pins in the homespun cloth so that she could be touched by hand. She pretended to be sleeping, and as Gilling was waking up and stirring, he flung out his hand towards her and touched her cheek. And when he was awake, he said, "Something awkward's happened here. I must have done you harm. It looks to me as if you're much fatter than you were."

She answered, "Keep this a secret, as best you can."

He answered, "I'll do no such thing—once our numbers increase, there's no way to hide it."

A little later, Snotra gave birth to a handsome boy, and named him Gautrek. Gilling said, "A dreadful calamity has happened, and there's no hiding it now. I must go tell my brothers." They said, "Now all our plans will come to nothing, thanks to this disaster that's struck. This is a serious violation of the rules." Gilling said,

> How stupid of me
> to stir my hand
> and feel that woman's face.
> Siring sons, I'd say,
> is a simple matter;
> that's how Gautrek was begotten.

They said that he wasn't to blame, since he'd repented and never wanted this to happen. He said that he was quite eager to go over Family Cliff, and added that it would be counted as a lesser calamity. They asked him to wait for what else might happen.

Fjolmod brooded over his wealth all day, and carried his bars of gold with him wherever he went. One day he was sleeping, and he awoke to see that two black snails had crawled over his gold bars. It looked to him like there were dents where they'd smeared dark slime on the gold, and he felt that his treasure had shrunk badly. He said, "This loss of money is a terrible thing, and if it happens again, it'll be no good going to Odin penniless. I will go over Family Cliff and not have to suffer this poverty any more, because my affairs have never looked so bleak since my father shared out his wealth with me."

He told his brothers of the calamity that had struck, and asked them to share out his inheritance. Then he said,

> Stumpy snails
> ate stone before my eyes,
> now everything's all wrong;
> I must mope,
> my money's all gone,
> since snails have shaved my gold.

Then he and his wife went to Gilling's Crag and went right over Family Cliff.

One day, Imsigul was walking through his fields. Right before his eyes, he saw the bird that's called a sparrow; it's about the size of a titmouse. He feared that matters had taken a turn for the worse. He went through the fields and saw that the bird had taken one seed from an ear of grain. Then he said,

> It was spoilage
> that the sparrow wreaked
> in Imsigul's acres.
> Stricken was an ear,
> stolen was a grain:
> that will trouble Totra's kin forever.

He and his wife left at once, and they gladly went over Family Cliff. They didn't want to suffer such losses any longer.

When Gautrek was seven years old, he was outside and saw the fine ox. As it happened, he stabbed the ox with a spear and killed it. And when Gilling saw that, he said,

7

The young lad struck down
the steer before my eyes,
these are baleful forebodings.
Never again
will I get such a jolly
treasure, as long as I live.

He said, "Now this is just unbearable." Then he went to Gilling's Crag and went right over Family Cliff.

Two people were left, Snotra and her son Gautrek. She readied herself and her son for a journey. They traveled until they found King Gauti, and he welcomed his son warmly. He was raised there in his father's household, and soon grew to manhood.[15]

Several years passed, until Gautrek had fully come of age. Then it happened that King Gauti fell ill, and he summoned his friends. The king said, "You have been faithful and obedient to me in everything, but now I think it's quite likely that this sickness I have will sever our friendship. I want to give this kingdom which I have owned to my son Gautrek, and the title of king along with it."

They were pleased with this. After King Gauti had breathed his last, Gautrek was raised to kingship over Gautland, and he is mentioned in a great many of the old sagas.

Now this saga turns to Norway for a while, and tells of the shire-kings who lived there at that time, and about their descendants. Later, this saga will return to Gautland, to King Gautrek and his son. The story is told in the same way throughout Sweden and more far-flung places.

CHAPTER III

Hunthjof was the name of a king who ruled over Hordaland. He was the son of Fridthjof the Bold and Ingibjorg the Fair.[16] He had three sons. Herthjof was the name of one of his sons, who later became king of Hordaland. Another was named Geirthjof, king of Uppland; and the third was Fridthjof, king of Telemark. These men were all mighty kings and great warriors, but King Herthjof stood above them in wisdom and shrewdness. He was away on raids for a long time, and from this he became very famous.

At that time, there was a king in Agder named Harald, a mighty king. He was called Harald the Agder-King. His son was named Vikar; he was young and promising at the time.[17]

There was a man named Storvirk, son of Starkad Ala-Warrior. Starkad was a cunning giant. He kidnapped Alfhild, the daughter of King Alf, from Alfheim.[18] King Alf called on Thor, so that Alfhild might return. Thor killed Starkad and brought Alfhild home to her father, but she was with child. [19] She gave birth to her son, who was named Storvirk, as mentioned earlier. He was a handsome man despite his dark hair, bigger and stronger than other men. He was a great raider. He came to the household of King Harald of Agder, and took charge of his lands' defenses. King Harald gave him the island in Agder called Thruma,[20] and there Storvirk lived. He was away on raids for a long time, but at other times he stayed with king Harald.

Storvirk kidnapped Unni, the daughter of Jarl Freki of Halogaland, and then went home to his estate in Thruma. They had a son named Starkad. Fjori and Fyri, the sons of Jarl Freki, pursued Storvirk and secretly came to his house at night with a host. They burned the house with Storvirk inside it, along with their sister Unni and all the men there, because they didn't dare open the door, fearing that Storvirk would escape. They sailed away by night and headed northwards along the coast. On the second day after their departure, a storm blew up. They sailed right into submerged rocks off Stad,[21] and all hands were lost.

Starkad, the son of Storvirk, was young when his father perished, and King Harald fostered him in his own household. So said Starkad about that:

> I was a boy, when
> there burned indoors
> full many seafarers,
> my father among them;
> beside the shore
> he sleeps on Thruma,
> the hardy hero
> of Harald Agder-King.

> The ring-breaker° was burned
> by his brothers-in-law,
> Fjori and Fyri,
> Freki's heirs,
> the brothers of Unni,
> my own mother.

ring-breaker: generous man

9

CHAPTER IV

Herthjof the king of Hordaland and his forces moved against King Harald at night and in secret. Herthjof killed him treacherously, but took his son Vikar as a hostage. King Herthjof subjugated all the realm that King Harald had held, and he forcibly took the sons of many powerful men as hostages, and claimed tribute from all the kingdom.

Grani was the name of a mighty man in King Herthjof's forces. He was called Horsehair-Grani. He lived on the island in Hordaland called Fenhring, at the estate called Ask.[22] He claimed Starkad Storvirksson and brought him to Fenhring. Starkad was three years old then, and he stayed on Fenhring with Horsehair-Grani for nine years. So says Starkad:

> When Herthjof
> had dealt with Harald,
> betrayed his trust
> through treachery,
> Agder's prince
> he deprived of breath;
> he bound his sons
> in bonds and fetters.

> Three winters old,
> I was taken
> to Hordaland
> by Horsehair-Grani;
> at Ask I began
> to grow in stature;
> for nine winters
> I knew no kinsman.

King Herthjof was a mighty warrior and traveled away on raids for a long time, and there was a great risk that his kingdom would then be invaded. He had beacons built on mountains, and he set men to tend them and to set them aflame if hostilities were to break out. Vikar and two other men tended the beacon on Fenhring. They had to light the first beacon if an invading host was sighted, and then each would be lit from the next one.

When Vikar had been tending the beacon for a short while, he went to Ask one morning and met his foster-brother Starkad Storvirkson. Starkad was incredibly large. He was a laggard and a coal-biter[23] and lay on the floor

beside the fire. At the time he was twelve years old. Vikar picked him up
off the floor and gave him weapons and clothes and measured his size,
because he thought that Starkad had grown amazingly tall since coming to
Ask. Starkad and Vikar then got a ship for themselves and sailed away at
once. So said Starkad:

> I gained strength
> in my growing arms,
> got lanky legs
> and a loathsome head,
> as I sat daydreaming
> down on the floor,
> an idle one,
> unaware of much.
>
> Until Vikar came
> from tending the beacon,
> Herthjof's hostage,
> the hall he entered;
> at our meeting
> he commanded me
> to stand up straight
> and speak to him.
>
> He measured my size
> with the span of his hands,
> reckoned my arms' reach
> to the wrist-joints.
> My hair had grown,
> hanging from my chin.

Here Starkad mentions that he had a beard when he was twelve.

Then Starkad got up, and Vikar gave him weapons and clothes, and
they went to the ship. After that, Vikar summoned warriors, twelve men all
together. They were all champion fighters, skilled at single combat. So said
Starkad:

> Then Harald's heir
> called Hildigrim
> and sent summons
> to Sorkvir and Grettir,

Erp and Ulf,
An and Skuma,
Hroi and Hrotti
Herbrand's sons,

Styr and Steinthor
from Stad in the north;
old Gunnolf Blaze
was also there.
Thirteen warriors
we were in all;
seldom was seen
a more splendid band.

Then King Vikar went with his men to face King Herthjof. When King Herthjof heard about this threat, he had his own men prepare themselves. King Herthjof had a great farmhouse, so well fortified that it was almost a castle or fort. There were more than seventy fighting men, not counting all the workers and servants. But as soon as the raiders came, they made such a fierce attack that they rattled the gates and doors, and they hacked at the door-posts so that the latches and bolts on the inside of the gates gave way. The king's men fell back, and the raiders forced their way inside. Then a great battle broke out. So says Starkad:

So we came
to the king's fort.
We shook the gates,
we smashed door-posts,
we broke the bars,
we brandished swords.
On the king's side
there stood against us
seventy heroes
of high degree.
All the thralls
were there as well,
working men
and water-carriers.

King Herthjof and his men defended themselves for a long time, because he had many brave men, but since Vikar had picked excellent champions for his own forces, King Herthjof's men grew fewer as they faced them. Vikar was always in the forefront of his men. So said Starkad:

> To stand beside Vikar
> was in vain to try,
> for first and foremost
> of fighters he stood;
> we hewed helmets
> and heads' crowns,
> we slashed mailcoats
> and splintered shields.

Starkad and Vikar together attacked King Herthjof furiously, and they dealt death to him. All of Vikar's champions attacked fiercely. Many men fell there, and some were wounded. So said Starkad:

> For King Vikar,
> victory was fated,
> but deadly strife
> ordained for Herthjof.
> We struck soldiers,
> and some we killed;
> I wasn't far from
> the fall of the king.

Vikar won a victory there, but King Herthjof fell, as was said before, along with thirty men. Many were fatally wounded. But none of Vikar's men fell.

Afterwards, Vikar took all the ships that King Herthjof had owned, and all the forces which he had assembled. Then he moved eastward along the coast with every man who would follow him. And when he reached Agder, those who had been friends of his father came over to him. Soon he had gathered a great following. Then he was raised to the kingship over all Agder and Jaeren, and he laid Hordaland and Hardanger under his rule, along with all the kingdom that King Herthjof had held. King Vikar soon grew powerful, and he was the greatest warrior. He went raiding every summer.

King Vikar traveled eastward into the Oslofjord with his host, and landed on the east side of the fjord. He raided all the way to Gautland

13

and accomplished many brave deeds there. But when he came up to Lake Vänern, a king named Sisar came against him. He came from Kiev in the east. He was a mighty champion and had large forces. King Vikar and Sisar fought a furious battle there, and Sisar advanced fiercely and killed many men in King Vikar's ranks.

Starkad was there with King Vikar. He went up against Sisar, and they traded blows for a long time. Neither one had any cause to doubt the strength of the other's blows. Sisar knocked Starkad's shield away, gave him two great wounds in his head with his sword, and broke his collarbone. Starkad was also wounded in his side above the hip. So says Starkad:

> You weren't with Vikar
> on Vaenir lake
> off in the east,
> early that day,
> when we sought Sisar
> on the slaughter-field,
> a more strenuous deed
> than it seems to you.

> He let his blade,
> bitterly sharp,
> smash through my shield
> and sorely wound me,
> slicing helm from head
> and hitting my skull,
> my cheek and jaw
> he chopped to the molars,
> leaving broken
> my left collarbone.

Starkad also took a deep wound in his other side from the bladed spear that Sisar fought with. So said Starkad:

> And in my side,
> the stalwart man
> bit with his blade
> above my hip.
> My other side
> he stabbed with his lance,

14

the icy point
plunged deeply.
Men still may see
my scars, now healed.

Starkad struck Sisar with his sword and sliced through his side, and he gave
him a terrible wound in his leg below the knee. Finally, he cut off his other
foot at the ankle, and King Sisar fell. So says Starkad:

On his other side
I sliced him up,
broke his body
with bitter edge;
I swung my sword
in the struggle's heat,
all my power
I put forth there.

Both sides suffered grievous losses in the battle, but King Vikar won
victory, and the Kievans turned and fled—those who survived. After this
victory, Vikar went home to his kingdom.

CHAPTER V

King Vikar heard that King Geirthjof had summoned great forces in
Uppland, intending to attack King Vikar with that host and avenge King
Herthjof, his brother. King Vikar called out the levy from his own kingdom,
and he went to Uppland with those men to face King Geirthjof. They had
such a huge battle that they fought for seventeen days without stopping.
King Geirthjof fell, and King Vikar had victory. Then King Vikar claimed
Uppland and Telemark for his own, because King Fridthjof of Telemark
was away from his own kingdom. Starkad states that this battle which he
won in Uppland was the third of King Vikar's battles:

For the third time
the thewful one
held a contest
of Hild's game,°   *Hild:* a valkyrie or battle-goddess; *Hild's game:* battle
before Uppland
was finally won

15

and Geirthjof
was given to Hel.

At once Vikar appointed men to rule the kingdom which he had won in Uppland. He went home to Agder and became a powerful king with a large following. He took a wife and had two sons with her. The older was named Harald, and the younger was named Neri. Neri was the wisest of men, and everything he set his mind to turned out well, but he was so stingy that he could not give anything away without regretting it at once. So said Starkad:

> The great king had
> begotten himself
> two sons and heirs,
> outstanding men.
> Harald was the name
> of his elder son;
> he was taken
> as Telemark's lord.

> Jarl Neri, it's said,
> was the stingiest man
> with gold, though giving
> goodly counsel.
> Vikar's son,
> seasoned in battle,
> was the Upplanders'
> only ruler.

Jarl Neri was a great warrior, but so stingy that all the stingiest men have been compared to him, and since then his name has been given to others.

When Fridthjof heard of the fall of his brothers, he went to Uppland and conquered the kingdom which Vikar had previously won. Then he sent word to Vikar that he should pay tribute from his kingdom, or else be invaded. So said Starkad:

> Fridthjof chose
> first to send
> a war-message
> to the wise leader:
> would Vikar suffer

invading foes,
or pay the prince
the price of tribute?

When this message came to Vikar, he summoned an assembly and discussed with his counsellors how to reply to this difficult question. They all set forth their counsel and deliberated for a long time. So said Starkad:

We took counsel,
discussed it long,
soon we became
stirred to anger.
The men chose this:
the mighty king
should press on
with the promised battle.

Word was sent to King Frithjof that King Vikar would defend his land. Then King Fridthjof set out with his host and intended to harry King Vikar.

Olaf the Keen-Eyed was the name of a king in Sweden, at the place called Nærriki.[24] He was a powerful king and a mighty warrior. He summoned the levy from his own kingdom and went to King Vikar's aid. They had huge forces and moved against King Fridthjof, deploying their battle-lines in the boar's-head formation.[25] So said Starkad:

Olaf the Keen-Eyed,
king most favored,
was sovereign lord
of Sweden in the east.
He called out
the kingdom's levy;
his share of soldiers
was said to be large.

There a fierce battle began, and King Vikar's men advanced boldly, for there were many champions in their ranks. The foremost champion was Starkad Storvirksson. Ulf was another, along with Erp and many other good warriors and great champions. King Vikar advanced fiercely. Starkad wore no armor, and he broke through the ranks and struck with both hands, as is said here:

We went forth
in the weapon-clash,
the king's men
were keen for battle;
Ulf was seen there,
Erp as well;
stripped of armor,
I struck with both hands.

And when King Vikar and his champions furiously attacked King Fridthjof, King Fridthjof's ranks were on the verge of breaking when he begged King Vikar for peace. So said Starkad:

Fridthjof decided
to sue for peace,
since Vikar refused
to fall back,
and Storvirk's son,
Starkad himself,
fought fiercely
before everyone.

That was the most furious and terrible fighting, and a great many of King Fridthjof's men fell. But when he begged for peace, King Vikar stood down his forces.

King Fridthjof came to a settlement with King Vikar, and King Olaf was to arrange a treaty between them. The agreement was that King Fridthjof gave up all his rule over Uppland and Telemark, and left the land. Vikar set his own sons over this kingdom. He gave Harald the title of king over Telemark, but to Neri he gave the title of jarl and the rulership of Uppland. He became friends with King Gautrek in Gautland, and it is said in some books that Neri held some of his realm in fief from King Gautrek—the region of Gautland which was closest to him—and that Neri was also a jarl of King Gautrek and advised him whenever it was necessary.

Afterwards, King Vikar went home to his kingdom and became very famous from his victories. He and King Olaf parted in friendship and held to it ever after. Olaf went east to his home in Sweden.

CHAPTER VI

There was a man named Rennir, a wealthy farmer. He had his residence on the island that has been called Rennisey ever since.[26] This island lies off the coast of Norway, north of Jæren. He had been a great raider before he settled on his farm. He had a wife and one boy-child, who was named Ref.

When Ref was young, he lay in the cookhouse and bit twigs and bark from logs. He was incredibly tall. He never cleaned the filth from himself, and he never lifted a finger to be of use to anyone. His father was a very wealthy man, and his son's slothfulness displeased him. Ref was very well-known, not for any cleverness or achievement, but rather for making himself a laughingstock to his other, more capable kinfolk. His father thought that he was unlikely to distinguish himself in anything, as was the custom for other young men at the time.

Farmer Rennir had one possession that he prized more highly than his other valuables. It was an ox, both large and showy on account of its horns. Its horns were carved, with gold and silver inlaid into the carvings and on the tips. A chain between the ox's horns was fashioned of silver, and there were three gold rings on the chain. This ox was far superior to other oxen that were in the land, on account of its size and all the expense of its trappings. Farmer Rennir was so fastidious about it that it could never be left unguarded.

Rennir was always by King Vikar's side in battles, and they were good friends.

CHAPTER VII

King Vikar became a great warrior and had many famous champions with him, but Starkad was the most valued of all of then and dearest to the king, where he was his highest-ranking liegeman and counsellor and defender of his lands. He received many gifts from the king. King Vikar gave him a goodly ring that weighed three marks, and Starkad gave him the island of Thruma, which King Harald had granted to his father Storvirk. He was with King Vikar for fifteen summers, as he said:

> Vikar gifted me
> with gold from far lands,
> this red-gold ring
> which rides on my hand,

three marks in weight—
and Thruma I gave him.
I followed the folk-king
for fifteen summers.

King Vikar sailed from Ogd northwards to Hordaland with a large host. He anchored among certain islands for a long time, but encountered strong headwinds. They cast wood-chips[27] for a favorable wind, and the omens showed that Odin wanted to claim a man from the host to be hanged, to be chosen by drawing lots. The men were assembled for the drawing of lots, and King Vikar's lot came up. Everyone fell silent at this, and it was planned that the counsellors should have a meeting about this difficult question on the next day.

That night, around midnight, Horsehair-Grani awakened Starkad, his foster-son, and told him to go with him. They took a small boat and rowed to a nearby island. They went up into the forest and found a clearing there. In the clearing were a great many people, and an assembly was seated there; eleven men were sitting on chairs, and the twelfth was empty. They walked forward to the assembly, and Horsehair-Grani sat down on the twelfth chair. They all greeted him as Odin. He said that the judges should set the fate of Starkad.

Thor spoke up, and he said, "Alfhild, the mother of Starkad's father, chose a cunning giant as the father of her son, rather than Asa-Thor. I shape Starkad's fate so that he shall never have a son nor a daughter, and so his lineage shall end."

Odin answered, "I shape his fate so that he shall live three human lifetimes."

Thor said, "He shall commit a vile deed in each lifetime."

Odin answered, "I shape his fate so that he shall own the best weapons and clothes."

Thor said, "I shape his fate so that he shall never own land nor estates."

Odin said, "I grant him this, that he shall have abundance of money."

Thor said, "I lay this on him: he shall never think that he has enough."

Odin answered, "I give him victory and prowess in every battle."

Thor answered, "I lay this on him: he shall receive a disfiguring wound in every battle."

Odin said, "I give him the art of poetry, so that he shall compose poetry as fast as he can recite it."[28]

Thor said, "He shall not remember what he has composed."

Odin said, "I shape this fate for him: he shall be most highly esteemed by the noblest and best men."

Thor said, "He shall be hated by all the common folk."

Then the judges passed sentence that everything that Odin and Thor had spoken should befall Starkad, and thus the assembly broke up. Starkad and Horsehair-Grani went to their boat. Then Horsehair-Grani said to Starkad, "Now you can repay me well, foster-son, for the help that I have given you."

"It is well," said Starkad.

Horsehair-Grani said, "Now you are to send King Vikar to me, and I will give you the plan."

Starkad agreed to this. Horsehair-Grani put a spear in his hand, and said that it would seem to be a reed sprout. They went out to their men as day was breaking.

The next morning, the king's counsellors assembled for deliberation. It was agreed that they had to do some sort of representation of the sacrifice, and Starkad told them his plan. There stood a fir-tree next to them, and a single high stump next to the fir. Low on the fir tree was a narrow branch, and it reached upwards to the crown of the tree. The servants were preparing food for the men, and a calf had been butchered and gutted. Starkad had them take the calf's intestines, and he stepped up on the stump and bent the slender branch down and tied the calf's intestines around it.

Then Starkad said to the king, "Now a gallows is readied for you, king, and it must not look very dangerous. Come here, and I'll place a noose around your neck."

The king said, "Should this device be no more dangerous to me than it appears, I suppose that it won't harm me. But if it's otherwise, then fate must decide what happens."

He stepped up on the stump, and Starkad laid the noose around his neck and stepped down from the stump. Then Starkad stabbed at the king with the reed and said, "Now I give you to Odin."

Then Starkad let the fir-branch loose. The reed-sprout became a spear and pierced the king through. The stump fell from under his feet, and the calf's intestines became strong withies. The branch sprang up and hoisted the king into the crown of the tree, and there he died. That place has been called Vikarsholm ever since.

Because of this deed, all the people found Starkad abhorrent, and he was first exiled from Hordaland for it. Afterwards he fled Norway and traveled east to Sweden. He stayed for a long time with the kings at Uppsala, Eirek and Alrek, the sons of Agni Skjalf's Husband[29], and he went raiding with them. When Alrek asked Starkad what tidings he could tell them about his kinsmen or himself, Starkad made the poem that is called "Vikar's Piece." Thus he told of the killing of King Vikar:

I fared with the troops,
the finest I knew—
in all my life
I loved this the most—
before we fared
one final time
to Hordaland,
haunted by trolls.

It was on this foray
that Thor fated for me
a mean reputation
and many hardships;
I, the base one,
was bound to wreak ill.

In a high tree
I had to offer
Vikar to the gods,
Geirthjof's Bane.
I stabbed the warrior
with a spear in the heart,
the most dismal deed
done by my hands.

From there I wandered
winding roads,
hated by Hordalanders,
my heart sorrowing,
lacking in rings
and lays of brave deeds,
deprived of my prince,
despairing in mind.

Now I have sought
the Swedish realm,
and Uppsala,
the Ynglings' seat;
the lord's own sons,
as I'll long remember,
say that I sit
as a silent thul.[30]

Concerning Starkad, it may be seen that he thought that his worst and most monstrous deed was that he killed King Vikar. We have not heard any stories that he settled down in Norway afterwards.

When Starkad was at Uppsala, there were twelve berserk mercenaries there. They treated him scornfully and mocked him, and the two brothers Ulf and Otrygg were the most vicious at it. Starkad kept silent, but the berserks called him a reborn giant and a worthless man, as is said here:

Among the lads
they let me sit,
savagely scorned,
snowy-browed;
the high ones mock me,
the haughty men
make the lord's creature
a laughing-stock.

On me myself
they imagine they see
the marks of eight
arms of a giant,
which Hlorridi° tore   *Hlorridi*: Thor
from Hergrim's Bane,
ripped with his hands
on rocks in the north.

The warriors laugh
to look at me,
my loathsome mug
and longish snout,

wolf-hoary hair,
hands all gnarled,
scabby neck
and scaly hide.

When King Eirek and King Alrek set out for home, Starkad set out raiding with the ship that King Eirek had given him, crewed with Norwegians and Danes. He traveled far and wide to many lands and fought battles and single combats, and always won victories, and he is no longer in this saga.

King Alrek didn't live long, and that happened in this way: King Eirek his brother beat him down to Hel with a bridle, when they had ridden out to tame their horses.[31] After that, King Eirek ruled Sweden alone for a long time, as will be told later, in the saga of Hrolf Gautreksson and his shipmates.

CHAPTER VIII

Now we move on to two stories. First it's time to tell the one that we left off earlier, concerning how King Gautrek ruled Gautland and became a mighty ruler and the greatest warrior. The king felt that the main thing lacking in his kingdom was that he wasn't married, and he wanted to look for a match for himself.

There was a king named Harald who ruled over the southern Baltic lands. He was a wise man, but not much of a warrior. He had a queen and a lovely and well-bred daughter named Alfhild. King Gautrek set out on a journey to the Baltic shore and asked to marry King Harald's daughter. His proposal received a favorable answer, and after all their discussions, it was concluded that Gautrek should marry the maiden. He brought her home to Gautland and held her wedding feast. And when they had not been together for long, Alfhild gave birth to a lovely daughter. She was named Helga. She was mature at an early age. She grew up with her father, and she was considered the best match in Gautland.

King Gautrek had many outstanding men with him. There was one man named Hrosskel, Gautrek's friend and a great raider. On one occasion he accepted an invitation to feast with King Gautrek, and at their parting, King Gautrek gave him worthy gifts. He gave Hrosskel a fine stud-horse, a gray stallion, along with four mares. They were all as pale as silk and the most handsome animals. Hrosskel thanked the king for the gifts, and they parted in great friendship.[32]

King Gautrek now ruled his kingdom for many years and lived in peace, until the queen fell ill, and her sickness didn't end until the queen was carried out dead. King Gautrek felt this to be the worst grief. The king had a burial mound raised for his queen. He was so grieved that he paid no attention to governing the kingdom. He sat on the mound every day and hunted with his hawk from there, amusing himself and whiling away the days.

CHAPTER IX

Now it is time to tell how Jarl Neri held the rulership of Uppland, as was said before. When he heard of the killing of his father King Vikar, he summoned his brother King Harald, and when they met, they discussed how to divide up their inheritance. It was decided between them that, since Harald was the elder brother, he should claim all the kingdoms that Vikar had formerly ruled and be king over them, but Jarl Neri should have Uppland, as before, along with Telemark, which his brother King Harald had formerly ruled. The brothers parted in harmony.

Jarl Neri was so wise that no one to match him could be found. Everything he set his mind to turned out well, whatever it might be. He never wanted to accept gifts, because he was so stingy that he begrudged giving anything in return.

As we mentioned before, it's said that Rennir the farmer went to the cookhouse one day. He tripped over the leg of his son Ref, and he said to him, "It's a terrible shame for such a son, that you want nothing better for yourself. Now you must go away and not come before my eyes or into my sight again, as long as you keep up this foolishness."

Ref answered, "Since you're driving me away, it'll be fitting for me to take with me the best treasure that you have, the one you'd think it worst to lose."

Rennir said, "There's no possession in my holdings that I won't give up to never see you again, because you're the laughingstock of your family."

After that they ended their conversation.

Not long afterwards, Ref stood up one fine day and prepared to leave. He took the splendid ox and led it to the beach. He pushed out the boat, meaning to go to the mainland. The ox got a bit wet, but he didn't care. He sat down at the oars, but tied the ox to the ship, and that's how he rowed to land. He was wearing a short cloak and ankle-length breeches,[33] and when he reached land, he led the ox behind him. He first went east along the coast of Jæren, and then followed the road towards Uppland. He didn't break his journey until he came to the estate that Jarl Neri owned. The jarl's retainers

25

told him that Refr Renni's Fool had arrived, leading the fine ox behind him. The jarl ordered them not to mock him. When Ref came to the doors of the hall where the jarl was accustomed to sit, he asked the doorkeepers to call the jarl to speak with him. They answered, "Your foolishness just doesn't quit. The jarl is not in the habit of rushing to speak with a peasant."

Ref said, "Take him my message, and let him decide on an answer."

They went to find the jarl, and said that Ref the Foolish was asking him to come out. The jarl said, "Say that I will meet with Ref. You never know what sort of luck each person brings."

The jarl went outside, and Ref greeted him courteously. The jarl said, "Why have you come here?"

Ref answered, "My father has driven me away. But here is an ox that I own, and I want to give him to you."

The jarl replied, "Haven't you heard that I accept no gifts, because I'm not willing to repay anyone?"

Ref answered, "I have heard that you're so stingy that no one needs to assume that he'll get anything valuable in return, even if he gives you a gift. Still, I want you to accept this treasure. Maybe you will do me good by your words, whatever the monetary reward is."

The jarl said, "I will accept the ox because of what you say. Come inside and be my most highly honored guest tonight."

Ref released the ox and went in. The jarl ordered him to be brought clothes, so that he wouldn't be shamed. When Ref washed, he was the finest-looking man. He sat there for a while. The jarl's entire hall was decorated with shields, so that each touched another where they were hung up. The jarl took one shield which was inlaid all over with gold, and he gave it to Ref.

When the jarl went to his feasting the next day, he turned to where the shield had been hanging. He then spoke a verse:

> The showy prize once shimmered,
> my shield against the hangings.
> The greatest sorrow grips me
> when I gaze in that direction.
> The chasm looks unlovely;
> I'll lose my riches quickly,
> once warriors win my shields
> without wiles, by their own gifts.

The jarl was so affected by the loss of his shield that he turned his high seat away. When Ref saw that, he went before the jarl, with the shield in his hand, and said, "My lord, cheer up, because here is the shield that you gave me. I want to give it to you because it's of no use to me, since I have no other weapons."

The jarl said, "You gave the finest gift of all, because it's a great ornament to my hall to have it back in the place where it formerly hung. But here's a treasure I want to give you, and it might be to your benefit if you follow my advice."

The jarl put a whetstone[34] in his hand—"and you won't think this gift valuable."

Ref said, "I don't know how this helps me."

The jarl said, "Here's how it is: I won't feed any man who sits there and doesn't busy himself with something. Now I want to send you to King Gautrek. Put this whetstone in his hand."

Ref said, "I'm not used to going between noble men, and I don't know what use this stone will be to the king."

The jarl said, "My cleverness wouldn't be of much use if I couldn't see farther forward than you. But the only trial for you will be to find the king, because you mustn't talk to him. I'm told that the king often sits on his queen's burial mound and hunts from there with his hawk, and often, when day is passing, the hawk droops. Then the king has to sweep around his chair with his hands to find something to throw at it. If it happens that the king doesn't get anything to throw at the hawk, put the stone in his hand. If he passes something in his hand to you, accept it and come back to me."

Then Ref left, as the jarl had instructed him, and came to where the king was sitting on the mound. It went as Neri had guessed: the king flung everything that he picked up at the hawk. Ref sat down by the king's chair, behind the king. At once he saw how things were. The king reached out his hand behind him. Ref stuck the stone into his hand, and the king threw it straight at the hawk's back. The hawk flew up sharply when the whetstone hit it. The king felt that he had done well, and he didn't want the one who had done him this service to lack what was rightfully his. He passed a gold ring behind his back, without looking at Ref. Ref took the ring and went to meet the jarl. He asked how it had gone. Ref told him and showed him the ring. The jarl said, "This is a fine treasure. Sitting around isn't more useful than winning such a thing."

Ref stayed there over the winter. When spring came, the jarl said, "What will you accomplish now?"

Ref said, "That's an easy decision. Now I can sell the ring for cash."

The jarl said, "I'll give you some more help. There is a king named Ælle. He rules over England. You must give the ring to him, and you won't lose money from it. But come to me in the autumn. I won't withhold food or advice from you, though it won't amount to another payment for the ox."

Ref said, "I wish you wouldn't mention that."

Then he traveled to England and came before King Ælle and greeted him fittingly. Ref was well fitted out with both weapons and clothing. The king asked who this man was. He answered, "My name is Ref, and I want you to accept this gold ring from me," and he laid it on the table before the king.

The king looked at it and said, "This is a great treasure. But who gave it to you?"

Ref answered, "King Gautrek gave me the ring."

The king said, "What did you give him?"

Ref answered, "A little whetstone."

The king said, "Great is King Gautrek's generosity, since he gives gold for pebbles. I will accept the ring, and I invite you to stay here."

Ref said, "Thank you for your invitation, my lord! But I intend to return to Jarl Neri, my foster-father."

The king said, "You must stay here for a while." He had a ship made ready, and one day he asked Ref to go with him. The king said, "Here is a ship which I want to give you, with all the cargo that's best for you, along with as many men as you need. I don't want you to be someone else's passenger in order to go where you like. Yet this is a small thing, compared to how King Gautrek rewarded you for the whetstone."

Ref said, "This is a magnificent reward." Then Ref made ready to board his ship with his lavish cargo, and he thanked the king with many fair words.

The king said, "Here are two dogs that I will give you." They were quite small and pretty, and Ref had never seen anything like them. They had on golden harnesses, and a gold ring was clasped around the neck of each one, with seven little rings on the leash between them. No one thought he'd ever seen such treasures of this sort.

Then Ref departed, and came to Jarl Neri's realm. The jarl went to meet him and welcomed him—"and come to me with all your men."

Ref said, "I have enough goods to pay our way."

The jarl said, "That is well, but you mustn't diminish those goods of yours. You must eat at our table, though it's not a great reward for the ox."

Ref said, "The only thing that bothers me is that you mention that."

Now Ref stayed with the jarl for the winter and became popular, and many men chose to follow him. When spring came, the jarl spoke with Ref: "What will you do now?"

Ref said, "Wouldn't it be easiest to set out raiding or trading, since there's no lack of money?"

The jarl said, "That's true, but I will meddle in your affairs again. You must now go south to Denmark to meet King Hrolf Kraki,[35] and bring him the dogs, because they aren't possessions for a commoner. Once again, you won't lose money from it, if he will accept them."

Ref said, "It's up to you, but I'm not short of money now."

CHAPTER X

Now Ref made ready and sailed to Denmark. He met King Hrolf and came before him and greeted him. The king asked him who he might be. He said that he was named Ref.

The king asked, "Are you called Gift-Ref?"

Ref replied, "I've accepted gifts from men, yet I've also given them now and again. I want to give you these little dogs, my lord, along with their harness."

The king looked at them and said, "Such things are great treasures. But who gave them to you?"

Ref answered, "King Ælle."

King Hrolf said, "What did you give him?"

Ref answered, "A gold ring."

"Who gave you that?"

Ref answered, "King Gautrek."

"But what did you give him?"

Ref answered, "A whetstone."

King Hrolf said, "Great is King Gautrek's generosity, since he gives gold for pebbles. I will accept the dogs. Stay with us."

Ref answered, "I have to return in the fall to Jarl Neri, my foster-father."

King Hrolf answered, "So be it."

Ref stayed with the king for a while, and readied his ship in the fall. Then the king said, "I've thought of a reward for you. You shall accept a ship from me, just like the one from the king of England, and the finest cargo and men shall go with it."

Ref said, "Thank you very much for a noble gift," and then he got ready to leave.

King Hrolf said, "Here are two treasures, Ref, that you should accept from me: a helmet and a mailcoat."

Ref accepted the treasures. They were both made of red gold. Ref and King Hrolf parted in good cheer, and Ref went to meet Jarl Neri, captaining two ships. The jarl welcomed him and said that his wealth had grown still more—"and you all shall stay with me over the winter. It's a small reward for the ox, but it wouldn't be seemly for me to withhold my advice, since it's helpful for you."

Ref answered, "I benefit from your guidance in all these affairs." Ref stayed there over the winter, highly honored, and he became a famous man.

CHAPTER XI

In the spring, the jarl asked Ref, "What will you do this summer?"

Ref answered, "Lord, you should see to that, but I'm not short of money now."

The jarl said, "I suppose that's true. Now there is just one expedition that I want to propose to you. There's a king named Olaf who goes out raiding. He has eighty ships. He sails out to sea, in winter and in warm summer. He is the most famous battle-king. You must bring him the helmet and the mailcoat. If he accepts, I expect that he will ask you to choose a reward for it. You must choose to command his forces for half a month, and take them wherever you like. But there's a man named Refnef[36] with the king, the wickedest of men. He is the king's counsellor. I can scarcely tell whether your luck or his sorcery might be greater, but you'll have to risk it, however it turns out. You must lead all your forces here, and then maybe I'll get you rewarded for the fine ox."

Ref said, "I think you mention that too often." Then they parted.

Now Ref went to seek King Olaf, and found him where he was anchored with his fleet of ships. He sailed for the king's ship, boarded the ship and greeted the king. King Olaf asked who he might be. Ref gave his name.

The king said, "Are you called Gift-Ref?"

He answered, "At times, noble men have given me gifts, and I have always given something in return. Here are two treasures that I want to give you, a helmet and a mailcoat, because these treasures will be quite fitting for you."

The king said, "Who gave you these treasures? I've never seen their like. I don't believe I've ever heard of these, though I have traveled far and wide through many countries."

Ref answered, "King Hrolf Kraki gave me these treasures."

The king said, "But what did you give him?"

Ref said, "Two dogs with golden harnesses, which Ælle the King of England gave me."

"But what did you give King Ælle?" said King Olaf.

"A gold ring that King Gautrek awarded me in exchange for a whetstone."

King Olaf said, "Great is the generosity of such kings, and yet King Gautrek's generosity excels above all others'. Refnef, should I accept these treasures, or not?"

Refnef answered, "I don't think it's a good idea for you to accept them, if you don't have the sense to give something in return." And with that, he seized the treasures and stepped overboard with them. Ref saw that he'd soon be badly played if he lost the treasures, and he went after him. They had a fierce fight, and in the end Ref got the mailcoat, but Refnef kept the helmet and dove to the bottom and turned into a troll down there. Ref came up, quite exhausted. Then this was said:

> I must reckon
> that Refnef's advice
> was rather worse
> than the wisdom of Neri;
> Gautrek didn't toss
> his treasure in the sea
> when he gave
> a gold ring to Ref.

King Olaf said, "You are a most excellent man."

Ref then said, "Now I'd like you to accept the remaining treasure."

King Olaf said, "I certainly will accept, and I am no less thankful for the one than I was for both. It was because of trickery that I didn't accept both right away. That's not surprising, since I listened to the counsel of a wicked man. Choose your reward for it."

Ref answered, "I want to command your ships and men for half a month, and send them wherever I want."

The king said, "That's a strange choice, but the ships shall be at your disposal."

At once they sailed to Gautland to meet Jarl Neri. They arrived late in the day. Ref secretly informed Jarl Neri's men that he wanted to meet him. The jarl went to meet Ref, and Ref told him all about his travels.

"Now things have come to the point, foster-son," said the jarl, "that it's time to find out whether you're a lucky man, because now I want to marry you into King Gautrek's family. You should marry his daughter."

Ref asked him to oversee this matter by himself. The jarl said, "The next time we meet, you must not show surprise at anything I might say, and respond according to what I hand you."

Then the jarl rode off and didn't break his journey until he had come to meet King Gautrek. The jarl arrived around midnight and told him that an overwhelming force had entered his kingdom—"these men intend to take your life and conquer the kingdom."

The king asked, "Who is the leader of these hosts?"

The jarl answered, "Someone we'd hardly suspect, but he won't listen to my advice at all: it's Ref, my foster-son."

The king said, "You must reason with him even more—but wouldn't it be best to summon forces to oppose him?"

The jarl said, "If you don't reach a settlement with them, I think it's very likely that they'll pillage the land before you can assemble your forces. I would rather go with a suitable message and find out if a settlement between you might succeed, because I believe my realm will be the first to be ruined when they come near."

The king answered, "We've heeded your counsel for a long time."

"I want you to listen in on our conversation, king," said the jarl.

The king said that that was up to him.

They traveled with some men until they approached the ships. The king saw that they had a vast host of warriors, and it would be difficult to withstand them. The jarl spoke, calling out from land to the men on the ships. "Is my foster-son in command of this host?"

"It's true," Ref said.

"Foster-son, I never thought that you would raid my kingdom, or King Gautrek's kingdom. Shouldn't we reach some sort of settlement, so that peace may come about? I want to arrange everything so that your honor may be greater than ever, and I believe that the king will want the same thing for his own heir. I want you to accept honors from the king and then leave his kingdom in peace. I know you'll be quite agreeable, and that's not surprising, because your mother's father was a powerful jarl, and your father a trusty champion."

Ref answered, "I shall accept good proposals, if they're offered to me."

"I know you won't trust a paltry offer," said the jarl. "I know what you're thinking. You must want to have the jarldom that I have held in King Gautrek's name, and you must want the king to give you his daughter into the bargain."

Ref answered, "You go and see to it, jarl. I will say yes, if the king will agree."

The jarl said to the king, "I believe it would be wiser to accept this solution than for us to risk our lives at the hands of these men from Hel. I see that they'll probably take your kingdom first, and then take your daughter as spoils of war. But it's the most suitable thing to do, to betroth your daughter to a man descended from jarls. I will give Ref my counsel. Let him be the overseer of your kingdom. May our wishes be done in this matter."

King Gautrek answered, "Your counsel has always been a help to us, jarl, and I want to have your foresight. And I believe that it would be far beyond our strength to engage this host."

The jarl said, "Now I will advise you to let Ref strengthen your kingdom and take him into your confidence." This was confirmed with oaths, and the jarl decided on all their arrangements, and King Gautrek went home.

Ref said, "You've granted me much help, King Olaf. You shall now go on your way, wherever you like."

King Olaf answered, "Wiser men than you have taken part in this." Then King Olaf sailed away.

And when the fleet had left, King Gautrek said, "I've had to deal with tricky men here, but I won't break my oath now."

The jarl said to Ref, "Now only your men are left, and you can see all the help I have brought you. This is the right thing for you to do. Maybe you've been repaid for the ox in full, but I haven't rewarded you as much as I might have, because you gave me all you had, while I have plenty of possessions left."

Now King Gautrek had a feast laid on, and Ref went to marry Helga, King Gautrek's daughter. Along with that, King Gautrek gave him the title of jarl. He was the most renowned of men for all his valor; his family was descended from noble men, and his father was the greatest warrior and champion. Ref ruled this jarl's realm, but he didn't live to be old.

Jarl Neri died suddenly, and nothing further is said about him in this saga. King Gautrek held the funeral feast for him. The king was becoming quite bowed down by old age. He was more famous for his generosity and valor, but it's not said that he was a deep thinker. Yet he was well-liked and quite generous, and the most mannerly of men.

And here ends the story of Gift-Ref.

THE SAGA OF HROLF GAUTREKSSON

Hrólfs saga Gautrekssonar

CHAPTER I

We begin this saga with King Gautrek, son of King Gauti who ruled Gautland. He was an excellent king in many respects, well-liked and so very generous that his generosity is always praised when ancient kings are mentioned. He had one daughter, and he betrothed her to Gift-Ref, Rennir's son, on the advice of Jarl Neri.

At that time, King Gautrek's queen had died. He was bowed down by old age, although he was the most valiant of men. The king always sat on the queen's burial mound, for her death was a terrible blow to him. His kingdom was quite without governance while the king grieved her loss most deeply.

Later on, the king's friends asked him to take a wife. They said that they would prefer for his descendants to rule over them, and they said that if he would take their worthy advice, it would be likely to do honor to them all and bring peace for a long time. King Gautrek welcomed their advice, and said that they always showed and had shown great good will towards him, both in counsel and in brave service. A little while later, King Gautrek prepared to go on his journey with eighty men, well equipped with weapons and clothes and the finest of ships. He took great care in organizing this expedition down to the last detail, as befitted his rank.

There was a powerful hersir[1] in Norway named Thorir, who had his seat in Sogn. He was an outstanding man of great worth, the mightiest of men. He was married and had one daughter, named Ingibjorg. She was both wise and lovely, and was thought to be the best match. Many powerful men had asked for her hand, and she had shown them all the door, because she felt that not one of them was a suitable match.

Now it happened that King Gautrek arrived with his men. They were welcomed there most warmly. Thorir went to meet him, and invited him and his retinue to stay for as long as he pleased. King Gautrek was given a fine feast with the best provisions and hospitality.

A certain prince had come there from his own country; he was named Olaf. He had a hundred men with him. This prince had asked for Thorir's daughter Ingibjorg, and she had responded favorably to his proposal. This man was young and handsome. When Gautrek heard of it, he paid no attention. When he had stayed there for a little while, he called Thorir to talk with him.

The king said, "I want to explain to you why I have come: It has been reported to me that you, Thorir, have a beautiful and wise daughter by the name of Ingibjorg. I have made up my mind to ask for her to be my wife, and thus establish bonds of kinship and friendship with you."

Thorir said, "I have heard it said clearly that you are a ruler of high degree, and for that reason I wish to give a favorable response to your request. I think it likely that my daughter would be well married if she were to come under your purview. But the word has gone out that a young and handsome prince has come here, by the name of Olaf. He has already asked to court my daughter, and we two have had some discussions about it. Now I must decline this obligation and let her choose her own husband, as she has previously asked to do." Both kings were well pleased with this answer.

A little while later, they and their comrades all went to Ingibjorg's bower. When she saw her father arrive with the two rulers, she greeted them all cheerfully and invited them to sit down.

Thorir began to speak. "The matter has come to this, daughter: these two kings have come here with me to meet you, as you may see. Both are on exactly the same mission, desiring to ask for your hand in marriage. Now since the old saying is quite true that 'one can't make two sons-in-law with one daughter', I want you to resolve the matter at hand by choosing which of them you wish to marry. I ask you to give them a clear answer and reach a decision that may befit you and suit us all."

Ingibjorg answered, "I believe it would be a most difficult matter for me, or for any other woman who is no more experienced than I, to resolve this case reasonably, or to be certain that I am able to choose as my spouse the man fit for me, for I feel that it is most likely that either of these two kings would be of high degree and much more than an equal match for me, whichever one's guardianship I enter. Rather, I may resolve this matter according to certain precedents: I may most readily compare these two kings to two apple-trees standing in one garden.[2] One is young, and it is quite likely that many large and sweet apples will grow there once it has fully come of age, and that signifies King Olaf. There is a second apple tree next to it, standing with its limbs thickly covered with foliage, and bearing apples of every sort. That apple tree signifies the rulership and authority of King Gautrek, who has long governed his kingdom with liberality and honor, and whose rule has lasted for the fullness of time. His bravery and generosity in every respect are known to us. Even were his rule to fail on account of his age, he might still beget bold sons, and it would be good to be happy with them, even were the king to die. Now although Olaf may be the younger man and a promising chieftain, it's surely a bad thing to pay for hope, and I'll not elaborate on the matter any further. I choose King Gautrek for myself, for joy and companionship, even though I already know that he may not live long, while Olaf may grow as old as a stone bridge. For my heart tells me that he will never become such a ruler—especially if he only lives for a little while."[3]

King Gautrek was overjoyed at the maiden's words, and he leaped up like a young man. He took the maiden's hand and married her, right next to King Olaf. King Olaf grew very angry at this, and said that he would take revenge on King Gautrek himself and on his men. King Gautrek said that he would just have to put up with misfortune that he couldn't change, and they parted with matters as they stood. King Olaf went away with his men, extremely angry.

CHAPTER II

Now when King Gautrek had stayed there for a while, which he enjoyed very much, he prepared to go home with his future wife Ingibjorg, because he wanted to celebrate his wedding at home in Gautland. Thorir sent his daughter away in grand style, and sent much gold and silver with her.

King Gautrek and his retinue went on their way home. One day, when they had come close to a certain forest, King Olaf attacked him with his own men. The fiercest battle broke out between then. When they had battled for a while, Olaf said, "King Gautrek, you must want me to give you the chance to save your life. Surrender the girl to me, along with all her dowry, and then you shall go in peace anywhere you want, because it's not right for such an old man to take a tumble with such a lovely maiden. This is the only way you can save yourself from death."

When King Gautrek heard his words, he said: "Though I have fewer men than you, before evening comes you'll find that this old man is no coward."

King Gautrek was so enraged that he often broke through Olaf's ranks, and he didn't stop until Olaf and all his men had fallen. King Gautrek won the victory and suffered few casualties. After that, he didn't break his journey until he came home to Gautland. This expedition had greatly increased his fame.

When he had been home for a short while, he commanded a great feast to be held, and he invited all the prominent men in the land. He drank to his betrothal to Ingibjorg with the strongest ale. When the feast ended, he presented suitable gifts to all the powerful men whom he had invited, and this brought him great renown. Warm love began to grow between him and his wife, and they lived peaceably in his kingdom.

Not long afterwards, Gautrek fathered a child with his wife. It was a male child, and he was brought to the king. The king had the boy sprinkled with water and named: he was to be called Ketil.[4] He grew up there in the household. Three winters afterwards, Ingibjorg bore another boy. He was big and handsome, and he was named Hrolf.

These boys were raised nobly, as was fitting for sons of a king, but each of the brothers had his own personality. Ketil was the smallest and swiftest of men, a noisy lad, ambitious and reckless, full of daring and most impertinent. He was called Ketil the Stunted because he was so little. Hrolf was the tallest and strongest of men, and handsome to see. He was taciturn, trustworthy, and not ambitious. If something were said or done to offend him, he pretended not to know at first—but some time later, when the other person least expected it, he would avenge the offense harshly. And when certain problems that concerned him were brought before him, he would pay no attention at first—but some time later, even several years later, once he had devised a solution to the problem, he made it known, whether it was to his advantage or not. Matters would then have to go as he wanted them to go. He was popular with all his people, and men loved him much.

Time passed until Ketil was ten years old, and Hrolf was seven.

CHAPTER III

In those days a king named Hring ruled over Denmark, a mighty and beloved king. He had a beautiful, wise queen. They had a son named Ingjald; he was young, but most promising. King Hring and King Gautrek were the best of friends. Each gave the other feasts and costly gifts and many royal honors, for as long as their friendship lasted. They had always gone raiding together when they were younger, and they never broke their friendship for as long as they treated each other fairly. But now their friendship began to be strained because of the intervention of wicked men who kindled strife between them. Matters came to the point that each of them was preparing to go to war with the other.

On one occasion, King Hring of Denmark came to speak with his queen: "As you supposed, it has been brought to my attention that King

Gautrek means to make war on our kingdom. I am not certain what excuse he will give us, but I think it's wiser to be the first to strike, for it is said that 'he who strikes first comes out on top.' I don't know whether he is guilty of the treachery which has been reported to me."

The queen said, "You're speaking unwisely if you believe such slanders from wicked men that you want to go to war with King Gautrek, since you know that the two of you have been the best of friends. It is an utterly unkingly act to want to vanquish one's own sworn brother. If it comes to that, let him be the one to break faith with you, rather than doing him any harm yourself and so losing his friendship. Do well, my lord, so that such paltriness may not be found in your breast that you would wish to throw down and trample on so many great deeds that each of you has done with the other. Be loyal to King Gautrek, my lord, with gallantry and boldness founded on good will, with love and perfect peace. Don't lose the friendship of such a good man on account of the slanderous words of wicked men. He has married a woman so wise and kind that she will mend your fellowship completely, and resolve whatever's gone wrong. And King Gautrek has such vigorous sons that they will quickly avenge any offense to their father. My lord, take the advice that I give you: Go yourself in one ship to meet King Gautrek, along with the wisest of your counsellors, and offer to foster his son Hrolf with you. If they're willing to accept, he may become an everlasting source of strength for you and for your kingdom, and bring us all worldly honors as well."

When the queen had finished her counsel, the king felt that she had spoken wisely and well, and he said that he would not ignore her advice. He had preparations made for his journey as the queen had advised. When he was ready, he set out and came to Gautland with all his goods.

When King Gautrek heard of his arrival, he called Queen Ingibjorg to speak with her, and he said, "I have been informed that King Hring has arrived in our kingdom from Denmark, in one ship. Since you have heard that we have been informed of his enmity, I shall pay him back for all that before we part. Now that he has fallen into my hands, I may well do this without any risk to my life."

When the queen heard his words, she spoke to the king in this way: "There's little wisdom in the words you've tossed out, if you want to cause any harm to King Hring, since I'd say that he's come to meet you as if he's expecting honor and good will from you, since you two once bound yourselves together. You can see that King Hring would not have come here with so few men unless he trusted you just as much as before. He must have been falsely accused of being your enemy. Now this is my advice: Send men to meet him and invite him to a fine feast with all his retinue. Be merry and cheerful with him, and when he has entered the hall with his men, pay close attention and see whether you find him in any way guilty of what he is accused of. And if there is any disagreement between you, resolve it all, with the counsel of the best men. Then keep your sworn brotherhood in spite of any disagreement, for as long as you both live."

When the king heard his queen's advice, he had a splendid feast laid on, and he began by inviting King Hring to come with all his retinue. He summoned many other mighty and wise men to this feast as well, whose counsel the king wanted to have. As the kings sat and made merry in the hall, they discussed how their friendship had been spoiled. When they both realized that there were no true grounds for disagreement between them, and found that it was the slander and evil rumors of wicked men, they renewed their friendship completely. As a new beginning, King Hring invited Hrolf Gautreksson to be fostered with him. Since King Gautrek accepted gladly, King Hring prepared to travel home with Hrolf, and he was sent off with worthy gifts. Both kings felt that matters had turned out well. Now the kings parted in love and joy, and they held to their friendship for as long as they lived.

Hrolf went to Denmark with King Hring, who fostered him in the noblest fashion. The king found the greatest master in the Northern lands for him, who taught him all the skills that brave and bold men were eager to learn at that time. Hrolf and Ingjald came to be the best of friends, and they swore brotherhood with each other. They grew up in Denmark, and Hrolf became the most outstanding man, superior to others in both strength and size.

Ketil grew up in Gautland with his father, and he was the shortest and most vigorous of men. Yet he was not much like King Gautrek in temperament, because of his boisterousness and energy.

CHAPTER IV

A king named Eirek ruled over Sweden. He had a wise and well-mannered queen. They had one child, a daughter named Thornbjorg. She was lovelier and wiser than any woman that anyone knew. She grew up at home with her own father and mother. Men have said of this maiden that she was more skilled than any woman that people had ever heard of, at any skill that a woman might turn her hand to. Besides that, she practiced jousting and fencing with sword and shield. She knew these skills just as well as knights who know how to wield their weapons well and skillfully.

King Eirek wasn't pleased that she was behaving like a man, and he asked her to stay in her bower like other princesses. She replied, "Since you have no more than one lifetime to rule the kingdom, and I am your only child and will inherit everything, I may well need to defend this kingdom from kings or princes, if I lose you. I would most likely find it bad to be married to one of them against my will, if that were to happen, and so I want to learn some knightly ways. Then I think it's more likely that I will be able to hold this kingdom with the strength and loyalty of good followers. So I ask you, father, to give me some of your kingdom to rule in trust while you are alive, and I will try my hand at ruling and overseeing such people as are given into my power. There's also this to consider: if any men ask for my hand in marriage and I refuse to consent, it's more likely that your kingdom will be left in peace from their tyranny if I respond to them, instead of you."

The king considered the maiden's words, and he found her overbearing and haughty. He thought there was a good chance that he and his kingdom would get into trouble from her arrogance and ambition. He decided to give her a third of his kingdom in stewardship, and he granted her a royal seat along with that, called Ullarakr.[5] In addition, he gave her fierce and bold men as followers, who were compliant and obedient to her will.

When she had received all of this from her father, she went to Ullarakr. At once she summoned a great assembly and had herself raised to kingship over the third of Sweden which King Eirek had agreed to let her rule in stewardship. She also gave herself the name Thorberg. No man was so bold as to call her a maiden or a woman—whoever did that would have to suffer harsh punishment. Then King Thorberg dubbed knights and appointed retainers and gave them pay, in the same way as her father King Eirek in Uppsala. Sweden maintained this arrangement for several years.

CHAPTER V

Now we turn to how King Gautrek of Gautland fell ill. He called his queen to speak with her, together with other powerful men, and he said to them: "Word has gone out that I have fallen ill, and since age weighs heavily on me, I probably won't ever suffer any more illnesses. I want to thank all of you men, with praise for the service and fellowship that you have offered me. As you know, I have two sons to inherit after me. One is here with us, but the other is in Denmark with King Hring. It is the law of this land that a king's elder son should rule as king after his father.[6] Now, in the case of my son Ketil, I do not wish to break the law through my own obstinacy, or on behalf of you men of this land. Yet I want to ask you all together to allow the son whom I believe is better suited to inherit the kingdom after me."

They said that they were quite willing to trust his insight, which had always served them well, and they didn't want to reject his advice in the end, since they had always taken it before and it had served them very well. The king said that he wanted Hrolf to take the kingdom, and said that he expected he would become an excellent man and a good leader of his people. The king asked for Ketil's approval. Ketil said that he wasn't greedy for the kingdom, and it would be well if Hrolf took it.

After that, they thanked him for the excellent peace and quiet that they had enjoyed for a long time, thanks to his lordly governance and royal management. The king arranged his affairs as he thought best. Each man went home, but those whose duty it was stayed by the king's side. It didn't take long before the sickness claimed his life. The queen felt this to be a terrible blow, and so did all the folk of the kingdom. He was deeply mourned by all the inhabitants, for no king had been more beloved, on account of his generosity and wisdom. Afterwards, he was buried in a mound, according to ancient custom.

Not much time had passed, when the queen prepared to go on a journey with a splendid retinue. She didn't stop her travels until she arrived in Denmark to meet King Hring. She brought before the king the grief and hurt that she had suffered from the death of King Gautrek. She told him all of the arrangements that King Gautrek had made before he died.

When the king had heard these tidings, he was deeply saddened by the death of his sworn brother King Gautrek. He asked Queen Ingibjorg to stay with him for as long as she liked.

The queen answered, "We didn't make this journey just to stay in your kingdom. But if you want to do something to honor us, my lord, then I ask you to come to Gautland at our invitation, with your foster-son Hrolf, so that he may become king there under your supervision, as King Gautrek had planned. Along with that, I want you to hold the inheritance-feast on behalf of King Gautrek, according to ancient custom."

The king said that it would be done as she asked. Not long afterwards, the king started out on his journey with a fine retinue, and he didn't stop until he came to Gautland, with Queen Ingibjorg and her son Hrolf with him. A splendid feast had already been prepared, and many of that land's noblest men were there. King Gautrek's inheritance-ale was drunk, and a great assembly was summoned to the feast. At the assembly, Hrolf was raised to the kingship, on the advice of King Hring and with the consent of all the people in the whole of Gautland. When everything was fulfilled and completed, King Hring returned to Denmark, and he was sent home with worthy gifts.

Hrolf began to rule the kingdom, and he made laws and rules according to his will. He soon became well-liked by his men. He was a wise ruler, and as generous as his father. He was twelve years old when he took the rulership of the kingdom. His brother Ketil stayed with him. Ingjald, his foster-brother, set out raiding in the summers, but always made his winter quarters in Gautland with King Hrolf. So matters went until Hrolf was fifteen years old.

CHAPTER VI

It's said that the brothers were conversing once, and King Hrolf asked what Ketil thought of his rulership. Ketil said that it was fine, in most respects.

King Hrolf answered, "Since you have insight into this, you must tell me how what I have achieved by my own will seems defective."

Ketil answered, "I can easily find the matter in which you seem to be lacking in good fortune. You're not married, and you would be thought a much greater king if you took a wife befitting your station."

The king said, "Where should I go to seek a wife?"

Ketil answered, "Your honor would grow if you were to ask for the hand of a princess who is both clever and foresighted. But I certainly wouldn't expect you to be rejected, no matter where you wanted to look."

The king replied, "I don't think much about such possibilities. This is a small country, and no one will think there's much profit in our kingdom. But where would you look first, kinsman?"

Ketil answered, "I have heard that King Eirek in Sweden has a beautiful and wise daughter named Thornbjorg. I have heard that such a match is not to be found in all the Northlands, for she is skilled in every art which may well adorn a woman. But she is also skilled at jousting and fencing with shield and sword, on an equal footing with bold knights. She is greater at that than any woman I have ever heard of. King Eirek, her father, is renowned for his might and for many other accomplishments which such a celebrated king may pride himself on."

King Hrolf answered, "We're not bold enough for anything like that. Such an attempt would draw more attention for rashness than for wisdom— as sometimes happens to you, kinsman. It's bad for someone who has no hope to be so conceited about how he might rise. If I go and ask for the daughter of King Eirek in Sweden, as you want me to do, I believe the woman would be refused to me, and I would probably be insulted. I would have to put up with all that, since I wouldn't be able to take vengeance because of how powerful the king is—and I wouldn't take that well at all."

Ketil said that it wouldn't happen that way. "We have no lack of men from Denmark and Gautland for an attack on King Eirek, if he denies you the girl."

King Hrolf said, "You don't need to taunt me, because I know how this would turn out if we attempted it."

As before, it happened again that King Hrolf's mind worked like this: He paid no attention to the matter and let it pass, as he did with many other things that were brought to his attention, and it wasn't clear what he was thinking. Later, he would take up this matter which had slipped everyone's mind. For some time, the sworn brothers stayed by turns in Denmark or in Gautland. They always went raiding in the summer, winning a great deal of wealth, and were the bravest of warriors, so that no one could withstand them. They became most famous for their heroic deeds. Almost everyone knew their names.

It is said of King Hrolf that he was the largest and strongest of all men. He was so heavy that he couldn't ride any horse for a whole day, without it suffocating or collapsing under him—he always had to change horses.[7] King Hrolf was the most handsome of men, courteous and well-shaped in every respect, with the finest hair of any man; a broad face and prominent features; the keenest eyesight, with blue and flashing eyes; a slender waist and broad shoulders. He was the most accomplished and well-mannered man in every respect, a better fighter than anyone, and more skilled in all sports and achievements than any other man in the Northlands in those days. He was the best-loved of men. King Hrolf was a wise man, foresighted in everything, intelligent and clear-sighted. He soon became famous far and wide for his rulership, near and far.

One spring, Ketil asked what King Hrolf intended to do in the summer. He answered, "Wouldn't it be a good idea to go to Sweden and try to become King Eirek's in-laws, as you once suggested?"

Ketil said, "You're unbelievable. First you ignore what's said to you and don't pay it any attention at the time—yet it's on your mind. Then you remember it later, once many years have passed, and act as if it had just been brought up. I feel the same way about it as I did then, and there's no need to delay."

The king said, "Have you heard anything about this maiden?"

Ketil answered, "Nothing at all, except for what I've already told you."

The king said, "I've heard that she is both wise and beautiful—and, as I've been told, that she is so haughty and proud that she wants no man to address her as a woman. She has been raised to kingship over a third of Sweden. Her seat is at Ullarakr, where she maintains a household like other kings. I've also heard it said that several kings have asked for her hand in marriage. Some she has had killed; some she has shamed in some way; some she has blinded, castrated, or had their hands or feet cut off; and she's received them all with ridicule and disgrace. This is how she wants to discourage people from courting her. I can also see that this journey could turn out either way. If we manage to arrange this marriage, the journey will increase our fame—but otherwise, we'll get shame and disgrace and be laughingstocks forever."

Ketil said, "Many men aren't enough for you, even if they've been brought together for you in full. It's completely ridiculous that you hardly have the confidence to propose to a woman. I think that the more arrogance she assumes, the more her ferocity will collapse once the time comes to put an end to it."

King Hrolf said, "Now that you're questioning my courage about this journey, I'll send you to Denmark to find my sworn brother Ingjald. I want him to make this journey with me."

Their conversation ended. Ketil went on his way to Denmark. Ingjald lost no time and traveled to meet King Hrolf. The king welcomed him warmly and told him his plan. Ingjald thought it was a good one, and said that with the king's luck, they could expect their mission to turn out all right in the end.

King Hrolf told Ketil his brother to stay at home and guard the kingdom. Ketil said, "It's your decision, lord, but I'm astonished that you're calling me worthless, since I'm not fit to join your retinue."

The king said, "Don't think of yourself that way, brother, because you shall make the journey if we need you in a difficult situation. But first, we will put forth this proposal calmly and patiently, if we're given the chance." But Ketil was most unwilling, and predicted that it would go badly.

King Hrolf set out on his journey, riding away from home with sixty men. Those men had been carefully picked, both for their courage and for their showy trappings of clothes and weapons. They rode away, as the road took them, and didn't stop their travels until they came to Uppsala.

CHAPTER VII

Now the story turns to King Eirek. He had a wise and beautiful queen, who set great store by dreams. Her name was Ingigerd.

One night, the queen awoke in her bed. She said to King Eirek, "I must have been thrashing around in my sleep."

"You were," said the king, "but what did you dream?"

She answered, "I was standing outside and looking around, and suddenly I could look out over all Sweden and much farther. I looked towards Gautland, and I could see so clearly that I saw a huge pack of wolves running from there, and I thought they were heading towards Sweden. A huge lion was running ahead of the wolves. After it came a white bear with red cheeks. Both beasts seemed peaceful, with their hackles down. They howled, but not fiercely—but that seemed odd, given how quickly the animals were coming here, and how clearly I thought I saw them. There didn't look to be more than sixty. I realized that they must be intending to come here to Uppsala. I thought that I called out to you to tell you about it, and at that moment I awoke."

The king said, "My lady, what do you suppose this means?"

She answered, "When I saw the wolves, those were men's fetches.[8] Since the lion ran ahead, that is a king's fetch, and he must be their ruler. A white bear was running next to him, and that must be some champion or prince accompanying this king, because the bear is strong and indicates powerful support. I think it's very likely that some noble king is seeking you out. That beast was much larger and stronger than I have heard could exist."

The king said, "When do you think this king will arrive? And how much damage do you think they will do in our kingdom?"

The queen said, "I would say that I expect that this king is coming in peace at this time, because these beasts were gentle. If I had to guess, I would say that the great lion must be the fetch of King Hrolf Gautreksson of Gautland, since that's where these beasts were coming from. I guess the white bear must be the fetch of Ingjald, his sworn brother."

The king said, "What could Hrolf the champion want, coming here to meet with us?"

The queen said, "It's all a riddle, but because the beasts seemed mild, I think that they are coming in peace with good intentions towards us. I think it most likely that King Hrolf will have the same mission that many others have had before: to ask for the hand of our daughter Thornbjorg. She is now the most famous woman in the Northlands."

The king said, "I didn't know that Hrolf intended such insolence, nor that other king who rules such a little kingdom—since high kings, with under-kings who pay them tribute, have previously asked for her hand. Don't go on with such daydreams, my lady."

The queen said, "Don't pay this any mind, unless what I think proves true."

The king said, "How shall I go to meet King Hrolf if he comes here, or receive his proposal, if that's his reason for coming?"

She answered, "You must receive Hrolf well if he seeks you out, and offer him the best cheer, because he is the most accomplished man in many respects. It's not certain that your daughter could get a more famous man, or so I'm told about him."

After that, they ended their conversation for the time being. Several days passed.

CHAPTER VIII

King Eirek was informed that King Hrolf Gautreksson had arrived with sixty men. The king got men to invite him to a feast in his hall. When the invitation reached King Hrolf, he went to meet the king, and he was welcomed well and suitably, but with no grace or good cheer. The high-seat across the table from the king was prepared for him.

They arrived late in the day. Once the tables and food were taken away, drink was brought in. When they had drunk for a while, many were quite cheerful, but King Hrolf was quite attentive and said little. King Eirek spoke to him and asked for news from Gautland or any other place from which he might have heard. King Hrolf said that there wasn't any news from Gautland.

King Eirek said, "For what reason have you come to us Swedes, riding with many men in the middle of winter?"

King Hrolf answered, "Whether we've been traveling on ships or horses, we have come here of our own free will, whatever comes of it from now on. Since you're asking about our mission, we had intended to mention it at a more leisurely time than now—but since you've found out, I suppose that we need not put it off, because it's true what they say, 'a shy man's request has to wait till evening'. My mission here is to propose becoming your son-in-law and marrying your daughter Thornbjorg. Now we would like to hear a clear and prompt answer to our proposal."

King Eirek answered, "I know the way that you Gauts tell jokes and speak very humorously when you drink, and I can't take it at all seriously.

I must have guessed the truth about you Gauts and your mission. I'm told that there is a great famine among you Gauts. It often happens; Gautland's a small country, with little income but a large population. You always provide food for a large host at your own expense, and you're openhanded and generous with your goods while they last. Now I realize that you must feel awfully hard-pressed, and that's why you've left home: you must be feeling terrible about suffering hunger and hardship. It's a dreadful misfortune when you can't keep up your strength, and so very difficult for men like yourselves to have to suffer. It was a very wise course to seek help at the likeliest place, rather than blundering around in misery. I think well of you for hoping for some help from us. I will quickly explain to you the help you can receive in our kingdom: we will permit you one month of safe conduct throughout our kingdom, if you're willing to stay here and be grateful. And if another king offers you such help, then I would really expect that you would go there and take all these people with you, instead of starving. Don't go spreading the nonsense that you asked for a woman's hand in marriage, neither my daughter's nor anyone else's, because that can't be anything but empty words as long as you're in such a state from poverty and famine. But when this time is over, matters will look more hopeful again when you go home, and you won't need to trouble yourselves about that."

CHAPTER IX

King Hrolf listened carefully to the king's words. When the king ended his speech, Hrolf said, "My lord, it's not true that we're short of food in our land, or that we need anyone's charity to help our people. Had this disaster struck us, we would rather have gone somewhere else than here. Your taunting seems uncalled for." The men saw that King Hring was getting very angry, though he said little. The kings parted right then, and the men went off to their beds. King Hrolf and his men were brought to an outbuilding to sleep.

King Eirek also went to his bed. The queen was already there, and they began talking among themselves. She asked, "Has King Hrolf come to meet us?"

"Certainly," said the king.

"What do you think of King Hrolf?" she asked.

"That doesn't take long to tell," said King Eirek. "I have never seen a bigger and stronger man, nor one more handsome and courteous, as I can see from his appearance. Nor have I seen anyone better shaped in every way."

The queen said, "I'm told that either you've discussed something with him, or else you've put his wisdom to the test."

The king told her how their entire conversation had gone. "And I think," he said, "that he is far ahead of other men, both in wisdom and in most achievements—and in patience."

The queen said, "Then this has begun badly, for you to have treated a ruler like King Hrolf so poorly. For that, you and your kingdom will suffer severe trouble from him for a long time. Although you may think he has a small kingdom, what I think is that his boldness and bravery, along with his kingly nature, would be of more use than the huge hosts of some other king in the Northlands, because I've been informed that he is far superior to other kings."

The king said, "Not only is he greatly superior to other men, you admire this king a great deal. What is your advice now?"

The queen said, "My advice is brief, my lord. I want for you to apologize to King Hrolf. I tell you truly that it will be difficult for you to match him in tenacity or in fighting ability, because he has support from the Danish king. He plans everything with King Hring, his foster-father."

The king replied, "Maybe we've misjudged the situation. What must I now say or do that will please him well?"

The queen said, "My advice is this: when they come to their seats in the morning, and you have all drunk for a while, you should speak cheerfully with King Hrolf and ask about the mighty deeds that he has accomplished. I guess that he'll be reserved, and your conversation will not have slipped his mind. Then you should ask why he's come here, and pretend that he had never brought up his mission to you. But if he hints or brings up anything you've said, then say that you don't remember that you two had talked about anything except in a fine and friendly way, but if you said anything wrong, say that you really wish it hadn't been said. And if he brings up his suit, I want you to agree to it, and not turn him away—assuming he can get her to say yes to his proposal. Be cheerful and easy-going in this matter, and I expect that it will go well between you. But I don't think it's certain just how easily the courtship will go, even if you consent." After that, they went to sleep for the night.

In the morning, when the men came to the table to drink, King Eirek was quite jovial and spoke very cheerfully with King Hrolf's men. When King Hrolf heard that, he paid attention, but spoke very little. When King Eirek noticed that, he said, "So the matter stands: Hrolf, you've come into our hall, as we invited you, and since it seems to me that you have no inclination to be cheerful, as is the custom of noble chieftains at feasts, we are eager for you to share with us the cause of your unhappiness, so that we may make your happiness complete. Thus may your kingly rank maintain its dignity, through the enjoyment of such things with which we may increase your honor. In exchange, we would like to hear from you some entertaining tales of your mighty deeds, such as are told daily about your heroic achievements and battles. We have been told a great deal about them already."

King Hrolf said, "It'll be like everything else that's said about me; it won't seem very worthy to you Swedes."

King Eirek said, "Much has been said to us about your handsomeness and your accomplishments, and we think that one could not tell too many stories about all your handsome looks, courtliness, and courtesy. How old are you, Hrolf?"

"I am now eighteen years old."

The king answered, "You are an outstanding man. But where do you intend to ride? What reason do you have for seeking us out?"

Hrolf was amazed that the king would ask that, and he thought that the king must want to taunt him a second time. He said, "We've made known our reason for coming here, and I don't think that the answer we got from you when we met has been forgotten by us Gauts."

The king said, "I don't recall that you had brought up any reason to us. It does not befit our kingly rank to speak with an equally worthy ruler, such as yourself, except in goodly fashion. If we have said anything that might displease you, then the saying must be true that 'ale makes a different man.' We wish to take all that back judiciously, leaving it as if it were unsaid. Now that I can guard my tongue, I want to answer your proposal favorably, and that's the way that matters will stand."

King Hrolf saw that King Eirek was calm. He brought up his proposal of marriage for the second time. He delivered it both well and swiftly. And when he ended his proposal, King Eirek said, "We want to answer this request favorably, because in all probability, no king more famous than you could ask to become our son-in-law. But you must have heard that our daughter does not live with us. We have given her a third of our kingdom, and she rules it just like a king. She is powerful and haughty and has a retinue, just like kings. Many kings and princes have asked for her hand. She has sent them all away with scornful words, and some she has had maimed. Now, since this conduct of hers is not to my taste, because she commits such great injustices, since no man may dare to address her in any way other than with the royal title, on pain of suffering hardship at her hands—now, if you wish to seek this woman's hand in marriage, whether by wits or by force, then we will give you leave on our behalf. In return, we would like to

51

have guarantees of peace and protection from you, for our men and all our kingdom, even should you need to engage in battle. Also, we are unwilling to force against her, and so we and all our retainers wish to remain at peace."

King Hrolf said that he could not have asked for more from the king, and they bound the agreement between them with oaths. Now they drank, happy and cheerful. King Eirek held the most lavish feast.

When three days had passed, King Hrolf prepared to leave, and the kings parted in warm friendship. He didn't stop traveling until he came with his retinue to Ullarakr, where Thornbjorg ruled. They arrived early in the day, and were told that the king was sitting at the table with all her household. The king chose twelve of his men to go with him—"and the rest of our men are to stand outside, with our horses ready."

King Hrolf spoke again with his men who were to go inside. "Here's how we shall line up: I will go in first, then Ingjald, then the rest in single file. If it happens that we're tested by an attack, defend yourselves as best you can, and let the man who came in last get out first. Let's go in as boldly as we can."

After that they went into the hall. As they came in, all the king's men were sitting on benches along both sides of the tables, and the hall was fully decked out. No one greeted them, but everyone listened carefully. King Hrolf went in before the high seat. He saw a most mighty person sitting there in splendid royal finery. This person was fair and handsome. Everyone sitting inside was amazed at the height and handsomeness of King Hrolf, but no one addressed any words to them.

King Hrolf took the helmet from his head and bowed to the king, but stuck the point of his sword in the table. He said, "Be well, my lord, and peace to all your kingdom." When the king heard his speech, she didn't say a word or even glance at him.

When King Hrolf saw the king's great hostility, he began to speak: "My lord, I have come here to meet with you, with the advice and consent of King Eirek your father, to seek honor for you and advancement for myself, by joining with you in delightful enjoyment which each of us may offer the other according to the bidding of our natures, without any grief or unrest."

The king stared at him and said, "You must be a complete fool to have come to visit us, whatever you're called back home. I can clearly see that this 'delightful enjoyment' that you're craving from us is food and drink. We won't withhold that from any man who is in need and will take it from us. For the trouble we're taking, you should follow this request of ours closely: Don't make us listen to such taunting, because I don't intend to be any man's steward or servant, not yours and no one else's. You and your comrades get

52

to your places quickly, so that you can ease your hunger and thirst. But leave us and all our trusted men in peace from your teasing."

King Hrolf said, "It's not true that we're craving food or drink from you now, because we've had plenty of that. But since we know that you're the daughter of the King of Sweden, rather than his son, we want to make our proposal in no uncertain terms, with your father's staunch agreement, and ask for your hand in marriage, to strengthen and rule our kingdoms in order to support and maintain all our offspring."

When King Thorberg heard these words from King Hrolf, she was so furious that she hardly knew what to do. She ordered all her men to arm themselves right there in the hall, and capture and tie up that fool—"he's offered us such a huge disgrace, which I assume is meant to slander and shame us, because never before have such disgraceful words been spoken to any king or champion who can wield a weapon. I'll pay him back, and discourage petty kings from making fun of us, or mocking our father the king so much."

This king and all her men were fully armored. She was the first to seize a weapon, and then one man after the other did the same. Loud clashings and battle-cries broke out in the hall, as each man encouraged the others. When King Hrolf saw the commotion, he set his helmet on his head and ordered his men to leave. The last man to enter was the first to leave. The entire household attacked King Hrolf with all the vigor they could muster. King Hrolf leaped backwards through the hall, holding his shield before him and swinging his sword as best he could. It's said that he killed twelve men in the hall, but when they got out, he saw that there was no chance of resisting the great host of men. All they could do was to ride away at once. Their opponents kept screaming battle-cries and catcalls after them, each one louder than the next.

King Hrolf ordered his men to ride away, and he soon got away, because the locals had no horses nearby for the pursuit. King Hrolf's men were quite glad to escape. Nothing is said about their journey until they came home to Gautland. Their journey had gone badly.

CHAPTER X

It's said that after the chase was over, the Swedes turned back to their own hall. The king had her hall cleaned and the fallen bodies carried out. The news was heard far and wide, and everyone felt that this journey had been completely ludicrous.

On another occasion, when the King of the Swedes had sat down with her household, she asked whether they knew anything about the man they had mocked. They answered that his name was Hrolf, king of Gautland. "He is easy to recognize," they said, "on account of his height and handsomeness."

The king said, "We quickly recognized him from men's reports. He is such a distinguished man, and he must also be a wise and patient man, and he seemed steadfast. I would think that he'll be cool-headed and persistent in pursuing the proposal that he made, so we should prepare for this man coming after us Swedes again. We'll seek out builders and have a rampart built all around our estate, immensely strong and well-built, and build it with such skill that it can't be attacked with either fire or iron, because I think that this king is plotting against us."

When all this was done as the king willed and planned, King Thorberg had engines of war built there, both catapults and flame-shooters. The stronghold was made so secure that most people thought it unlikely that it could be taken, as long as there were bold men on the ramparts. The king now thought that she had a secure place to stay. She waited, cheerful and happy with those of her men who were at hand. No one could get in to see her without her leave.

CHAPTER XI

Now the story turns to how King Hrolf came home to Gautland, not content with his journey. His brother Ketil went to meet him and asked how it had gone. Hrolf told him about all their dealings.

Ketil said, "It's such a terrible disgrace to suffer being chased by a woman, like a mare in the stud-herd or a dog in the milking-shed. I'm sure that if I had been there, this journey would not have turned out so laughably. We should have all fallen there, one across the other, before letting ourselves be chased like cowardly goats before wolves. You must not mean to let this lie unavenged for long. You must summon all your fighting men at once, those who'll support you."

King Hrolf answered, "We don't care for your recklessness and thoughtlessness. Our journey would have gone much worse if we'd had your impatience and rashness to deal with. You can be sure that I intend to summon my men, but I don't intend to go to Sweden this summer."

Ketil said, "This is terrible. The Swedes have beaten all the courage out of you, so you don't dare avenge yourself."

The king said that he didn't care about his anger or rebuke. He said that he would go ahead with his own plans. The king was tight-lipped about those and many other things, whether they pleased or displeased him.

Winter passed, and in the spring the king prepared to set out from his land. When he was prepared, he set out raiding for the summer. He had five ships, all large and fully crewed. Both Ketil and Ingjald were with him. They raided far and wide throughout the western lands, in Shetland, the Hebrides, Orkney, and Scotland. They won plenty of wealth, and when summer had passed, they meant to go home.

One evening they anchored in the lee of an island and put up awnings over their ships. When they had set them up, King Hrolf crossed the island with some men. They saw nine ships lying together off the other side of the island. They saw that these were Viking ships.

The king went back to his own ships. He ordered Ketil his brother to launch the boat and find out who the captain of these ships was. Ketil did so; he rowed to the ships and asked who the captain was. A tall and handsome man stood up on the afterdeck of one of the ships and spoke up: "If you're asking for the captain of this ship, he's called Asmund, and he's the son of King Olaf of Scotland. But who sent you?"

Ketil answered, "King Hrolf Gautreksson sent me to find you and tell you that he'll come here in the morning. He wants to have your wealth and ships, and butcher you for the wolves, unless you surrender everything you own into his hands."

Asmund answered, "We know that King Hrolf Gautreksson is famous for the many deeds that he has accomplished on raids. But now, since I am a king's son and I have plenty of men, I say to King Hrolf that we will not surrender without a fight. We'll pit five ships against your five ships,⁹ and we'll win this fight without sorcery."

After that, Ketil went back and told King Hrolf what had happened, saying that the man was the handsomest man and the finest warrior.

In the morning, both sides prepared for battle. Asmund had four of his ships anchor nearby, and they began to fight at once. It was a hard and long and fierce battle. Asmund advanced with great bravery, and Hrolf thought that he'd never had to deal with braver men. Many fell on both sides. King Hrolf saw that this was no time for half measures, and he and his men rushed on board Asmund's ship. Then there was a great slaughter. Asmund urged his men on and charged forward most bravely. King Hrolf came against him, and many men fell on both sides, but more on Asmund's side. Both men traded blows, going at it with all their might. Hrolf ordered that no man should interfere in their combat. Asmund was badly wounded in their encounter, and when King Hrolf saw that he could no longer fight wholeheartedly, he said, "I want us to rest and talk a while."

Asmund asked him to explain. Hrolf said, "I have been raiding for several summers, and I have never found your equal in bravery. Now, since many of your men are wounded and dead, there are two options at hand. One is for you to crew your ship a second time with unwounded men, if you want to fight longer. Then we will fight to the end. The other option is for us to call a truce. Then I will offer to swear brotherhood with you, and thus we will make our friendship firm."

Asmund replied that he wanted a truce—"if you will spread no slander about me or my men."

Hrolf said that he had never met braver men.

After that, King Hrolf ordered them to cease fighting. The peace-shields were held up.[10] Both of them anchored alongside the island and bound their men's wounds. Two of Asmund's ships, and one of Hrolf's, had been cleared of fighters. Afterwards, each man swore faithfulness to the other, and vowed never to be parted except by the consent of both men. Then Asmund arranged his surviving forces: he equipped one ship very well with men and weapons, and the rest of his men he sent to Scotland. Two of his ship's crews had fallen, and one of Hrolf's. But the men whom Asmund thought were his best and bravest followers, he kept with him on one ship, and he sailed with King Hrolf to Gautland.

Asmund was considered the boldest and bravest man, and came nearest to King Hrolf in all his achievements—yet he still came up short. They all stayed together that winter in Gautland, in perfect peace and with much good cheer. Asmund kept reminding King Hrolf to go back and see to his proposed marriage in Sweden, strongly urging him to make the journey. The king was always tight-lipped about this journey, but he had grief from his brother Ketil, who urged him on eagerly.

When spring came, King Hrolf prepared to leave his lands. He had seven ships, all well equipped, and the boldest men. King Hrolf made it plain to his men that he meant to go to Sweden. Then the king asked his brother Ketil not to stay behind, and all the sworn brothers went on this journey. They set a course for Sweden with all their forces.

CHAPTER XII

On the night they arrived in Sweden, Queen Ingigerd had a dream. She told the dream to King Eirek: "I seemed to be standing outside, and once again I could see for a long distance. I looked to the sea and saw that no small number of ships had landed, and from the ships there ran many wolves, but a lion ran ahead of the wolves. Two white bears ran with him, very large and handsome. All these beasts came side by side, but beside the lion on the other side, there was a boar charging ahead. He was not as large as he was savage. I had never seen anything like him. He rooted up every hill and howled as if he would turn inside out. Every bristle on him was sticking out. He acted as if he would attack everything and bite whatever came in reach. Now I realize that the lion is King Hrolf's fetch, since I saw him before. But now he was scowling much more fiercely than before. All the beasts were much more ferocious, and they charged onto land, heading for Uppsala."

King Eirek said, "Who do you suppose has the wicked boar you saw as a fetch? That fetch wasn't here on their first journey, and there was no more than one bear then."

The queen said, "I've heard it said that King Hrolf has a brother named Ketil, the smallest and most impetuous of men, full of rashness and violence, and the most eager for warlike exploits. I suppose this boar must be his fetch, because he wasn't here before with his brother King Hrolf. Since there were two white bears, I guess that King Hrolf has taken some great man into his following, a king or a prince. Act rightly, my lord, and keep all your agreements with King Hrolf. He must now intend to come and see about his proposal of marriage. Many men would already have taken vengeance for outrages like those that were done to him when he went to Ullarakr, as we heard. As much as you promised to do as he wished the last time, you must now promise even more firmly, because he is now completely bent on harming us if he doesn't make the marriage that he agreed on." The king said that it would be done.

Now the king was informed that King Hrolf had arrived in the land. King Eirek invited him to a splendid feast, along with a hundred of his men, and King Hrolf accepted. Eirek the king of Sweden and all his household went to meet him with great good cheer. They stayed there for several nights, honored most highly. King Eirek offered them anything they might be lacking, with the greatest good will.

One day, when they had sat down to drink, King Eirek asked whether King Hrolf intended to pursue his marriage proposal. He said that he would risk it, however it might turn out.

The king said, "Now it will go as I told you before; to accomplish anything here, you'll need both cunning and bravery. We've been informed that the king has built great defenses. She's had the strongest fortifications built, with great skill and all sorts of traps, and we don't think that they will be easy to conquer. I will fulfill every promise which I have made to you, King Hrolf, and grant you rulership over the kingdom that we gave her to rule, until we leave off governing. Then you shall claim all this kingdom after we are gone—if you manage to win her."

King Hrolf thanked King Eirek for his noble speech, and said that he could not have asked for more from his hands.

CHAPTER XIII

Not long after, they prepared to leave, and they didn't stop their journey until they reached Ullarakr. Certain knowledge of their coming had gone ahead of them for their entire journey, and the Swedish king had had strong fortresses built, so that there was no way to get in. When King Hrolf arrived with his men, there was no lack of uproar and clashing of weapons coming from the fortresses. They saw the strong defenses there. King Hrolf ordered his men to pitch their tents and camp, saying that they wouldn't stay there for long. King Hrolf then spoke with his brother Ketil and asked him to take the fortress with sudden attacks and taunting speech. Ketil said that he intended to attack without holding anything back, and so did each of his men.

They slept that night, and in the morning King Hrolf made a request, saying that he wanted to speak with the King of the Swedes. He asked her to come out onto the ramparts, so that each of them might hear the other's words clearly. This was told to the king, and she went out onto the wall with all her retinue. When King Hrolf saw the king, he said, "Sire, I ask you to hear and heed the words which we will speak to you. You may remember the last time we came to meet you, what our purpose was, and what shame and disgrace you did to us. Now, if we receive no better answer than before, I shall burn this place and kill every mother's son in it, or else I shall die here."

When the king had heard his words, she said, "You'll be a Gautlandish goat-herd before you'll get any authority over this place or anyone who protects us. Go home with all your men and be glad that you got away unhurt." Then the king beat on her shield and said that she didn't want to hear another word out of King Hrolf, and all her men did the same. When King Hrolf saw that his negotiations with the king had come to nothing, he ordered his men to arm themselves and attack boldly. They did as the king ordered, but soon retreated without accomplishing anything. They couldn't do anything without facing a counterattack. They carried fire to the walls, but water poured down from hollow logs set into the ramparts. They thought they could take the fort with their weapons by digging, but their enemies poured blazing pitch and boiling water on them. Large stones were dropped on them as well, bruising them all, because there was no shortage of defenders. Some men were killed there and many were hurt, and they went away both exhausted and wounded. There was grumbling among the Gauts, and they didn't like this fight. The Swedes came out of the fortress, jeering and laughing at them, and questioning their courage. They brought out velvet and silk and many precious treasures and showed them off, inviting the Gauts to try and get them.

King Hrolf asked his brother Ketil how he thought things were going. Ketil said that it seemed rather hard work—"I believe this king of the Swedes is pissing very hot." The king said that perhaps more than just bragging was needed.

They stayed there no less than half a month. Then Asmund said to Hrolf, "We've been attacking this stead for a long time, and every day we've had severe troubles. We've lost many men, and some are wounded. Now, my lord, we want you to come up with some plans which will help. If not, our men want to go home, because we've gotten mockery and laughter for our pains."

King Hrolf answered, "We don't see any way to make it certain that this fortress will be won. But let's try going to the forest and tying up big bundles of sticks. We'll make a huge wickerwork out of them, and put big logs under it. Then we should carry this wickerwork so high that men can easily stand underneath it and prop it up from below with posts. We must pick all our strongest men for this. Then some will have digging tools and dig holes in the walls, and we'll find out if we can get through the walls that way."

They all felt this was a good plan. When they had brought this device, they carried it under the ramparts. It was so strong that nothing hurt the men behind it, neither stones nor pitch, so that in a short time they had breached the fortress walls. When King Thorberg had figured out their trick, she ran into an underground passage with all her men, and that's how they escaped into the forest. King Hrolf broke into the fortress with all his forces, but when they came inside, everyone had fled. They found it very strange not to find any men when they came into the quarters—but food and drink stood prepared in every room, and clothes and treasures were all there, ready to hand.

Ketil said, "This king's a coward at heart, if she's abandoned such a huge store of treasures, along with food and drink prepared for our enemies. We've had a great stroke of luck for our trouble. First we should drink and eat, and then divide up our loot."

When King Hrolf heard his words, he said, "Now you've snapped at the bait that was set for you, paying more attention to filling your belly than capturing the king. No one is to delay here so that the king can get away. Instead, we must search this place, in case we find any underground passages that might lead away from here."

They did as the king ordered, and they found an underground passage in the fortress. King Hrolf went in first, and then one man after another followed. They walked until they came to an upwards passage, and by then they had reached the forest. There before them was the Swedish king with all her household. A battle broke out. King Hrolf advanced boldly and bravely, and so did all the sworn brothers. The Swedish king and all her men fought bravely, because her followers were hand-picked for their valor, and she had a much larger force. But as soon as the sworn brothers entered the fray, they charged fiercely and killed many men. The Swedish king urged her men on and said that they were no help if they couldn't drive away a petty king. King Thorberg fought with a keen heart, and she and her champions killed many men, yet the battle was turning very much against the Swedes.

King Hrolf spoke with Ketil, his brother. "I want you to attack the king of the Swedes, and capture her if you can. But don't use a weapon against her, because it's the worst disgrace to wound a woman with a weapon."

Ketil said that he would do it if he could. Just then, the Swedish ranks broke and ran. By then, Ketil had come so close to the king that he slapped the king's crotch with the flat of his sword blade. He grabbed her and said, "My lady, this is how we'll scratch that itch in your crotch. Now that's what I call a foul blow."[11]

The king said, "That blow won't bring you honor." She struck Ketil under the ear with the blunt side of her axehead,[12] so hard that she knocked him head over heels, and said, "That's how we always beat our dogs, if they're too eager to bark."

Ketil leaped to his feet, ready to avenge himself. At that moment, King Hrolf came up and seized the king and said, "Lord, lay down your weapon; you are now in our power. I will grant a truce to you and all your men, if you will agree to be governed by your father."

The Swedish king said, "You probably think you have power over us and all our men, King Hrolf, but it will do you little credit that we will never willingly consent, even if you force us into this."

King Hrolf said, "My lord, we've come together because I want to ask for your hand honorably. I ask that our engagement be decided by your father's judgment. If he resolves matters between us, it will be said that you have honorably upheld all of our glory."

The Swedish king said, "You must be a wise and experienced man, because many a man in your position would think to force us to his will— but you want to go ahead with this arrangement between us. Now that we and our men are in your power, we will agree to this, and so release ourselves from this bondage for now. Now, King Hrolf, we wish to follow the custom of courteous men if they are beaten and overcome: we want to invite you and all your men to rest and enjoy a grand feast, and so reward you for granting a truce to our men. But just now, we want to ride to Uppsala with all our surviving picked troops, and meet our father King Eirek for a complete consultation, because it is our honor to keep his advice."

The kings bound themselves to this agreement with strong oaths. After that, King Hrolf turned back to the fortress, and as soon as he had come there, he accepted a feast there for three nights. But the King of Sweden rode to Uppsala with all her retinue. As soon as she arrived, she went before King Eirek her father, lay her shield down before her feet, took the helmet off her head, bowed to the king and greeted him. She said, "My dear father, I have been driven from the kingdom which you gave into my keeping. Because I have been overcome by strong warriors, I ask you to make whatever arrangements you please for my marriage."

The king said, "We strongly desire that you stop this fighting, and we want you to take up womanly activities and go to your mother in the bower. Then we will betroth you to King Hrolf Gautreksson, because we know no one who is his equal throughout all the Northlands."

The princess said, "We wouldn't want to come to meet you for your guidance, but then be unwilling to trust your wisdom."

After that she went to the bower, giving the weapons she'd borne over to King Eirek for safekeeping. She sat down with her mother to embroider. She was fairer and lovelier and more courteous than any maiden, so much that there was no one as lovely to be found in the northern half of the world. She was wise and beloved, eloquent and shrewd and haughty.

CHAPTER XIV

After that, King Eirek sent men to meet King Hrolf and invite him and his warriors to a feast. King Hrolf lost no time and went to Uppsala. When King Eirek heard of King Hrolf's arrival, he went with all his retinue to meet him. He led him to the high seat beside him in his own hall, and arranged the seats for his sworn brothers. They drank, happy and cheerful. Then they discussed what had become of their arrangement, and they came to complete agreement. After that, King Eirek had his daughter summoned into the hall. When her father's message reached her, she dressed herself in the best finery and entered the hall with her mother and many other refined ladies. When Eirek saw his daughter come in, he stood up to meet her, and he led her to a seat on his other side, along with the queen and all the women in her train.

When the kings had been drinking for a while, King Hrolf brought up his proposal of marriage, so that the young maiden could hear. There's no need to make a long story of how King Hrolf was betrothed to the young maiden. The feast was made even grander, and a multitude of men was invited from all over the Swedish realm. This feast was magnificent and lasted half a month. And at the end of the feast, King Eirek gave noble gifts to all mighty men with glad good will, and then each man went to his home by the cheerful consent of King Eirek.

King Hrolf stayed behind in Sweden with his wife, and good love began to grow between them. King Hrolf sent his brother Ketil to rule over Gautland. Ingjald went to his father in Denmark. King Hrolf began ruling the realm which the princess had formerly ruled. Now they all stayed in peace, each in the place to which he had come.

CHAPTER XV

The next spring, messengers came to King Hrolf from Denmark. They said that King Hring was dead, and that Ingjald had asked King Hrolf to come visit him and share the inheritance-feast in memory of King Hring, who was his foster father. As soon as Hrolf heard the news, he prepared for this journey, and his sworn brother Asmund went with him. When they were ready, they set their course for Denmark. They had two ships, well crewed with men and stocked with weapons. Ketil came to join them, and he had one well-equipped ship. They came alongside Zealand late in the day and tied up along an island, spreading awnings over their ships.

King Hrolf landed on the island with some men. They saw ships anchored along the other side of the island, five ships all together. Four were longships, and the fifth was a dragon-ship, both large and beautiful. The king thought that he had never seen a more beautiful ship. These ships were tented over with black awnings.

The king said, "Who can be the captain of that costly ship? I have never seen a ship that I would rather own than that one."

Asmund answered, "That's certainly a prize ship in every respect, and as such it would be a king's treasure. But I think there's only one man who can be the captain of this ship, and you'll have to exert all your strength before you get it. The one who owns it must think well of himself."

The king said, "Do you know who owns the dragon-ship?"

Asmund answered, "His name is Grimar the son of Grimolf, and he is the worst Viking. He sails on warships both in winter and summer. He looks huge and wicked, but in truth he's even worse. No iron bites him or any of the twelve men that follow him. They eat all their meat raw and drink blood.[13] It's truly said that they're more trolls than men. One summer, we encountered each other off the Hebrides. I had ten ships, all well crewed, and they had five ships. We fought one day, and the battle quickly turned against us. All my men fell there, but I jumped into the sea and escaped. I've never gone on a worse expedition than that one."

The king said, "Do you think there's any point in fighting them with the forces we have?"

Asmund asked the king to decide. "We must trust in your luck, if it will help." Ketil strongly urged them to attack, and he said that it would be good to test themselves and win wealth and fame.

King Hrolf said, "Since they are wicked and greedy, but they have the treasure that I truly want to own, we will prepare for battle and load stones onto our ships."

It was done as the king ordered, and they prepared as best they could. The king had them go up onto the island and cut great clubs.[14] After that they put on their armor, and then they rowed at them silently.

It is said that Grimar's ships were all anchored side by side, and the longships lay closer to the island, with the dragon-ship on the outside. There was a wide gap between the ships and the island. They headed first for the longships, knowing that if those were taken before they moved against the dragon-ship—"I think we'd win, if our men had no longships on the other side when they attack the dragon-ship." The king ordered them to fight hardest while the other side was least expecting it, and to know how to deal with them as quickly as possible. He ordered them not to shout, but to move as silently as they could. They did as the king ordered.

There was fog and thick darkness. The men on the longships noticed nothing until the awnings were pulled away and they themselves were beaten with stones and weapons. They all sprang to their feet and counterattacked with great bravery, because they all kept their weapons with them while they were lying down, yet they suffered many casualties before they managed to arrange their forces for defense. When they had fought for a little while, King Hrolf and his men boarded the ships. There was such a terrible slaughter that in a short time they cleared the ship that they'd boarded. They killed some men, and others jumped into the sea and drowned. They cleared three ships in this way, killing every mother's son. At that, Grimar awoke and ordered his men on the dragon-ship to attack. There were loud shouts and battle-cries, as each man encouraged the others.

King Hrolf said to his brother Ketil: "Now you shall attack the remaining longship, and Asmund and I shall attack the dragon-ship." Ketil said that they would do so.

King Hrolf and Asmund attacked the dragon-ship on both sides. They had taken few losses, so they had many men. Grimar stood up on the dragon-ship and said, "Who's attacking so boldly?"

The king answered, "If you're curious, I'm called Hrolf son of Gautrek. The other is called Asmund, the son of the king of Scotland."

Grimar said, "We've seen that man. The last time, we parted in a way that must have left him with little nostalgia for our meeting, when we drove him overboard wounded, and killed every last one of his men. Doesn't he remember now?"

Asmund said, "Before evening comes, you'll find out that it hasn't slipped my mind."

Grimar spoke: "We're not afraid of your threats, but we know that King Hrolf is famed for his bravery, and so we're willing to offer him a choice that we haven't given anyone else, because it's a shame for such a man to be killed. King Hrolf, I invite you and all your men to land on the island, and you may keep your weapons and fine clothes. But the money you have, I'll take in exchange for the men you've killed before my eyes—and that's still far too little. But I've never made such a good offer to any man since I began raiding."

When King Hrolf heard his words, he said, "That must certainly be a kind offer. But since it's not clear to us that we're at your mercy, with you offering terms to us instead of us offering them to you, we don't want to lose our money by any means."

Grimar said, "I see that you must not be as wise a man as we thought, since you don't want to save your life, because I tell you truly that this is the last day of your life if you intend to fight me. I'd thought that you should be allowed to enjoy your life longer, because I'd been told that you were brave and popular. I had meant to show you more warriors' honor than the others. I thought I could increase my own fame for showing you more mercy than you deserve."

King Hrolf said, "You'll get no thanks from us for that. Prepare yourself quickly, because we're willing to risk finding out which of us will be offering terms to the other before evening comes. We've also overcome some of your men, and you have to avenge that."

"Now you've made the choice that you'll always regret afterwards, and you deserve it."

After that the battle broke out, fierce and hard. Grimar and his men were both strong and hardy, and so ferocious that the king's men couldn't do anything but defend themselves. It was difficult to take the fight onto the dragon-ship, because it was as high as a castle, and strong and skillful men defended the ship, striking downwards in front of themselves. Iron didn't bite any of these twelve, as Asmund had said. King Hrolf's men were falling, both from exhaustion and from wounds.

It's said that Ketil Gautreksson attacked the remaining longship. The man who captained the ship was named Forni, the bravest of men. Each attacked the other boldly, and their encounter was savage. Ketil made a fierce assault and boarded the ship with his men. The fighting was furious there. Forni and Ketil traded blows, and Forni fell before Ketil. Then they killed every man on the ship, and Ketil won high praise from his men. After that they sailed at the dragon-ship, and the brothers met. Ketil asked how the fighting was going. King Hrolf had little to say, but he said that things couldn't go on as they were, and added that this was a dreadful enemy to deal with. He ordered Ketil to row to the island and bring large tree trunks out to them, because there was no lack of deep forest there. Ketil did so, and did everything quickly.

When they came back, the king had the trunks fall onto the side of the ship. They were so large and heavy that the ship listed to the side. At once, King Hrolf and his men boarded the ship, and the dragon-ship's crewmen began falling, both from stones and from weapons. The battle turned against Grimar and his crew. King Hrolf headed for the ship's stern, holding a great club and striking left and right. Asmund and Ketil followed him, and their enemies fell, one across another. The king had superior numbers, and Grimar's forces fell until twelve men were left standing: Grimar and his champions. They were attacked with vigor and bashed with clubs. Many of them fell.

When Grimar saw that his side would be beaten, he leaped overboard into the sea. Asmund was standing nearby and plunged in right behind him, and swam after him to the island. When King Hrolf saw that, he swam to shore at once, wanting to help Asmund so that it wouldn't be just the two of them in the fight. When Asmund came to shore, Grimar was on land, and when he saw Asmund, he seized a stone and flung it at him. Asmund ducked into the sea, and when he came up, Grimar meant to throw another one, but at that moment he was hit with a club and fell down at once. King Hrolf had arrived, and he struck him some more blows, and there Grimar lost his life.

They headed out to the dragon-ship, where Ketil had finished the job for them. They cleared the dragon-ship, flinging the fallen into the sea. Then they went to the island and bandaged their wounds. Their men were both weary and wounded, and a great many had fallen. They stayed there for several nights. The king wasn't much hurt, but Asmund and Ketil were badly wounded.

After that, they prepared to leave. They took the dragon-ship, *Grimar's Gift*, but they could hardly manage to crew it because they were short of men, and they left all their other ships behind. They sailed to Denmark, and when Ingjald heard of King Hrolf's coming, he invited them to the feast which he had arranged—the inheritance-feast in memory of his father. They all drank King Hring's inheritance-feast together, with full honors. Nothing was discussed as much as their killing of Grimar, because everyone felt that to be the mightiest of brave deeds.

When this was finished, King Hrolf had a great assembly summoned. At that assembly, Ingjald was raised to kingship over all Denmark, after his father. He stayed there and ordered his kingdom as King Hrolf advised. After that, King Hrolf prepared to leave Denmark, honored with great gifts from King Ingjald. He went on his way until he reached Sweden, safe and sound. King Ingjald stayed quietly in his kingdom in Denmark, and they parted with the greatest joy. Ketil went to Gautland and stayed there in peace.

King Hrolf stayed for a long time in Uppsala, keeping up warm friendships with his kinfolk. King Hrolf spent a large sum to decorate the dragon-ship *Grimar's Gift*. He had it all painted above the waterline with various colors: yellow and red, green and blue, black and blended. He had the dragon's head ornamented with gold, along with the carvings and the entire prow, and he caulked the planking with molten gold wherever it seemed to be an improvement. It was more ornate than any ship,[15] and it was felt to excel every ship just as King Hrolf excelled other kings in the Northlands. He became greatly famous everywhere for his rulership and wisdom. Many powerful men sought him out and became his liegemen and rendered him faithful service. We have heard that no ship at that time had ever been crewed with more famous champions than the dragon-ship *Grimar's Gift*, although we don't know their names or anything to tell about them.

King Hrolf stayed in Sweden for a year, with great good cheer and splendor. Queen Thornbjorg loved King Hrolf very much. The king found that she was wiser than any other woman, and more outstanding in every respect. Asmund was well maintained by the king and proved to be the boldest man, brave in every way. The king valued him the most of all his men.

King Hrolf held a third of Sweden in stewardship. In the summer, he always made an expedition beyond his lands, seeking fame and renown for himself. The summer after the battle with Grimar, King Hrolf went out raiding. He raided far and wide in the western lands and won much wealth and fame. In the autumn, the king set his course for Sweden and spent the winter at peace.

CHAPTER XVI

At that time, a king named Halfdan ruled over Russia, a wise king with many friends. He had one beautiful daughter named Alof. King Halfdan loved his daughter very much. She was thought to be the best match in all Russia and even farther beyond.

There was a man named Thorir, who held the high seat in King Halfdan's hall. He was both tall and strong, and he was called Iron-Shield. For a long time he had served as guardian of the king's lands.

There were twelve berserks with King Halfdan. They were wicked and overbearing. Iron didn't bite any of them. Two of them are named: one was called Hrosskel, and the other was Hesthofdi. It is said of them that they waded through fire and walked freely on blades when the berserk fit came upon them. They killed both men and cattle and everything in front of them that didn't get away, and they spared no one while the madness was on them. But when it left them, they were so weak that they had nowhere near half their strength, and they were as weak as men who were stricken by illness. That lasted a day or so. King Halfdan had a great deal of trust in their fighting spirit, so that no kings had the courage to go to war with him.

The king loved his daughter much, and although kings asked for her hand, they all ran away because of the mockery and abuse which the berserks flung at them. Those who escaped this abuse thought themselves lucky. Thanks to this, the princess grew fussy and didn't want to say yes to anyone, even if he asked her. They lived in peace now, because everyone was weary of her answers.

CHAPTER XVII

On one occasion, Queen Thorbjorg was talking with King Hrolf. "What do you intend to do in the summer?"

The king answered, "I intend to go raiding."

She asked, "Have you heard anything about the travels of Ketil, your brother?"

He said that he had not heard anything—"can you tell us about it?"

She replied, "I have heard that Ketil went east to Russia to ask for the hand of King Halfdan's daughter. I've been told that he sailed from here with two ships, and he entered the king's hall with twelve men. I've heard that he stated his case well and frankly, and pressed his suit with many eloquent words, but he got answers from the king and the young lady that he found rude. The berserks leaped up with a battle cry and a great commotion and drove them out of the hall, chasing them to the ships with roaring and unheard-of howling. They were both battered and wounded, and they only escaped by 'buying their lives with their feet.' That's what we've heard about it. Now it's come to our attention that Ketil had no better luck asking for her hand than he had on your journey the first time you visited us, and his journey ended up much more shamefully. He will soon come to meet you and ask you to go with him to avenge his disgrace."

King Hrolf answered, "It's not easy to advise men like him, what with his fierceness and boldness. It'd be just as well now for him to give up his own stubbornness, since he didn't want to proceed with our supervision."

She asked him not to talk like that, and said that he was obliged to offer his brother help on his journey. At that point they broke off their conversation.

A little later, Ketil came to meet King Hrolf and explained about all the disgrace that he had suffered in Russia. King Hrolf said that the way it had gone was only to be expected—"because you thought you'd accomplish everything by your own ambition."

Ketil asked King Hrolf to go on the journey with him—"because I think I have too few forces to set right the dishonor that was done to me." Ketil was in a competely foul mood.

The king said to him that all his hot-headedness and bragging would come to nothing—"I don't think you're likely to get vengeance against such men as we have to deal with, because you'll need both numbers and firmness. First, you should go home to your kingdom and gather ships and men. Send word to King Ingjald in Denmark for him to do the same. Both of you come here in the summer, and then we'll see what seems the best course."

And after that, Ketil went home to his realm. Everyone made plans and preparations for this expedition.

CHAPTER XVIII

It's said that when summer and winter had passed, Ketil and Ingjald came to Sweden with forty ships, well equipped with men and weapons. King Hrolf had readied thirty ships, with his dragon-ship in the forefront. All these ships were crewed with a huge host of well-armed men, and they awaited a favorable wind. King Hrolf asked the queen how she felt in her heart about how their journey would turn out. She said that she expected it would end well, but said that she had dreamed that they would be in dire straits on one occasion on this journey, such that they'd be put to the test.

When the wind turned favorable, they hoisted their sails and set out at once, each as he was ready. There was very little wind at first. King Hrolf was the last to set out. The dragon-ship moved little, because it needed a strong wind. They sailed along the route to Russia. When they had sailed for a while, the wind began to pick up, and the dragon-ship swiftly followed the other ships. Then the wind grew strong. The king ordered them to tie the ships together and find out whether they could hold out like that, but when they tried to do it, such a gale broke out that the ships were separated at once. They had to take in their sails and run before the wind. After that came a wild northeaster, and they couldn't run before the wind any longer, and they had to reef almost all of the sail. Such a great gale blew up that their rigging tore, the mast-stays and the halyards broke, and so much water came at them that few of the crewmen expected to live. When this storm was at its most furious, King Hrolf's dragon-ship tore loose and drifted towards an island. But because there was a good harbor, the ship was trusty, and the crewmen were skilled, they reached land safe and sound. It was late in the evening; the wind fell, and the weather grew very mild. King Hrolf said that he wanted to land on the island and find out if he could see anything new. Asmund went with him, along with eight more men, but he ordered the rest of his men to wait by the ships and told them to wait till noon of the next day, if he didn't send them word before then.

After that, they went up onto the island. It was large and thickly covered with forest. When they had been walking for a while, they found a hut on the island, both large and strongly built, and they thought they had never seen a house so tall. The door was closed. The king ordered them to open it.

They took turns charging at the door but couldn't get it open.

The king said, "Whoever usually opens this door must have strength in his claws. I'll find out whether it opens." The king walked up to it and opened it with one hand.

They went right in and searched around and found a fire; they lit torches and carried them around the hut. They saw that there was no lack of all sorts of goods. There was a bed there, very well made and enormously large. The king lay down on the bed. He saw that, even if someone as tall as he were to lie down at his feet, the bed would still be much longer. They realized that the master of this house was no little man.

There was a single pillar in front of the bed, reaching up underneath the roof-beam. A very large sword was hanging on it, so high up that the king couldn't reach it. King Hrolf said, "Should some of our men spend the night here and wait for the man who is master of this house, and dare to find out what he's like at home? Or do you want to go to the ship and not risk meeting him?"

They asked him to decide, but said that they weren't willing to stay.

The king said, "I am more inclined to wait for the man of the house, but it may be that he'll find us too large a multitude, and he will be shy of so many guests. I shall now divide our forces. Four men shall go to the ship, but Asmund and I and four more shall stay behind. The four men should explain what's keeping us. If we don't come to the ship before breakfast, then be off on your way. There'll be no point in waiting then, because I suppose that a multitude wouldn't be of use against this man, for he'll overcome many just as well as few, if he is as brawny as I think. People will understand rather more clearly what became of Hrolf Gautreksson and his companions if you can get away and tell what you've seen. It seems to me that that the fellow who lives in this hut may have planned for our coming, and he wants our meeting to go ahead. I shall stay here all night."

After that, those whom the king had addressed left, and went to the ship and told what they'd heard from the king. They were all very afraid of what would happen to him.

CHAPTER XIX

Now we turn to how King Hrolf and his men were in the house at evening. The king said, "I would like to get that great sword which is hanging up."

"What is your plan?" said Asmund.

The king said, "You are to climb up on my back, and find out if you can manage to take down the sword if you stand on my shoulders."

Asmund said, "I think that sword is so heavy that I wouldn't be able to handle it."

The king said, "Steady yourself against the pillar with one hand, and lift the sword from below with the other hand. As soon as you feel that it's loose, let it fall down against the pillar. Then I'll take it."

Asmund did as the king asked. He got onto his shoulders and lifted the sword from below, and the king got it.

The evening passed. They heard a loud clatter outside, and just then a man came in. Then they didn't wonder why the hut was tall and grand, because the man was the most fearsome giant. None of them had ever seen so large a man before. He wasn't so ugly as to be monstrous, although his features were coarse. He was dressed well, and he was carrying a gray bear on his back and a huge bow in his hand. He was extremely tired, and they thought that he must have walked a long way. He went to the other side of the fire and flung down the bear. King Hrolf greeted him, but he acted as if he didn't hear. He swiftly and skillfully butchered the bear, hung up the kettle, and boiled the meat. After that, he took a table, spread out a cloth and set out the food and drink. Everyone thought that he had arranged things well. After that he began his meal, eating and drinking quite boldly.

Once he was fed, he looked around at everything that was going on. It is said that he set the table a second time, much more courteously; he set out wash-basins with clean towels.[16] After that he began to speak: "You must not think I've been very hospitable to you, up to now, but now it's time to come dine with your men, King Hrolf. I am not so poorly off that I would regret giving some men food for the night, even less distinguished men than you. You are very famous from the many brave deeds which you have accomplished, more so than other kings."

The king said, "This is well offered, in grand style, as it's likely that you are of a grand nature, both in this and other things. But we had enough food and drink before we left the ship, and we don't need them right now. What is your name?"

He answered, "I am called Grimnir, and I am the son of Grimolf, and I am the brother of the Grimar whom you killed. There you took many treasures which I wanted to own. Now it's true that you deserve nothing good from me, and you shall have no good from me, and even if you were here with all your forces, you should never get away. I invited you to dine because I supposed that you wouldn't be terrified by it. That great storm that caught you, I sent at you and Asmund and the dragon-ship's crew, until the ship broke loose. I didn't think much of the other ships, and they've gone wherever they want, because I gave them gentle winds. But now you've come here with your men, safe and sound, since you were on the dragon-ship, and you shall never get away, because it's the best ship in your fleet. I shall also take savage vengeance for my brother, even without axe or sword, because it's all too easy for you to fall before my weapons. I'll give you and Asmund a truce for the length of the night, and then devise tortures for you that will test your resolve most severely. But as soon as I knew that you had separated from your men, I gave them a gentle wind, and they've gone where they wanted, because I didn't care to have any trouble from your huge host."

The giant had thrust an iron poker into the fire, and one end was split, resembling a pair of spears. That was a dangerous implement.

"I didn't know," said King Hrolf, "that I had struck so near to your heart. It's true what they say, 'there's compensation for everything,' and it must be so in this case. Will you accept compensation for your brother?"

The giant said, "You're afraid now, little man. That's to be expected, because now I shall show you the little game that I play with small boys who come here."

He brought up the iron poker and stabbed the points through two of the king's men and threw them dead into the flames. After that, he skewered another two, and threw them dead on top of the others. Then he shook the poker so hard that there seemed to be four points on the shafts. He said, "There's no need for you to be so afraid, king. You'll have so much longer and worse tortures when the morning comes."

King Hrolf said, "'When evil's on the way, it's best to delay.' I find it amusing to watch these games of yours, or any others."

The giant said, "There's an animal skin laying on the seat, which you two may spread under yourselves where you lie down for the night, because I am a light sleeper, and I wouldn't enjoy listening to your muttering over me."

King Hrolf said, "We'll make our beds here by the fire, and spread skins under us as well, because we'll fall asleep quickly."

The giant said, "If you two can sleep, you're much less afraid than I thought." Then he slammed the door and said, "Now I'm sure you won't escape our hut."

King Hrolf said, "We won't try. We think we've found such a good householder that it's no use for us to do anything other than what he asks."

"You two can think about this," said the giant, "that you'd be best off if you didn't give me any trouble and lie as quietly as possible." They said that they would do so.

Now both of them lay down to sleep. The giant had grown weary, and he fell asleep quickly. King Hrolf said, "How's your situation, sworn brother Asmund?"

"Seldom worse that this. I think that troll's bad to deal with, and not in the mood to be helpful."

The king said, "This enemy of ours will never overcome us. Some other fate must lie in store for us."

The king then took a plank and knocked it against the partition next to the giant. The giant woke up and told them to lie still, "or else I'll strike you both down into Hel with my fist." After that he fell asleep. King Hrolf knocked again with the plank. The giant turned onto his other side without waking up; he said nothing to them and fell asleep soundly. The king knocked a third time as loudly as he could, and the giant didn't wake up at that.

King Hrolf said, "Now we have to follow this plan. First I want to get the sword, and I think it likely that it will bite the giant.[17] Now we'll proceed as we did this evening." They did so, and King Hrolf managed to get the sword. He said, "Now our chances look more promising to me. We have to follow this plan. You must stick the giant's poker into the fire and get it glowing, and I want you to put the two points into the giant's eyes at the moment when I stab him with the sword. If it goes off, we'll save ourselves as quickly as possible under the bed."

King Hrolf drew the sword. The king picked up a stick and boldly went to the bed and stripped the bedclothes from him, and he looked dreadfully trollish. The king stabbed with the sword so forcefully that it went right through him at once, under his left arm. Just as quickly, Asmund stuck the poker into his eyes.[18] After that they hurried under the bed. King Hrolf flung the stick out the door, and it hit the woodpile and knocked against it loudly. The giant ran at the door hard and furiously, fumbling with his hands and trying to grab them and squeeze them without mercy, but with his terrible wounds and mighty struggles, he collapsed onto the door, shattering it into small pieces. They ran up and bashed the giant with huge logs until he was dead, though he held on to life strongly. After that they carried him out of the hut, and they had to dismember him before they could get out.

The morning was well along, and they prepared to leave. They hadn't gone far before they saw their men coming to meet them, clashing their weapons loudly. They were glad to see the king unharmed. They had meant to find the giant and avenge their lord if necessary, and they didn't think it better to outlive their king. They carried a great store of wealth out of the hut, and many good treasures. The king kept the sword, Giant's Gift. It was so large that no man could wield it except for King Hrolf, and it was heavy even for him.[19]

CHAPTER XX

After that brave deed, they sailed away and got a favorable wind, and arrived in Russia near the king's seat, early in the morning. There they recognized their own men. There was a joyful reunion. Ketil and his men had also just arrived. They asked about King Hrolf's journey, and he told how it had gone. They felt that things had turned out luckily for him, yet splendidly, and everyone praised his exploit and his boldness.

Ketil asked his brother King Hrolf whether they shouldn't go at once, fully prepared for war, and make an attack on the king. The king said that he didn't want to do that. "I will send men to meet the king and tell him that I have arrived, and what our errand is. I want you to make this journey, Asmund. Tell King Halfdan that if he will not make my brother Ketil his son-in-law, he will have our enmity. We will wait for the king for half a month; let him summon his forces and prepare for battle. But we intend to win the hand of the maiden for Ketil."

Asmund now went with some men, and he came to the halls where the king was sitting at the drinking-table with his household. There was great merriment. Asmund came into the hall, pushing past the unwilling guards at the doors. He went before the king and set forth his errand, well and frankly, as King Hrolf intended.

King Halfdan answered, "We have heard that King Hrolf Gautreksson is an excellent man. But since we've already refused this engagement to Ketil, we do not see fit to agree, even though you've arrived with larger forces than Ketil had at the time. We choose to decide this matter in battle, since King Hrolf has well said that we may summon our forces."

Then said Thorir Ironshield, the king's chief man, "My lord, my advice is that you not fight with King Hrolf, because that will take all your strength. Your daughter is quite honorably married if Ketil weds her; he is a brave man and full of courage. Wherever King Hrolf is, you will have trusty supporters, because we know of no one in the Northlands more famous for all his boldness, wisdom and bravery. I tell you the certain truth that your honor would be lost if you were to fight him. But since you do not wish to heed my advice, there's no chance that you'll get any help from me, and I will not bear my shield against King Hrolf."

The king's twelve berserkers all jumped up together, with Hrossthjof in the lead. He said to Thorir, "These words of yours are unmanly, even cowardly, to not help the king with all your might, and to not dare to fight one petty king. For such words, you are unworthy to receive honors from our lord. Even if our king had no more men than us twelve berserks, nonetheless he would send this one to Hel with all his men, and not one mother's son would get away. I mean to marry King Halfdan's daughter myself and butcher King Hrolf for the ravens and eagles. Go away quickly, you messengers, if you don't want to be beaten and injured. Tell your king that he can expect a fierce battle from us, before King Halfdan would give his daughter to the man whom we know is the most wretched weakling and dullard in every way—if he makes the attempt. It's incredible that Ketil would dare to present his suit again, when he was chased and beaten like a dog by a kennel."

Asmund answered, "Hrossthjof, I can tell that you and all your fellows have spoken with the mouths of doomed men, for King Hrolf wouldn't fear you even if you were men, but far less now that you're screeching like nanny-goats cowering in the woods. You may expect evil from evil, if you urge your king to take the worst advice."

Asmund turned away from the hall, but the berserks howled and bellowed at them. The king ordered them to be silent and quit shrieking and raising a racket, and he said that it was a manly deed to put forth a proposal from one's own king.

Asmund came back to meet the king and told him how it had gone. He said that they had to prepare for battle. King Halfdan summoned his forces, and a huge host assembled in a few days. Both sides made preparations, and on the same day when they were to fight, King Halfdan sent his host against King Hrolf. The berserkers led the host, walking a bit in front of the other men, because they only wanted to make it known that they were superior to other warriors, because of their overbearing nature and great might.

King Hrolf spoke, ordering Ingjald and Asmund and Ketil to deploy their forces to meet King Halfdan, but he said that he wanted to find the berserks by himself. They called that unwise. The king said that he would decide that, and he went to meet them by himself. When they met, the king asked who they might be, shouting so loudly— "are you going out ahead of the king's battle lines?"

Hrossthjof said his name.

Hrolf said, "I'm quite familiar with your family. Your father Hrosskel was a great friend of my father King Gautrek, and they used to exchange gifts. But since you're threatening to fight me, I want to tell you a little story and make your lineage known to you. Your father came to Gautland once, as he often did. My father welcomed him warmly and invited him to a feast, and he accepted and was received most richly. He stayed there for a long time. My father had splendid treasures. One was a stud horse, a large and beautiful stallion, dapple-grey in color, along with four mares. At their parting, King Gautrek gave your father many splendid and costly treasures, and he gave him this stud-horse. Your father was very pleased with the treasures and gifts, but most of all with the horses, and he thanked King Gautrek for the gift with many fine words. They parted, and your father went home with the horses. He took care of them carefully and visited them every day. And it wasn't long before men found out that your father didn't find the stallion as good as before. Men also heard that he found the mares to be just as good, or better. One day, when he came to the horses, he found the stallion killed, run through with a spear. He didn't care about this. Everyone was surprised that he didn't take it hard, losing such a treasure as the stallion was. But he went to the mares all the more often, and all the more closely. One of the horses was pale in color. He found it the best of all the horses, and in springtime, everyone who saw the pale mare thought that she must be pregnant. They say that time went on until the mare foaled, and the result was quite unexpected; it was a baby, not a foal. Your father had the baby taken and raised, and it was big and handsome. He had this boy called Hrossthjof and called it his son. And it's no wonder that you're puffed up, since you're the son of a mare.[20] Your father himself killed the stallion, and I don't know whether he had more sons with these mares, but I've heard it said that he had another son named Hesthofdi, and he was also of horse-kin. But since you're much like each other, all wicked and unlike other men, then it's likeliest that you were all begotten that way."[21]

At the king's words, all the berserkers leaped up, bellowing and howling. They all wanted to attack the king at the same time. Hrolf drew the sword Giant's Gift and struck the leader first. The sword cut their bodies as if it were slicing water, because none of them were wearing armor, since no weapon had ever hurt them before. By the end of their encounter, King Hrolf had killed them all and wasn't seriously wounded.

Then he saw that the battle lines of King Halfdan and those of the sworn brothers were crashing into each other. King Halfdan had much greater forces. King Hrolf turned to the battle against King Halfdan, which was both hard and long. The sworn brothers were the fiercest of fighters, and wherever King Hrolf advanced, King Halfdan's ranks turned and fled, and a multitude fell.

As for Thorir Ironshield, it's said that he didn't want to fight King Hrolf because Halfdan didn't value his advice. The princess went up into the highest tower and watched the battle. She saw her father's brave men killed. She then went back and entered the hall. She saw that Thorir sat alone on the high seat, muttering with his head in his hands. He had been her foster-father. She came before him and said, "It would be best, foster-father, to arise and help my father, because I see that he needs your support."

Thorir looked at her and didn't answer and sat as before, and she went away. When a little time had passed, she came before him and said, "How can it be, foster-father, that you sit so still and don't help my father, since he is in so much need? That is most unheard of, and it will be considered behavior unbecoming a warrior, since you sit on his high seat and have received many gifts from him and had your way in everything you wanted."

He looked at her angrily and didn't answer and sat as before. The maiden went away, and her foster-father seemed to be scowling. She went to look around, and she saw that King Halfdan and his ranks were advancing, and she saw King Hrolf striking to right and lefts. She doubted whether she should ask her foster-father again, but as before, she bravely turned back to him and laid her arms around his neck and said, "My beloved foster-father, I beg you to help my father and me, so that I may not be married against my will. You have sworn to grant me one favor, when I ask you. I want you to go into that battle now and help my father according to your strength, and I know that you'll help him well."

Ironshield shoved the maiden hard onto the hall floor. He looked so angry that she didn't dare to talk to him. Then he leaped to his feet. She heard him sigh loudly. He seized his weapon and dressed himself quickly and deftly.

At once he strode into battle. There was no lack of terrible slaughter and hard fighting. Thorir advanced so fiercely that everyone recoiled from him. When some time had passed, King Hrolf looked around and saw that Ingjald and Ketil's ranks were giving way. The king headed in their direction and ordered Asmund to fight under their banner until he came back. When the brothers met, the king asked how the fight was going. Ketil said it was proving to be difficult: "Such a terrible enemy has come here that no one can withstand him, and he's more like a troll than a man."

The king said, "He must be a man, but maybe he's somewhat bolder than other men."

The king struck to right and left with Giant's Gift, and he met none so brave, strong, or proud that he didn't quickly get death in exchange for life. Ketil followed him bravely and killed many men, and they broke right through the ranks. After that, Thorir disappeared, but the king got his lines back in order.

When they had fought for a while, the king saw that Asmund was falling back in disarray. The king returned at once to his own banner. King Hrolf had his banner brought forward and followed it, attacking mightily. King

Halfdan advanced well and was the boldest in battle and the bravest of warriors, and he killed many men. Thorir had also arrived there, and he advanced boldly with mighty blows and quickly dealt with everyone who moved against him. As soon as he saw King Hrolf, he moved away quickly to face Ketil and his men. There he advanced vigorously and felled one man across another, so that no one withstood him. The battle quickly turned against the sworn brothers.

Ketil saw that things couldn't go on as they were. He went to find his brother King Hrolf, and said, "I find it unbelievable that you're not attacking that ogre who's doing us such great harm. We would have had victory long ago if that troll hadn't gone up against us. Up to now, we've never found you to be anything but completely bold, always rushing to where the greatest danger is—except for today, when your courage is failing against this blackguard. It looks to us as if each of you is avoiding the other. Now, since you don't want to overcome this man—if I can call him a man— give me the sword Giant's Gift and find out whether my courage will fail me if I get in reach."

The king answered, "You're a great man for boldness, and you'd advance well if you were as foresighted as you are eager. Do you think you could fight with this weapon, which I can hardly carry?"

Ketil answered, "I can clearly see that the sword is no weapon for me, but I had to encourage you somehow."

The king and Ketil returned to the fight. It wasn't long before there was the fiercest battle and great attacks. Thorir Ironshield faced them; he struck to right and left and felled many men to earth. The king and some men turned to face Thorir, and there was a hard fight. The king saw that things couldn't go on as they were, but he noticed that Thorir didn't want to attack him and was always moving away. The king got so close to him that he struck down the man who stood in front of him, and in the next moment he stretched his hands out over Thorir's shoulders and killed the man at his back. Then a man fell before the king's feet, and he stumbled and almost fell. At that, the king stabbed the sword at Thorir as the rush of battle pressed them together. Thorir turned away and wrapped his clothes around himself. A little later, the king didn't see him anywhere. He had disappeared from the battle.

The king urged on his men to advance, and he himself attacked King Halfdan. It was easy to see what was happening everywhere: the survivors were fleeing one after another. King Halfdan fled to the fortress with the men who had gotten away, but a multitude had fallen. Many of King Hrolf's men had also fallen. The king ordered his men who were wounded to go to the ships.

King Hrolf ordered Asmund to go with him. They went to the forest, but the rest of their men went to the ships. Asmund said, "What do you want to investigate in this forest?"

The king said, "When the battle was at its fiercest, I scratched a tall man with my sword, who was making the most terrible slaughter of our men. I very much want to find him, because I think he went into this forest."

Asmund said, "Don't you think that he's dead of the wound? I know you must want to kill him."

The king said, "That's not it. I want to find him, and I very much want to heal him if I can, because I'd rather have him in my company than ten other men, even if they were champions."

Asmund said, "It's likeliest that that troll has gone into the crags and you won't find him."

The king said, "That can't be. I'll see whether he can be found."

When they had walked through the forest for some time, they came into a clearing, and under an oak tree they saw a man lying. The ground all around him was very bloody. He was terribly pale. His weapons lay next to him. The king went up to him and said, "Who is this man who's lying here?"

He answered, "I recognize you clearly, King Hrolf Gautreksson, on account of your size and your handsomeness. I realize that you must have come here because you must want to kill me. Maybe you can claim enough reasons. But I won't hide my name from you. Men call me Thorir Ironshield."

The king said, "Did you fight against us this day and kill many of our men?"

Thorir said, "That's true, and I might well have done you more harm if I had wanted. But because I knew that King Halfdan would suffer defeat from you, I was unwilling to fight in this battle, because I realized that one of us would sink before the other. So I stayed away as best I could, because it seemed an irreparable harm to your kingdom if you should be overcome, so I didn't oppose you with all my strength. And even though I took this wound, that wasn't what you wanted."

King Hrolf said, "You must be an excellent man in battle. Will you accept a truce from me?"

Thorir answered, "I don't think that will be of much help."

The king said, "Are you badly wounded?"

Thorir said that it was very slight. "I got a scratch from your sword that's made me a bit stiffer than before, but I don't suppose it's serious."

The king asked him to show him. He pulled off his clothes. The king saw that his entire belly was slit open, and everything was slashed down to the inner membrane.

The king said, "Your wound is so severe that you can hardly be healed. But since your guts haven't fallen out, I will seek out healers for you and ask them to heal you, if you will become my man and render me help and service."

Thorir said, "If I must serve a man, then I'd choose no other man than you.[22] So I will accept life, provided that you grant a truce to King Halfdan and all his men, because he couldn't withstand your attack."

The king said that he would do that, if King Halfdan would submit to him. Then he cleaned the wound, and after that he took a needle with silken thread and sewed up the wound. He put on all the ointments that he thought would be most likely to do some good. He bandaged and treated it with everything that seemed most promising. That seemed to take away all the burning and pain. He thought that Thorir was almost able to travel wherever he wanted. They went to the ships and stayed there for the night.

Early in the morning, King Hrolf readied his forces and went to the fortress. There was no resistance there. King Halfdan was captured, but King Hrolf granted him a truce as a favor to Thorir, on the condition that King Hrolf alone should set all terms between them. Then King Halfdan agreed to grant Ketil his daughter.

King Hrolf went to the ships and had his men's wounds bound, and buried the fallen in a mound. But King Halfdan had a feast prepared and invited many powerful men in his kingdom, and at the agreed time, King Hrolf came to this feast with all his men. Everyone drank together, happy and cheerful, in warm friendship and perfect concord. This feast lasted for seven nights, with the greatest magnificence. At this feast, Ketil took Alof to be his wife, with her full consent and also her father's consent. As her dowry, her father gave much wealth in gold and silver and many costly treasures. At this feast, King Hrolf gave his brother all of Gautland, and the title of king along with it. When this feast came to an end, King Hrolf sailed away with all his retinue, honored by King Halfdan with many precious gifts. One of those treasures was a horn so magnificent that it was called Hringhorn.[23] Its nature was that if it were drunk dry, it howled so loudly that it could be heard for a Welsh mile, if important events were about to happen—but one couldn't get any more drink out of it than before, if it wasn't correctly drunk down. There was a huge gold ring on the horn's narrow end. It was considered a great kingly treasure. King Hrolf would have nothing else but that Thorir should come with him, and King Halfdan felt it was best to allow it. The kings now parted in the greatest good cheer, and King Halfdan realized that King Hrolf was far superior to other kings. Everyone felt him to be a most worthy man, on account of his strength and hardiness, since he alone had beaten and overcome twelve berserks whom they'd thought he couldn't hurt, and who had always won great victories before.

After that, they sailed away from Russia with the bride and many other fine treasures, and came home to Sweden. All the people were glad to see them and held a splendid feast to welcome them. Afterwards, Ingjald went home to Denmark, and Ketil went to Gautland. He established himself in his kingdom, arranging and ruling matters with much glory and honor. King Hrolf stayed in Sweden with Asmund.

That same winter, King Eirek died in Sweden. King Hrolf claimed all that kingdom, and became sole king over Sweden and all the kingdom that King Eirek had ruled. King Hrolf had fathered a son with his queen; he was named Gautrek. He was big and promising at an early age. All these kings ruled their own kingdoms for a while, at peace and in perfect concord, and so it went for several years.

CHAPTER XXI

A king named Hrolf ruled over Ireland. He was powerful and hard to deal with, and he sacrificed to the heathen gods. He had one daughter, named Ingibjorg. She was a wise woman and beautiful, and it seemed that there was no better match in Ireland. Many noble princes had asked for her hand, but her father didn't want to marry her off. They had tried to win her both by diplomacy and by war, but King Hrolf could foresee the future so well that he knew of their arrival in advance by means of his wickedness and evil religion, and he always had overwhelming forces when they thought they could catch him unawares. He himself was the worst berserk in battle, so that he had felled many champions in single combat who had challenged him to duels. For these reasons, he had become so infamous that no kings had any desire to contend with him. He had been left in peace for a long time without any king attacking his kingdom, because they were all afraid of his ferocity.

It is said that Asmund once came to speak with King Hrolf Gautreksson: "The word is going around, my lord, that I want to make my rule secure and marry. My father has become quite elderly, and I have to assume the rulership after him."

King Hrolf replied "Where would you go to find a wife, sworn brother?"

Asmund answered, "There is a king named Hrolf who rules over Ireland, a notable man. He has a lovely and wise daughter named Ingibjorg. I want to marry her and to use your strength and hardihood to get this match for me."

King Hrolf answered, "You can't be unaware of King Hrolf. He is full of magic and spells, and no one can catch him unawares. And it's a bad idea to attack Ireland with a host of foreigners. It's densely populated, and there is such a vast shoal in front of the shore that you can't reach the place except in small boats.[24] I have heard that many prominent men have asked for this maiden's hand and gotten nothing but shame and disgrace from this king. Know this, sworn brother: It won't do for us to go on so many courting expeditions where we have to fight battles and lose so many men. Even if the kings themselves weren't willing to resist us, the women themselves would start fighting us, using many tricks. We'll have to try to find something easier than going into King Hrolf's clutches. And I suppose that the Swedes and Gauts and Danes are of the same mind: they'll find it's high time to give up this senseless raiding and not have to pay such a high price, summer after summer."

Asmund found that the king flatly refused and listed all the drawbacks to this expedition. He also knew that the Irish king was hard to deal with, and that he had shamefully treated those who had gone there and asked for the maiden's hand. But Asmund couldn't think of anything else to do. He kept bringing it up before the king and begged him to lend him the forces and give him advice, even if he didn't want to go himself. The king said that he thought it would come to nothing, except that he'd suffer even more casualties.

When Asmund saw that the king was firmly opposed to the proposal and refused to listen to his request, he asked the queen to plead his case. He told her what he wanted, and he also told her about his conversation with the king. The queen said that she would be glad to do as he wished in every way that she could. "But I can't add much weight to this request of yours, because I don't know what advice to give that might increase your fame or honor, since you have to deal with an evil man like King Hrolf of Ireland, because he's a fierce and ill-natured man. King Hrolf Gautreksson will see it this way, since he is wise and foresighted and predicts many things accurately."

CHAPTER XXII

It's said that on one occasion, King Hrolf and his queen were talking. She asked whether he had avoided making the journey to Ireland with his sworn brother Asmund. He said that he certainly had done that.

She said, "You do that wrongly, because I don't know anyone whom you should honor more than him. He has helped you long and well, and served courteously, and been with you on many war expeditions, and suffered with you through thick and thin, and always proved himself to be the boldest of men."

The king said, "Winning brides isn't so easy for us, even if we don't have to deal with men from Hel like King Hrolf of Ireland. We have to stop setting off on these bridal quests. But since you're so eager for these journeys, what plan do you see that is likeliest to succeed in our case?"

She said that she knew no advice to give, but said that they would succeed— "thanks to your good luck and guidance, my lord, if you proceed with this journey. My advice is for you not to take large forces on this journey. I want Ketil and Ingjald to stay behind, and for you not to take any men from their kingdoms, because imposing this levy will seem heavy-handed to them. I want Thorir Ironshield to stay behind and guard the land while you are away. You and Asmund should go, and have no more than ten ships and a hundred men on each ship, and the dragon-ship shall be the eleventh. I think that if your return is delayed, Ketil and Ingjald will not stay here quietly. And I find it more likely that you will be avenged, if necessary, if men such as they are alive."

Then King Hrolf said to Asmund, "Now, sworn brother, since I'm going with you on this expedition, however it turns out, you have to do something. I'm told that your father has a beautiful daughter named Margret. You must agree to let me arrange her betrothal." Asmund said that he was quite willing, and said that he trusted that the king would oversee the business much better than himself.

After that, they made plans for their journey, and at the height of summer, the sips were all ready, along with the men who had to accompany the king. Thorir wanted to go on this journey, but the king didn't want him to. Thorir said that he would make his own expedition wherever he liked, as soon as the king was away. He said that he wouldn't be in the king's company unless the king wanted him, but he didn't like it that he couldn't decide for himself where he was going to go. The king ordered him to govern the kingdom. Thorir said that he thought King Hrolf would need more help before he came back from this journey, and they parted rather coldly.

King Hrolf had another young son with the queen, who was named Eirek. Hrolf's son Gautrek was eleven years old when his father left the land.

CHAPTER XXIII

Now it is time to tell how they sailed away from Sweden and westward out to sea, as soon as they were ready. They made little headway, but got strong gales and unfavorable winds. They were covered by thick darkness, and the going became quite difficult. They had to put in along islands and capes for a long time, and they always encountered Vikings—but in their encounters, King Hrolf always won victory.

It is said that they reached England as summer was passing. At the time, King Ælle ruled England. He was a mighty and splendid king. When he heard of the coming of King Hrolf Gautreksson, he sent men to meet him and invited him to a feast with as many men as he wanted. King Hrolf brought the invitation before his men and asked whether they found it agreeable to go to the feast. They asked him to decide. The king said that he meant to go, and he prepared to go with a hundred of his men.

It's said that King Ælle owned a certain beast, so fierce and savage that it spared nothing that it was set on to. It was both huge and strong. It was a lion. They had trained the beast so that it didn't hurt anyone, except for those who showed aggression towards the king and whom he wanted to set it on. But it was gentle and calm to all the king's household, and all those whom the king wished to stay with him in peace and quiet. The king felt that the beast was a splendid possession, because as soon as there was an attack on his kingdom, he had the beast turned loose, and in a short time it would strike down a multitude of men, amounting to hundreds. It was so fearless in defense of the kingdom that no kings had the confidence to attack England, as soon as they found out about this beast's behavior.

Two men in King Ælle's household are named; one was named Sigurd, and the other was Bard. They were highly esteemed. They took care of this beast; every day it was bound strongly with iron fetters. These brothers were very unjust men, and rather eager to behave wickedly. And when they found out that King Hrolf was invited to come with his retinue, Sigurd said, "How can we plot for this king, who is praised so much by everyone, to lose his honor? For I find it bad that he should get any sort of advancement from our king."

Bard answered, "This is my best advice: we should go into the forest that lies along their route and take the king's beast with us, and turn it loose when we see them coming. This king won't be mighty enough to beat the beast; instead, it will do him harm. May it go as it must and as I wish."

They went into the forest with the beast and concealed themselves until they saw King Hrolf coming. They had already driven the beast mad with wine and all sorts of the strongest drink. They turned the beast loose at once and let it run, but hid themselves.

CHAPTER XXIV

Now the story turns to King Hrolf. He landed with a hundred men, intending to meet the king. When they had walked for a little while, they heard a crackling and an awful roaring in the forest. Asmund spoke up. "Lord," he said, "what's that noise we hear?" The king ordered them to hold still and figure out what noise that must be, but none of them could make anything of it, except that it seemed loud and hideous to listen to.

The king said, "I've heard that the king of England owns a beast that is very large and fierce and hard to deal with. It may be that we haven't been dealt with entirely in good faith. Now I want you to stay here, but I want Asmund to go forward with me and find out what noise that must be."

They did as he said, and when they had gone for just a short time, they saw the beast playing in the forest. The lion was showing its strength, casting its own tail in a ring around oak trees and pulling them up by the roots. Then it grabbed them with its claws and tossed them up in the air, like a cat playing with birds.

Asmund said, "How can that monster be acting like that?"

The king said, "I suppose the beast must be playing because it's been driven crazy by drink."

Asmund said, "I see that we'll never get past this enemy."

The king said, "We must try something different. Off the path here stands a tall tree trunk. There is thick forest alongside the road. You must go up the tree trunk and stand there. I'll use you as bait for the beast, but I shall hide myself nearby. When the beast charges at you, leap into the forest, and I'll see if I can manage to reach it. I think it's possible that it will get itself stuck in the forest, because it's very thick. You must squeal as loudly and as much like a pig as you can, because the beast can't stand to hear that, and I know that that's the only thing it's afraid of. That's its nature."[25]

Asmund did as the king asked. Now it went as the king thought it would: as soon as the beast saw the man, it rushed at him with ferocity and savagery, right between the oaks. Asmund did as he was told, and squealed as loudly as he could. When the beast heard this noise, it stopped still and clasped its head between its feet and pressed at its ears with its paws, for it didn't want to hear the pig squeals. King Hrolf then rushed up and struck with his sword and cut through the beast's back, right in front of the hips, and the beast died in its tracks.

When the brothers Sigurd and Bard saw that, they ran home to the hall as fast as they could, and told King Ælle the unheard-of news of how King Hrolf had beaten the beast which they had thought couldn't be hurt. The king asked how this had happened, and they told him everything. The king grew furious with them on account of their scheme, and said that it wasn't for them to test their luck against King Hrolf. He had them both seized and fettered. King Ælle himself went out to meet King Hrolf with many men, and said that King Hrolf would probably think that what his men had undertaken was a trick of his own.

After killing the beast, Asmund and Hrolf returned to their men, and King Hrolf said, "We shall go on as we'd already planned, because I think that this was not King Ælle's idea. What I think is that he'll find the beast's death a terrible loss, and I will tell him myself."

They went on, until they came out of the forest and could see that a great host of men was coming towards them, well armed. They thought that fighting would break out. King Hrolf said, "It's one of two things. Either this king is full of falsehood and cunning and has plotted to deceive us from the beginning, like a coward—or else this isn't his plan, and some bad men have taken it upon themselves to create hostility between us, which I think is no less likely. Let's prepare ourselves as stoutly as we can, and let's go to meet them boldly and show no signs of fear, whether they wish us well or ill—and if necessary, let's die with honor rather than live in shame."

They steeled their courage and said that whoever didn't do all he could should never prosper. They advanced in battle formation. King Hrolf marched in the center of his ranks and held the naked sword Giant's Gift, and they behaved like true warriors. When King Ælle saw that, he had peace-shields held up, and he himself rode to meet King Hrolf. He welcomed him warmly and repeated his invitation to King Hrolf. When King Hrolf saw King Ælle's cheerful expression, he accepted gladly, and they all went together to the fortress, where the heartiest welcome and a most excellent feast had been readied for them.

The kings talked with each other. King Hrolf said, "I want to let you know that we must have done you grievous harm when I killed a certain beast, since I've been told that that would be such a terrible blow to you. I thought I had to defend myself, and that's why we did it, but without any feeling of resentment against you. For everything that you find to be an offense, I will compensate you in a way that pleases you."

King Ælle answered, "You show true wisdom in this, as in many other things, that you offer compensation for what others would have to compensate you for. Because you did not blame this on our faithlessness,

I will give up the men who did this for your judgment and punishment." Then he had the brothers Sigurd and Bard sent for. They were both led in before him, bound, and they themselves admitted their plot. After that, King Ælle asked King Hrolf to judge their case, or else decide the deaths that he wanted them to have.

King Hrolf answered, "You judge your own men, lord, for all the law-breaking that they commit. But if you are willing to let me intercede, I would like you to spare their lives, but expel them from your kingdom, and let them have that for their untrustworthiness."

King Ælle said, "It's true to say that few kings are your equal in generosity. It shall be done as you wish." The king had them released and gave them a ship and some money, and they left the country and are out of this saga.

After that the kings began to talk among themselves. King Ælle asked about King Hrolf's journey, and he told him all about what they intended. The king said that it was quite a hopeless journey, and said that King Hrolf of Ireland was most fierce and bad to deal with, and asked King Hrolf not to attempt this journey that summer. He invited King Hrolf to stay with him with a hundred men, and they would lodge the rest of his forces nearby in England. King Hrolf accepted this invitation. King Ælle had prepared and arranged everything at great expense.

King Hrolf stayed in England with all his forces, with much good cheer. The king provided that most lavishly. Some time passed.

CHAPTER XXV

It's said that King Hrolf and Asmund left from the hall one day to amuse themselves. When they meant to go back to the hall, an old woman came towards them. She walked with two crutches. The old woman turned up her nose and said, "Who are these honorable men?"

They said their names. The old woman said, "Is this the noble king Hrolf Gautreksson? If I've found him, I would be blessed."

The king said, "What do you want from King Hrolf?"

"It seems to me, just as it is said, that you are more handsome and courteous than every king, and superior to other kings in all respects. What I want is to receive a favor from you, and your advice."

The king asked what she might need from him.

She answered, "I'm a poor woman. I'm alone in my house with my daughter, who has waited on me, and she is the loveliest of women to look at. But now she's worse for me than not having anyone, because a man has got into the habit of seducing her. I'm strongly opposed to it. She doesn't pay attention to anything because of him. He is a tall man and handsome, but I don't like him. My lord, I want you to come and talk with this man. He'll do what you say and leave off seducing my daughter."

King Hrolf answered, "I shall certainly come to visit you some day, old woman."

The old woman showed them the way to her house. The king went home to the hall, and several days passed. One day, the king said to Asmund that the time was right to visit the old woman. Asmund answered, "I suspect the old woman is wicked and wily, and I don't like her."

The king said that it was necessary that the man cause her no trouble. Asmund said that he didn't care, even if the man was screwing both women.

After drinking all day, they went to the old woman's house. There was a little room where the woman, young and pretty, sat on a raised platform. A tall, bold-looking man was sitting next to her. He sat fully armed and conversed with the woman. The old woman sat in the corner of the platform, wearing a cloak and a ragged mantle wrapped around herself. The women welcomed the king warmly, and when the old woman realized that the king had arrived, she jumped up and grabbed both her crutches and came forth on the floor. She said, "My lord, I beg you to drive out my shame and kill this wicked man, who has done me such great harm that he has seduced and shamed my daughter."

The king said, "Don't be so mad, dearie. Maybe you'll come out ahead, even if the two of us just have some fun."

"That won't do," said the old woman. "They have worn me out so much with this affair that I can't stand the way things are any longer, now that I can hope for some help."

The old woman picked up her crutch and tried to strike the man on the ear. The man blocked the old woman's blow with his shield, and she struck the shield so hard that her crutch broke. King Hrolf grabbed the old woman and said, "I came to find you in order to take charge of this business of yours." He set her down, next to himself.

The king asked, "Who is this man who's giving the old woman such trouble?"

He replied, "My name is Grim."

"What sort of man are you?" asked the king.

"My father's name is Thorir. He is a free man who lives in the village a short way from here."

The king said, "You're a handsome man, but how often do you usually come to the old woman's house?"

He said that he was always coming there.

The king said, "This old woman has complained to me a bit. She finds that you're chatting too much with her daughter. She thinks that she won't come off well in this business, and she said that you're endangering the means of support for both of them. Now I want to ask you to stop provoking the old woman. It's petty to cause her trouble like this, and it does you no credit. I'm glad that I don't need to discuss this any further. In return, I will offer to grant you another favor."

Grim said, "I hadn't intended to change my habit of coming here, no matter who might interfere. But in accordance with your offer and your will, I shall do as you wish. I won't soon get a request from a nobler man than you, and I also won't delay in asking you a favor in return. This is what I ask: for you to accept me among your men, and for me to travel with you in summer. I am eager to test myself. I've never been in battle before."

The king said, "I will certainly grant you this. You have a good and lucky look about you. Come join us in the summer." Grim left at once, and they parted cheerfully.[26]

Then the old woman stood up and thanked the king for his counsel. She said, "Could any king grant better favors than you? Do you know anything that will cure old age, my lord?"

The king answered, "I don't know how to do that. I don't know what it is."

Asmund said, "It's often found in a peasant's house, but not in a king's. I know a cure for your old age, woman, if you'll accept it from me."

She said that she was eager for it. "But will you do it in bed?"[27]

He answered, "Come to me. I'll proceed as I think best."

The old woman flung off her mantle and walked up to Asmund. He had a timber axe in his hand. He told the old woman to bow before him. She did so, thinking that he wanted to speak with her privately. Asmund let the axe fall onto her neck so that it cut her head off, and he said, "Now I've cured your old age."

King Hrolf hadn't been paying attention to their conversation, but he noticed the head flying off. King Hrolf became so angry at this that he was on the verge of attacking Asmund. He said that such a wicked and outrageous deed had been done that they would never recover from the disgrace, and their shame for having killed a poor old woman in a foreign land would be spread all around. Asmund said that it was unbelievable that he was taking it so badly. They argued about it, and they went back to the hall.

When men had come to the table to feast, King Ælle noticed that King Hrolf did not look happy, and at once he asked the king what had happened.

King Hrolf told how it had been, and said that this had been the worst of misfortunes. King Ælle told him not to say that— "because she was the worst old crone and the whiniest, and full of deceit and lies. It's much better that she's been put to death."

Asmund said that he had never seen King Hrolf so angry over a small matter.

CHAPTER XXVI

It is said that some high-ranking men in England attempted to slander King Hrolf Gautreksson to King Ælle, and told the king to prepare for treachery from him. The ringleaders of this wicked plot were two jarls, along with many other powerful men. They said that King Hrolf intended to take over the kingdom in any way he could. King Ælle was unwilling to believe it, but for some time they made their accusations where the king could hear. The king behaved in the same way to King Hrolf, completely cheerfully, and said that it must be the greatest lie. But in the end the king began to have doubts, because the jarls proved their accusations with many false witnesses. Men soon found that the king's temperament changed, and he became more reserved with King Hrolf next to him than before. King Hrolf took no notice, and some time passed in this way.

On one occasion, the jarls came to speak with King Ælle and brought up this treachery. The king answered, "Since you think you've discovered this man' treachery against us, I give you leave to arrange for fitting vengeance on him. But since King Hrolf is here at my invitation, I have no mind to attack him as long as he is not clearly guilty of treachery against us, and I will stay out of your dealings." The king spoke of this because he suspected they might be lying. The jarls said that they would ask no more of the king. At once they agreed on a time to attack King Hrolf. They said that they would attack him with both fire and iron. The king told them to do as they liked.

That same evening when the jarls expected to attack, King Ælle heartily served the drink, and behaved most merrily with King Hrolf. Almost everyone became very drunk. King Hrolf always drank least when others were the most drunk. King Hrolf slept in an outbuilding with his men. It was always his custom to go to sleep early, and so he did that evening.

King Ælle said, "King Hrolf, you have stayed in our kingdom for a while. We have always observed your behavior, and that of your men, to be excellent conduct and courteous manners, every day. Now I want to sleep tonight in your lodgings and observe the behavior of your men. no less at night than by day."

King Hrolf answered, "You are certainly welcome to do so. If you will deign to do this, we will accept with thanks." And when the tables were taken up, King Ælle went to the outbuilding with King Hrolf, and they lay down and were soon asleep.

When they had slept for a short while, King Hrolf awoke when he heard a huge din and commotion and clashing of weapons outside. Just then. the building was set on fire. King Hrolf ordered his men to wake up and arm themselves: "It's a terrible misfortune for us that King Ælle should be in this peril right alongside us, because these men must think they have grievances against us. It's a bad thing for such a good and just king to suffer on our account."

King Hrolf wanted to awaken the king and couldn't manage to do it; the king was sleeping so soundly that he wasn't aware of the commotion. King Hrolf said, "I must be quick to devise a plan, before this house burns down around us. We must break down the house's roof posts and batter down the wall-planks, so that we can escape."

The king organized his strongest men and had King Ælle lifted up, fully dressed, and carried out, and ordered the men to carry him to his own bed—"and take the greatest care that the king is protected, because our honor depends on it." When they got out, they saw that a huge multitude had arrived, and the fiercest battle broke out. But when King Ælle was carried out, he shouted and ordered his men to fight no longer. Then he told King Hrolf what had happened, and said that to some extent it had been his own idea. He begged King Hrolf to forgive him for this scheme, and said that the ones who had stirred up this trouble should be killed. King Hrolf said that they shouldn't be killed for that. For that, he became very popular with the men of England.[28]

The kings resumed their friendship. From then on, King Ælle feasted King Hrolf even better than before, because he felt that he'd proved that King Hrolf was unlike anyone else in his uprightness. Now the winter passed, and summer came.

CHAPTER XXVII

Early one morning, King Hrolf got out of bed by himself, and walked some distance away from the outbuilding. He had few clothes on, but he never went anywhere, neither by night nor by day, without taking the sword Giant's Gift. The king looked all around, and when he meant to go back to the building, he saw a man riding very swiftly. He was well armed, not a large man on horseback, yet quite vigorous. When he saw where the king was standing, he turned towards him and pulled up before King Hrolf and jumped off the horse's back and greeted him suitably. The king accepted his greeting and asked who he might be. He said that he was called Thord and owned a farm farther inland. The king asked where he meant to ride. Thord answered, "I don't intend to ride any farther, now that I've found you."

The king asked, "What do you want with me?"

He answered, "I'm in quite a difficult situation. For the past three winters, a man named Harek has come to me—if he can be called a man, for he's no less like a troll. He is the greatest berserk, and an overbearing man. I have a sister named Gyda, and she is the finest match. This man wants to take my sister as a concubine, and I don't want that. He challenged me to single combat, and I agreed. Now I see that it's not possible for me to fight that ogre. I have heard about your many deeds of bravery, my lord. Now I want to ask you to release me from this danger, and slay the berserk."

The king said, "You're in a bad situation, and I will certainly find this man. I must go inside and get my weapons and clothes."

Thord said, "That can't be. You have to go there at once, as you are. I'm afraid that the berserk has come. He will think that I'm so cowardly that I didn't dare to wait for him, and he'll carry off my sister. Now get up on this horse, lord, and take these weapons and clothes here." He had these ready for him and was in the greatest hurry. All the king had to do was to get on the horse and ride, and Thord ran in front of the horse. It was not a very short distance inland.

When they came to Thord's farm, Harek hadn't arrived. The king saw that it was a good farm. They went into the living room, and there was a high seat made ready for the king. There were many people. Gyda looked most fetching to the king. When they had stayed there for a while, Harek arrived with eleven other berserks,[29] and they spoke most arrogantly and asked whether Thord was ready for the combat. He answered, "I have got a man to fight for me, as was agreed between us."

Harek asked who would be so rash as to offer resistance to him. Thorir told him that it was King Hrolf Gautreksson.

Harek said, "I've heard mention of King Hrolf, and few kings are more famous now, for bravery and skills and all accomplishments. It's much more fair for the two of us to fight each other. I don't think it's any great matter to face you. You'd better stand up, King Hrolf, since you will stake your honor under my blade."

The king said that he didn't think it a great risk to go up against Harek. After that, they went outside, and a cloak was spread out under their feet, and the berserk pronounced the law of combat. The king had no weapon but the sword Giant's Gift. Thord held the shield before the king.[30] With the first blow, the king swung down and struck the berserk on the shoulders, and he fell down dead to earth. Thord thanked the king for this victory and gave King Hrolf splendid gifts, for he was a wealthy man. The king asked him not to marry off his sister before he returned from Ireland—if he was fated to return—and Thord promised him this.[31]

After that, Thord went home with the king. There was a great commotion on the king's estate. Asmund had woken up a little after the king had left, and had searched for him at once throughout all the estate. He was not in a good mood. But when the king returned, his men were quite glad to see him. King Ælle asked where he had gone. King Hrolf told him everything that had happened. King Ælle said that King Hrolf had done a fortunate deed and beaten the worst berserk in all England, who had treated everyone most unfairly with his tyranny and robbery. He thanked him very much.

King Hrolf resolved many other conflicts through the winter, and he traveled around England far and wide with King Ælle. He arranged and settled cases that King Ælle had the right to judge, because King Ælle was very old at the time. Everyone was willing to sit down or stand up as King Hrolf wished. His popularity spread throughout all England.

CHAPTER XXVIII

Now it is time to pick up where we left off, as Queen Thornbjorg stayed behind in Sweden. She heard no news of King Hrolf's expedition. By now, twelve months had passed since he went away. She was quite heartsick about their journey.

It is said that one day, Thorir Ironshield was sitting in the high seat in the hall, as was his custom, with a few men next to him. The queen entered the hall, bearing the excellent horn in her hands. Thorir was astonished when the horn was brought in, because he had not seen it since King Hrolf went away. Then Thorir was astonished that the queen was serving him drink, because she had never done that before. But when Hrolf left Sweden, Thorir had promised to kill the person who told him of the fall of King Hrolf Gautreksson.[32] Thorir stood up to meet the queen and welcomed her. He accepted the horn and drank it down. Once he had drained it, a loud howl came from the horn, as always happened when important events were coming, or else had happened. This noise signified great battles and the deaths of noble men. Thorir Ironshield threw the horn away and glared at the queen and said, "Are you telling me of the death of King Hrolf Gautreksson?"

She answered, "That's not what I'm doing. Rather, I hear that the horn is telling you of some significant news, wherever it comes from and whatever it pertains to. I have dreamed that King Hrolf will need help before this summer is over."

"Now, queen, since you have shown me your thoughts concerning King Hrolf, which your heart sorrowfully tells you—and because I have to repay him for so much goodness, as you know—I shall leave this kingdom and not return until I know what has become of King Hrolf, whether the king is alive or dead. I cannot enjoy food or drink as long as I don't know what has happened to him and I have no knowledge of his actions."

After that, he got a small ship and a few men, and he sailed away from Sweden. By the time he came to England, King Hrolf had left and gone to Ireland. Thorir didn't stay there, and he meant to come to King Hrolf's aid. He didn't stop until he came to Ireland, but not to the place where King Hrolf had landed.

Thorir spoke with his men: "You must wait for me here, and I will go ashore alone. I will not fix the time of my return for you. You must not mention my name at all, even if you think you hear something plausible about my journey. It may be that I'll do something that may not make you popular with the inhabitants. You must say that you're merchants, and say little about yourselves, until I come back."

With that, Thorir left his ship that night and went so far ashore that he didn't alert anyone that he'd come. He headed for the king's seat. And when he didn't think it likely that anyone had found out about his journey, he started killing both men and cattle. Everyone who saw him thought that the mightiest troll must have come to the land, and anyone who met him ran away, so that not a spear was raised against him.

CHAPTER XXIX

Now it is time to tell of King Hrolf. As soon as spring came, he summoned his forces and prepared to travel to Ireland. King Ælle offered him men from his own kingdom, as many as he might want. King Hrolf left his dragon-ship and all his larger ships behind, and took more and smaller ships. They had thirty ships from England, all of them small. Grim came to meet the king, as they had agreed. The kings parted cheerfully, and when King Hrolf's forces were ready, he sailed away from England. They got a favorable wind and reached Ireland late in the evening. They anchored there for the night. It's said that Hrolf the king of Ireland had found out about the coming of his namesake by means of his own sorcery and wisdom, and he had summoned many men.

In the morning, when the sworn brothers awoke, King Hrolf said to Asmund, "Wouldn't it be best to bring forth our request for the maiden's hand, and hear King Hrolf's answer?"

Asmund said that that was certainly what he wished for.

The king said, "We shall go in peace, with no fighting or raiding, as long as no hostility is shown us."

Then the king ordered a hundred men to come with him, and he ordered his men to arm themselves and be prepared for any fighting, if necessary, and to land and go into a forest near the fortress. King Hrolf traveled until he was approaching the fortress, and then they saw that men were coming to meet them, ready for battle. The king ordered his men to go forward. The men of the fortress came towards them, and when they met, it was the King of Ireland who had come there with six hundred men.

Hrolf the king of Ireland spoke: "I know very well who you are, Hrolf Gautreksson, and Asmund your sworn brother, son of Olaf the king of Scotland. I also know why you've come here; you don't need to bring that up. I shall give you a quick choice, King Hrolf, because you're more handsome and noble than any other king: I shall let you go home with all your men, safe and sound, and never come back on this mission, because there have been many bolder and nobler men who have come with the same intent and gotten nothing but shame and injury. If you're not willing to agree to this offer of ours, then you'll be dealt with, all the more shamefully since you think you are more worthy than other men."

At the conclusion of Hrolf the Irish king's speech, King Hrolf Gautreksson answered, "Because you are such a wise and foreseeing king that you know matters that have not yet happened, and the mind and intentions of every man, I suppose that it would be more prudent to accept this offer. But since I and my men have traveled from my home in Sweden, and I have promised my support and faithfulness in this matter to my sworn-brother Asmund, I can't bear to turn back and leave matters as they stand, without putting your strength and might to the test any further."

The King of Ireland said that he had made the worse choice for him and his men. King Hrolf warned his men and ordered them not to be slow to support each other. King Hrolf Gautreksson assumed that the Irish king couldn't have more men than the ones they saw, and thought that his plans were well in hand. The Irish king had an overwhelming force, and Hrolf's men didn't know about it. But the Irish king also didn't know that King Hrolf had men in the forest.

The Irish king ordered his men to attack. King Hrolf Gautreksson ordered his men to save themselves and retreat. A little while later, he charged the Irish king's men. The Irish king ordered his men to retreat to the fortress. Many Irishmen fell before they made it into the fortress. King Hrolf's men hotly pursued them into the fort.

When all of King Hrolf's men had entered the fortress, men charged at them from all sides. Both sides formed up for battle. It's said that the odds were no less than six Irishmen for every Swede. Many of them lost heart and felt that the odds were daunting for them to go up against such a huge mob. The battle broke out, and it was both long and hard-fought. The Irish attacked with great ferocity and in huge numbers, because they saw that their chieftain was a fearsome killer. The Irish king was shooting so fast that they saw two arrows in the air at once, and every one struck a man.

King Hrolf Gautreksson fought with a brave heart. All his men followed him staunchly and bravely and won glory as they died, although we aren't able to tell of each man's defenses and attacks. It was clear that many of them had been the greatest warriors. As long as they had their strength, they felled many men to earth and never turned to flee, even though the odds were greatly against them. Grim, whom we have spoken of before, distinguished himself in this battle. He was both skillful and valiant, and the boldest in attacking. King Hrolf Gautreksson advanced with great fierceness in this battle, and struck right and left with the sword Giant's Gift. He never protected himself with a helmet, nor a shield, nor a mail coat. He sent many men to Hel and always broke through the opposing ranks, on account of his great courage. Asmund advanced in similar fashion, and he struck often and strongly and wrought great destruction as he defended himself. The fighting grew fierce, and the most terrible slaughter occurred on both sides. But it happened there, as it always must, that the men of the land got the upper hand. The slaughter turned against King Hrolf Gautreksson and his men, and as soon as the Irish found that the killing was turning against their enemies, they boldly charged forward. King Hrolf Gautreksson's men fell, one across the other. They were attacked on all sides, with battle cries and shouts of encouragement.

When King Hrolf saw that his men were falling so that few were left, he ordered them to retreat to the fortress walls and let them be their protection. His men said that they would flee and find out if they could reach their ships. The king said that he didn't want to flee, and said that he would rather fall with all his men. For that reason, none of his men fled; instead, each fell at the feet of the others, all together, so that no more than twelve men were standing, and they were badly wounded and terribly exhausted.

King Hrolf said to Asmund, "Now, sworn brother, it's more than likely that we'll need to work a bit to become the Irish king's in-laws, which you were so eager to achieve for us. I've felt slow and sluggish on this expedition. Now I shall not hold back from helping you with all my strength and fetching the maiden's dowry home."

King Hrolf Gautreksson clasped his sword's grip with both hands, and struck to right and left, both frequently and powerfully, and he brought quick death to many. Asmund and Grim gave him able assistance. It's said that they piled up so many dead men all around them that they could hardly fight. All of King Hrolf's men had fallen except for Asmund and Grim, and by then they were so badly wounded and terribly exhausted that they could hardly stand up. Shields were pressed on them from all sides. Before they captured King Hrolf, he had killed fifteen men in front of them. But in the end, as the saying goes, 'one can't withstand great numbers'. They were all captured and stripped of clothes and weapons. They had fought all day and much of the night, and so many of them fell that not a one escaped, and they had striven to do nothing but give their king the best assistance they could. So many of the Irish king's men had fallen that there were no more than five hundred survivors, and all were wounded and weary.

Now Hrolf the Irish king boasted of his victory. He said to King Hrolf, "Now it's gone as I thought it would: you and all your men have been overcome. It would have been better for you to have gratefully accepted the choice that was offered to you, and so kept your men unhurt."

King Hrolf Gautreksson answered, "You haven't improved your reputation. You have prevailed more through tricks and craftiness than manliness or boldness, on account of the great host that you sent against us. It may yet be that you will be paid back for that."

The Irish king said, "You'll cling to your pride for a long time, because you don't understand what you have to deal with, because there's nothing nastier in this place than what you're going into."

King Hrolf Gautreksson said, "Truly you now have us fellows in your power. The way for bold men to die is to have their heads cut off."

The Irish king said, "First I shall put you in my guest-house, and there you'll starve all the way to Hel.[33]"

He had them brought out into the yard. There they clearly saw a deep pit down in the earth. Many men were needed before they could fling King Hrolf down in the pit. It was quite deep, and if they had thrown the king down on his head, he would have quickly lost his life, but he landed on his feet. There was a foul stench, and human corpses under him. Asmund and Grim were also flung down. The king caught them in midair and set them down next to him. Then a great slab was brought over the pit, so large that ten men could hardly manage to move it. The Irish king's men went away and took their rest.[34]

CHAPTER XXX

King Hrolf Gautreksson said to Asmund, "Sworn brother, I think my namesake means for you to sleep here, rather than next to his daughter Ingibjorg. What do you think of these preparations for us?"

Asmund said that he found them terrible—"I would rather have fallen today, under the weapons of brave men, than be in this calamity. We must be meant to suffer here until we die."

King Hrolf said, "Well spoken, sworn brother. But as the saying goes, 'it's always darkest before dawn.'[35] There may yet be something good in store for us." They were standing barefoot on human corpses, in their undershirts and linen breeches.

The daughter of the Irish king had watched the battle that day, and saw how bravely King Hrolf and his men fought. She was much grieved that such a noble king should lose his life so soon. She had a bower and lived in it with many handmaids. She was wise and well-beloved and very lovely and courteous. She had one chambermaid whom she trusted more than all the others. This maid was the daughter of a powerful man in Ireland, and she was named Sigrid. When the battle was all over, she called the maid to her and said, "You must go to the pit where King Hrolf Gautreksson is with his men, and ask what he most wants that I can offer him."[36]

She went, and she called down into the pit and asked whether anyone was alive there. The king answered, and said that three men were alive. The maid said, "The daughter of the Irish king told me to ask you, King Hrolf Gautreksson, what she can give you that you would most readily choose to help you."

The king said, "That's an easy choice. I would most want her to get my sword. It is easy to recognize among the slain bodies, on account of its length and size. When I was captured, I took care of it by throwing it as far as I could among the fallen bodies, where I think it lies."

The maid ran to the bower, found Ingibjorg and told her what had happened, and said that this must be a completely stupid man, if out of all things he chose what was of no use to him, as badly off as he was. The princess said, "Yet we've heard that King Hrolf is wiser than anyone. Now you must go look for the sword."

The maid said that she didn't dare to search the fallen alone at night, wading through blood and stepping on corpses. She said that that was no errand for a lady. The princess ordered her to go, and said that they wouldn't hurt her. With her encouragement, she went, but she went timidly. She searched for the sword but didn't find it. She came back and said that dead men were walking all around. The princess said that she was timid and foolish if she was afraid of dead men—"Now I shall go with you." They both went out and searched the slain. The princess went quite boldly, and she found the sword. They dragged it behind them to the bower.

The princess spoke again to the maid: "Go to the pit and ask King Hrolf what he would most prefer, of all that I can give him." The maid went and found the pit and asked what they needed most, and said that they had gotten the sword. The king said that matters were looking more promising.

The maid said, "Now what would you choose above all? Tell me."

The king replied, "Most of all, we would like to have some cloth under our feet. It's cold and nasty, standing on dead men's corpses. I see that there's a hatch under the slab on one side. It can go in there."

The maid went and told their request to the princess. Ingibjorg answered, "King Hrolf has shown further that he is braver and nobler than any other king. Many would be more impatient for help, if they could get it in a situation such as he's in now. And it's a bad thing that such brave men should end their lives so soon."

Now she took them all the things that they needed: food and drink, good ointments and healing herbs, clothes and torches and everything they needed. She went with her maid and brought them these things. They had a rope, and they lowered these things down to them. They brought King Hrolf's sword in the same way. He was overjoyed at this, and thanked them with fair words. Now he felt the wounds of Asmund and Grim, and neither of them had deadly wounds. At once they dressed and made themselves comfortable, and then they ate and drank. They felt that their situation looked promising, but they were still in a tight squeeze.

CHAPTER XXXI

Now it's time to tell about what happened in Sweden, Denmark, and Gautland. Thorir Ironshield held the stewardship of Sweden after King Hrolf went away, as was mentioned before. Ingjald and Ketil took it very badly that they had stayed behind. But after Thorir left Sweden, Queen Thornbjorg sent word to Ketil and Ingjald to summon forces and help King Hrolf Gautreksson. They lost no time and called out the levy from

Denmark and Gautland, and the queen assembled a host from Sweden. Then she took a shield and sword and rode off on the journey with her son Gautrek. He was twelve years old at the time, and the most handsome man, tall and strong.

They all met together at the appointed place, with many men. The queen took command and organized their forces. Again it happened, as often before, that Ketil showed more impatience than foresight or caution. He wanted everything on his journey to happen all at once. Now let's let them set off when they like.

CHAPTER XXXII

It had happened in Ireland one day, after Hrolf the King of Ireland had summoned all his forces and found out through his sorcery that King Hrolf Gautreksson had come, and thus called his men together half a month before King Hrolf arrived, that a huge troll came to the country around the king's residence, so evil and fierce that no one raised a shield against him. He slaughtered men and cattle and burned farms, and spared no one, but struck down every living being and did the most wicked deeds. Those who survived fled into the woods and forests.

The morning after the battle of the kings, he came to the town. King Hrolf of Ireland had been drinking for a long time that night. Then he and all his men went to sleep. In the morning, when the men intended to go outside, such a huge troll was blocking the doorway that no one thought he'd ever seen such a huge troll. It was fully armored and had an iron shield so large that it completely covered the hall doors. This troll was so fierce and terrifying that no one dared to try to go out, and the beast caused such great terror that he robbed the king of all his wits along with his strength and guile, so that no one was more terrified than he. Men found this dreadful; it was the worst disaster for them to have to bear with such a monstrosity. The troll acted as if it would charge into the hall at them at any moment. The king ordered that no one should be so rash as to face that troll, and he said that he expected that it would go away after a while. The men stayed there all day, disturbed by the troll, and it wasn't much fun for them.[37]

CHAPTER XXXIII

Princess Ingibjorg's chambermaid had gone to the hall that day, and when she came near the hall, she saw that great troll. She rushed back to the bower, shrieking and flailing wildly. The princess asked why she was acting so foolishly. She said that a troll had come to the doors of the hall—"there's nothing that could be like it."

The princess said, "Are you sure that it was a troll, and not a large man?"

She answered, "There can't be any troll like it. It howled so fiercely, as if it would not spare anyone who came at it."

The princess said, "It can't be a troll, even if it howls trollishly. I think it might be fierce in mind and think it must come here to seek vengeance. Now I'll send you to the hall. You shall take food with you and offer it to the troll. Maybe it won't be so fierce, and will yield to people instead."

The maid said, "Now you're saying something horrible—that I, a little maiden, must go to this troll which no one dares to face, when your father the king, as great a champion as he is, doesn't dare to go outside, and neither do any of his men, and they'd rather suffer till death. You must be bewitched by this monster who goes about in broad daylight in the middle of summer, since you want to give it food, and it wants to kill the king, your father."

But though she said such things, she didn't dare to go against the princess's will. She carried a plate in the palm of one hand, and a great horn in the other hand. When she came close enough that she thought it could hear, she shouted, "Eat your food, troll!"

It turned towards her. She was terribly frightened. She rushed back to the bower with a terrified shriek. She spilled the food out of the dish and splashed the drink out of the horn and said that it was unbelievable that she should be sent into the troll's clutches. "What have I done, that you want to kill me?"

The princess said that she didn't want her to suffer harm or death because of her plans. "You won't come to any harm. My heart tells me that this can't be a troll. Now you shall go a second time."

The maiden went, although she wasn't willing. When she came so close that she could see the troll clearly, she said, "Will you take food, you big troll?"

He turned towards her and glowered at her. She ran away and told the princess that she had now seen clearly that it was a male troll.

The princess said, "How did the troll look to you? Did it try to say anything to you?"

She answered, "I've never seen a troll before, but it didn't look wicked, so much as huge. It's scrawny and thin, as if it's been starving for a long time. I'm amazed that it's not eating the dead men that lie all around the town. It may be, my lady, that it's a mongrel and not a purebred troll. Now I'm not as afraid as I was."

The princess said, "How is the troll dressed?"

She answered, "It has such a big shaggy cape that I could see neither hands nor feet. It had a shield of iron, so big that it completely spanned the hall doors. It had a terrible spear, and was stabbing it into the hall, next to the shield."

The princess said, "Now I will tell you what to do. You shall go and offer it the food, and say that King Hrolf Gautreksson is alive, and find out what effect this has."

She went much more bravely than before. When she came to him, she held out the dish and said, "Eat your food, troll, Hrolf Gautreksson is alive."

He looked at her happily. He reached out and took the dish, ate and drank. She saw that he was very eager for the food, but he didn't gobble it like a slave. When he was fed, she went away. The night was ending, and she told the princess what had happened, and how when he took the dish, "under his cloak there was a red sleeve, and a thick gold ring on it."[38]

Now the night passed. The men couldn't get out of the hall, and everyone was quite out of his wits because of this giant. In the morning, the maiden came back with food and brought it to him, and when he reached out for the dish, he took the maiden by the hand and set her on his knee. She screamed out loud. He told her not to be afraid—"but tell me where King Hrolf Gautreksson is, and who has saved his life."

She answered, telling him everything that had happened on their expedition, and how matters stood. He said, "Tell the princess that I will come there tonight to meet her. I want us to discuss something."

Then he turned the maiden loose. She rushed back to the bower and told the princess that the troll had managed to touch her, and said that he had told her many things—"and he intends to meet you tonight."

The princess said that would be fine. She said that she had no need to fear him if he was alone.

That night, he came to the bower. It's said that the princess showed no sign of fear, even when she saw the troll. At once they began to talk. She asked what his plans were. He said that all he wanted to do was to burn the king inside the hall with all his household. "But since King Hrolf Gautreksson is alive, and you have helped him, I will do as you advise."

She answered, "I'd much prefer some other alternative to having my father smothered indoors, like a red fox in a crevice or a white fox in its burrow. I have dreamed that he will be attacked soon. What I think is that more mighty men will come to King Hrolf Gautreksson, and he won't have long to wait."

Thorir said, "I am most eager to find King Hrolf, my sworn brother."

She said that she could easily take him to speak with Hrolf and his men, but said that they couldn't get out, unless they had a multitude of men.

They went to the pit at once. When Thorir saw the slab which was shutting them in, he heaved it up with his great strength and threw it many fathoms out into the field. Then he let down a rope and hauled them all up. There was a very happy reunion, and each thought the other had been pulled out of Hel. They all went to the bower and drank there, glad and cheerful.

King Hrolf asked what plans they should make. Asmund said that this was an easy decision—"the first thing is to set fire to the hall and burn the king inside, with his men."

The princess came up and said, "I want to ask this of you, King Hrolf: that you grant my father a truce, even if you have him in your power."

The king said that he would certainly agree to what she wanted, on account of the bravery and courtesy that she had shown him. He said that she deserved to have her favor granted.

CHAPTER XXXIV

Now it's time to tell about the journey of the kings: Ketil, Ingjald, and Queen Thornbjorg. They set sail with their forces and had sixty ships, all large and well crewed. Their journey went quickly, and they landed in Ireland on the same night that King Hrolf was taken out of that hellish dungeon into which he had been placed, intended for an ignoble death by King Hrolf of Ireland. But King Hrolf didn't dare to go outside, and neither did any of his men, because of the huge troll.

When Ketil and the others arrived, they saw a great fleet of ships, and recognized many of the ships that King Hrolf Gautreksson had owned. There was no one aboard the ships. This grieved them terribly, for they realized what must have happened there. They traveled to the hall in a furious uproar, and soon they saw the signs of what had happened. Many a man was distressed.

Queen Thornbjorg asked what plans they should adopt. Ketil said, "We must go ahead with my plans. I'll set fire to every building, house and village, and I'll burn up everything before us."

The queen said, "That's not what I advise. There must be just enough men left here that we'll have enough forces to deal with them. King Hrolf and his men must have left matters like that, before he lost his life. But it may have happened that they've set up some sort of refuge here, which we don't want to damage any more than we'd want to harm ourselves. And I see that the town hasn't been cleared of the dead men who have fallen in this battle."

Ketil said that he would attack. At once a fire was kindled and carried everywhere.

CHAPTER XXXV

It's said about King Hrolf and his men that they were sitting down to drink, glad and cheerful. Outside they heard a great uproar and clash of weapons, and suddenly the bower where they were sitting was set on fire. It so happened that the queen herself was leading those men, with her son Gautrek.

King Hrolf then said, "Thorir my comrade, I should have known that your shield would be little defense against the king's men. They must have come out with their forces. Let them know our weapons now, before we are overcome."

They leaped up and armed themselves. Then the princess spoke: "King Hrolf, before you go out, make sure that those aren't the men of the Irish king, but rather your friends and kinsmen. And keep well all your oaths to us."

They took a stump and threw it at the bower door, and at once it broke apart and they came out. King Hrolf immediately recognized Gauts and Swedes. One man stood before him, fully armed and most warlike. He took off his helmet and stood back, and King Hrolf recognized that it was Queen Thornbjorg.

The king said, "It's hard enough to trust women like you, and now you want to burn me indoors like a fox in its burrow."

She answered, "You might appreciate this better if you wanted to, King Hrolf, because we didn't do this out of ill will. Now we all have victories to boast, since you're all unhurt—our worthiest men. Let's start doing what's most urgent for everyone."

King Hrolf ordered the fires to be put out as quickly as possible. News traveled quickly through the ranks that King Hrolf was well and unharmed, and Asmund as well, and that Thorir Ironshield had come. There was a great rejoicing of all the chieftains and warriors. It took only a short time to put out the fires, which had been kindled in only a few places. When the Irish king noticed that enemies had arrived and the troll wasn't at the hall doors, he and his men rushed out and defended the hall bravely. King Ketil was there to meet the attack with both fire and steel. There was some killing before Hrolf Gautreksson came out and ordered the fires to be quenched. Ketil went about it with vigor and strength and had King Hrolf of Ireland captured. But they killed everyone who tried to protect him.

When these deeds were done, King Hrolf Gautreksson said, "It's come to this, my namesake: for a few nights you had my life in your hands, and you had planned a rather harsh death for me, had our situation not improved. Now matters have changed, so that I have you and all your affairs in my power. You will have to abide by our judgment. Will you now grant Asmund, my sworn brother, son of the King of Scotland, kinship with you, and win life for yourself and peace and freedom for your men?"

King Hrolf of Ireland said that he would agree. King Ketil Gautreksson and the other warriors found it incredible that King Hrolf of Ireland would not lose his life at once, since he had done such harm to their men. They had lost many good warriors and men of great worth. But King Hrolf Gautreksson said that he would do all he could on behalf of the princess, and said that she had done well for him and his comrades. He said that King Hrolf of Ireland was of no worth, and that he was a wicked and arrogant king, and he said that it was thanks to his sworn brother Thorir Ironshield that he had done no harm by working his magic, as he usually did, but rather had received shame and harm, as was fitting.

After that, the Irish king bestowed much gold and silver and all sorts of treasures on his daughter, because they wanted to leave Ireland as soon as possible, and they didn't want to grant the Irish king the honor of holding the wedding for his own daughter. They treated him most disgracefully; although he kept his life, they took his goods and gave him no thanks. Then they sailed away from Ireland with all the ships they could get away with, and quite a lot of wealth. Now there was great joy among their men. They had rescued their king and the rulers whom they loved most dearly, and won a beautiful and wise woman like Ingibjorg, along with the men whom she most wanted to have with her. They set sail for England.

King Ælle welcomed King Hrolf Gautreksson most warmly, and recompensed him well for the loss of life which he had suffered. After that they sent their entire force home, and appointed three chieftains to lead it. One was Aki, who was Danish; the second was Bjorn from Gautland, and the third was named Brynjolf, of Swedish descent. They were all the mightiest of men, and they were to hold the guardianship and rulership of the kingdoms, until the kings should come home.

The kings kept twelve ships, fully crewed. They stayed in England for a long time. Grim Thorkelsson married Gyda, the sister of Thor who was mentioned earlier, on the advice of King Hrolf. He wanted to go with King Hrolf and never be parted from him. King Ælle asked King Hrolf for Thorir Ironshield to stay behind in England to defend and strengthen his kingdom. Thorir was willing, and King Hrolf granted that to King Ælle.

Thorir married Sigrid, the same chambermaid who had served Princess Ingibjorg. She was the daughter of a mighty man in Ireland and seemed to be the best match. Thorir now became the most powerful man in England, and was always the greatest champion and brave man. But we can't tell much about his journey to Ireland, and about whether he had kept his oath or not. Men often survive for a long time on many things that can't quite be called food, such as many herbs and roots. Thorir and King Hrolf Gautreksson parted with good cheer, and he is out of this saga.

CHAPTER XXXVI

After that, King Hrolf prepared to leave England. King Hrolf and King Ælle parted the best of friends, and King Hrolf sailed to Scotland. When King Olaf heard of the coming of King Hrolf and his son Asmund and all the sworn brothers, he prepared a splendid feast in their honor and invited King Hrolf with all his men. The king himself went out to meet them and welcomed them splendidly, with the greatest cheer. And on the advice of King Hrolf, King Ingjald brought forth his suit and asked for King Olaf's daughter's hand in marriage, and with Asmund's support, the suit easily won the king's consent. The most splendid of feasts was laid on, and they celebrated the marriage of Ingjald to Margret, the daughter of King Olaf of Scotland, and of Asmund to Ingibjorg, the daughter of the King of Ireland. At the end of the feast, King Hrolf quartered his men in Scotland, but the kings sat in honor and state next to King Olaf, and they were all quite content.

That winter, King Olaf of Scotland died. He was very old, and had been the most excellent of rulers. Asmund assumed the kingship of Scotland and became a good and beloved ruler.

At the height of summer, the kings prepared their ships. Asmund stayed behind. He invited Gautrek, King Hrolf's son, to stay with him, and Gautrek accepted with the consent of his father. Gautrek lived for a long time afterwards with King Asmund, and he got a ship from him, set out on raids and became the most famous man. We have also heard that he invaded Ireland with support from King Asmund and won the kingdom of King Hrolf of Ireland. Asmund thought that he would rule there, since Ingibjorg was the only child of the Irish king. King Asmund and Gautrek won this kingdom thanks to their friendship and sworn brotherhood with King Hrolf.

Now King Hrolf prepared to leave Scotland. Asmund gave him splendid gifts, and they parted with the greatest good cheer and were firm friends ever after. King Hrolf returned home to Sweden. Men were very glad to see him and welcomed their lord warmly. Ketil and Ingjald stayed for a little while in Sweden. King Ingjald went home to Denmark, and Ketil returned to Gautland.

King Hrolf left off most of his raiding and stayed at home for a while. Eirek his son grew up there and became the most excellent man, both for his size and handsomeness and for all his accomplishments. When he came of age, King Hrolf gave him a ship. He took the dragon-ship, *Grimar's Gift*, and all the host which his father King Hrolf had had. He set out on raids with great strength and bravery. He became an excellent man, famed far and wide.

CHAPTER XXXVII

It so happened in Russia that King Halfdan died, and then men claimed the kingship who were not entitled to it. When King Hrolf and his brother Ketil heard that, they went right away and drove out those who had ruled, killing some. They brought peace and freedom to everyone. Ketil became king there. He was known more for boldness and forwardness, stubbornness and impetuousness, than for wisdom or foresight. Yet he was well-liked and had the greatest confidence from King Hrolf his brother. Then King Hrolf took Gautland under his rule and stayed there for a long time. Grim Thorkelsson held to his friendship with King Hrolf.

King Hrolf stayed in Sweden. He was considered the foremost of all kings, on account of his achievements and his generosity, which he had inherited from his father. No kings dared to encroach on his kingdom. He was more powerful than any other king, and many established friendly relations with him and hoped that in return they might have peace and freedom from his kingdom, rather than aggression and violence, as many had to suffer. For that reason, no one dared to contend with him.

King Hrolf grew old, and he died of an illness. Eirek took the kingship after him, and all the realm that King Hrolf his father had ruled. He became a famous king, and was much like his father.

People say that this saga is true. Although it hasn't been inscribed on tablets, wise men have nonetheless kept it in memory, along with many of the brave deeds of King Hrolf that aren't included here. His heroic deeds will be slow to fade.

Concerning this saga, like many others, it happens that not everyone tells it the same way. But there are many men and they travel widely, and one hears what another one didn't hear, yet both accounts may be true, if neither has quite gotten to the truth. People shouldn't be surprised that men were once more outstanding in size and strength than they are now. It's true that they could only reckon a few generations since the giants. Now the human race has all become the same, since the lineages are all blended. It's true that many smaller men could fall at one blow of a mighty man, since their weapons were so heavy that weaker men could hardly lift them from the ground. One may note that smaller men would not be able to stand if mighty men struck at them with great strength and sharp blades, which would smash everything even if the weapon didn't bite.

I think it's best for those who can't improve the story not to find fault with it. Whether it's true or not, let him have enjoyment from it who can, and let the others enjoy something that they like better.

Here we end the saga of King Hrolf Gautreksson.

THE SAGA OF BOSI AND HERRAUD

Bósa saga ok Herrauðs

FOREWORD

This saga does not originate from the nonsense that jokers make up for fun and games, full of useless twaddle. Instead, it proves its own truth by means of correct genealogies and ancient sayings that people often take from the matters that are described in this tale.[1]

CHAPTER I

There was a king named Hring who ruled over East Gautland. He was the son of King Gauti, the son of Odin who was a king in Sweden and who had come from Asia, from whom the most famous royal lineages in the Northlands are descended.[2] This King Hring was the half-brother of Gautrek the Generous on his father's side, and his mother's lineage was noble.

King Hring married Sylgja, the daughter of Jarl Saefari of Smaland, a beautiful and mild-mannered woman. Her brothers were Dagfari and Nattfari,[3] retainers of King Harald Wartooth, who at that time ruled Denmark and the greater part of the Northlands.[4] They had one son who was named Herraud. He was tall and handsome, strong and so accomplished at skills that few men could equal him. He was popular with everyone, but he didn't have much love from his own father, and the reason was that his father had another son by a concubine, whom he loved more. This son was named Sjod.[5] The king had sired him in his youth, and by now he was fully grown to manhood. The king gave him an important position: he was the king's counsellor and collected his taxes, levies and land-rents, and he was in charge of all revenues and outlays. Most people found him greedy when collecting payments, but tight-fisted when paying others. But he was loyal to the king and always had his best interests in mind. An expression based on his name came into use: someone who earns the most profit for someone else, and best takes care of it, is called *Sjóð-felldr*, meaning lucrative. Sjod

110

collected little sacks, which ever since then have been called money-purses, to keep the silver that was collected as taxes to the king. The money that he took above what was owed, he put into small purses and called that profit. He diverted this for his own expenses, but without affecting the taxes. Sjod wasn't popular with the people, but the king loved him very much and let him have his way in everything.

CHAPTER II

There was a man named Thvari, called Brynthvari.[6] He lived a short distance from the king's royal seat. In his early years he had been a great raider, and while he was on a raid, he met a shield-maiden named Brynhild, the daughter of King Agnar of Noatun.[7] They fought, and Brynhild suffered wounds until she was disabled. Thvari claimed her for his own, along with a rich share of plunder. He had her healed, but ever since then, she was bent and crippled. For that reason she was called Brynhild the Crooked. Thvari held a wedding feast and married her, and she sat on the bridal bench in her helmet and chainmail. All the same, they loved each other well.

Thvari gave up raiding and settled down on a farm. He had two sons. The elder son was named Smid; he wasn't a very tall man, but he was the most handsome of men and well-versed in all skills, so clever that he could turn his hand to anything.[8] Their other son was named Bosi. He was tall and strong, with a dark complexion, not very handsome, and like his mother in mind and body. He was cheerful and joking, and persevered at whatever he started, and he wasn't very gentle with the people he had to deal with. His mother loved him very much, and he was nicknamed after her and called Crooked Bosi. He also knew a lot of tricks, using both words and actions, so the name fit him.

Busla was the name of an old woman. She had been old man Thvari's concubine and had fostered his sons. She knew much magic. Smid was quite a follower of hers, and learned many things from her. She offered to teach Bosi spells, but Bosi said that he didn't want it written in his saga that he'd achieved anything underhandedly that should be attributed to his manliness.

The king's son Herraud and the farmer's son Bosi were nearly the same age, and they were close friends. Bosi was always at the king's estate, and they made a pact of fellowship. Sjod objected to Herraud giving Bosi his own clothes because Bosi's were always torn. Bosi was considered a rough player if he was playing games with them, but no one dared to object on account of Herraud, for he always stuck up for Bosi.

Sjod asked the king's retainers to knock Bosi out of the games.

CHAPTER III

On one occasion the king's retainers held a ball game,[9] and the men were playing vigorously. They went up against Bosi, but he countered them fiercely and dislocated the arm of one of the king's men. The next day he broke another man's leg. On the third day, two men came against him, and many were shoving him. He put out one man's eye with the ball, and knocked the other one down and broke his neck. The men rushed for their weapons and wanted to kill Bosi, but Herraud stood by him with the men that he could get. They were on the verge of fighting when the king arrived. On the advice of Sjod, the king declared Bosi an outlaw, but Herraud got him away so that he wasn't captured.

A little later, Herraud asked his father to give him warships and brave men to go with him, because he said that he wanted to leave the country and win more fame, if that was his destiny. The king brought the matter before Sjod, who said that he thought the treasuries would be drained before Herraud was outfitted for the journey as he wanted. The king said that they had to try, and it had to be as the king willed. Herraud was readied for his journey at great expense. He took painstaking care over everything, and he and Sjod didn't agree on much. He left with five ships, most of them old. He had bold men with him, and plenty of gold and silver money. He sailed away from Gautland and headed south to Denmark.

One day, in a gale, a man was standing on a cliff and asking for passage. Herraud said that he wasn't going to turn around to pick him up, but passage was available if he could reach the ship. The man leaped from the cliff and landed on the tiller just in front of the rudder, and that was a leap fifteen ells long.[10] The men recognized that it was Bosi. Herraud welcomed him warmly and said that he was to be the steersman on his ship. They sailed to Saxony and raided wherever they went, gaining plenty of wealth. They traveled in this way for five years.

CHAPTER IV

Now the story returns to Gautland. While Herraud was away, Sjod looked after his father's treasuries. All the chests and trunks were empty, and he often repeated the same words: "I remember when this treasury looked completely different," he said.

Sjod prepared to leave to collect the king's taxes and land-rents, and most of his demands for payment were greedy. He came to old man Thvari and requested a levy for war, as he did at other places. Thvari said that he was too old to go to war, and that he wouldn't pay the levy. Sjod said that he had to pay a larger levy than other men, and said that he was the cause of Herraud leaving the country, and demanded compensation for the men that Bosi had injured. Thvari said that a man who went to the games had to look out for himself, and he wouldn't throw away his money for such a thing. A quarrel broke out between them. Sjod broke down Thvari's storehouse and took away two chests of gold, along with much more wealth in the form of weapons and clothing. With that done, they parted. Sjod went home with a great store of wealth, and he told the king about his journey. The king said it was wrong of him to rob old man Thvari, and said that he thought that would turn out badly for him. Sjod said that he couldn't be blamed for that.

Now it is time to tell how Herraud and Bosi were preparing to sail home from their raiding. They had heard that Sjod had robbed old man Thvari. Herraud intended to intercede for Bosi and make peace between him and the king. They were struck by such a strong wind that their ships were separated, and all the ships that Herraud had brought from home were lost, but he escaped to the Elfar Skerries[11] with two ships.

Bosi was driven to Wendland[12] in one ship. There was Sjod with two ships, anchored in front of him. He had just come from the Eastern realms and had bought costly treasures for the king. When Bosi found out about that, he ordered his men to arm themselves, and he set out to meet Sjod and asked how he would compensate him for robbing Thvari. Sjod said that he was foolhardy for daring to say such a thing, since he had been outlawed by the king, and he told him to be happy that he wasn't missing any more. Both sides went for their weapons, and a fight broke out. In the end, Bosi killed Sjod. He granted a truce to the survivors, but claimed the ship and everything on it.

When Bosi got a favorable wind, he sailed around Gautland and found his sworn brother Herraud and told him the news. Herraud told him that that wouldn't improve his popularity with the king. "But why did you come to find me, since you've struck down such a close kinsman of mine?"

"I knew it was no use avoiding you, if you wanted to retaliate," said Bosi. "But I thought I could trust someone like you completely."

"I might say that Sjod was no great loss, even though he was my kinsman," said Herraud. "I will go meet my father and try to reconcile you."

Bosi said that he didn't expect much relief from the king, but Herraud said that not trying wouldn't do any good.

Herraud went to meet his father and came before him and greeted him worthily. His father received him, because he had already heard of Bosi's fight with Sjod. Herraud said to his father, "There's a need to see about compensation for you, from my comrade Bosi, because he's committed a great mishap. He's killed your son Sjod, and although there may be some cause for that, we want to offer a settlement and as much money as you choose for yourself, and along with that, our support and favor and whatever service you want to demand of him."

The king answered angrily, "You've got a lot of nerve, Herraud, supporting that evil man. Many would think it better for you to help avenge your brother and our dishonor."

Herraud replied, "Sjod was no great loss. And I don't know whether he was my brother or not, even though you loved him very much. I don't believe that you respect me much, since you don't want the settlement I'm asking you to accept. But I think that I'm offering a better man in place of Sjod, considering the service that he did."

The king said, very angry, "All your pleading for Bosi is making matters much worse. As soon as I manage to capture him, he shall hang far higher than anyone has ever seen. No thief has ever been hanged so high."

Herraud answered, very angry, "Many will say that you don't know how to accept honor done to you. Now since you aren't willing to respect me, you may assume that Bosi and I will share the same fate, and I will defend him as myself, for as long as my life and my courage last. Many will say that it's a rather steep price to pay for one concubine's son, if you give us up for him."

Then Herraud turned away in a rage. He didn't stop until he had met Bosi and told him how he and his father had parted.

CHAPTER V

King Hring had a trumpet blown to summon his forces, and went to find the sworn brothers. Fighting broke out between them at once, and the king had two or three times as many men. Herraud and Bosi advanced bravely and killed many men, but all the same they were overwhelmed and captured, clapped in fetters and thrown in a dungeon. The king was so enraged that he wanted to have them killed right then, but Herraud was so popular that everyone dissuaded him. First, the booty was divided up, and the dead were buried.

The next day, many men held an assembly with the king, so that he might reach a settlement with Herraud. Herraud was led before the king. The king offered him a truce, and many men agreed, but Herraud said that he wouldn't accept a truce unless Bosi could be guaranteed safety for both

114

life and limb. The king said there was no hope of that. Herraud said that he would kill the man who caused Bosi's death, and not spare the king any more than others. The king said that it wouldn't be wrong for the one who was asking for trouble to get it. The king was so furious that no one could get in a word with him, and he ordered Herraud to be led back into the dungeon, and for them both to be killed in the morning, because the king would have nothing else. Most felt that the matter had turned hopeless.

That evening, the old crone Busla came to speak with Thvari. She asked whether he meant to offer money for his son. He said that he didn't want to throw his money away, and he said that he knew that he'd never be able to buy life for a man who was doomed to die. He asked what could have become of her magic if she couldn't offer Bosi some help. She said that she wouldn't go around like a beggar, like him.

That same evening, Busla came into the chamber where the king was asleep, and began the prayer which ever since has been called Busla's Prayer and become widely famous. There are many wicked words in it, which Christians have no reason to speak. Still, this is the beginning of it:

Here lies King Hring,
helmsman of Gauts,
the most mulish
man of them all.
You plan to slaughter
your son yourself;
such a heinous deed
will be heard, far and wide.

Hark to Busla's prayer,
and hear it sung,
soon it shall echo
through all the world,
harmful to all
who hear its words,
most fearsome to them,
as I will foretell.

May wights go wandering,
may weird go awry,
may cliffs be quaking,
may the country go mad,

115

may the weather worsen,
may weird go awry—
unless you, King Hring,
grant Herraud peace,
and offer shelter
to my son Bosi.

I shall torment
and trouble your breast
so that vipers will gnaw
and devour your heart,
your ears be stopped
and stricken deaf,
your eyes askew
and your sight befuddled,
unless you offer shelter
to my son Bosi,
and give up your hatred
of Herraud.

If you hoist sails,
may the hawsers break,
and may the rudder
be ripped from its mount,
may the sails be shredded
and slammed to the deck,
and all your tackle
be torn to pieces,
unless you give up your hatred
of Herraud,
and seek to settle
with my son Bosi.

If you go riding out,
may the reins tangle,
the horses hobble
and the hacks break down,
and may all the streets
and straight pathways

carry you right into
the clutches of trolls,
unless you offer shelter
to my son Bosi,
and give up your hatred
of Herraud.[13]

May your bed burn you
like blazing straw,
and your high seat
heave like the waves;
yet for you it will
be worse by far,
if you want man's pleasure,
playing with maids:
you'll lose the way—
do you want more?

The king answered, "Shut up and go away, you demon, or else I'll have
you maimed for your curses."

"Now that we've met," said Busla, "we won't part before I get my way."

The king wanted to stand up, but he was stuck fast to the bed, and his
pages didn't wake up. Busla spoke the second third of the prayer, and I'll
pass on writing it down, because no one has any need to repeat it, and it's
least likely to be repeated if it's not written. Still, this is the beginning of it:

May trolls and elves
and treacherous norns,
bogies and bluff-giants
burn your halls,
storm-giants hate you,
stallions hump you,
straws sting you,
storms madden you,
woe be to you,
unless my will is done.

When her recitation was done, the king said to her, "Rather than having
you curse me any longer, I'll spare Herraud's life, but Bosi is to leave the
country and be killed when I get my hands on him."

"Then I'll do you one better," said Busla. She began the verse that's called "Syrpa's Verse."[14] The most powerful magic is hidden in it, and reciting it after sunset is not allowed. This appears near the end:

> Six men come here.
> Say their names to me,
> all unbound,
> as I will show you.
> If you don't solve this
> so it seems correct,
> then hounds from Hell
> shall harry you,
> and your soul
> sink into torment.

ᚱ·ᚠ·ᚦ·ᚴ·ᚤ·ᚾ· ||||| · ♦♦♦♦♦♦ : ᚿᚿᚿᚿᚿᚿ : ||||| : ᚱᚱᚱᚱᚱ :

"Interpret this name correctly, or else all the worst things I have prayed for will take effect on you, unless you do my will."[15]

When Busla had finished the prayer, the king hardly knew how to respond to her persuasions. "What is your will now?" said the king.

"Send them on a dangerous mission," said the old crone, "where it's doubtful whether they'll succeed, and let them answer for themselves."

The king ordered her to leave, but she wouldn't do that until the king swore an oath to her in good faith that he would keep his promises, and then Busla's Prayer would have no effect on him. Then the old crone went away.

CHAPTER VI

The next morning, the king got up early and had the assembly summoned, and Herraud and Bosi were led there. The king asked his counsellors what he should do with them. Most of them begged him to spare Herraud.

Then the king said to Herraud, "You don't respect me, but I will now do as my friends ask, so that Bosi shall be assured of safety for both life and limb. He must leave this land, and not return before he has brought me a vulture's egg, inscribed all over with golden letters on the outside. Then we two will be reconciled. If he does not, he is to be called worthless by everyone. Let Herraud go wherever he wants, travel with Bosi or make whatever plans for himself he wishes, because we will not be living together."

Bosi and Herraud were both set free. They went to Thvari's home and stayed with him over the winter. When spring came, they prepared to leave the country. They had one ship and a crew of twenty-four men. They traveled in much the way that Busla suggested, and headed for the Eastern realms and arrived at Bjarmaland,[16] where they anchored alongside a desolate forest.

CHAPTER VII

Harek was the name of the king who ruled over Bjarmaland at the time. He was married and had two sons; one was named Hraerek, and the other was Siggeir. They were mighty champions, retainers of King Godmund of Glaesisvellir and guardians of his lands. The king's daughter was named Edda. She was lovely to see, and quite knowledgeable about most things.

Now we must tell how the sworn brothers reached Bjarmaland and the forest called the Dvina Forest. They pitched their tents on land, very far from the traveled regions. In the morning, Bosi told his men that he and Herraud would go ashore and search the forest and find out what they could. "You should wait for us here for a month, and if we don't come back, you should sail wherever you want to." Their men felt this was terrible, but it had to be as they wanted.

Then the sworn brothers went to the forest. All they had for food was the animals and birds that they shot, and sometimes they had nothing but berries and tree sap. The forest quite ruined their clothes.

One day they came to a certain farmstead. There stood an old man outside, splitting planks. He greeted them and asked their names. They told him their real names and asked his name, and he said that he was called Hoketil. He told them that a night's lodging awaited them if they wanted it, and they accepted. The old man went with them to the main room of the house, and there weren't many people there. The lady of the house was rather elderly. They had a beautiful daughter; she took off their guests' clothes, and they were brought dry clothes. Then washbasins were set out, and the table set for them. They were given good ale to drink, and the farmer's daughter served them. Bosi often glanced and smiled towards her, and touched his feet to hers, and she played the same game with him.

In the evening they were shown to their rest in soft beds. The husband slept in a bed-closet, and the farmer's daughter in the middle of the house. The sworn brothers were shown to a bed at the gable-end of the house, up against the doors. But when the folk were asleep, Bosi stood up and went to the farmer's daughter's bed and lifted the covers off her. She asked who was there. Bosi told her his name.

"Why have you come here?" she said.

"Because my bed wasn't comfortable"—and he said that he wanted to get under the covers next to her.

"What do you want to do here?" she said.

"I want you to battle-harden my jarl," said Bow-Bosi.

"What jarl is that?" she said.

"He's young, and has never been put to the test before. But a jarl should be tested at a young age."[17]

He gave her a gold ring and got into bed next to her. She asked where the jarl was. He asked her to reach between his legs, but she pulled her hand back and said to hell with his jarl, and asked why he was carrying that frightening thing with him, as hard as a log. He said that it would soften up in the dark hole. She asked him to go on in any way he wanted. Now he set the jarl between her legs. The path there wasn't very wide, but he succeeded in his journey, all the same.

Now they lay for a while, as they pleased, before the farmer's daughter asked whether the battle-hardening had succeeded for the jarl. He asked whether she wanted to harden him again, and she said that she'd like that very much, if he felt that he needed it. It isn't said how often they played that game that night, but it's said that Bosi asked whether she knew "where they should search for the vulture's egg, with golden letters written on the outside, which we sworn brothers have been sent to find."

She said that the least she could do to repay him for the gold ring and the night's excellent entertainment was to tell him what he wanted to know. "But who was so angry with you that he wanted you dead and sent you on this dangerous mission?"

"Not everything goes badly, and no one wins fame from doing nothing," he said. "And many things often turn out to bring good fortune, though they begin perilously."

CHAPTER VIII

"Here in this forest there stands a huge temple. King Harek, who rules over Bjarmaland, owns it. The god named Jomali is worshipped there,[18] and there's plenty of gold and treasures. The king's mother, who's named Kolfrosta, rules over the temple. She's been made so powerful by sacrifices that nothing takes her unawares. She knows by her magic arts that she won't live through the month. For that reason, she shape-shifted and traveled to Glæsisvellir, and stole away Hleid, the sister of King Godmund, intending that she should be the temple-priestess after her. But that's a terrible thing,

120

for Hleid is the loveliest and most courtly of all maidens, and it would be better if she could be spared."

"What sorts of dangers are in the temple?" said Bosi.

"There's a vulture there," she said, "so baleful and fierce that it kills everything that gets close to it. It directly faces the doors and notices anything that comes in, and whatever encounters its talons or venom has no hope of surviving. There's a slave in the temple who sees to the priestess's food. She needs a two-year-old heifer every time she eats. Under this vulture is the egg that you've been sent to get. There's a bull in the temple that's received so many sacrifices that it's been turned into a monster. It's fettered with iron bands. It's supposed to mount the heifer, and venom will be mixed into her, and everyone who eats her meat will be turned into a troll. She's going to be fed to Hleid the king's sister, and then she'll turn into a troll just like the temple-priestess had been. I don't think you're likely to beat these monsters, with such powerful sorcery as you'll have to deal with."

Bosi thanked her for her story, and banged her one more time[19] as a reward for her entertainment. It was good for them both. They slept until daylight. In the morning, Bosi went to Herraud and told him what he had heard. They stayed there for three nights, and the farmer's daughter told them how to get to the temple, and she wished them well when they left. They went on their way.

Early one morning, they saw a tall man walking, wearing a gray cloak and leading a cow. They realized that that must be the slave, and they crept up on him. Bosi struck him with a club, so hard that it killed him. Then they killed the heifer and flayed off her skin and stuffed it with moss and heather. Herraud put on the slave's cloak and dragged the cowskin after him, and Bosi spread his own cloak over the slave and carried him on his back until they saw the temple. Then Bosi took his spear and stuck it up the slave's arse and all the way through his body, so that the point was left sticking out between his shoulders.

Now they went to the temple. Herraud entered the temple wearing the slave's outfit. The priestess was inside, asleep. He led the heifer into a stall and turned the bull loose. The bull mounted the heifer, but the moss-stuffed skin wasn't weighted in front, and the bull drove his head into the wall and broke off both horns. Herraud gripped him by both ears, and by the lips, and wrenched his neck until it broke.

The ogress awoke and leaped to her feet. At that moment, Bosi entered the temple, carrying the slave on the spear up over his head. The vulture reacted quickly and plunged out of its nest, wanting to gobble up the man who'd come in. It swallowed the slave all the way to his waist. Then Bosi thrust the spear so that it went up the vulture's neck until it stuck in its heart. The vulture dug its claws into the slave's buttocks and battered Bosi about the ears with its wingtips, knocking him unconscious. Then the vulture collapsed onto him, and its death-struggles were dreadful.

Herraud attacked the priestess, and their fight was the fiercest. The old crone had wicked nails and tore his flesh to the bone. They fought all the way to the spot where Bosi had fallen and the floor was covered in blood. The vulture's blood made the floor slippery for the old crone, and she fell on her back. She and Herraud wrestled so hard that first one and then the other was underneath.[20] Bosi woke up and seized the bull's head and smashed it into the ogress's nose. Then Herraud cut off her arm at the shoulder, and her wrestling ability began to weaken. But her death struggles caused a massive earthquake.[21]

Now they went through the temple and ransacked it. In the vulture's nest they found the egg, inscribed all over with gold letters. They found so much gold that they had quite enough to carry. They came to the altar that Jomali was sitting on. From him they took a golden crown set with twelve gemstones, and a necklace worth three hundred marks of gold. From his lap they took a silver bowl, so large that four men couldn't drink it dry, and filled with red gold.[22] The velvet hangings around Jomali were worth more than three cargoes from the richest galleon that sails the Mediterranean. They took them all for themselves.

They found a side room in the temple, in a well-hidden location. There was a stone slab in front of it, firmly set, and it took them all day to break it up before they got in. They saw a woman there, sitting on a chair. They had never seen another woman more beautiful. Her hair was tied to the chair-posts and was as fair as threshed straw or gold ingots. An iron fetter was securely fastened around her waist. She was crying hard. When she saw the men, she asked what had caused the commotion that morning—"and why do you find your lives so wretched that you have any desire to come here, into the clutches of trolls? Because the ones in charge here will kill you as soon as you're spotted."

They said that they'd explain later,[23] and asked what her name was and why she was there, imprisoned so cruelly. She said that she was called Hleid, the sister of King Godmund of Glæsisvellir in the east. "The troll-woman who ruled here kidnapped me with her sorcery, intending for me to lead the sacrifices in the temple and be the abbess here when she was dead. But I'd rather be burned to death."

"You'd be good to the man who freed you from here," said Herraud.

She said she knew that it couldn't be done.

Herraud said, "Will you marry me, if I bring you away?"

"I don't know of a human so repulsive," she said, "that I wouldn't marry him instead of being worshipped in this temple. But what is your name?"

"I'm called Herraud," he said, "son of King Hring of East Gautland. You don't need to be afraid of the priestess, because Bosi and I have sung a Requiem over her skull.[24] You may assume that I think I'll get benefits from you, if I release you from here."

"I have nothing more to pledge than myself," she said, "if my kinsmen are willing."

"I'm not asking them for a dowry," said Herraud, "and I'll have no delay, because I think I'm no less well-born than you. But I shall release you, all the same."

"I don't know a man I'd rather marry than you," she said, "of all the men I've seen."

They released her. Herraud asked whether she'd rather go home with them and be married to him, or have him send her east to her brother so she'd never see him again. She chose to go with him, and each pledged their troth to the other.

After that, they carried the gold and treasures out of the temple. They set fire to the temple at once and burned it to the ground, so that not a particle was left but ashes. They left with their spoils and didn't stop until they came to farmer Hoketil's home. They didn't stay there long, but they gave him much wealth, and they carried the gold and treasures on many horses to their ship. Their men were glad to see them.

CHAPTER IX

They sailed away from Bjarmaland when they got a favorable wind, and nothing is said about their journey until they arrived at home in Gautland. They had been away for two winters. They came before the king, and Bosi brought him the egg. There was a crack in the shell, but it was worth ten marks of gold.[25] The king used the shell as a drinking cup. Bosi gave the king the bowl that he had taken from Jomali, and now they were reconciled.

At that time, the queen's brothers, Dagfari and Nattfari, came to the king's household. They had been sent there by King Harald Wartooth with a request for help, because the time had been appointed for the Battle of Bravellir, the largest battle in the Northlands, as it says in the saga of Sigurd Hring, the father of Ragnar Shaggy-Breeches.[26] King Hring asked Herraud to go in his place, and said that in the meantime he would look after his bride, and they would be reconciled over everything that had happened between them. Herraud did as his father asked, and he and Bosi went with the brothers and five hundred men, and met King Harald. King Hring fell in that battle, and a hundred and fifteen kings fell with him, as it says in his saga, along with many other champions greater than kings. Dagfari and Nattfari fell there. Herraud and Bosi were both wounded, but they survived the battle.

By then, events in Gautland had taken a new turn while they were away, which must be told about.

CHAPTER X

Since it's not possible to tell more than one story at a time, we must now explain what's previously happened in the saga. We must begin with Hleid, King Godmund's sister, and her disappearance from Glæsisvellir. When the king missed her, he had her searched for both on sea and land, but he couldn't get any news of her.

Hraerek and Sigurd were brothers who were with the king. The king ordered Siggeir to lead the search for Hleid, and he'd earn betrothal with her. Siggeir said that he didn't think it would be easy to find her, if the priestess of Bjarmaland didn't know about her. They prepared to leave; they had five ships, and traveled to Bjarmaland. They met King Harek and told him their mission. He told them to go to the temple, and said that she wouldn't be easy to get, if Jomali or the priestess didn't know where she was. They went to the temple and found a heap of ashes, and not a particle of what had been there.

Now they traveled through the forest and came to Hoketil's farm, and asked whether they knew who had destroyed the temple. The old man said that he didn't know, but that two men from Gautland had been anchored by the Dvina Forest for a very long time, and one was called Herraud and the other Crooked Bosi. He said that they seemed likeliest to have committed such an outrage. The farmer's daughter said that she had met them on their way to the ship, and they had Hleid with them, the sister of King Godmund of Glaesisvellir. They told her that if anyone wanted to find her, they could look for them.

When the brothers found this out, they told the king. They summoned forces from all Bjarmaland, and got twenty-three ships. They sailed to Gautland at once, and arrived at the time that the sworn brothers were fighting in the Battle of Bravellir. King Hring was at home with only a few men, and they ordered him to fight or else give up the maiden. The king chose to fight, but the battle soon took a turn for the worse. King

Hring fell there, with the greater part of his forces. The brothers took the maiden, plundered all the wealth, and went away. They didn't stop until they came home to Glaesisvellir. King Godmund was glad to see his sister, and thanked the brothers well for their expedition, which was thought to be quite successful.

Siggeir asked for Hleid's hand, but she was reluctant, and said that it was fitting for the one who had freed her from the trolls' clutches to have her. The king said that Siggeir had won her fairly, and said that he himself had to decide whom she'd marry—"and no foreign chieftain has a chance of marrying you, even if you won't abide by our decision." It had to be as the king willed.

Now we'll let them get ready for the wedding, because they think they're doing well—but it's possible that the guests' comfort will be spoiled at the feast.

CHAPTER XI

Now it's time to tell how Herraud and Bosi came home to Gautland half a month after Siggeir and Hraerek had sailed away. They missed their friends there and took counsel among themselves, and Bosi sought out his father for advice. He said that they would be too late if they summoned large forces—but instead, they might get the king's daughter with deep-laid plans and fast action. They made their plans, readying one ship with thirty men. Smid was to come with them and have complete command of their journey. The old man gave them plenty of advice, as did Busla.

They sailed as soon as they were ready. Smid always had a favorable wind when he steered,[27] and their journey was faster than seemed likely. They arrived at Glaesisvellir more quickly than expected, and anchored their ship alongside a desolate forest. Smid cast a magical helm of protection over their ship.

Herraud and Bosi went onto land. They came to a humble little house where an old man and woman lived. They had a beautiful and knowledgeable daughter. The farmer offered them a night's lodging, and they accepted. It was a good household. There was good hospitality for them, and then the tables were taken away and ale was served to them. The farmer was taciturn and didn't ask any questions. The farmer's daughter was the kindest one there, and she poured ale for the guests. Bosi was cheerful and cast little flirting glances at her, and she did the same back to him.

In the evening they were shown to their beds, and as soon as the light was extinguished, Crooked Bosi came to where the farmer's daughter was lying and lifted the bedclothes from her. She asked who was there, and Crooked Bosi told her his name.

"What do you want here?" she said.

"I want to water my foal at your wine-spring," he said.

"Will that be easy, my man?" she said. "He's not used to the kind of well-house that I've got."

"I'll lead him forward," he said, "and shove him in the well, if he won't drink any other way."

"Where's your foal, my dear?" she said.

"Between my legs, my love," he said, "and you can hold him—but gently, because he's very skittish."

She took his cock and stroked it and said, "This is a frisky foal, but he's very stiff-necked."

"His head's not well set," he said, "but he tosses his mane better once he's had a drink."[28]

"Now it's up to you," she said.

"Lie with your legs as far apart as you can," he said, "and stay as still as possible."

Now he watered his foal so very lavishly that he was completely submerged. The farmer's daughter was so completely carried away that she could hardly speak. "Aren't you drowning the foal?" she said.

"He has to have all he can stand," he said, "for I often find that he's unmanageable when he doesn't get to drink as much as he wants."

He set to doing what he liked, and then they rested. The farmer's daughter wondered where the wetness in her crotch had come from, because the whole bed underneath her was lathered. She said, "Could it be that your foal has drunk more than was good for him, and he's thrown up more than he's drunk?"

"Something or other's affecting him," he said, "because he's as soft as a lung."

"He must be sick from drinking ale," she said, "like other drunkards."

"That's certain," he said.

Now they amused themselves as they pleased, and the farmer's daughter took turns on top and underneath. She said that she'd never ridden a more steady-paced foal than this one.

After plenty of fun and games, she asked who he was. He told her the truth, and asked in return what was happening in the land. She said that the latest news was that the brothers Hraerek and Siggeir had captured the king's sister Hleid and killed King Hring in Gautland. "They've become so famous from this expedition that no one in the Eastern realms can compare to them, and the king has betrothed his sister to Siggeir, though it's quite against her will. The wedding has to be held within three nights. But they're so cautious that they have spies on every road and in every port, and they can't be taken unawares. They don't believe they can ever rule out that Herraud and Bosi might come after the maid. The king has had a hall built, so large that in it are a hundred doors, with the same distance between all of them: a hundred men can sit comfortably between each door. There are two door-wardens at each door, and no one can come in who isn't recognized at one of the doors. Whoever isn't recognized at any of the doors is taken into custody until it is shown who he is. A bed stands in the center of the hall, and to reach it you have to go up five steps. The bride and groom are to lie there, and all the household has to keep watch all around, and no one can come upon them unawares."

"What people are with the king whom he esteems most?" said Bosi.

"The one called Sigurd," she said. "He's the king's counselor, and such a master at playing musical instruments, especially the harp, that you'd never find his equal, though you were to search far and wide. He's gone to see his concubine. She's the daughter of a farmer here, near the woods. He has her sew his clothes as he tunes his instruments."

Their conversation ended, and they slept through the night.

CHAPTER XII

Early in the morning, Bosi came to Herraud and told him what he had found out that night, and at once they prepared to leave the farmer's home. Bosi gave the farmer's daughter a gold ring. They traveled according to her directions, until they saw the farm where Sigurd was. They saw him walking with a servant, heading home to the hall. They got onto the path ahead of Sigurd. Bosi ran him through with a spear, and Herraud strangled the servant to death. Bosi then flayed the skin off them both and went to the ship at once, and told Smid what they had accomplished. Now they made their plan. Smid put a mask made from Sigurd's face onto Bosi, and wore the servant's face himself. He dressed in the clothes that the servant had worn, and Bosi wore those that Sigurd had worn. They told Herraud everything that he was to do, and they went to the fortress and came to the doors of the hall, with King Godmund standing before them. He thought he recognized Sigurd, and welcomed him warmly and led him in. Sigurd took charge of the king's treasuries and ale-vessels and cellars, and decided which ale would be served first, and told the cup-bearers ahead of time how keen they should be to pour the drink. He said that it was most important that the men should get as drunk as possible on the first evening, because the effects would last longest that way. Then the chieftains were arranged on their seats, and the bride was led in and seated on a bench, and many courtly maidens with her.

King Godmund sat in the high seat with the bridegroom by his side. Hraerek served the bridegroom. The tale doesn't say how the chieftains were placed, but it's said that Sigurd played the harp before the bride and her ladies. When the ale for the memorial toast was brought in, Sigurd played so well that men said that his like would never be found, but he said that it wasn't worth notice at the beginning. The king asked him not to quit. And when the ale blessed to Thor was brought in, Sigurd struck up a tune again. Everything that was loose began to stir, knives and dishes and everything that no one was holding. Many men jumped out of their seats and danced on the floor, and this went on for a long time.[29]

Then the ale hallowed to all the gods was brought in. Sigurd began playing again and tuned his harp to such a pitch that the echo resounded in the hall. Everyone inside stood up, except for the bride and groom and the king. Everything moved around throughout the hall, and it went on like this for a long time. The king asked if he knew some other tunes, and he said there would be some ditties later, and asked the people to rest first. The people sat down to drinking. He played "Song of the Ogress", "The Braggart," and "The Lay of Hjarrandi."

Then the ale for the toast to Odin was brought in. Sigurd opened up the harp, which was so large that a man could stand up straight in its belly; it was all worked with gold. He picked up white gloves, embroidered with gold. He struck up the tune called "Headdress Blower", and the headdresses flew off the women and danced above the cross-beam.[30] The women and all the men jumped up, and not a thing there stayed still.

When that toast was drunk, the ale that was blessed to Freyja came in, and that one had to be drunk last. Sigurd touched the string that lay across the other strings,[31] and told the king to prepare for "The Powerful Tune." This startled the king so much that he leaped up, and so did the bridegroom and the bride. No one danced more nimbly than they did, and this went on for a long while. Smid took the bride's hand and danced more nimbly than anyone. He took the table settings from the tables, whenever he saw one within reach, and tossed them into a bedsheet.

Concerning Herraud, we may relate that he had his men damage all the ships that were moored by the sea, so that none was seaworthy. He had some go to the fortress, and they brought the gold and treasures to the shore which Smid had ready for them. Now it was quite dark. Some were up on the hall roof, watching what was going on inside, and they hauled out of the window what had been tossed into the bedsheet. Some carried it to their ship and turned their prow away from the land.

CHAPTER XIII

As they were dancing most merrily in the hall, a strange new thing happened: a man walked into the hall. This man was tall and handsome, wearing a scarlet tunic and a silver belt and a gold band around his forehead. He was unarmed, and he went dancing like the others, until he came before the king. Then he raised his fist and punched the king in the nose so fast that three teeth flew out of his mouth. Blood gushed from the king's nose and mouth, and he collapsed unconscious.

Sigurd saw that. He flung the harp up into the bedsheet, and drove both fists between the shoulders of the man who had just come, but turned and ran. Sigurd ran after him, along with Siggeir and everyone else, although some people stayed and fussed over the king. Smid took the bride by the hand and led her up into the bed-sheets and locked her inside the belly of the harp,[32] and the men outside hauled her out of the window along with Smid. They brought them to the ships and boarded. The man who'd struck the king had already arrived. Sigurd also ran out onto the ship that he'd reached, and Siggeir came after him with a drawn sword. Sigurd turned to face him and pushed him overboard; his men had to haul him to land, nearly dead. Smid cut the moorings, and the men hauled up the sail and set to both sailing and rowing and got to sea as fast as they could. Hraerek rushed to his ship with many more men, but when the ship was launched, the deep blue sea flooded in, and they had to make for land. They just had to deal with it, since everyone was completely befuddled from drinking.

The king came to now, but he had little strength. People tried to nurse him, but he was quite weak. The festivities had turned to sadness and sorrow. But when the king recovered his strength, they made plans, and they agreed to not let the crowd of people scatter, but to prepare as quickly as possible to pursue the sworn brothers.

We'll let them make their preparations, but turn the story back to Bosi and Herraud's company. They sailed until they reached the point where the paths diverge, and one led to Bjarmaland. Bosi asked Herraud to sail home to Gautland, but he said that he had a mission in Bjarmaland. Herraud said that he wouldn't part with him—"but what is your mission there?" He said that that would become clear later. Smith offered to wait for them for five nights. Bosi said that that would suit them well.

The two of them together sailed to shore in a boat, and they concealed the boat in a hiding place. They went to a house where an old man and woman lived; they had a beautiful daughter. They were well received, and were given good wine to drink that evening. Crooked Bosi kept looking and smiling at the farmer's daughter, and she kept making eyes at him in return.

A little later, people went to bed. Bosi came to the farmer's daughter's bed. She asked what he wanted. He asked her to put a ring around his stump. She asked where the ring might be. He asked whether she didn't have one. She said that she had none that would suit him.

"I can expand it, even if it's narrow," he said.

"Where's your stump?" she asked. "I know pretty well what I can expect from my ring's bore."

He asked her to take it between her legs. She pulled back her hand and said to hell with his stump.

"What does it feel like to you?" he asked.

"The balance arm of my father's farmyard scales, but with the ring broken off."

"You keep finding fault," said Crooked Bosi. He slipped a gold ring from his hand and gave it to her. She asked what he wanted in return.

"I want to push a stopper into your wineskin," he said.[33]

"I don't know what you're talking about," she said.

"Lie with your legs spread as widely as you can," he said.

She did as he asked. He got between her legs and thrust up into her belly, all the way up under her ribs. She gave a start and said, "You forced the stopper right through the bunghole, man."

"I'll get it back out," he said. "How was it for you?"

"I'm as dizzy as if I'd been drinking fresh mead," she said. "You keep mopping the hole, as fast as you can."

He didn't hold back, until she felt so hot all over that she was about to be sick, and she asked him to stop. They took a rest, and she asked who he might be. He told her the truth and asked whether she might be at all friendly with the king's daughter Edda. She said that she often went into the king's daughter's bower and was well received there.

"I'll take you into my confidence," he said, "and I'll give you three marks of silver for you to bring the king's daughter to me in the forest."

He took three walnuts out of his purse. They looked like they were made of gold. He gave them to her and asked her to tell the king's daughter that she knew of a certain grove in the forest where such nuts were plentiful. She said that the king's daughter wouldn't be readily taken, and said that a eunuch always went with her—"his name is Skalk[34] and he's so strong that he has the strength of twelve men, whatever test he's put to."

Bosi said that he didn't care, as long as those were the only hazards to watch out for.

Early in the morning, the girl went to find the king's daughter and showed her the golden walnuts. She said that she knew where plenty of such nuts could be found. "Let's go there right away," said the king's daughter, "and the slave can go with us." And they did so.

The companions went into the forest and came upon them. Bosi greeted the young maid and asked why she was here all alone. She said that it wasn't dangerous. "This is how it's going to be," said Bosi. "Do whichever you want: come with me willingly, or I'll marry you quickly right here in the forest."

The slave asked what insanely rash ruffian this was, to be babbling such threats. Herraud ordered that foul-smelling oaf to shut up. The slave swung a huge club at Herraud, but Herraud brought up his shield. The blow was so heavy that the shield shattered. Herraud rushed under the slave's grip, but the slave quickly spun to face him. They wrestled powerfully, and the slave never went back on his heels. Bosi came up and yanked the slave's feet out from under him, and they put a rope around his neck and hanged him on an oak tree. Then Bosi lifted the king's daughter in his arms and carried her to the ship, and they set out from land and traveled until they found Smid. The king's daughter was dejected, but as soon as Smid had a word with her, all her despair left her. They sailed home to Gautland.

CHAPTER XIV

While this was happening, the brothers Hraerek and Sigurd had completely readied their forces, and they had countless men. But Herraud's punch had been so hard on King Godmund that he was in no shape to make this journey, and the brothers had to take on both the glory and the responsibility. They sailed from Glaesisvellir with forty ships, and increased their fleet with still more ships that joined up along the way. They came to Bjarmaland and met their father King Harek, just as Herraud and Bosi had left. King Harek was fully aware that they had taken his daughter away. He had readied his forces and had fifteen great ships. Now he joined the brothers on their journey, and all together they had sixty ships. They sailed towards Gautland.

Now we must tell how Herraud and Bosi summoned their forces as soon as they arrived at home. They wanted to be prepared in case they were pursued, and hold the wedding when they had the leisure for it. Thvari had ordered spears and axes and arrows to be made while they were away. A great multitude of men assembled. They had heard that King Harek and his sons had invaded their land, and they didn't stay quiet about it. Herraud ordered the ships to sail out against them; he had a large and fine force, though much smaller than Harek and his sons had. Thvari's son Smid steered his ships to face the king, but Bosi faced Hraerek, and Herraud faced Siggeir. There was no need to ask the reason; the fiercest of battles broke out between them, and both sides fought most furiously.

The battle hadn't gone on for long when Siggeir boarded Herraud's ship and quickly started killing men. Herraud's forecastleman was named Snidil. He flung a spear at Siggeir, who caught the spear in the air and flung it back at the thrower. The spear flew right through Snidil and so far into the ship's prow that it pinned him against it. Herraud turned to face Siggeir and stabbed at him with a great spear, piercing his shield, but Siggeir twisted the shield so hard that Herraud lost his grip on the spear. Siggeir struck at Herraud, and the blow landed on his helmet and cut off a quarter of it, along with his right ear. But Herraud seized a large beam from the deck and smashed him in the nose, so that his helmet visor was driven into his face, his nose broken and all his teeth knocked out. He leaped backwards into his own ship and collapsed unconscious and lay there for a very long time.

Smid was fighting bravely. King Harek boarded his ship with twelve men and mowed down anyone in his way. Smid turned to face him and struck at him with the knife that the old crone Busla had given him, because only charmed weapons would bite him. The blow hit him in the teeth and knocked all of them out, breaking his upper jaw and splitting both lips, and plenty of blood gushed from his mouth. He reacted to this blow so violently that he turned into a flying dragon and spewed poison over the ship, and many men died. He dived at Smid and gobbled him up and swallowed him down.

Now the men saw a bird flying down from the land, the kind called a skerry-vulture. It has such a huge and hideous head that it's compared with the devil. It rushed at the dragon, and their attack was terrifying. Their encounter ended when they both fell down; the skerry-vulture fell into the sea, but the dragon landed on Siggeir's ship. By then Herraud had boarded the ship and was swinging his club left and right. He struck at Siggeir, and the blow landed under his ear and his entire skull was shattered. He was knocked overboard and never came up again. King Harek came to his senses and suddenly turned into a wild boar. He seized Herraud with his tusks and tore off all his armor, and sunk his teeth in his breast and ripped off both his nipples down to the bone. Herraud struck at the boar's snout in return and cut it off in front of the eyes. Herraud was so exhausted that he fell on his back, and the boar trampled him underfoot, but couldn't bite him because his snout was cut off. Then a huge and deadly bitch-hound with great big fangs came onto the ship. She tore a hole in the boar's groin and pulled out his intestines and leaped overboard. Harek turned into human shape and plunged overboard after her. They both sunk to the bottom, and neither one came up after that. People think that that must have been the old crone Busla, because she was never seen again.

CHAPTER XV

Crooked Bosi now boarded Hraerek's ship and fought most manfully. He saw his own father floating on a plank, completely worn out. He jumped overboard and helped him and got him up into his own ship. By then Hraerek had boarded the ship and killed many men. Bosi boarded the ship and was very weary, but all the same, he attacked Hraerek and struck his shield, splitting it completely in two and cutting off the front of his foot. His sword hit the windlass and split it down the middle. Hraerek struck back. Bosi spun on his heel and dodged the blow, but the sword slipped off his helmet and landed on his shoulders and completely ripped off his mailcoat, wounding him on the shoulder-blades. It kept going down his entire back so that all his clothes were ripped off, leaving him completely naked.[35] And it cut off his left heelbone. Bosi seized a beam, but then Hraerek wanted to jump overboard. Bosi cut him in two against the gunwale, so that each piece fell in a different direction.

By then, most of Hraerek's men had fallen, and the survivors accepted a truce. Bosi and Herraud mustered their own men—there were no more than a hundred able-bodied men left. The sworn brothers had a great victory to boast of. Now the men divided the booty, and those who could be healed were healed.

CHAPTER XVI

Then Herraud and Bosi prepared for their wedding, and there was no lack of provisions both excellent and plentiful. The feast lasted a month, and men were sent home with worthy gifts. Herraud assumed the title of king over all the realm that his father had ruled.

A little while later, they mustered their forces and traveled to Bjarmaland. Bosi asked for a hearing and reckoned that Edda, who had now become his wife, was to inherit the land after her father. He said that he could best compensate the inhabitants for the slaughter they had suffered at his hands by being king over them and making them stronger with laws and legal amendments. As they had no ruler, they saw no better option than to accept him as king. Edda and all her good ways were well-known to them. Now Bosi became king over Bjarmaland.

Bosi had a son by the lover with whom he had battle-hardened his warrior. He was named Svidi Bold-Attacker, the father of Vilmund the Outsider.[36]

Bosi went east to Glaesisvellir and reconciled King Godmund and Herraud. Herraud and Hleid loved each other very much. Their daughter was Thora Fortress-Hart, whom Ragnar Shaggy-Breeches married. It's been said that a little gold-colored serpent was found inside the vulture's egg that Bosi and Herraud searched for in Bjarmaland. King Herraud gave it to his daughter as a tooth-gift. She laid a gold ring underneath it, and it grew so huge that it lay coiled around her bower, and so fierce that no one dared to come near it, except for the king and the man who brought its food. It required an old ox for every meal, and it was considered the most harmful beast. King Herraud swore an oath to betroth his daughter Thora to the one man who dared to enter the bower to speak with her and do away with the serpent. But no one dared to do that until Ragnar came, the son of Sigurd Ring. This Ragnar was later called Shaggy-Breeches, and he took the name from the clothes that he had made for himself when he vanquished the serpent.[35]

And here we now end the saga of Crooked Bosi. May Saint Busla bless everyone who has listened, read, and written, or who has given some charity or done good deeds. Amen.[36]

THE SAGA OF STURLAUG THE HARD-WORKING

Sturlaugs saga starfsama

CHAPTER I

All men who are truly knowledgeable about history know that the Turks and Asians settled the Northlands. Then the language originated which has spread through all lands since then. The leader of this folk was named Odin, from whom men reckon their descent.[1]

At that time, a king named Harald Goldmouth ruled over Trondheim in Norway. He had a queen, but they had no children. In his kingdom there was a jarl named Hring, whose residence was at Kaupang[2] along the coast. He had a daughter who was called Asa the Fair, because she excelled all the young maidens of her day as pure gold excels pale brass, or as the sun outshines the other heavenly bodies.

Ingolf was the name of a powerful man who ruled over the shire of Namdalen.[3] He had a son named Sturlaug. Sturlaug was exceedingly tall in stature from an early age, fair of hair and skin, courteous in all his conduct and well-formed in all his body, cheerful in his speech with his men, even-tempered, and free with his money. For those reasons, he was blessed with a great many friends. He practiced archery and swimming and all manner of sports. Ingolf, his father, had his seat at the estate called Skartastadir.[4] He was the most magnificent man, and maintained a great many men in his household. He had another estate on the island called Njardey,[5] and there were also many people there. He owned four more estates.

There was a man named Asgaut who lived at the estate called Tunglaheim,[6] a man of much importance. He was married to a woman named Grima. They had two sons. One was named Jokul, and the other was Guttorm. They were sturdy men, and well-bred like their father.

There was a man named Thorgaut, who lived on the island called Loka.[7] His wife was named Helga. They had two sons. One of the sons was named Soti, and the other was named Hrolf Nose.

There was a man named Hrafn, a farmer who lived on the island called Urga. His wife was named Helga. They had a son named Sighvat. He was physically strong and well-mannered.

There was a woman named Jarngerd who lived at the estate called Berg, not far from Ingolf. She had a son named Aki, who was a very mighty man.

Of the men at that time, he came closest to Sturlaug in all accomplishments. Aki and Sturlaug were playmates in childhood.

All these men that we have listed played together as children. They took up all kinds of sports and skills that it was customary for men to teach their sons back then, and they swore brotherhood with each other. They all lived prosperously with their fathers.

CHAPTER II

There was a woman named Vefreyja[8], stately and wealthy. She had settled at the estate called Ve.[9] She had two sons. One was named Raud, and the other was Hrafn. Both of them were big strong men, and well outfitted with weapons and clothes. Vefreyja's foster-son was named Svipud, and both he and she were knowledgeable and wise about most things.[10] She had a fine house, with two doors in it. She sat there every day and turned to face a different door each day. Few things came upon her unawares. She was always spinning linen and sitting on a chair. She had grown very red-eyed from old age, yet she saw anything that came to her yard, whatever it was, because few things caught her unawares. Asa the Fair stayed there as her foster-daughter when she was young, and she learned knowledge there. Vefreyja loved her deeply, and Asa loved her.

CHAPTER III

On one occasion, Ingolf said to Sturlaug and his sworn brothers, "How long will this go on that you sworn brothers play children's games, like girls flirting with men? It would be the way of bold warriors to try to do some renowned deeds instead, or at least to ask to marry a wife and settle down on a farm, and administer the land and livestock with your fathers."

Sturlaug said, "Where should I ask for a wife, since you're pushing this so hard?"

Ingolf said, "Jarl Hring has a daughter named Asa the Fair. She is a beautiful woman and gifted with wisdom."

Sturlaug said, "I'm still not very old for courting a wife, and not very keen on it in my mind, but I'll try this. Yet I expect that it won't amount to much."

Now they prepared for their journey, sixteen men all together, well provided with weapons and clothes and horses. They went on their way, and came at evening to Jarl Hring, and they were received warmly. The jarl held a fine and splendid feast in their honor. They stayed there for three nights.

And one day, they went with the jarl to Asa's bower, and Sturlaug carried out his errand and asked Asa for her hand in marriage. The jarl turned to her and told his daughter about the men, and said, "You have to answer your suitor now, daughter."

Asa said, "Why would I marry a man who's always milking the cows at home with his mother, doing nothing to distinguish himself?"

Sturlaug was very angry at these words, and he rode away to his home.

CHAPTER IV

In the spring, the sworn brothers sailed away with ten ships. They raided in the Eastern realms and always won victory, wherever they went. They let merchants go in peace, but they forced robbers to submit to them.[11] They were out on raids in the summer, but went home in winter to stay with their fathers.

Now they wished to leave this occupation and divide up all their booty. The sworn brothers took their wealth and brought it to their fathers, but they let their men set out raiding in their own ships. Sturlaug and his sworn brothers stayed there peacefully.

CHAPTER V

The next thing to tell is that King Harald's queen became ill and breathed her last. The king felt that that was a terrible loss, because he had grown so old, and he was distressed by her death. The king's counselors and retainers advised him to ask a woman to marry him and be queen—"and then you might forget about your lady's passing, and no longer pine for her."

The king said, "Where should I go to ask for a woman's hand in marriage?"

They said, "Jarl Hring has a daughter named Asa. If you wanted, you could have her as soon as you like."[12]

The king said that it would be so. He prepared for his journey, taking a hundred men with him. They rode until they came to Jarl Hring. He was outside, and men were playing sports before him. The king rode up so swiftly that men had to jump out of the way in both directions. The king gave him two options: betroth his daughter to him, or be killed on the spot.

The jarl said, "Let's go to Asa's bower and talk with her, so that we can find out what her answers are."

"No," said the king, "I don't want to wait around for your daughter. Choose quickly, one or the other."

138

The jarl thought it over, and realized that he would be overpowered. He extended his hand and betrothed his daughter to the king. She would have to stay betrothed for three years.[13] The king turned away and rode home, well pleased with his journey. The jarl stayed behind, not very content with his lot. He stood up and went to Asa's bower, sat down and sighed sadly. Asa said, "What grief has come to you, my father, that you are so silent? Have you any new tidings to tell?"

"Here's some important news," said the jarl. "I had to betroth you, against my will."

"Who is the man?" she said.

"King Harald has betrothed you," he said, "and you must stay engaged to him for three years."

She answered, "He's not the least important man to offer his hand, but one never knows what this news might mean. I may be meant to marry someone else, and things may change in a moment. Be cheerful, father."

The jarl said, "I think it would be better if you were betrothed to Sturlaug."

She answered, "I don't know what would be for the best."

Now time passed, and matters were quiet for a while.

CHAPTER VI

One day, it so happened that Jarl Hring was out on the playing field, and his retainers were with him. They saw a huge man come riding out of the forest. His horse was fully armored and so was he, with a black shield at his side and a hewing-spear[14] in his hand. He rode so swiftly that men had to jump out of the way in both directions. He rode up, mounted on his horse, and he aimed his spear forward right between the horse's ears, and said "Greetings, lord."

The jarl accepted his greeting and asked who he might be.

He said, "I am called Kol the Crooked,[15] and I've come here to ask for your daughter Asa's hand in marriage."[16]

The jarl said, "Don't you know that she is betrothed to King Harald?"

Kol said, "It's no worse for me to have her. Now do one of two things: break off the engagement, or I'll run you through with the spear."

The jarl thought it over, and realized that neither choice was good. He chose to live, but felt that nothing but grief would come of it. He didn't concern himself with how badly the confrontation between King Harald and Kol would go, and he broke off her engagement to Harald.

Kol said, "Tell King Harald that I challenge him to single combat, eastwards along the Gota River, when half the winter has passed. Let him who wins have the maiden. Should he not come, or should he not dare to fight, then may he bear a coward's reputation in the eyes of every man, as long as he lives. Stay well, lord." At once Kol turned his horse around and rode away, thinking that matters had gone well.

The jarl was not very content with his lot. He stayed behind for a while, and then stood up and went to his daughter's bower. He sat down next to her and could hardly speak. Asa said, "Are you sick, father?"

The jarl said, "It would be better to be sick and die quickly, than to suffer such shame as to betroth one's own daughter against her will."

Asa said, "To whom am I betrothed now?"

The jarl said, "He is called Kol the Crooked."

She said, "Rather than marrying the worst man, matters may change for the better. Our situation may improve from what we can expect now. One of them must win, but not both. And it might happen that neither of them will win, if we are lucky. Be cheerful, father."

The jarl said, "It would be well if it could be as you say, but I'm afraid that that won't happen if they kill each other—but that would be what I'd prefer." Now they parted for the time being.

CHAPTER VII

King Harald now heard this news, and he felt that matters were no better than before. He sought advice on the matter from his friends. In the end, the king sent his men to find Heming and invite him to the Yule feast, and to tell him that he would not go away without gifts. He got a certain man named Kolli to take the message. Now they went north to Namdalen to meet Heming, and they greeted him and brought the king's message. Heming had been the greatest dueler, but now he was bowed down by age, and he had had a falling-out with King Harald for some time.

The messenger spoke his message. Heming answered, "I don't recall that the king has invited me to his home before. There are two choices at hand now: to stay home and ignore the king's invitation, or else to get to the bottom of this. Since an old man has nothing to lose,[17] let it happen as it may. Someone will survive, as long as my son Sighvat lives."

Now Heming prepared for his visit, with twelve men, and they arrived on the first evening of Yule and went into the hall before the king, and greeted him well. The king accepted their greeting warmly and cleared the high seat and seated Heming next to himself, and they gladly drank the Yule toasts, highly honored. But on the last day of Yule, the Heming and the king took counsel together. The king said, "I have been summoned to single combat, and I was looking to you to redeem me from Kol the Crooked."

Heming said, "I don't know that you've offered me so much that I'd risk my life for you. I suspect that we're not dealing with a strong man, but rather with a troll."

The king said, "I've sought out your help because I believe that you were the greatest champion in the land. I think it likely that if you fall short, such a man as you are, then no one can do it. And if you come back from this journey, I will richly reward you with gold or silver."

Heming said, "It's true what they say: an old man has nothing to lose. But 'an old tree can be expected to fall', and I will go on your errand."

The king said, "Bravest of all warriors on sea or land, I expect that you will succeed."

Now Heming prepared to go on his journey, and rode off on his way and didn't stop until he came to the east bank of the Gota. Kol was there ahead of him. When they met, Kol asked what Heming was going to do. Heming said, "I mean to fight you."

Kol said, "That would be a shameful end for me, if you killed me on the field. I have killed men who were stronger and more promising than you are. Go back home, but give me your weapon and admit that you were overcome and didn't dare to fight me."

Heming said, "I would rather die than bear the name of coward before any man."

Kol said, "I won't hold back from killing you, dog, if that's all you want."

In the evening, they put up their tents and went to sleep for the night. In the morning, Heming stood up and saw that Kol had gone to the island where the duel was to take place.[18] He went to the island with his men. They spread a cloak under their feet, and Kol pronounced the law of combat.[19] Then they came together and fought, and in the end Heming fell before Kol.

Kol said to Heming's men, "Now you must go back to the king and tell him to do one of two things: come to fight me himself, or get a man with some fortitude to come on his behalf, if he wants the woman for himself. Otherwise, he must give her up." The men who had left their home turned back quickly and went north to Namdalen, to meet with King Harald and tell him about all these events and Kol the Crooked's declaration.

CHAPTER VIII

The king felt this was bad news. Again he sought out advice, and he adopted a plan to send Kolli the messenger to Sturlaug and his father, and invite them to a feast lasting half a month, with as many men as they wanted to have with them. These words passed between father and son: Sturlaug asked his father whether they should accept the invitation. His father said, "I want us to stay home and not go anywhere."

Sturlaug said, "I have no mind to ignore the king's invitation, but I know that there must be something behind it. Yet I want to go. The saga about us will be short, if we can't visit another man when we are invited. One never knows whether what happens on our journey might bring us honor."

Ingolf said, "You'll want to decide about our travels, whether they go well or badly."

After that, they prepared for their journey. They were sixty men all together, all well provided with weapons and clothes. They rode to meet King Harald and came there on the first evening of Yule. The king welcomed them gladly and set them on the high seat next to himself, and the finest feast was set. But when Yule was over, the king went to take counsel with Ingolf and his son Sturlaug.

Sturlaug told his men, "Make ready our horses while we talk." They did so.

The king said, "I have been summoned to a single combat. I see that you, Sturlaug, such a man as you are, might redeem me from going to fight Kol the Crooked, because I am an old man."

Sturlaug said, "Give over to me the betrothal that you forced from Jarl Hring, because this won't be without a price."

"The price you've set seems high to me," said the king.

"If you accept it, then I'll risk it," said Sturlaug, "however it goes between me and Kol."

The king said, "I wasn't aware that you would impose this condition. It would be the greatest disgrace for me to agree to it."

Sturlaug said, "It's time to choose which option seems better for you."

The king said, "Yet I will choose for you to go and fight the combat with Kol. It will go with us as it's fated to go."

Sturlaug replied, "Give up your betrothal first."

The king did so, though he was unwilling, because the company of sworn brothers seemed paltry to him.

They rode away to meet with Jarl Hring. He welcomed them, and invited them to accept his hospitality. They told him how their dealings had gone, and how it had gone with them and King Harald. The jarl cheered up to hear that, and invited them to go to Asa's bower, and so they did. And when they arrived, Asa welcomed them well.

Hring said, "You have to receive and give your answer to a suitor here, daughter."

"Who is the man?" she asked.

"His name is Sturlaug."

Asa said, "I'm not short of husbands now."

Sturlaug said, "It's been decided that I won't wait for your answer any longer."

Asa said that it would be as they willed. A splendid feast was prepared, and nothing needful was spared. Sturlaug went to marry Asa the Fair, and right away they went to lie in the same bed. The feasting continued, and men were sent home with good gifts. Ingolf and his men rode home, and Asa and Sturlaug stayed behind and were quite content with their marriage.[20]

CHAPTER IX

One morning, as Asa and Sturlaug were lying in their bed, Asa said to Sturlaug, "Have you been challenged to single combat, Sturlaug?"

"It's true," he said.

"With whom?" she said.

"With Kol the Crooked," he said. "What can you tell me about him?"

She answered, "Go and find Vefreyja, my foster-mother. Take her advice, and it will serve you well. Here is a gold ring that you must bring her as a token. Tell her that it's very important to me for her to receive you well."

Sturlaug now went with his sworn brothers, twelve all together. They rode until they came to the home of the old woman. Sturlaug leaped from the back of his horse and rushed through the doors to the old woman. He laid his arms around her neck and kissed her, saying, "Greetings and blessings, my lady."

She quickly turned away from him and stared at him. "Who is this son of a bitch who treats me so disgracefully? No one has ever dared to do anything like this. I'll pay you back frightfully for this."

Sturlaug said, "Do not be so angry, my lady, for Asa has sent me here to you."

"What do you have to do with Asa?" said the old woman.

"She is my wife," he said.

She asked, "Is the wedding over?"

"It is," he said.

"Now that's a shabby trick," said the old woman, "that I wasn't invited to the wedding. But I'll do as Asa asks. Take off your clothes. I want to see the shape of your body."

He did so. She stroked him all over, and he felt himself growing very strong because of it.[21] Then she gave him a cup to drink from, and they went to the sitting-room. The old woman was most helpful that evening. She asked whether Sturlaug wanted to lie alone that night, or next to her—"but I certainly won't betray my dear Asa."

Sturlaug said, "I think it would be better, lady, if I were near you."

Then the old woman put a log between them,[22] and they both lay together on the same pillow and talked through the night. Sturlaug said, "What advice can you give me, since I have been summoned to a single combat with Kol the Crooked?"

"I believe that things have taken an unlucky turn," said the old woman, "because no iron will cut him. I can hardly advise you here."

In the morning, the sworn brothers prepared themselves for their journey. When they were ready, the old woman said to Sturlaug, "Take this shaggy cape[23] which my father's family owned, and this short sword—good fortune has always gone with it. And test whether there's any strength in you."

Sturlaug accepted the sword and struck at a stone that stood in the courtyard, and he cut off a corner of the stone. The rust fell off the sword, and it was as bright as silver. The old woman said, "You must bring that sword to the combat with Kol the Crooked. But you must not show him that sword, if he asks to see what you have to strike with."[24]

Then the old woman said, "Farewell, my Sturlaug, and may everything turn out to bring you victory and prosperity as long as you live. I lay upon you all the luck which our kin has had, as much as I may. Yet I am afraid of how Kol the Crooked might deal with you. I have two sons, whom I want you to take into sworn brotherhood."

"So be it," said Sturlaug, and they swore brotherhood with each other. Then they turned away. When they had gone a short distance, the old woman called out after them and said, "You will want my foster-son Svipud to come with you, my dear Sturlaug. He is fleet-footed."

"I am willing," said Sturlaug. The old woman put a little purse into Svipud's hand. He stuck it into his clothing and then he rushed out in front of their horses. Now they rode on and didn't stop until they had gone east to the Gota River. Kol hadn't arrived. Sturlaug pitched his tent where Kol usually pitched his tent.

CHAPTER X

Kol arrived a little later. Sturlaug went to meet him and greeted him. Kol said, "Who is this wicked son of a bitch, who is so impudent that he dares to pitch his tent where I usually pitch mine?"

Sturlaug said, "You know very well who the son of a bitch is, because he wasn't here before you got here. But if it's my name you're asking for, I'm called Sturlaug."

Kol said, "What do you mean by coming here?"

Sturlaug said: "I intend to fight you."

Kol said, "Now this is hardly a fair move. You're far too rash to have such arrogance, since I have killed so many warriors who have fought me. What drove you to do this?"

Sturlaug said, "This above all: Asa the Fair is my wife. You won't take the maiden, even if I should fall before you."

Kol said, "Listen to this outrageous thing that's come into your rascally[25] head to do. Just for that, I won't show you any mercy, and soon you'll lose your life. It's too late for you. Yet it's a shame for such a man as you."

Sturlaug said, "Never shall I turn tail before you."

Kol pitched his tent on another site that evening. When Kol had gone inside to eat, Svipud came into his tent and took the old woman's little purse out of his cloak and shook it in the tent, and this created much smoke. Kol glared at him and said, "Go away, you wicked dog, and don't come back, because you must be up to no good." Svipud turned away, so that no one knew what had become of him. They slept that night.

In the morning, Sturlaug got up early, along with his sworn brothers. They went to the island, sat down and waited for Kol. Hrolf Nose stood up and went into the forest and cut himself a great big club. He picked it up and went back to his fellows. Kol got up in the morning, and the sun was shining all over the meadows. He said, "I suppose that wretched slave who came here yesterday evening had some sort of magic which hasn't done us any good. This may truly be called a death-sleep that we've slept. Let's go to the dueling-ground."

They went to the dueling-ground and cast a cloak under their feet. Kol pronounced the law of combat between them, and each of them had to stake twenty marks of silver. Whoever won was to have it. And when they were ready, Kol spoke up: "Sturlaug my lad, show me the sword that you have." He did so. Kol saw the edge and stared at it, and said, "You won't beat me with that sword. Go home at once and say that you've been beaten. Give

me your weapon, and send me Asa the Fair. Tell her that you didn't dare to
fight me, or to withhold her from me."

Sturlaug said, "You won't beat me with words alone, because you're
overcome with terror. Soon you'll die a wretched death."

Kol was angry at his words and said, "You'll find out that I won't show
you mercy, you wretched dog."

Then Sturlaug threw away the sword that he had shown to Kol, and he
took Vefreyja's Gift from under his cloak and drew it. Kol said, "Where did
you get Vefreyja's Gift? I would not have challenged you to combat had I
known."

Sturlaug answered, "It makes no difference to you. Things have gone
badly for you if you're afraid before you need to be."

Sturlaug struck at Kol and split his shield completely. Kol struck back
and split his shield in the same way. Then Sturlaug struck a second time
against Kol's helmet, and sheared off all the flesh from his cheek, and the
stroke went on down to the shoulder and stuck in his shoulder-blade. Kol
stood straight and didn't pay any attention to the blow. Then Hrolf Nose
rushed at him with the club and pounded the sword's point, so that the
sword drove down into his body. Kol fell there, and Sturlaug won the victory
and became famous for this deed.

Sturlaug rode to Vefreyja. The old woman was outside, and she greeted
Sturlaug warmly. Svipud was there ahead of him. They stayed there for the
night. The old woman was pleased with this deed. "And it's true," she said,
"that my Asa is blessed to have such a man as you, and from now on your
wise plans will turn out well for you, if you're careful. I am afraid of how
things will turn out, but I hope that it goes well with you. This old woman
won't be worse than nothing to you."

Sturlaug rode away to meet Jarl Hring. He welcomed them all gladly, and
Asa was happy to see her husband. This news reached King Harald. The
king was upset at what had happened, as later events will show, but all of
Sturlaug's kinsmen thought that he had been pulled out of Hel.

CHAPTER XI

One day when Jarl Hring was at the games with his men, as Hring and
Sturlaug were playing before them all, they saw a man ride at them out of
the forest, fully armored and riding a red horse. He was very tall, with a
helm on his head, girded with a sword, with a gold-enameled shield at his
side and a spear in his hand. He rode up to the jarl and greeted him warmly.
He welcomed him in the same way, and asked who he was. He said, "I won't

withhold my name: I am called Framar, and Kol the Crooked and I were half-brothers. I have come here because I want to challenge you to combat, Sturlaug, for I will not carry my brother in my purse."[26]

Sturlaug said, "I'm quite ready for combat whenever you want. You're obliged to seek redress on behalf of a wicked man, such as Kol was."

"That's true," said Framar, "but he was my kinsman, and for that I want to fight you where Kol fell, east on the Gota River, when half the winter has passed."

"So be it," said Sturlaug. Then Framar went on his way, and the others stayed behind. Summer passed.

One night, as Sturlaug and Asa lay together in their bed, Asa said, "Have you been challenged to combat, Sturlaug?"

"It's true," he said. "What advice can you give me about that?"

Asa said, "Go and find Vefreyja, my foster-mother, and take her advice."

"So be it," said Sturlaug. He went to meet Vefreyja. The old woman was outside, and she greeted him warmly, and they stayed there for the night.

In the morning, Sturlaug asked the old woman for advice. The old woman said, "Whom do you have to battle?"

"His name is Framar," said Sturlaug, "the brother of Kol the Crooked."

"They're not like each other," she said, "and it's too bad that you two have to bear deadly spears against each other, because Framar is the bravest man and comes of the best family, but Kol was the worst man and descended from thralls. And it would be fortunate if it could come about that you two might become friends, rather than enemies. I can't help you with that, and it must go with you as it's fated. But Svipud, my foster-son, shall go with you."

Now they went their way, and didn't stop until they came east to the Gota, and Framar rode to the other bank. They met each other there and asked each other for news. They dismounted, and each set up his tent with the other's help, and they slept there for the night.

CHAPTER XII

In the morning they got up early and went to the island and sat down on a log. Framar said, "What would you like, for us to test each other first, or for our men to fight?"

Sturlaug said, "I think it would be a good idea to be entertained by my men."

Hrolf Nose stood up and said, "I'll go up against you, black man."[27]

Hrolf quickly prepared himself for wrestling. At once they attacked each other and wrestled with powerful grips, and their combat was both fierce and long. They were badly mismatched in strength, because the black man could carry Hrolf in his grip wherever he wanted. The berserker wanted to throw Hrolf down, but he always got his feet under himself. This black man was as large as a giant, as broad as a bull and as black as Hel. He had such large claws that they were more like vulture's talons than human nails. Now he carried Hrolf towards the log, and the black man wanted to throw Hrolf down onto his own club, but Hrolf put his feet down so hard that they fell away from each other. The black man landed on his back, and there was a stone underneath him, and his back broke. Hrolf quickly leaped to his feet and seized his club and quickly bashed him down into Hel. Hrolf was all bruised and bloody, and his flesh was torn from his bones. Sturlaug thanked him very much for his ferocity.

Next there was a man with Framar who was named Thord, a tall man and a strong one, from Sweden in the east. Hrafn the Tall went up against him, and they had a single combat with mighty blows, but in the end Hrafn fell before Thord.

Now Jokul went forward and said, "Who will stand up to me?"

A man named Frosti stood up and said, "Wouldn't it be fitting for me to take you on, since frost hardens a glacier?"[28]

They fought for a long time until Jokul fell before Frosti. Sturlaug felt that it was a great grief to lose his sworn brother, but it had been stipulated that no one could help anyone else.

There was a certain Finn[29] with Framar, and it was arranged that he would face Svipud. They attacked each other and fought so fiercely and quickly that the eye couldn't follow them, and neither one wounded the other. But when men looked their way a second time, they had vanished, and there were two hounds who bit each other furiously. And when everyone least expected it, the hounds vanished, but men heard some sort of commotion up above, and they looked up and saw that two eagles were flying at each other in the air. They tore off each other's feathers with their claws and beaks, so that blood was falling to earth. In the end, one of them fell down dead on the ground, and the other flew away, and no one knew which one that was.[30]

CHAPTER XIII

Framar said, "Now it's time for the two of us to test each other."

"I'm ready for it," said Sturlaug.

Now they spread a cloak under their feet. Sturlaug drew Vefreyja's Gift, and when Framar saw that, he said, "How did Vefreyja's Gift come to you?"

Sturlaug said, "It's none of your business where it came from."

Framar said, "I would not have challenged you if I had known that. Still, I have never had fear in my breast."

Framar pronounced the law of combat, and Sturlaug had to strike first. He struck Framar right on his helmet and cut off the part that he hit, and his stroke went on into his shield and split it all the way down to the pointed end,[31] so that the sword sank into the earth. The point cut through Framar's mailcoat into his chest, and it also gashed his forehead and scratched the bone. Blood ran into his eyes so that he couldn't see, and the wound swelled up terribly.

Then Framar struck at Sturlaug and split his shield completely in two. Then Sturlaug struck at Framar a second time, and it went the same way as the first stroke, and Framar was out of the fight. He sat down and said, "You have the greatest enemy in your hands, because your sword is full of venom and evil. Cut off my head as soon as possible, because I don't want to live in torment."

Sturlaug said, "Will you accept your life from me?"

Framar said, "I would find it good to accept my life from you, but my life has now been destroyed."

They carried him off the island and into his tent, and there was little hope for him. And at that moment, they heard a great rumbling noise outside, and when they came out, there was Vefreyja in a wagon. She asked how it had gone for them. They answered that Framar was on the point of death.

The old woman said, "Carry him out here. It doesn't matter where he dies." It was done as she ordered.

Sturlaug said, "Will you let more men go with you?"

"I won't," said the old woman. "I am quite capable of doing this by myself."

The old woman drove off with Framar, and the others stayed behind. The night passed, and in the morning, Sturlaug got ready for his journey. Frosti came to Sturlaug and said, "I would willingly go on the journey with you and your sworn brothers."

Sturlaug said, "I suppose that I would be compensated for Jokul if you took his place," and Frosti became Sturlaug's sworn brother. At once they rode away and didn't stop until they came to Vefreyja. When they arrived, there were Svipud and Framar, both completely healthy. They stayed there for the night and were well received.

In the morning, Vefreyja spoke up: "My dear Sturlaug, I want you and Framar to swear brotherhood, for he is the boldest man in every respect."

Sturlaug answered, "It's your decision, old woman. That will benefit me the most." Now Sturlaug and Framar swore brotherhood with each other. Each one had to avenge the other, as if they were brothers by birth.

CHAPTER XIV

After that they rode off, until they were approaching the estate of Jarl Hring. They thought that something strange was going on: the hall was completely surrounded by men. King Harald had come there with four hundred men, intending to burn Jarl Hring and his daughter Asa the Fair inside the hall. They saw that flames were licking over everything, and that King Harald was burning all the estate. Then Sturlaug and his men saw people coming up out of the ground in a certain clearing, and when they headed over there, they realized that Jarl Hring had escaped with all his household, and Asa the Fair was there with him. There was a happy reunion for them all.

After that, they all rode to meet the king, where he was at the burning. They were fully armed and their horses were wearing chainmail. Sturlaug said, "It's better for us to meet here than at sea, king. But things have gone badly for you, because you're both cowardly and treacherous."

The king replied, "I'll pay no attention to your wicked words, but I must say to you, Sturlaug, that you shall never stay in this land unafraid, unless you bring me the aurochs horn that I once lost. I'll give you a name along with the quest. You shall be called Sturlaug the Hard-Working. That name will stick to you, because from now on, hard work will always be the fate of you and your sworn brothers, as long as you all live, if you come back from this journey—which won't happen."

Sturlaug said, "Where shall I look for it?"

The king said, "Figure it out yourself."

Sturlaug said, "It's unworthy of me to go on your quest. But I'll stake my life on any task that you think is heavy to set before me."

The king didn't attempt to attack them, since he felt that the band of sworn brothers were tough opponents, both in strength and in armor. Neither one wished the other farewell, and they parted leaving matters as they stood. Sturlaug and all his men rode north to Namdalen together and stayed there through the winter.

CHAPTER XV

One day, Asa came to speak with Sturlaug, and she said, "Has a quest been laid on you?"

"It's true," he said. "What advice can you give me on where I should search for this horn?"

Asa said, "Find my foster-mother Vefreyja, and take her advice."

On the next day, they prepared to leave home and rode to Vefreyja. She was outside and welcomed them well, and they stayed there for the night. In the morning, Sturlaug said to Vefreyja, "What can you tell me of this horn, which is called an aurochs horn?"

The old woman said, "I cannot tell anything about it, and I won't."

Sturlaug said, "Do you know anyone who is able to tell me about it? For I'm eager to know."

Vefreyja said, "There is a woman named Jarngerd; she is my sister. Go to her and find out what she has to say."

They rode away now and didn't stop their journeying until they came to where Jarngerd had her home. They spent the night there. Sturlaug asked Jarngerd whether she could tell him about the aurochs horn. She said, "I cannot tell you, but I know a woman who will know."

Sturlaug asked who that was. "Snaelaug is my sister's name. She is married to King Hrolf of the Hundings. But it isn't safe for you to go there, because this journey will turn out to be a serious matter when you return."

Thus informed, the sworn brothers rode home.

CHAPTER XVI

The next thing to tell is how, a little later, Sturlaug and all his sworn brothers prepared for their journey. They had a hundred men and one ship. Sturlaug talked with Jarl Hring and also his own father, and asked them to look after Asa's affairs and all the property that he left behind while he was away.

Now they sailed north, along the coast of Halogaland and Finnmark and Vatnsnes and into Austrvik.[32] They dropped the anchors and tied up there, and settled in for the night. Then they drew lots for standing watch. Aki was chosen to stand watch for the first third of the night, Framar for the second, and Sturlaug for the last third.

When all the men were asleep on the ship except for Aki, he took a boat and rowed along the coast out to the cape. He heard someone walking up on the beach. Aki spoke up and said "Who am I addressing here, a man or a woman?"

He heard a reply: "Of course it's a woman."

"What's your name, sweetheart?" said Aki.

"My name is Torfa," she said, "but who is in the boat?"

"His name is Aki," he said.

"It can't be Aki, the son of Jarngerd, who has come here?" she said.

"The very same," he said.

"Won't you make a deal with me, my dear Aki?" she said.

"What's the deal?" he said.

"For you to take me to that island, a short distance off the coast. My father has died there, leaving a lot of money. We are three sisters and we have to divide the inheritance between us. I want to come out ahead of them. I will give you a day and a night of favorable winds when it will be most useful."

"So be it," said Aki.

She stepped into the boat, and he rowed out into the channel. When he had rowed a short distance, she spoke up: "Now I can easily wade to land. Fare well and good luck to you, and I will keep my agreement with you in full." Now she hitched up her tunic of skins and stepped overboard. Aki rowed back to the ship and woke up Framar, and lay down and quickly fell asleep.

Framar stepped into the boat and rowed out along the cape. He heard someone walking on the beach at low tide. Framar said, "Is that a man or a woman on land?"

He heard an answer: "There's no question it's a woman."

"What are you called, rich and lovely lady?" he said.

"My name is Hild," she said, "and what is your name, my boy?"

"My name is Framar," he said.

"That can't be Framar, the brother of Kol the Crooked, who has come here?" she said.

"That's the man," he said.

"You two aren't much alike," she said. "I want to make a deal with you."

"What kind of deal?" said Framar.

She said, "You must carry me to the island here, nearest to the land. There my father has died and left much wealth, and we three sisters are claiming our inheritance, and I will be cut off if I come too late."

Framar said, "Will you give me a day and a night of favorable winds, then?"

"I will," she said.

Now she got in the boat, and the boat seemed to sink down quite a lot when she came aboard. She said, "Do you want me to row with you?"

"There's no need," said Framar.

But when they'd gone a third of the way, she spoke up: "You don't need to carry me out any longer. Now there are just channels all the way to the shore. I can manage to wade them just fine."

She stepped overboard, and so she waded to the island. Framar went back to the ship and woke up Sturlaug. He quickly jumped to his feet, and Framar lay down to sleep.

Sturlaug stepped into the boat and rowed out along the cape. And when he came north around the cape, he heard something walking along the beach, and he saw that fire flew out from the gravel underneath this being. It had a thrusting-spear in hand. It seemed to him that it was no common weapon that the monstrosity carried.

Sturlaug asked, "What am I hailing here, a woman or a man?"

She said, "Can't you tell what you're looking at? It's a woman. What's your name?"

"I am called Sturlaug," he said.

"Where have you come from and what do you want, Sturlaug the Hard-Working?" she said. "I'm called Hornnefja.[33] What about the men with you? Is a certain Hrolf Nose with you? I've been told that he is a fine man, and swifter than any animal."

"You've hit it on the head," he said.

"Something's amiss," she said. "Will you make a deal with me?"

"What kind of deal do you want?" he said.

"I want for you to bring Hrolf Nose to me, so that I may see the shape of his body and his face, because much has been said to me about his fair appearance. I will give you this treasure that I have in my hand. It's a thrusting-spear."

Sturlaug said, "What's so fine about this treasure that you're offering me?"

She said, "It cuts everything that it hits. It can become so little that you can pin it in your clothes, like a needle. You will never find a place where it won't be easy for you to succeed with it, whatever you may want or need."

Sturlaug said, "Then we'll make a deal."

Sturlaug now went to his sworn brothers and woke up Hrolf Nose and asked him to go with him. They went off to a cliff, where the woman was down below. Hrolf sat on the edge of the cliff and let his legs dangle over. He was outfitted in a hairy goatskin coat, with a thick calfskin on his head, and the tail stuck up out of the middle of his head. Soot from a kettle was smeared all over his face, and he had a stick shoved into his mouth so that his cheeks were puffed out like huge balls. He had an ox-horn in his hand and pigskins on each foot. He was decked out so that he didn't look handsome at all, where he sat on the cliff and gawked at the moon because it was shining brightly.[34]

After that, Sturlaug went to meet Hornnefja. She greeted him and asked, "Where is Hrolf Nose?"

Sturlaug said, "Look up on the cliff and see where he's sitting."

She turned around fast and saw where he was. Then she held her hand above her eye and examined him carefully, and said, "It's true to say that the man is most handsome. It's no exaggeration what has been said about him, that he's so noble."

Now the crone swelled up enormously and stretched herself right up the cliff. She thought that she could never manage to see him clearly where he was. "All I can say is that the woman who had this man would seem lucky to me."[35]

Then Sturlaug saw that she would get a grip on Hrolf's feet, and he didn't want to wait for that. He leaped out of the boat onto a rock and stabbed her with the thrusting-spear, so that it ran her through. She fell on him. He jumped into the water and swam out from under her, but the boat capsized. She lost her life there, and he righted the boat. With matters as they stood, they went back to their fellows and told them how things had gone. They approved.[36]

CHAPTER XVII

After that, a favorable wind always blew for them, and they sailed until they saw land. It was heavily overgrown with forest. There was one hidden fjord that they came to, and they sailed into this fjord and laid up in a hidden bay and dropped the anchors. The sun was in the south, and they went onto land. Sturlaug asked, "What land do you suppose this is, that we've come to?"

Framar said, "The land of the Hundings, according to my brother Kol's account. Three of us will go onto land: Sturlaug, Aki and myself. You all must wait for us here until the third sun has set. If we don't come back, you'll have to decide for yourselves what to do."

Now they went ashore and entered a thick forest, and they carved on the oak trees to show where they had been. After a while, they came out of the forest and saw many large estates, forts, and castles. They saw one fortress and hall much larger than the others. That's where they went. Men were standing in the doorways, and their chins were grown down to their chests, and they barked like dogs.[37] Now they realized where they were. The guards barred their entry. Sturlaug drew the spear Hornnefja's Gift and chopped the door guardian in two, and his sworn brothers killed the other.

After that, they went into the hall and stood on the outer edge of the hall floor. Aki saw women sitting on a dais. One of them was noteworthy because she was much more beautiful than the others. Aki recognized this woman from his mother's stories. He went to the dais and laid both arms on her neck and said, "Greetings, kinswoman." She accepted his greeting and turned to him. King Hundolf saw this and didn't take it well, because he could not bear to see that men were looking at his queen. Now you may imagine how angry he felt, that an outlander should fling himself onto her neck and kiss her before his eyes and do such a monstrous thing. He pushed the tables away and called for his guards, and trumpets sounded through all the streets.

Aki said, "I have come here to find you, kinswoman. I want you to tell me about the aurochs horn, and where to look for it."

She said, "Who are these men?"

They said their names.

She said, "It's too bad that you've come here, because death awaits you all, so there's no need to tell you about the aurochs horn."

Aki said, "Even if we're to be killed on the spot, it's better that we know the truth of what you can tell us about the horn."

She said, "First of all, it is said that a temple stands in Bjarmaland.[38] It is hallowed to Thor and Odin, Frigg and Freyja, and skillfully made from the costliest wood.[39] One set of doors faces to the northwest, and the other faces southwest. Inside, there is only a statue of Thor. The aurochs horn is there on a table before him, as fair to see as gold. But only Sturlaug must enter the temple, because luck will hold out for him alone. Yet he must not pick up the horn with bare hands, for it is full of venom and sorcery. But it will come to nothing for you, because you are all certain to die, and it's a great shame to lose men as brave as you sworn brothers."

Sturlaug said, "When we are all fallen, these Hundings will find that they'll have bloody noses, even though we're few."

And at that, the Hundings charged into the hall, fully armed, and attacked them fiercely. They defended themselves well and bravely and killed thirty men before they were captured. They were stripped of all their clothes except for their linen underpants, and herded out of the hall with whips and prodded with spear-points and driven out to the forest. They came into a clearing where there were two stones, hollow inside. They were put inside the smaller stone, and covered over with the larger stone. The intention was that they should starve to death there. These stones stood on a certain hill.[40] Now the Hundings went away, and thought that they had well avenged their disgrace.

Now it's time to tell of Sturlaug and his men inside the stones. Sturlaug said, "How do you like this?"

They said they were fine, as long as they were all quite healthy.

Sturlaug said, "What did I stick myself with in the back of my calf, a moment ago, when we were stripped of our clothes?"

He reached out with his hand and found a piece of iron as small as a needle. It was his thrusting-spear. He said that it had to become so large that it would be easy for him to succeed in what he needed to do. It quickly became so large that he chopped at the stone until he and all his men got out. Now they hurried to their companions, and there was a joyous reunion.

CHAPTER XVIII

Now they prepared to depart, and they sailed out of the fjord. Aki said, "I suppose that I'll never be in greater need of favorable winds than now."[41] At once a wind sprang up, and they sailed until they came to Bjarmaland, to the mouth of the Dvina River. They saw that the land west of the river was a level field, and there was a temple, shining so brightly that it seemed to light up all the field, because it was built with gold and precious stones.

Sturlaug said, "Now we must turn the ship about, and the stern must face the land. We'll tie up with only one rope, in case we need to make a fast start. Have poles ready for pushing off, and let's be prepared for anything. Framar and I will go onto land."

Now they went onto land, along with Hrolf Nose, and they went to the temple. And when they came to the temple, the doors were arranged as they had been told. They went to the doors on the northwest side of the temple, because they alone were open. They saw that inside the threshold there was a pit full of venom, and next to it a large crossbeam fitted over the entrance, and inside the doors the pit was walled all around, so that the furniture wouldn't be damaged by the venom spilling out. As soon as they reached the temple doors, Hrolf Nose came up. Sturlaug asked why he had come. He said, "I don't want to begrudge myself the honor of going into the temple with you."

"There's no chance of that," said Sturlaug. "I alone must enter the temple."

"You want to deprive me of the honor," said Hrolf.

"That's not my intent," said Sturlaug.

He looked inside the temple and saw an enormous idol of Thor sitting on the high seat. In front of him was a splendid table, covered with silver. There he saw the aurochs horn, standing right before Thor on the table. It was as lovely as if it were made of gold, and filled with venom. He saw a game board and pieces standing there, both of them made of brilliant gold. Shining hangings and gold rings were fastened up on poles. Sixty women were in the temple, and there was one who stood out from all the rest. She was as huge as a giant and as black as Hel, but as fat as a mare, with dark eyes and an evil expression. All the same, this woman was well dressed. She served at the table. The women recited this little ditty when they saw Sturlaug:

> Here comes Sturlaug
> the Hard-Working
> to seek the horn
> and stores of rings;
> here is the horn
> and holy offerings
> of gold and treasures.
> Grim are our hearts.

Then the temple's high priestess responded and said, "He shall never escape with his life if I may prevail, either by my faith or my curses." She said:

> He shall relish
> his rest in Hel,
> once he's suffered
> all sorts of torture.
> Then hero Sturlaug,
> the Hard-Working man,
> will be butchered to bits
> by blades of the gums.°   *blades of the gums:* teeth

After that, Sturlaug prepared himself to go in, forbidding his sworn brothers to follow him. In the temple there stood three slabs of stone, so high that they reached to his breastbone, and there were deep pits full of venom in between them. He had to leap over them before he could get to where the aurochs horn stood. Sturlaug pulled himself up and leaped over all the slabs, skillfully and boldly, hastily grabbing the horn from the table without any hindrance. He turned and headed back the way that he'd come. The temple-priestess stood nearby, swollen with rage and holding a double-edged knife. It seemed as if flames were blazing from the edges. She howled at him horribly and gnashed her teeth at him most ferociously, yet she lacked the courage to to attack him.

When Sturlaug came to the slabs, he saw that Hrolf Nose was leaping in over the slabs. Hrolf turned to the space in front of Thor and Odin, grabbed the game-board and threw it into the front of his tunic, and dashed back through the temple. But he saw the temple-priestess leaping after him, gnashing her teeth. He leaped onto the slabs and tried to get out over them, but the temple-priestess seized him by the tunic and swung him aloft and threw him down on the slabs, so that his back was broken at once. Hrolf Nose laid down his life there, with great valor.

After that, the temple-priestess rushed outside and screamed with such dreadful madness and frenzy and menace that it echoed from every crag and mound in the area. She saw now where Sturlaug had gone, and she rushed at him and stabbed at him. He defended himself well, with great valor and skill. Just then Sturlaug saw a man coming out of the woods, and then another and a third, and then men were coming from all directions. Sturlaug turned and fled, but the more men she saw crowding in, the more viciously she attacked. He charged at her with Hornnefja's Gift and drove it into her midriff, so that the point stuck out between her shoulders. She spun away so fast that he let go of the spear, and that delayed him, but she was killed at once.

Sturlaug now leaped onto the ship and immediately cut the rope, but the Bjarmians attacked Sturlaug's ship in force with their own ships. Then Framar said, "I now pronounce that the favorable wind should come, which fierce Hild promised me." And at once, such a wind sprang up that it strained every rope, and they sailed away. The Bjarmians pursued them as long as they could; some were driven off by the gale, but some perished by weapons. Those who managed to come back thought themselves fortunate.

CHAPTER XIX

Sturlaug and his men sailed out into the ocean. Nothing is said about their journey until they came to Värmland. They landed and asked for news. They were told that Jarl Hring had left his country for Sweden. Right away, they went to meet King Harald. They entered the hall and went before the king and greeted him. Sturlaug stood before the king and held the aurochs horn. The king sat in his high seat, so swollen with rage that he could not speak a word.

Sturlaug said, "Now I have returned from this quest, king, though you didn't mean for that to happen. You must admit this. Accept this horn which I have brought."

The king didn't answer and kept his hands close to his sides. Then Sturlaug threw the horn at the king's nose, so that blood gushed from his nose and four teeth were knocked out of his head.

After that, Sturlaug went east to Sweden and found Hring his father-in-law, and Asa his wife, and his own father. At that time, the king in Sweden was named Ingvi-Frey.[42] Sturlaug took charge of the defenses of his land, as did all his sworn brothers, and they raided lands far and wide and always had victory, wherever they went. That went on for twelve years. Then King Ingvi-Frey gave the title of king to Sturlaug, and a large kingdom along with it, and the sworn brothers took charge of its defenses.

CHAPTER XX

On one occasion, Sturlaug let it be known that he wanted to go to Bjarmaland. He summoned a great host, and his sworn brothers came to him. Nothing is said about that journey until they came to Bjarmaland and set fire to everything there and burned as much as they could. They did one wicked deed after another. Rondolf, King of Bjarmaland, found out about this and summoned his forces right away, but he was very short of men. And as soon as they met, the fiercest battle broke out. There one might see many stout shields cloven, mailcoats sliced through, hewing-spears broken from their shafts, swords shattered asunder, and many headless men collapsing to the ground. And the battle ended this way: King Rondolf fell there, and many of his men with him.[43] After that great deed, Sturlaug subjected all Bjarmaland to his own rule. He recovered and brought back the spear Hornnefja's Gift, and many more fine treasures.

When this great and mighty deed was done, he intended to invade the Hundings' country, against the king of the Hundings. Sturlaug made fresh preparations for an expedition with his forces, and nothing is told of it until they came to the Hundings' country. They killed men and seized riches, burning farms and all dwellings wherever they went. King Hundolf heard of this and summoned his forces and moved out against Sturlaug at once. As soon as they met, battle broke out, with fierce attacks and mighty blows. Sturlaug often broke through their ranks. He had both arms bloody to the shoulders, dealing them mighty blows, sweeping many of them to the ground headless, and the devil took them.

It is said that King Hundolf made an advance in force. Sturlaug saw the king cut his banner down. This displeased him, and he pressed forward at King Hundolf with the short sword Vefreyja's Gift drawn. He struck him on the helmet with the sword and cleaved him completely, splitting his skull and body and mailcoat and horse down the middle. The sword plunged down into the ground. Sturlaug and his sworn brothers killed countless Hundings, and King Sturlaug won a fine victory. Then they turned back, and Snaelaug went with them. Nothing is said of their journey until they came home to Sweden.[44]

CHAPTER XXI

The next winter, Sturlaug held a Yule feast and invited many prominent men. And when men had taken their seats on the first evening of Yule, Sturlaug stood up and said, "It is the custom of all men to try their hand at new entertainments for the amusement of some of the guests. Now I'll begin the oath-swearing, and my oath is this: I shall discover the origin of the aurochs horn before the third Yule has passed, or else die."[45]

Then Framar stood up and spoke this oath: he would get into bed with Ingibjorg, the daughter of Ingvar the king of Russia in the east, and have kissed her before the third Yule, or else die. Sighvat the Tall swore an oath to go with the sworn brothers wherever they wanted to go, or set off to. Whatever oaths the other men swore aren't recorded. Yule passed, and nothing noteworthy happened, but after the feast each man went home with fine gifts.[46]

It is said that Sturlaug went to Vefreyja, and she gave him a warm welcome. He told her of the oath he had sworn. She gave him good advice, as will later be revealed. Sturlaug went home from there and was satisfied with his journey. Time passed, and all was quiet.

CHAPTER XXII

It is said that one day, Sturlaug called Frosti to him and told him, "I have devised a quest for you." He asked what it might be. "You shall go north to Finnmark and lay this rune-carved stick[47] in the lap of the daughter of King Snaer.[48]" Frosti agreed to make the journey.

After that, Frosti prepared to leave. He traveled by sea. He came to Finnmark, and came before King Snaer and greeted him. The king accepted his greeting and asked his name. He said that he was called Gest,[49] "and I ask that you take me into your household." The king said that it would be done.

Gest kept to himself and didn't meddle in anything that happened. He was there through the winter, and the king thought well of him.

A short distance from the hall was a bower, with two plank fences so high that nothing could get over them except a flying bird. Frosti always sat by the fence and wanted to see the king's daughter Mjoll, but he never could manage it. The winter passed, and nothing of note happened.

One day, when the king and his men were playing sports, Frosti went to the fence and saw that it was open, and so was the bower. He went inside and saw that there sat a woman on a chair, combing her hair with a golden comb. Her hair lay all around her on a feather pillow, as beautiful as silk. He saw her face, and he thought that he had never seen a more lovely woman than this one. He could not keep still, and he could not accomplish what he wanted to, but he took the stick and cast it into her lap. She swept her hair back and took the stick and looked at it. And when she had looked at it and read it, she looked out at the fence and smiled and seemed very pleased about what was carved on the stick. Her serving-maids came into the bower, but Gest left and went back to the hall. He could enjoy neither sleep nor food because of the concern which he felt for his mission.

When all the men were asleep, there was a touch on Frosti's chest. He followed the hand upwards. A golden ring fell forward from the arm. He stood up and went out. There was Mjoll the king's daughter, and she said, "Is that true, what is carved on the stick?"

"It's true," he said.

She said "Sturlaug and I agree on this, because there is no man under the sun's home whom I am more pleased with. I would gladly be his concubine if he wished. I will not refrain from offering him all my charms, with embraces and seemly caresses, kisses and endearments."

"He will graciously accept all of them," he said, "if you come to him."

"Then are you ready, Frosti?" she said.

"I've been ready for a long time," he said.

She went to the hall doors and spoke a certain spell before she went out. After that, they set out, and Frosti could hardly manage to follow her. She said, "You're a very slow traveler, my dear Frosti. Put your hands under my belt." She went so fast that he felt as if the wind were filling him up. There is nothing more said of their journey until they came to Sweden. The women took Mjoll the king's daughter into their bower. Frosti found Sturlaug and told him about their journey and how it had turned out.

Sturlaug said, "Now the fox has gotten out of a tight squeeze. You must now celebrate your wedding to her, and go wearing my best finery. She will think that it is I, because the two of us look much alike in every way."

Frosti said, "I will go along with all your plans."

Sturlaug said, "When you get into bed with the king's daughter Mjoll, Frosti, I want you to ask her what the origin of the aurochs horn is, because she alone knows that. I will stand behind the tapestries while you two talk about it."

He said that he would do so. Now he went into the hall with a multitude of men in fine clothing, and sat in the high seat, and everyone thought he was Sturlaug.[50] Mjoll looked at the bridegroom with smiling eyes and felt very good about the marriage.

The evening had passed when they got into bed together. Then the bride turned to her husband[51] and spoke most cheerfully with him.

Frosti said to her, "How do you think your marriage has turned out?"

"I think it's going just as I wished, my dear Sturlaug," she said. "Don't you think so?"

"I feel the same way," he said, "but there is one thing that I want you to tell me."

"What is it?" she said.

"It's like this," he said. "I swore an oath that I must find out the origin of the aurochs horn."

"I can tell you that," she said. "The first thing to tell is that King Harald raided far and wide through the lands, and always won victories wherever he went. But terrible famines always struck throughout the lands and Bjarmaland most of all, so that both livestock and men perished. Then the Bjarmians took an animal and sacrificed to it, and called it an aurochs. It gaped its maw at them, and they threw gold and silver into it. They made it so powerful with magic that it became the most harmful and dangerous of all beasts.[52] It began to eat men and cattle, and it trampled everything underfoot and laid waste all the land west of the Dvina River, so that no living thing got away. There was no champion who dared to go against this beast, until King Harald heard the news and found that he might expect to gain a lot of money, and he sailed there with three hundred ships and came to Bjarmaland. There it so happened that King Harald was asleep. A woman came to him, bearing herself most splendidly. She said to the king, 'Here you lie, and you think that you'll conquer our beast, which is called an aurochs.'

"The king said, 'What is your name?'

"'Godrid,' she said, 'and I'm on land, not far away. If you'll take my advice, you should go on land in the morning with half of your forces. Then you will see the beast. It will be afraid of a multitude of men and will run away to the sea. You must rush at it there, with all your men, and bring a big log and beat it with that. The animal will run away, out to sea. Then Godrid will slip in front of it, and I will force it down into the sea and hold it down.[53] Later it will come up, dead. You shall take it, but I am to have the most precious thing from the beast, and that is the horn that extends from its head.'[54]

"'So be it,' said the king.

"The night passed, and everything happened as she had said, and thus they managed to defeat the beast. Then this woman came and took that horn. That is the same horn that you sought in the temple in Bjarmaland, my dear Sturlaug. Now I have told you the origins of the aurochs horn."

"You've done well," he said.

After that, Sturlaug left, and a fire broke out in the bower and burned Frosti and Mjoll to ashes, and so they lost their lives there. This was all Vefreyja's plan, because Mjoll was such a sorceress that she would have immediately cast a spell on Sturlaug and Vefreyja, if she had found out.[55]

CHAPTER XXIII

The next thing to tell is how King Sturlaug and Aki sent Sighvat the Tall east to Russia to ask for the king's daughter Ingibjorg. He had ten ships, and after that he sailed to Gotland. His journey went well and bravely, until he came to Russia and went to meet the king, greeting him well and worthily. The king accepted his greeting warmly and asked who he was. He answered, "My name is Sighvat, and I've come here to ask for Ingibjorg, your daughter, to marry Aki, my sworn brother."

"Not only do you sworn brothers think you're mighty," said the king, "but you think that you're better than kings. You think that I would throw away my wealth and women, lands and servants, to give my daughter to the thralls of King Sturlaug. Capture them, and they shall hang from the highest gallows."

Sighvat quickly turned and left the hall and got away to his ships. He ordered his men to travel quickly, until they came home and told Sturlaug what had happened on the journey. Sturlaug quickly made ready, and the sworn brothers went with him eastward to Russia.[56] King Sturlaug captured King Dag, because he had no strength to resist them, and gave him two options: he could betroth his daughter to Aki, or die. Since the king realized that he was overpowered, he chose to betroth his daughter to Aki. Aki was engaged to Ingibjorg, and then the feast was prepared. Aki went to marry the king's daughter Ingibjorg, and he lived there afterwards, and he is out of this saga. Then Sturlaug went home to his own kingdom and stayed there quietly.

CHAPTER XXIV

Now it is time to relate how Framar wanted to fulfill his oath. He prepared to sail away from the land, and he had sixty ships. He set sail for the eastern realms and raided through the summer and brought his forces to Ladoga.[57] King Ingvar ruled there, a wise man and a great chieftain. His daughter was named Ingigerd. She was more lovely to look upon than any woman, and wise in her mind. She was a good healer, and many men sought her out when they needed healing.[58] It was said of her that she herself would choose the man she would marry. Many chieftains had asked for her hand, and she had sent all of them away with courteous answers.[59] Framar sent his men to Ladoga to meet King Ingvar and ask for his daughter's hand. The king replied to them that he would summon an assembly, and he invited Framar to come—"and she herself shall choose her husband."

Framar waited there until the day came for the assembly. Framar dressed in all his royal finery, and went to the assembly with many men. He had a chair placed under him. King Ingvar came there with many mighty men. The king asked, "Who is that man who comports himself so splendidly?"

"I am called Snaekoll[60]," he said, "come on this errand here to you to ask for your daughter's hand."

The king said, "Where are your lands and retainers, great stores of wealth and honors?"

"I mean to seek both honor and wealth from you, if I marry into your family," said Framar.

The king said, "Have you not heard that she herself must choose her husband?"

"I have heard that," he said.

Then Ingigerd was sent for, and when she came to the assembly, she greeted her father. He welcomed her well and fittingly. "You have a suitor here to greet, my daughter," he said.

"Who is he?" she said.

"His name is Snaekoll," said the king.

"Maybe," she said, and she went before this tall man and turned to face him for a moment, and then said, smiling, "You're quite a bold man, but you and your sworn brothers think that you outrank kings. I recognize you clearly, Framar, and you don't need to conceal your identity from me."

After that, the assembly broke up.

CHAPTER XXV

Framar went to the ships, and he sailed out to the islands that lay closest to land. Framar had tents spread over his ships there. Then Framar put on merchant's clothes, and went to the hall and asked for winter lodgings for himself. The king granted him that, and he took the name Gest. Often he watched for an opportunity to get into the king's daughter's bower, but he never managed to do it.

So it went on, until one day when he was walking away from the hall down a certain road. He heard human voices coming from down in the earth next to him. He saw the opening of an underground house, and went down and saw that there were three sorcerers.[61] He said, "It's a good thing that we have found each other. I shall inform on you."

They said, "Don't do that, Framar. We will do what you want, in whatever way you want."

Framar answered, "You must cast leprosy on me, but I must become healthy as soon as I want."

"So be it," they said. "It's not hard for us to do this." Then they altered all his flesh, so that he was nothing but scabs and sores from his feet to his neck. He turned away and went to the king's daughter's bower and sat down by the fence. The king's daughter Ingigerd sent one of her serving-maids to the hall, and when she saw this wretched man, she turned back, telling the king's daughter about this man, "and he must be in need of your mercies." They went to the fence and the king's daughter turned and looked at this pitiful man for a long time. They had not seen anyone with a sickness like his.

The king's daughter said, "This man is wretched and very ill. But you'll need to put on a better show before you can trick me—because I will recognize you, Framar, as long as both your eyes are whole in your head, whatever abomination you spread over yourself."[62]

She went back to her bower, but Framar went away to the sorcerers, and they took that loathsome illness from him. He went away and stayed quiet about what happened.

CHAPTER XXVI

Framar went to the woods and walked down a road. He saw a man coming towards him, very tall, and clutching both hands to his stomach.

165

He was wearing a mailcoat and had a helmet on his head, and his sword-strap hung against his chest. It was Guttorm, his sworn brother, who had come. There was a joyous meeting between them. Framar asked where he had come from. He said that he had fought with Snaekoll the Viking and had lost both men and wealth there, but that he himself had escaped by swimming. He asked whether it was a long way to the bower of the king's daughter.

Framar said, "It's now a day's journey there."

"That's a very long way," said Guttorm.

Framar said, "How long have you traveled like this?"

Guttorm said, "Two days, before we met."

Framar said, "There's quite a difference in valor between us. I was bemoaning a maiden and didn't get her, and I haven't gotten into any battles, but I can see that you're walking with your guts hanging out.[63] But I want you to get me into her bower, if she'll accept you."

"So be it—if I can," said Guttorm.

Now they traveled the same way that Framar had gone before, until they came to the fence. There was little hope for a man in Guttorm's condition. When they arrived, Framar went away. At that moment, one of the maidservants had gone out into the yard to pee. She saw this man whose intestines were hanging out, and she went back into the bower and told the king's daughter what a state the man was in. The king's daughter wasted no time. She and her other maidens, twelve all together, came to the gate. The king's daughter saw this wretched man and how terribly far gone he was, with his intestines falling out. She asked him his name. He said that he was named Guttorm.

"Are you a sworn brother of King Sturlaug?" she said.

"The very same," he said, "and I would like to ask you to grant me some help."

She said, "How could I get closer to Sturlaug than to heal his sworn brother? But don't trick me."

After that, they carried him into the bower. The king's daughter had a small house of healing, and it was very delightful inside for poor sick creatures to be next to such compassionate ladies with soft hands. Guttorm was in the king's daughter's house of healing for some time, and he was treated very well. The king's daughter herself and her maidservants were there for a long time, and they healed Guttorm with their skill and care, as she had done so often, curing and making whole many wealthy and poor people, women as well as men.

One day, the king summoned his daughter. She went straight to the hall with her maidservants. The bower was left open, and the fence was shut, but the gate wasn't locked. Framar was waiting for this, and Guttorm came there and led him into the bower and into the house of healing, and he stood there behind the tapestries. The day passed until the king's daughter came into the bower, and at once she went to Guttorm and loosened the bandages from the wound, and it was much better. "You've been outside today," said the king's daughter, "and you must have deceived me."

And as they were talking, Framar leaped out from behind the tapestries and put one hand under her chin and the other under her neck and gave her a kiss. She took this badly and ordered them to go away at once. "I don't want you two to be killed here before my eyes, as you deserve. Guttorm has been here for a while, and he's lucky to have Sturlaug, because you would have earned the loss of your lives for this scheme of yours—except that I think well of Sturlaug, because of his accomplishments."

They left, as she had ordered them. Framar went away immediately to his ships and set his course for Sweden. He told King Sturlaug how his dealings had gone, and he asked him now for help.

CHAPTER XXVII

Sturlaug was pleased, and had forces mustered throughout his kingdom. He readied a great fleet: three hundred ships, well prepared for anything. They sailed directly to Russia with great good cheer and splendor. And when they landed, their forces rushed onto the land. They slaughtered and killed, fire-raising and burning men and cattle. When this had gone on for a while, they became aware that their opponents had summoned their forces, and that Snaekoll and King Ingvar were aware of them. Each side prepared to meet the other.

When they met, there was the fiercest battle, and each side launched harsh attacks against the other. Sturlaug advanced without armor, as was his custom. The sworn brothers did many brave and warlike deeds. The battle lasted for three days, with a terrible slaughter of men. King Ingvar and Snaekoll fell together before Sturlaug in this battle. Hvitserk[64] managed to flee, and many men with him. Sturlaug then had the peace-shields lifted up and went to Ladoga with all his forces. There was much merriment and cheering and clamor of victory shouts in Sturlaug's ranks, and all the town was in their power. All the townspeople sued for peace and put themselves into Sturlaug's hands.

CHAPTER XXVIII

Sturlaug gave the king's daughter Ingigerd to Framar. The feast was splendid in every way that was needful, and after the feast the foremost men were sent away with fine gifts. Thus they parted, and each one returned to his own home. Then Sturlaug gave the town of Ladoga to Framar, with all the wealth that King Ingvar had owned, and along with that the title of king. Framar settled down with his lands and riches, and ruled his kingdom with the best counsel in the land. From Framar and Ingigerd are descended a large family and many great men, although they are not told of in this saga.

After that, Sturlaug went back to Sweden and stayed in his own kingdom, wise and wealthy. Sturlaug was always at peace with the High King of Sweden, and the king found him to be a staunch man in all trials, because his sworn brothers kept their friendship and loyalty to him as long as they all lived.

Sturlaug and Asa had two sons. One was named Heinrek, and the other was Ingolf. They were both great and promising men and enter into many sagas.[65] They took up all sorts of skills and sports at a young age. They were both kings after their father Sturlaug, and many great families are descended from them. Sturlaug died of old age, after the death of Peace-Frodi.[66]

Here ends this saga.

THE SAGA OF HROLF THE WALKER

Göngu-Hrólfs saga

FOREWORD

Men have composed many tales for entertainment, some according to ancient lays[1] or the knowledge of learned men, and sometimes according to old books, which originally were set down briefly, but were later filled out with words, because most events are quicker in the telling. Men are never equally well informed, because it often happens that what's seen and heard by one isn't seen and heard by another, even though they're present at the same event. And it's also in the nature of many foolish men to believe only what they see with their own eyes or hear with their own ears. They find that what came of the schemes of wise men, or the mighty strength or surpassing skill of great men, is far beyond their own natures—and this is no less the case concerning trickery, or wizardry and mighty magic, when they conjured up eternal misfortune or loss of life for some, and for others, worldly reputation, riches, and honors. Sometimes they stirred up the elements and sometimes calmed them down—men such as Odin was, and the others who learned spellcraft or healing from him. There are even cases where certain bodies have been able to move through the inspiration of an unclean spirit, such as Eyvind Split-Cheek in the saga of Olaf Tryggvason, or Einar Cormorant, or Frey whom Gunnar Half-and Half killed in Sweden.[2]

Now neither this, nor anything else, can be made to suit everyone's tastes, since there's no need to place more trust in such things than seems fitting. The best and wisest thing is to listen while it's being told, and be cheerful rather than grieved, because it's always the case that men don't think of other, sinful things while they are enjoying the entertainment. And it doesn't sit well for bystanders to criticize, even if the words go unwisely or clumsily, since few things which are as trivial as this are done perfectly.[3]

CHAPTER I

This story begins with a king named Hreggvid who ruled over the realm of Novgorod, which some men call Russia. He was tall and strong, the handsomest man and the boldest fighter, courageous and a great warrior, wise and shrewd, most generous to his friends, but severe and stern to his enemies. In most respects he was well gifted. He had been married to a queen of noble descent, but she isn't named and doesn't come into this saga. He had one child with his queen, a daughter by the name of Ingigerd. She was the loveliest and most refined of all the women there were in all Russia, and even beyond. She excelled everyone in wisdom and eloquence. She knew all the skills that suited a woman and which ladies of quality plied near and far. She had hair so long that it might well conceal all her body, and it was as fair as gold or straw.[4] The king loved his daughter very much. She had a home all her own, inside the town. It was a splendid dwelling, built strongly and soundly, and beautifully wrought with gold and gemstones. She stayed in this house every day, along with the other maidens who served her.

King Hreggvid was quite elderly at that time. It is said that when the king was young, he had frequently set out raiding, and he had conquered the region around the Don River, which flows through Russia.[5] From there, he had raided various realms in the East, and so acquired rare treasures. (This river is the third or the fourth largest in the world. Yngvar the Far-Traveler searched for the source of this river, as is told in his saga.[6]) King Hreggvid was on that journey for seven years all told, and men thought he was dead—but then he returned to Russia and settled down quietly. He had acquired a horse who could understand human speech. His name was Dulcifal. He was as swift as a bird, as agile as a lion, and as huge as a wolf. There was no horse like him in size and strength. If his rider was destined for defeat, he wouldn't let himself be caught—but if he was fated to win victory, then he carried him as his own master.[7]

He had a suit of armor, and there was none other like it, for the helmet was all set with gemstones and was so hard that it was invincible. His entire mailcoat was forged from three layers of the hardest steel, as bright as silver. The shield was so broad and thick that iron couldn't bite into it. The lance that went with it was stiff and tough, and rang like a bell if it were knocked against the shield—but if defeat were certain, it gave no sound.[8] The sword was never checked in its stroke, and was enchanted to bite steel and stone as easily as soft flesh. It was made of iron from the fjord called Ger, which can neither rust nor break. Dulcifal was related to the dromedaries, a type of horse.[9] King Hreggvid had never suffered defeat since he got the horse and these weapons. His kingdom was constantly being invaded, and he and his men were always fighting huge battles.

The king had many counsellors and picked men with him. One of them was named Sigurd, called Wool-Yarn.[10] He was the grandson of Halfdan

Red-Cloak who was the son of Burned-Kari. He was quite fearless, well-liked by all the people, and elderly. He had stayed with the king for a long time and served him well in many dangers.

CHAPTER II

There was a king named Eirek, a sea-king and a Gastriklander by birth. Gastrikland is ruled by the King of Sweden. Its inhabitants are strong and resemble giants; they are fierce and unruly, and gifted in sorcery. King Eirek was a tall and powerful man, with a dark complexion and a very gaunt appearance. He sailed out in winter and summer with a fleet of ships, raiding in various lands. He was the greatest fighter and very warlike. He had a beautiful sister named Gyda, and she was always with him.

Eirek had many berserks and champions in his forces, and four of them are named. There were two brothers; one was named Sorkvir and the other was Brynjolf. Big and strong they were, unruly and skilled in sorcery, and so full of spells that they could blunt blades in battle.[11] Sorkvir was the stronger of the two, and an excellent jouster. The third man was a kinsman of the king named Thord and called the Bald Man of Hlesey, a big strong man. His family came from Hlesey[12] in Denmark, and he had grown up there. His foster-brother was named Grim, called Aegir. This man was strong and wicked in every way. No one knew his origins or his family, because Groa the seeress had found him washed up in the beachwrack on Hlesey. She was Thord's mother, and she had fostered Grim and raised him and taught him all sorcery, so that no one in the Northlands was his equal, because he was unlike all other men by nature. Some men believe that Grim's mother must have been some sea-hag, because he could travel through both the sea and lakes if he wanted, and for that reason he was called Aegir.[13] He ate raw meat and drank blood from men and livestock alike. And he often turned into the likeness of various animals, shapeshifting so quickly that the eye could hardly follow it. His breath was so hot that men found that it burned even if they were wearing armor. He could also spew either venom or flames at men, and in this way he killed both men and horses, and thus no one could withstand him. King Eirek had great confidence in him, and in all of these men. They never held back from doing wicked deeds.

CHAPTER III

At that time, King Eirek invaded King Hreggvid's kingdom with his host. They killed men, burned buildings, and stole livestock. When the people of the kingdom found out about the invasion, they went to find King Hreggvid and told him what had happened. When he heard the news, he had the war-arrow[14] carved, and summoned all fighting men to join him. But he only raised a small force, because the invaders were coming on swiftly, and most people had dark forebodings about what was to come.

On the morning of the battle, King Hreggvid clad himself in his full armor. He clasped a gold necklace around his neck; it was a splendid treasure. Then he girded himself with his good sword. He took the lance and struck the shield, and it made no sound. The stallion Dulcifal also wouldn't let himself be caught. Many men chased him, and in the end he was brought into a high-walled pen. The king came to him and wanted to take him, but as soon as the stallion saw the king, he leaped out over the gates and ran off into the forest. Everyone felt this was a dreadful portent and thought that defeat was certain, and they made no effort to search for him. King Hreggvid took a different horse, shield and lance for himself, but he gave his daughter his own shield and lance for safekeeping. Then he and all his host prepared for battle.

King Eirek drew up all his host and ordered every man to work as a warrior should, and not to hold back any sort of strength which he might bring to bear. Grim Aegir said, "My lord, each of us is obliged to do the best he can. But if we beat King Hreggvid, we want to settle here, and I want to have a land to rule and the title of jarl. Your kinsman Thord shall come with me and shall take precedence over me, but Sorkvir and Brynjolf shall go with you and defend the land for you." The king agreed to Grim's proposal and said that it would be done.

Now both sides formed their ranks and advanced towards each other. King Eirek led one wing of his battle lines, and Grim led the other. The odds were much in their favor, as they had four warriors for each one of the local men. King Hreggvid arrayed his forces against King Eirek, and Sigurd Wool-Yarn faced Grim Aegir. Then the fiercest fighting broke out, with strikes and blows, arrows fired and stones flung. Every man on either side advanced with shouts and cheers. King Eirek's berserks advanced ahead of the ranks and mowed down King Hreggvid's men like brushwood, and they fell one across another. Sigurd Wool-Yarn saw that, and he struck left and right until he encountered Thord the Bald Man of Hlesey. He struck at him, but Thord blocked the blow with his bald head and the sword didn't cut.[15] After that, Thord struck Sigurd his death-blow, and he fell, winning great glory.

King Hreggvid saw that, and he was grieved at Sigurd's fall. He spurred his horse and fiercely rode forward, slashing and stabbing men and horses right and left, so that everyone shrank back before him. The sword cut as if it were slicing water. The scabbard was all wrought with gold wherever that seemed to improve it, and on the pommel of the sword's hilt there were loose life-stones, which drew poison and burning out of wounds if they were shaved into them.[16] He charged towards King Eirek's banner, so furiously that he had both arms bloody to the shoulders. At times he killed two or three men at one blow, until Grim Aegir and Thord came against him. They both struck at him at the same time, but the king defended himself so well that he wasn't wounded. At that moment, Grim blew with such powerful sorcery that the king's horse stumbled. The king jumped off the horse's back, still striking to left and right. He piled up a ring of bodies around himself so high that it came up to his belt. He struck with both hands at Grim Aegir, but Grim blew at him so that his sword flew out of his hands. Then the king seized an axe and struck Thord on his bald head with the blunt end of the axehead, so that he lay unconscious for a long time. At once the king lifted himself up and leaped over the heap of slain. King Eirek came up against him and struck at Hreggvid with his sword, so that the blade broke in two but didn't cut the armor. At that instant, Grim Aegir stabbed him with a sword from beneath, under the mailcoat, piercing him through. The king fell there, with great courage and great glory, and it seems that there has hardly been a more famed man in Russia than King Hreggvid. All his surviving men fled, though most of his men had fallen. Many in King Eirek's forces had also fallen. The peace-shield was held up, and those who wanted to save their lives were granted a truce, but the rest, who didn't want to serve King Eirek, were killed. And now the battle was over.

After that the dead were stripped of plunder, and the king went into the town with his retinue, and they had all manner of merriment, with drink and musical instruments. So passed the night. In the morning, the king called to Grim Aegir and his fellows that they should find the princess, and they did. When they entered her quarters, she greeted King Eirek, yet she was weeping and woeful. King Eirek cheered her up and said that they would compensate her for the loss of her men, and for the harm she had suffered—"and you shall receive any boon from me that you wish to request and that is seemly for us to offer, if then you will come to terms with us and do as we wish."

Princess Ingigerd said, "He may not rightly bear the title of king who does not keep his promise to a young maiden. I will come to terms with you and do your will, if you will keep your word and offer me the favor that I ask of you. But I would rather do away with myself quickly than marry some man unwillingly, and then no one would enjoy me."

The king's heart was filled with great love for her. He said, "May he who does not keep his word to you become a worthless wretch. Choose this very moment, and I shall grant it."

"My first request," said the princess, "is that a burial mound be raised for my father, large and well built inside, with a high plank fence around the mound. The mound shall stand a long way from here, in the wilderness. I shall bear gold and fine treasures into the mound next to him. He shall be dressed in his full armor and girded with his sword. He is to sit on a chair, with his fallen champions arranged on both sides of him. None of your men are to catch the horse Dulcifal; he must run as he wishes. For three years, I and those whom I shall appoint to stay with me will rule over a quarter of the kingdom. Those who belong to my household must all be left in peace and tranquility. Every year, I shall get a man to joust with you, or with Sorkvir your champion. Should I not find one of my men so excellent that he can knock Sorkvir from the back of his horse, you shall marry me and rule the entire kingdom. But if Sorkvir is beaten, you both shall go away with all your retinue and never enter Russia again, and I shall claim the realm and the rulership after my father, as is rightful."

Grim Aegir said, "This request can hardly be granted, because it comes from deep insight and long forethought. I don't think you'll stand for being kept waiting so long for an answer from any woman, my lord. But you may trust Sorkvir well that he will cause you no harm, along with my counsels and cleverness."

The king replied, "I didn't think that you would ask for this, princess. Yet I must keep my word to you, because I trust Sorkvir well. You will not find a more excellent man than him." They bound their agreement with oaths and ended their discussion.

Grim Aegir said, "A plan has come to mind that will help us. We must cast a spell and work sorcery[17] so that no one can beat Sorkvir, neither in jousting nor in single combat, unless that man has all of King Hreggvid's armor and weapons. But the mound must be built so strongly, with walls and bricks, that it can never be opened by any human being. You'll want to keep all your word to the princess. You should keep sending men after the armor, and promise your sister Gyda to the man who manages to get it. Then the armor and weapons will be in your grasp—or else the men won't come back alive."

The king and all his men felt that this was good advice. The mound was raised, and King Hreggvid was laid inside. Ingigerd was the last to leave of the mound. She secretly had a second set of armor brought there and laid it in her father's lap. The mound was closed and fenced off as Grim Aegir directed. Then the kingdom was divided according to their arrangements, and everything done that was said before. The princess couldn't find anyone who dared to challenge Sorkvir. The king sent many men to the mound, and not one came back.

Grim Aegir ruled Ermland.[18] That is a royal estate in Russia, and all those who served under him were unhappy with their lot. He and Thord the Bald Man of Hlesey always had great struggles with the men from the towns of Jotunheim, beyond Aluborg.[19] How they fought each other, with spells and magic and huge battles, would take many stories to tell. Both were the worse for it, and neither was the better. Sorkvir and Brynjolf set out raiding in the summers, and took charge of the defense of King Eirek's lands. Princess Ingigerd stayed in a safe castle[20] in her kingdom, with her picked men, and was quite heartsick over her lot.

CHAPTER IV

At the time when these matters that we have told of were taking place, Sturlaug the Hard-Working ruled Ringerike in Norway. He married Asa the Fair, the daughter of Jarl Eirek. They had many well-bred sons. One was named Rognvald, another was Fradmar, a third was Eirek, and the fourth was named Hrolf. He was named after Hrolf Nose, Sturlaug's sworn brother, who died in the temple in Ireland[21] when Sturlaug sought to get the aurochs horn there.

Sturlaug's son Hrolf was the largest of men in both girth and height, and so heavy that no horse could carry him for a whole day. For that reason he was always walking. He was the most handsome of men in appearance. He wasn't sociable, and he wasn't much for merriment and amusement, except that he found it most enjoyable to practice archery or jousting. He was so heavy and strong that no one could knock him out of the saddle, but he was awkward with weapons and never carried them. He was both harmless and useless to most people. Hrolf wasn't like his brothers, and there was never any warmth between them.

One day, Sturlaug and Hrolf were talking, as they often did. Sturlaug said, "It looks to me as though your destiny will be a pitiful one. The way you behave is more like a woman than a man. So I think it's best for you to get married and settle down on a farm and become a cottager in some remote valley where no one will find you, and live out your life for as long as it's fated to last."

Hrolf said, "I won't settle down and I won't get married, because I don't need women. And I can clearly see that you're trying to lay the blame so that you can quit having to feed me. So I'll go away, and not come back until I have won just as large a kingdom as you have now—or else am lying dead. I believe that your holdings are a peasant's estate, and there's little to share with us brothers. Neither you nor they will have the benefit of me from now on."

Sturlaug said, "I can give you both a ship and good traveling companions, if you will set yourself some quest that might bring you fame or honor."

Hrolf said, "I don't care to drag men after me until they're missing your sons. I won't get involved with battles, because I can't stand the sight of blood. And I don't want to crowd into a little boat with so many people that they make it sink and we all drown."

Sturlaug said, "I won't provide you with anything, because I can tell that you're both stupid and stubborn." That said, they parted in disagreement.

Hrolf went to his mother Asa and said, "Mother, I want you to show me the cloaks that your foster-mother Vefreyja made for my father, so long ago."

She did so, opening up a large chest, and said, "Here you can see the cloaks. They haven't aged much."

Hrolf picked up all the cloaks. They were made with sleeves, a hood, and a mask in front of the face. They were both wide and long. No iron could cut them, and poison could not damage them. Hrolf took the two largest and said, "I don't have very much of my father's estate, but I have these cloaks."

Asa said, "You mustn't go away so quickly, son, without weapons or companions."

Hrolf went away without a word, and a few days later he left, so that no one knew what became of him. Neither his father nor his mother nor any of his kin wished him well. No one knew which way he went. It's not said that Sturlaug took any notice of Hrolf's departure. Some time passed, while Sturlaug stayed quietly in his kingdom.

CHAPTER V

Now the saga turns to Thorgnyr. He held the rulership of Jutland in Denmark and had his seat there, but he claimed tribute from more kingdoms. He was a strong ruler and had good men with him. He was very old when this story takes place. His queen was dead, but their two children survived her. Stefnir was the name of his son, and Thora was his daughter.

Both of them were handsome and well-mannered. The jarl's son Stefnir was physically strong and the most accomplished at sports, and was gentle and mild-mannered every day. Thora was the most skillful woman. A bower had been built for her, and she stayed there with her ladies in waiting.

There was a man named Bjorn. He was the jarl's counsellor and dearest friend, wise and kindly and knowledgeable about matters of warfare. Ingibjorg was his wife's name. She was courteous and accomplished, and Bjorn loved her very much. He had a farm a short distance from the fortress, though he stayed most often with the jarl.

Jarl Thorgnyr had loved his queen very much, and her burial mound was near the fortress. The jarl often sat there in good weather, or whenever he held councils or games. The jarl was usually at his leisure, ruling a peaceable kingdom.

CHAPTER VI

Now we must return to Hrolf leaving Ringerike, as we mentioned before. He had no weapons but an oaken club. He wore the cloak Vefreyja's Gift, and carried the other cloak. The roads were unknown to him. He traveled more often through mountains and forests than through settlements. He headed east into the Eidskog Forest,[22] intending to go up to Sweden. He couldn't find the way, and he wandered far and lived outdoors for a long time.

Late one spring evening, he found a strongly-built hut in the forest. The door was hanging open. He set his club against the wall and went inside the hut. There was a bed for one man, and seats next to it. There were some furs, but few other things of value. Hrolf lit a fire. When the sun had set, a very tall man came inside the hut, wearing a dark cloak and a rust-colored hood. He was swarthy, with a thick beard. He wore a sword at his belt but walked holding a spear. He said, "Who is this thief? Where did you come from?"

Hrolf said, "There's no need for you to speak so harshly. I don't feel like concealing my name. I'm called Hrolf. I've come from Ringerike."

The hut-dweller said, "No one who comes from there should escape unharmed. But get away from the fires and sit up in the chair and rest."

Hrolf did so, and when he had sat down, the hut-dweller said, "Now I won't conceal my name. I am called Atli Otryggson[23], from Ringerike by birth. I recognize you clearly. You are the son of Sturlaug the Hard-Working. Now you'll pay for that, for your father made me an outlaw when I killed one of his retainers."

He seized the spear with both hands and stabbed Hrolf's chest so hard that the spearhead crumpled, but it didn't pierce the cloak. Hrolf wanted to stand up, but couldn't because he was pressed into the seat. Atli said, "You're not going to show your sorcery now. I'll take your club and bash you into Hel[24] with it."

He rushed out of the hut. Hrolf realized that he was in a bad way, and he smashed against the walls until the plank he was sitting against came loose, just as Atli came with the club. Hrolf rushed underneath Atli, who threw away the club, and they began grappling with each other, wrestling powerfully. Hrolf went at it with all his might, but Atli fought with full force until he fell backwards. Hrolf pinned him with his knee in the stomach and gripped his neck and windpipe with both hands, so that he couldn't speak a word. Atli struggled mightily, but Hrolf held his grip until Atli was dead.

In the hut, Hrolf found a large purse of money and took it with him. He took the sword and spear, but left the club behind. Hrolf got Atli out of his mantle, because he thought it would be lighter for traveling than his cloak, and he carried both cloaks. He burned Atli's body and spent the rest of the night there. In the morning he went on his way and traveled through the forest for many more days.

One day, he came out into a clearing and saw eleven fully armed men. One of them was best equipped, and Hrolf thought he must be their leader. When they saw Hrolf, this man said, "Here comes Atli the Evil. All of you, stand up and kill him as quickly as possible. Let's pay him back for his robbing and murdering."

Hrolf didn't get to say anything on his behalf, and they attacked him fiercely, slashing and stabbing. Hrolf turned on them manfully, by turns hewing or striking with the spear. He dealt them heavy blows, because his spear was the best weapon, but Hrolf suffered some wounds on his hands and feet. They fought for a long time, and in the end Hrolf killed them all. By then he was exhausted and had many minor wounds. He bound his wounds and threw away the mantle, because he didn't want to get the same treatment again. He suspected that these men must have come from Varmland[25] and gone out to hunt wild animals, or else to pursue Atli.

Then he went on his way, and nothing is said about his journey until he entered Gotaland along the Gota River. He saw a ship floating alongside the bank—a great longship, completely tented over between the bow and the stern. The gangplank extended onto land, and at the end of the gangplank was a fire where men were cooking food. Hrolf took down his cloak's hood and went up to the men by the fire and greeted them. They accepted his greeting and asked him his name and where he had come from. He said that his name was Stigandi[26] and that he had come from Varmland. Hrolf asked who owned the ship and whom they served. They said that he was named Jolgeir, descended from a family from Sylgisdal in Sweden.

Hrolf said, "It must be good to serve such a man."

They said that whoever served him was worse off, "because he is a sorcerous berserk, and iron doesn't bite him. He is ferocious and the hardest man to deal with. There are eighty of us on the ship. We all serve him unwillingly because he has killed our chieftain, who owned the ship, and forced us to swear oaths of loyalty. He accomplished all this with deceit and sorcery. Now he intends to go raiding in the Eastern realms."

Hrolf said that they had entertained him well. He walked right out onto the ship and came before Jolgeir and greeted him. Jolgeir was sitting on the ship's afterdeck, looking most unsightly to Hrolf. He accepted his greeting and asked him his name and his reason for coming.

Hrolf said, "I'm called Stigandi, and my reason for coming is to take service with good men. I'm not averse to working hard at what's needed, but I'm no warrior. I have heard good things about you, that you are a great chieftain who doesn't refuse food to men who need it."

Jolgeir said, "You've heard truly that I don't withhold food—but I don't like you, because I believe you're a wicked man. But you can come with us, if you like." Hrolf thanked him, and that was the end of their conversation.

They went raiding all through the summer. Hrolf dealt out silver from his purse with both hands, and everyone liked him except for Jolgeir, because Hrolf was both lazy and sleepy, and he didn't know how to do anything on the ship. He was never in battles, nor in any difficult trials. Jolgeir's raids went badly, and he usually robbed farmers and merchants,[27] but they raided most often in Courland[28] and gained a lot of money.

On one occasion, Jolgeir assigned Stigandi to stand watch on their ship. The ship was tied up along the shore, and the gangplank was out. The weather was bad, with storms and rain. They went to sleep on the ship, but Hrolf stayed on land at the end of the gangplank. The night passed, and as morning approached, Hrolf began to grow sleepy, and he wrapped the cloak Vefreyja's Gift around himself.

When Jolgeir awoke, he armed himself and went onto land with a sword in his hand. He saw Hrolf lying down, fast asleep and snoring by the coals. Jolgeir was furious. He drew his sword and swung it down at Hrolf's belly with both hands. That would have been the death of him if the cloak had not saved him. Hrolf awoke in a fright and leaped up, but Jolgeir tried to strike another blow at his head. Hrolf ducked under it. Jolgeir came at him, and a fierce wrestling bout broke out. He rushed at Hrolf in a frenzy, but

Hrolf let himself be carried towards the ocean, until they both fell over a cliff and into the sea. Each pulled the other into the water, and they were down for a long time. Many a time they plunged down deep. No one wanted to intervene, even though they all liked Hrolf better than Jolgeir. The fight ended when they came back up towards the shore. Hrolf got his feet under him, and the sea bed dropped off steeply in front of him. The water came up to Hrolf's waist, but Jolgeir couldn't touch bottom. Hrolf seized him by the shoulders and shoved him down into the water and held him under until he had drowned him.

Hrolf walked out onto land, completely exhausted. Jolgeir's men all thanked him for this deed and said that he was an excellent man to have beaten such a berserk. Hrolf said, "You may want to take me as chieftain over you now, in place of Jolgeir. I won't treat you any worse. Now I want to let you know you who I am, because my name is Hrolf, and Sturlaug the Hard-Working is my father, the ruler of Ringerike in Norway."

They all welcomed him and said that he was no commoner, since he might be the mightiest champion. Then they held a council and decided to follow Hrolf, and took him as their ship's captain. Hrolf didn't withhold the money that Jolgeir had gathered, and he paid them well for their service. They soon came to like him very much. They fought many battles, and Hrolf always won victory.

When autumn began, they sailed out of the east. Hrolf said that they would set course for Denmark. They came late in the autumn to Jutland, not far from Jarl Thorgnyr's fortress. They laid up in a hidden bay, anchored their ship and put up awnings. Hrolf told his men to wait there until he came back—"but I will go down from the ship by myself to see what's happening."

CHAPTER VII

It's said that one day in Jutland, as Thorgnyr was sitting at his feasting table, the hall doors opened and a man entered the hall. He was both tall and stout, wearing a long shaggy cape and holding a huge spear in his hand. Everyone in the hall was amazed at his great size. He came before the jarl and greeted him worthily. The jarl accepted his greeting and asked what sort of man he was. He said, "Hrolf is my name, and my father's name is Sturlaug, who rules Ringerike. I have come here because I want to know your customs, because I've been told that you are a great chieftain."

The jarl said, "I know all about your family and lineage, and I am quite willing for you to be made welcome in my kingdom and receive everything you ask for which is seemly for me to give. How many men do you wish to have serving you each day?"

Hrolf said, "Eighty men are on my ship, and they will come with me. I have enough money to pay our expenses. I would like to have some castle, not far from you, to house my men and defend your lands, if you're willing."

The jarl said, "I'm thankful that you came. Everything shall be done as you wish, that your honor may be increased."

Hrolf thanked the jarl for his words and went to his men. The jarl gave them a castle to hold. Hrolf stayed in the castle quietly and maintained his men well, but most of the time he went on raids and manfully defended the jarl's realm. Stefnir and Hrolf became firm friends. Bjorn the Counsellor was also dearest to Hrolf. Some time now passed, with nothing of note happening.

CHAPTER VIII

There was a man named Tryggvi, the son of Ulfkell. His family came from Buchan in Scotland. He was the greatest champion and berserk, and he sailed out with a fleet of ships in both summer and winter. He had a sworn brother named Vazi, who was also the worst troll on account of his size and his strength alike. Thorgnyr had killed Tryggvi's father when he was raiding. Tryggvi had now acquired twelve ships, all well equipped with men and weapons. He sailed with this host to Denmark, wanting to avenge his father on Jarl Thorgnyr. Vazi was with him, and many other champions. As soon as they reached Jarl Thorgnyr's realm, they invaded it and pillaged farms, killing men and stealing all the livestock they caught. When the jarl heard this news, he had the war-arrow carved and summoned his men. But because he was old, he appointed Hrolf and Stefnir to lead his forces. This was the second winter of Hrolf's first stay in Denmark.

Hrolf and his forces sailed with ten ships to find Tryggvi. They encountered each other alongside an uninhabited island. They didn't exchange many greetings. Fighting broke out at once. Tryggvi and Vazi had a great dragon-ship. They were ferocious fighters. It was difficult to carry the fight up into the dragon-ship because of how high its sides were. They dropped stones over the sides of the ship onto Hrolf and his men. Many of Hrolf's and Stefnir's men fell, and many were wounded, and the battle was turning against them. Stefnir and Hrolf were wearing the cloaks, Vefreyja's Gifts, and no weapon hurt them. They steered their ships at the dragon-ship and attacked manfully. Hrolf had the spear Atli's Gift and a great oaken club under his belt. Stefnir had a good sword in hand, and was the boldest of men.

When the attack was at the height of fury, Hrolf leaped up into the prow. He forced his way before him, stabbing with the spear so powerfully that the men opposing him either fell, or else they were run through. Stefnir leaped up after him, swinging his sword to left and right. They quickly cleared the prow of men. Then each of them moved sternwards along one side of the ship, and everyone fled back towards the sail. By then the day was mostly over.

When Tryggvi and Vazi saw this, they charged right at them. Vazi had a thrusting-spear in his hand, and Tryggvi had an axe. Hrolf went up against Vazi, and each one stabbed at the other. The thrusting-spear stuck in Hrolf's shield and split it all to pieces, but Hrolf wasn't wounded. Vazi brought up his shield against Hrolf's blow, but the spear glanced off the shield and pierced Vazi's thigh, making a severe wound. Vazi struck at the spear-shaft. Hrolf then seized his club and defended himself with that, smashing Vazi's entire shield. They fought for a long time, until Hrolf broke the thrusting-spear's shaft. At that moment, Vazi rushed at Hrolf so that he almost fell. Hrolf threw away the club and turned on him. They wrestled long and hard. Hrolf thought that he'd never had to deal with a stronger man who wasn't a shape-shifter. In the end, Hrolf carried Vazi out onto the gunwale and broke his back.

Stefnir and Tryggvi had been fighting all this time. Stefnir was worn out by exhaustion and heavy blows, but he wasn't wounded. Tryggvi was badly wounded. Hrolf hurried over there, and when Tryggvi saw that, he didn't want to wait around for him and stepped overboard. They couldn't search for him because of the darkness.

The battle ended, and a truce was granted to every survivor. Six ships were cleared of all their crews. They took much wealth there and headed for home, leaving matters as they stood. The jarl thanked Hrolf very much for his efforts. They didn't find Tryggvi at the time, and so they parted with him.

CHAPTER IX

It happened one day, as it often happens, that two unknown men walked into the hall. They were tall and bold-looking, but not well fitted out with weapons or clothing. They went before the jarl and greeted him. He accepted their greeting warmly and asked their names.

The larger man said, "We two are brothers. My name is Hrafn, and my brother is Krak, and our family comes from Flanders."

"It was a bad day for good names," said the jarl, "for such brave men to be called such things."[29]

Hrafn said, "We would like to lodge here over the winter, because we've been told that you are good to men who've stayed with you for a long time."

The jarl said that they would be welcome, and arranged for them to sit in the middle of the bench, to the outside of the king's greatest champion. They stayed there, highly honored by the jarl. They didn't take part in much good cheer or fun with other men.

There were always ball games going on.[30] Many men invited the brothers to come play. They said that they'd always played ball and were considered rough players. The jarl's men promised to take responsibility for whatever happened.

The next morning, the brothers went to play. They always kept the ball, all day long. They shoved men and knocked them down hard, and struck some. By evening, three men had broken arms, and many were beaten and injured. The jarl's men thought they had come off badly. This went on for several days.

The jarl's men decided to ask the jarl's son Stefnir to go to the games and even their odds a bit, and he agreed. The next morning, Stefnir went to the playing field. As soon as Hrafn saw him, he said, "Are you so strong that you're not allowed to play with other men,[31] or do you think you're so great that no one will dare to play against you?"

Stefnir said, "I'm neither so strong nor so arrogant that I'm not allowed to play this game."

Hrafn said, "Then I invite you to play against us brothers three nights from now, with the teammate of your choice, if you dare."

Stefnir said, "You can be sure that I'll come to the game."

He left at once. He took a horse and rode until he came to Hrolf's castle. This was the second winter of Hrolf's stay in Denmark. As soon as Hrolf knew that Stefnir had arrived, he went to meet him and welcomed him most cheerfully. Then they sat down to drink.

Stefnir said, "I've come here because I'd like to invite you to play on my side, against the men my father has taken in for the winter, known as Krak and Hrafn."

Hrolf said, "I've been told that they have injured many men and killed some, and that they are strong men. And I don't know how to play games. Still, I'll go with you, if you want."

They went to the fort, and the jarl welcomed Hrolf warmly. The next day, Hrolf and Stefnir went to the games. The brothers had also arrived. Hrafn took the ball, and Krak took the stick, and they played as they usually did. The jarl sat on a chair and watched the game. When they had played for a while, Hrolf managed to get the ball. He grabbed the stick away from

Krak and gave it to Stefnir. Then they played for a long time, keeping the ball away from the brothers.

On one occasion, as Hrafn was rushing after the ball, someone stuck out his foot so that he fell. It was a young man with a habit of playing pranks on others, a kinsman of the jarl's. Hrafn became very angry. He jumped up quickly and grabbed the man who'd tripped him and lifted him up and flung him down on his head, breaking his neck. The jarl shouted to his men and ordered them to seize Hrafn and kill him. Hrolf rushed at Hrafn and grabbed him. Krak and Stefnir were fighting elsewhere, and Hrolf forbade anyone to interfere with them. They hadn't wrestled for long before Hrolf picked Hrafn up against his chest and threw him down, knocking him unconscious for a long time and scraping the skin from his shoulder-blades.

But when Hrafn came to, Hrolf helped him up and said, "I see that you have the look of a man of rank. My lord, I ask you to grant these men a pardon, because I know that they come from noble kin."

Stefnir had gotten the better of Krak, and asked his father to give Hrolf what he asked for. The jarl was furious for a long time, yet he gave them a pardon, as Hrolf and Stefnir had asked. The brothers were very stiff, and walked off to their quarters without a word. They did not appear at the table that evening.

The men now left off playing and went to drink. Hrolf said to Stefnir, "Now you must take the finest cloth we have and give it to your sister Thora. She must sew clothes for the brothers, and have them ready early in the morning."

Stefnir did so, and went to Thora with the cloth and told her how she should make the clothes. When Stefnir left, she began to sew the clothes. The night passed, and early in the morning Thora sent the finished clothes to Hrolf. He took them and went to the brothers' lodgings and saw that they were lying down. Hrolf said, "Why is the raven so late in flying, since there's plenty of carrion, and eagles and other scavengers are full now?"

Hrafn said, "They can hardly fly if they've been plucked, or if they're molting."

Hrolf took the clothes and tossed them at them and left at once. The brothers put on the clothes and went into the hall and sat at the table.

The winter passed. It's not said that Krak and Hrafn thanked Hrolf for the clothes, or for saving their lives, although they were well treated. Towards the start of summer they left, so that no one knew what became of them. Many felt that they'd acted strangely.

Hrolf and Stefnir both went on raids through the summer, winning plenty of wealth and fame. They came home in the autumn, safe and sound, but there's nothing to tell about their mighty deeds.

CHAPTER X

The next summer, Hrolf stayed with Jarl Thorgnyr and was honored highly. One day in the autumn, as Jarl Thorgnyr was sitting on his queen's burial mound and games were being played before him, a swallow flew over him and dropped a silken handkerchief down into his lap and flew away.[32] The jarl took it and untied it, and saw a human hair inside, as long as a tall man and the color of gold.

That evening, the jarl sat down at the feasting table. He showed his men the hair which the swallow had let fall. Most of them thought that it must be a woman's hair. The jarl said, "This oath I swear: to win that woman whose hair this is—if I can find out which estates to search, or what land she is in—or else die."

Everyone felt that this was a mighty oath, and the men looked at each other.[33]

Some nights later, the jarl summoned an assembly of many men. He stood up in the assembly and informed the men of the oath he had sworn, and asked whether anyone could recognize this woman, or knew where she would have to be searched for. The hair was also shown, to see if anyone could recognize it.

Bjorn the Counsellor said, "Gladly will I speak and act, my lord, that it may bring honor and glory to you and your kingdom, rather than any sort of harm or discredit. I judge your sworn oath to be a weighty matter. I think that this woman is not fated to be yours, but I can nearly guess at who she is, though I have never inquired about her before. There was a king named Hreggvid, ruling over Russia. He had a daughter named Ingibjorg, fairest and finest in all respects. I have heard that it's true that no woman in the Northlands has ever excelled her, nor has had longer and fairer hair than she. My suspicion is that the hair must be hers, whatever the device by which it came to us. Now you all must have heard the truth about what happened to the princess when King Hreggvid fell before King Eirek. She must have a man to joust against the king's champion Sorkvir and thus rescue her. I think that few would be eager to contend with such a man. Even if someone were to unhorse Sorkvir, I don't think that the princess would be any easier to get out of Russia than before."

Everyone there thought that it must be as Bjorn had said.

CHAPTER XI

After Bjorn had given his advice, Jarl Thorgnyr was silent for some time. Then he said, "To the man who will go to Russia and joust against Sorkvir and win the hand of this maiden for me, I shall give Thora my daughter, and a third of all my kingdom. I will withhold neither ships nor men for the journey, for the man who is willing."

All the men fell silent at this proposal. No one answered the jarl, until Hrolf stood up and spoke: "This is a paltry thing, failing to answer a ruler such as we have. My lord, because I have been with you for some time, highly honored and receiving many boons from you, I will go on this journey and try to get the princess, or else lie dead. But even if I return from this journey, you should give your daughter to whomever you want, because she's well worthy of a good match, but getting married is not to my taste."

The jarl thanked Hrolf very much, and asked him to take as many men as he wanted. But Hrolf said that he didn't want anyone, "because one man arouses less suspicion than a crowd, wherever they go."

Stefnir asked to go with him, but Hrolf didn't want him to. Now the assembly broke up. Hrolf returned to his castle, and everyone went back to his own home.

CHAPTER XII

Shortly afterwards, Hrolf left the castle without anyone finding out, and his men stayed behind. He wore the cloak Vefreyja's Gift, and traveled with the spear Atli's Gift. He had a bow and a quiver of arrows on his shoulders. Nothing is said about what road Hrolf took, but one day, once he had gone most of the way through Denmark, he saw a man coming. He was very tall, and fully armored down to his hands and feet. He came towards Hrolf with a drawn sword in hand. Hrolf greeted this man and asked him his name. He said, "I am called Vilhjalm, and my ancestry I don't care to recite for you. You are to choose one of two options. One is to tell me who you are and where you wish to go and what your errand is. The other is for me to kill you, and then you'll travel no farther."

Hrolf said, "There's no need for you to give me a hard choice, because my chances are no worse than yours, however we test each other."

Vilhjalm struck at Hrolf with the sword, but Hrolf blocked it with the spear and it didn't cut. Hrolf threw away the spear and rushed at Vilhjalm, who turned to face him, and their wrestling lasted a long time before Vilhjalm fell.

Hrolf said, "Now the advantage is all mine. You'll have to tell me what your errand is and where you're from."

Vilhjalm said, "I come from here in Denmark. I'm the son of a farmer, but I wanted to go to Russia and break into the mound of King Hreggvid and take his weapons and thus win the hand of King Eirek's sister Gyda. Now I want to become your servant. I'm gifted at may things, because I'm both smart and well-spoken. It'd be best for you to let me live. I'll faithfully serve you. You'll benefit from me."

Hrolf said, "You're a promising man, and I certainly don't care to kill you if you'll follow me. But you don't have trustworthy eyes."

Hrolf let him stand up, and took him into his complete confidence and told him all about his journey. They went on their way. Vilhjalm's horse was close by. Vilhjalm wouldn't stand for walking while bearing armor and weapons, and he was a very showy person in his clothes and saddle-trappings. Vilhjalm always pointed the way as they traveled through Denmark.

CHAPTER XIII

One day, they saw a fine large house up ahead of them. Vilhjalm said, "We'll get good lodging at this farm this evening, because my kinsman is in charge. His name is Olvir, and he's a good farmer who keeps many servants."

When they came to the farm, the farmer came out to meet them and welcomed Vilhjalm and his companion, asking who the large man might be. Vilhjalm said, "His name is Hrolf and he is my master. He's big and strong, of good family, and a great champion."

The farmer invited them in to drink. They were quite at ease. Vilhjalm would trust no one else but himself to serve Hrolf, and he praised him with every word. There was good ale and much cheer. As the evening went on, they kept drinking for a long time. When Hrolf got drunk, he wanted to go to sleep. A fine bed was prepared for him. He took off his clothes and lay in the bed and quickly fell asleep.

But as the night was passing, Hrolf awoke—and not with pleasant dreams, because he was bound hand and foot and tied firmly to a pole. He had no clothes on and had been carried to the edge of a huge bonfire. There was his servant Vilhjalm standing over him, with the farmer and all the men of the household.

Vilhjalm said, "Now it so happens that I've overpowered you, Hrolf, and you must not have suspected that for a while. You have two choices. One is to be burned on this bonfire and never see the sun—or else you are to follow me to Russia and serve me in every way and call me your master and affirm the truth of everything that I say about myself. You are to do all the tasks laid before me, until the king agrees to betroth his sister Gyda to me. Then you shall be free from my service. You are never to take vengeance on me for this disgrace, nor on any of the men who are here. You shall take an oath to keep all the conditions which I have set out, or else you'll burn in the flames right here."

Hrolf said, "Since there's a way for me to be freed from bondage to you, I would rather agree to it than lose my life, for I know that I'll wouldn't accomplish much of the jarl's mission if I die here. I also want to stipulate that you say nothing about what I intend or who I am, or else all our agreement is void."

Vilhjalm said that they would do so. Hrolf was now untied, and he swore an oath according to the customs at that time. Hrolf now served Vilhjalm and acted like a worthless man. They left Olvir, and Vilhjalm rode, but Hrolf walked in front of the horse. They traveled through Sweden and from there to Russia. There's nothing said about what road they took, until they came to Novgorod. It was early in the winter, and King Eirek was residing in the town. They took lodgings, and then came before the king.

CHAPTER XIV

They arrived as the king was sitting at the table. They greeted the king, and he welcomed their greeting and asked what sort of men they were. Vilhjalm said, "I am called Vilhjalm, and this is my servant who's come with me. He's called Hrolf. I'm the son of a certain jarl from Frisia, and I've been exiled from there because I was cheated out of the earldom by the inhabitants themselves. I have come here because I have heard of your generosity and magnificence, and I would like to have winter lodgings here."

The king said, "I won't withhold food from you, but are you a man of great accomplishments?"

Vilhjalm said, "I know plenty of skills. The first is that I am so strong that my strength never fails. The second is that I am swifter than all beasts and four-legged animals."

"That's a fitting accomplishment for thieves," said the king, "yet it often comes in handy."

Vilhjalm said, "I'm not lacking in skill at archery and fencing, swimming and board-games and jousting, wisdom and eloquence. I lack nothing upon which a man may pride himself."

"I can tell that you're not lacking in audacity," said the king. "Tell your skills, Hrolf, because I don't trust him any less than you."

Hrolf said, "I can't tell them, lord, since there aren't any."

"Many things are shared unequally between you," said the king, "if one has everything and the other has nothing. Take your seats in the middle of the lower bench."

"It's your decision, my lord," said Vilhjalm, "but I've never had such a lowly seat before."

They went to their seats. Sorkvir and Brynjolf weren't there at that time; they had gone to Jotunheim with Grim Aegir. Vilhjalm and Hrolf were honored highly. Vilhjalm swaggered everywhere, but Hrolf was always taciturn and silent, never playing games with the other men. Vilhjalm put off demonstrating his skills, but the king was a great hunter and enjoyed pursuing animals with his household. Since coming to Russia, he was always left in peace, since most men were unwilling to invade his kingdom because of the champions who stayed with him, and especially because of the spells and sorcery of Grim Aegir.

CHAPTER XV

One day, King Eirek and his household went to the forest to hunt animals and shoot birds, as was his custom. They saw such a huge and lovely stag that no one thought he had ever seen a more handsome beast. Most thought that it had to be a tame animal, because its horns were carved all over, with gold inlaid in the carvings, and a silver bar was set between the horns, with two gold rings hanging from it. Around its neck lay a silver cord, and hanging down from that was a silver bell, which rang out loudly whenever the stag stirred itself and dashed.[34] The king wanted to catch the stag and ordered all his hounds to be turned loose, and it was done. Every man leaped into the saddle and rode as best he could. They wanted to catch the stag, but it swiftly dashed away from the hounds, and they never got any closer. They chased it all day, and in the evening, after dark, they couldn't tell what became of it. This went on for three days: they would find the stag but couldn't manage to catch it.

That evening, when the king came to his feasting table and his men had taken their seats, he said, "I don't think you're showing us much ability, Vilhjalm, because you don't engage in games or sports with the other men, and you don't go to the forest with us."

Vilhjalm said, "Competing with your men wouldn't be much fun for me, my lord, because I can tell that no one here knows any kind of sports. And I always had other men bring me venison when I lived at home in my kingdom."

The king said, "We have chased one stag for three days, and we can't catch it. If you catch the stag and bring it to us alive with all its trappings, then I will give you my sister Gyda and a great kingdom, because I have never seen anything that I want more. You can easily do this if you're as fleet-footed as you've said. But you must also accomplish two other tasks that I will set before you. Then I shall increase your honor in all respects, and win back the kingdom you once lost with my own forces. And if there is any other man in my household who can accomplish this, he shall have the same reward."

Then Vilhjalm said, "No one can do this except for me, so you must have meant for me to do it. And I'll accomplish it, or else lie dead."

They clasped hands to seal the bargain, as was the custom. Hrolf paid no attention. Then men went to sleep and took their rest. Hrolf served Vilhjalm in every way, as was said before.

Early in the morning, Vilhjalm and Hrolf got up and prepared to search for the stag. They went into the forest and soon saw where the stag had gone. Vilhjalm began to run as fast as a bird flies. The stag dashed all the faster. Hrolf lumbered after Vilhjalm, and he thought that Vilhjalm was swift at the beginning of the race. They ran for so long that Hrolf always came to the next hill and found Vilhjalm farther ahead—until Vilhjalm threw himself down and said, "It's no good running yourself to death to win a woman, wealth, or a kingdom."

At that moment, Hrolf came up to Vilhjalm and asked why he let the beast get away. Vilhjalm said, "I could easily run longer if I wanted. But I think that you should catch the animal and do all the work for me, according to our agreement—if you're man enough."

Hrolf didn't answer. He rushed forward after the animal and chased it for a long time, until he drew nearer to it because the stag had grown quite exhausted.

At last they came out into a glade. By then the day was over. In the middle of the glade there stood a hill, both wide and high. The glade was lovely and covered all over with thick grass. And when Hrolf came forward up to the hill, it opened up, and he walked all around it. A woman came out, wearing a dark blue mantle[35] and holding up a torch. She said, "You've got a poor job, Hrolf. You're the slave of a slave, and you have to steal another's livestock, because I own this animal that you want to catch. You will never get it unless I allow it.[36] Now I shall give you a chance to catch the animal. You must come into the hill with me. I have a daughter, and a spell has been laid on her so that she cannot give birth to the child she's pregnant with, unless a human being lays his hands on her.[37] She has now lain on the

191

floor for nineteen days and cannot give birth. I sent the stag into your sight because I knew that you would all want to catch it and would chase it here. I trust that you have the stoutest heart to come into the hill with me. But the king will get no benefit from the stag, even if it's brought to him."

Hrolf said, "I'll do it. I'll go into the hill with you, if I can have the stag to bring to the king. I don't care what happens to it afterwards."

The elf-woman was glad to hear that, and they went into the hill. Inside, there was a home, splendid and beautiful to see, and many wondrous things appeared to him. He came to where the woman was lying, and she was doing poorly. But no sooner had Hrolf laid his hands on her than she gave birth quickly. They thanked him with fair words and wished him good fortune.

The elf-woman said, "No reward for you could equal the gift of my daughter's health. But here is a gold ring which I will give you. You will need this when you go to Hreggvid's mound. If you wear it on your hand, you can never get lost, by night or day, on sea or land, in any darkness that you are in, and you will succeed in all the struggles that lie before you. But you must never trust Vilhjalm once you part from him, because he'd gladly see you dead."

Hrolf thanked her, and they came out of the hill. She touched the stag, and Hrolf laid it on his back and found it exceptionally beautiful. Each wished the other well. Hrolf headed homewards until he found Vilhjalm, who welcomed Hrolf warmly and ordered him to carry the stag home to the fortress. Hrolf did so, but he never told Vilhjalm how he had caught the animal.

They reached the fortress late in the evening, when the king was sitting at the table. Vilhjalm said, "Now we shall go into the hall. I'll carry the animal before the king. You are to confirm my story so that the king believes what I say."

Vilhjalm took the animal and put it on his back, and he fell to his knees. Still, he managed to bring the beast into the hall before the king, and he flung it on the floor. He was breathing very hard, and he said, "Now I think I am entitled to be betrothed to your sister. The stag has been brought here, and not many who could manage a deed such as I've done would offer to become your brother-in-law."

The king said, "I suspect that you didn't catch the stag. You'll have to do more bold deeds before you get her."

"There's no need for you to question my courage, because I'm superior to most men. My lad Hrolf knows that he was far off when I captured the stag."

192

Hrolf said, "Not only was I of no help to Vilhjalm, he didn't spare himself in any way."

Vilhjalm said, "I want to do everything myself because I want to claim the reward myself. What more tasks will you set before me? Because I'm ready to accomplish them."

The king said, "Now you must go to Hreggvid's mound and seek the arms of King Hreggvid. That's not a great test."

Vilhjalm said, "Now you want me dead, because no one who has gone there has come back."

"I certainly want you to come back," said the king, "but it's true that no one whom I have sent there has returned. I very much want to have those treasures back that were brought into the mound. And I shall only give my sister to a man who excels over other men."

Vilhjalm said, "I'll do it, for I don't think it takes effort to rob dead men to win a girl." Vilhjalm went now to his seat, and with that said, they parted.

CHAPTER XVI

After a few days, Hrolf tapped Vilhjalm on the legs one night and said, "It's time to win the maiden's hand and go to the mound."

Vilhjalm stood up quickly. Hrolf was dressed, wearing Vefreyja's Gift and holding the spear Atli's Gift, but Vilhjalm wore full armor. He rode, but Hrolf walked in front of his horse. They traveled on in this way until they came to a forest, and they found an ancient footpath. But when they had gone a short way, such a howling gale blew up against them, with snowstorms and frost, that Vilhjalm couldn't stay on horseback. Then Hrolf led the horse, and Vilhjalm walked behind it for a while, until the blizzard grew so strong that the horse couldn't walk. Hrolf dragged it flat behind him, steadying himself with the spear. He looked back and saw that Vilhjalm had disappeared, and the horse had been dead for a long time. He left the horse there and went forward on the path. The blizzard was so strong that oak-trees were snapping from their stumps and falling from a great height. They often struck Hrolf with severe blows which would have brought death to most men, and there was such lightning and thunder that he thought he would have been killed if the cloak had not protected him. This went on all night until dawn. Towards daybreak, such a terrible stench came at him that he would have choked if the face-mask hadn't saved him. Hrolf realized that the blizzard must have killed the king's men, and that it must be a storm sent by magic. He thought that he had never faced such a trial.

But when the day was brightest, the blizzard abated and the weather calmed, and the stench disappeared. Hrolf saw a mound as high as a mountain, and a tall stockade ringing it. He gripped one of the posts with his hand and vaulted over the stockade. Then he walked up onto the mound, feeling that it would be very difficult to break into. When he looked around, he saw a very tall man in royal vestments on the north side of the mound. Hrolf went up to him and greeted him as befitted a king and asked him his name.

He said, "I am Hreggvid, and I live inside this mound with my champions. You're welcome here. You must know, Hrolf, that I don't control these blizzards and stenches or other strange happenings, and I haven't killed anyone. Sorkvir and Grim Aegir are the cause of all of these, and they have caused the deaths of the king's men. Still, their wisdom sometimes falls short when they need it most. If they knew that you were here, they would want you dead. I went to Jarl Thorgnyr in the likeness of a swallow, with a hair from my daughter Ingigerd, because I knew that you of all the jarl's men would search for her and you alone were the man to free her, if luck is with you. I give you permission to enjoy her in the best way if you will joust against Sorkvir, for you lack neither boldness nor bravery. But Grim Aegir has promised Sorkvir that no one shall overcome him except for the man who bears my armor. That's why this mound is made to be unbreakable, and why there are barriers to entry—because he thought that no one should be able to get the armor. Now I shall get you everything that you want from the mound. I will give you two sets of armor, identical to each other except for the quality. You shall give the king the worse set. You must not let anyone see the other set until you need it, and you must take great care of the sword, because you'll seldom see another one like it.[38] My daughter Ingigerd is guarding all my jousting weapons and the horse Dulcifal, who's unlike most other horses in many respects. You must ride him when you fight Sorkvir, and you're certain to win victory if he lets you catch him. The lance and the shield will also keep their nature. You must not trust Vilhjalm even when you are out of his service, because he will betray you if he can. You'll want to keep your oath, but it's better if he's put to death sooner rather than later, because he will put you in danger."

After that, Hreggvid gave Hrolf the treasures and weapons, and finally the necklace from around his neck.[39] Then Hreggvid said, "It is fated that I may leave my mound three times, and there's no need to close it up until the last time. Now you shouldn't encounter any obstacles when you return home. Go well, and may everything go for you as you might wish. But if you come back to Russia, visit me if you need a little something."

Hreggvid turned back into the mound, and Hrolf took the treasures and kept them carefully. He returned from the mound by the same path, and wasn't aware of any strange happenings. When he came out of the forest, Vilhjalm came to meet him. He had slipped under some tree roots and lain there all through the snowstorm. He could hardly speak for the cold. He fawned on Hrolf and said, "I don't believe that too much could ever be said of your bravery and the good fortune that's with us, now that the mound is broken open and the gold and treasures have been found. Now I see that nothing can stand in our way, although that was such a great storm that I barely managed to survive. Now I think I'm entitled to marry the king's sister. You must give me the treasures and weapons, because I want to hand them over to the king myself."

Hrolf said, "You won't win much fame, and you'll pay me back poorly, even though I risked my life for you. Take the treasures and bring them to the king. I will keep my word to you and affirm your story, even though you're not worth it."

Hrolf had hidden the other set of arms in the forest, and Vilhjalm didn't see them. They went on their way until they met the king, sitting at his evening meal at the feasting table. Vilhjalm greeted the king and pretended to be quite exhausted. Everyone in the hall fell silent at their return.

Vilhjalm said, "I can hardly believe that there could be a harder struggle, all told, because Hreggvid is the worst of trolls, thanks to his sorcery, and the mound is difficult to break into. I've been fighting with King Hreggvid all night. I was terribly hard-pressed before I got the arms."

Then he took the sword and the necklace and lay them on the table before the king. The king said, "The treasures have certainly been found, and all of them look worse to me now than before, except for the necklace, which is flawless[40]—but I think that Hrolf must have gotten that, not you."

Hrolf said, "I tell you this: I didn't go into the mound. You may judge how likely that is. I wouldn't object to gaining such honors or others like them, if I had a choice."

Vilhjalm said, "It amazes me, my lord, that you doubt my story or the excellence and boldness of my manliness. We can quickly make a test and let Hrolf and me fight, and he won't get close to me, because first of all, he can't stand the sight of human blood. When I went into Hreggvid's mound, he had to hold the rope, and when he heard the commotion and loud crashes inside the mound, he was so terrified that he abandoned the rope. The only thing that saved me was that I had tied the end of the rope around a big stone, and I hauled myself up out of the mound by the strength of my own arms."[41]

The king answered, "Well do I believe his words, Hrolf, but the treasures would not have been brought here if they hadn't been found in the mound." The king had the arms guarded very carefully, thinking that they would do no harm to Sorkvir.

It's said that the stag got away one night, so that those who had to guard it didn't realize it. The king felt that this was the worst loss. It was searched for near and far, but not found. Hrolf realized that the elf-woman must have found it.

Vilhjalm boasted about himself and was always going to chat with the king's sister. Their conversations went well. He didn't hold back from bragging a lot about himself in every way. So the winter passed until Yule, and nothing noteworthy happened.

CHAPTER XVII

There was a king named Menelaus, a mighty and splendid king who ruled over Tartary. Tartary is said to be the largest of all realms, and the richest in gold, among all the kingdoms of the East. The men there are large and strong and fierce in battle. Many kings and men of high degree were subject to King Menelaus.

It's said that between Russia and Tartary there lies an island called Hedinsey, a jarl's realm. Wise men say that King Hedin, the son of Hjarrandi, first anchored off that island when he sailed from India to Denmark, and the island has been named for him ever since.[42] The king of Tartary and the king of Russia were always fighting over this island, although it was subject to the crown of Tartary. King Eirek had raided this island and done many warlike deeds there before he came to Russia.

King Menelaus had appointed a man named Soti to rule the island. His mother's family came from the island, and his father's family came from the realm of Novgorod. Soti wasn't on the island when King Eirek raided there. He was the worst of trolls on account of his strength and size, and his appearance matched his name.[43] He raided far and wide and always won victory. Soti had an elderly and sorcerous foster-mother, who had made a bath for him so that no iron could bite him ever after. That's why he went into battle without armor.[44] She had also told him that his chances of getting revenge against King Eirek were best that autumn, since none of his champions were at home. When Soti realized that, he went to King Menelaus and got many men from him. Then he headed straight for Russia with many thousands of warriors. A man named Nordri[45] accompanied Soti. He was tall and strong and the greatest of champions, who always carried his banner.

When King Eirek heard that Soti had invaded his land with a huge host, he had the war-arrow sent out in all directions and ordered everyone who could to join him, and he raised a huge multitude. King Eirek summoned Vilhjalm and said, "You've accomplished two tasks that I have set before you, and I don't know whether you did them. Now you must accomplish the third task: killing Soti the berserk while I'm standing nearby. I won't object to you marrying my sister if you accomplish this, and I shall keep all my agreements with you, as we discussed."

Vilhjalm said, "I'm ready to face Soti. I think it's good for you to see now what a valiant man I am. You must pick out all your best weapons and your strongest steed for me, because I will put them through a severe test before this battle is over."

It was done as Vilhjalm asked. Hrolf went with him, walking as he usually did. The king marched with his host until he encountered Soti on a level plain, with thick forest on the other side. Both sides prepared for battle, forming a huge host all together. With a great fanfare of trumpets, the ranks charged towards each other, and both sides screamed battle cries.

CHAPTER XVIII

King Eirek was in the center of his front line, advancing in the forefront of the battle. Soti arrayed his forces against him. The fiercest fighting broke out as both sides advanced. As soon as the fighting began, Vilhjalm rode off into a glade in the forest. Hrolf said, "Vilhjalm, now's the time for you to ride forth and win the hand of the maiden and kill Soti."

Vilhjalm said, "I'll get the woman and kingdom if it's my destiny, but I'm not about to risk my life in such a battle. What will a girl or a kingdom matter to me if I lose my life? It's much more suitable for you to free me from oppression and slavery. Take my weapons and horse. Ride out and kill Soti, or else you'll have to serve me for the rest of your life."

Hrolf took Vilhjalm's horse and weapons and rode into battle. The battle was a dreadful slaughter and was turning very much against King Eirek, because the Tartars were charging fiercely. Soti and Nordri ferociously cleared the way, and everyone fell back. Soti had a bladed spear to fight with, slashing and stabbing by turns. Nordri had a good sword and advanced boldly. King Eirek had led an all-out attack on the center of Soti's forces, until Nordri and many Tartars came against him. They attacked the king furiously. Many of his men fell, so that he was hard-pressed in the midst of his foes.

Now Hrolf rode forward with Vilhjalm's weapons, so boldly that Soti's battle-lines retreated before him. He slashed and stabbed to left and right and killed many men until he reached King Eirek. There Hrolf killed more than thirty men. When Soti saw that, he was outraged. He turned to face Hrolf and stabbed at him with his spear. Hrolf defended himself with his shield, and he countered by stabbing at Soti's chest. His spear didn't bite, but its shaft broke. Soti struck at Hrolf with both hands. The blade landed in the middle of his shield and split it, and it cleaved his horse in two just ahead of the withers and plunged into the earth. Hrolf got to his feet and was very weary, because he had been fighting hard that day. King Eirek was fighting Nordri, and they were attacking each other forcefully.

Just then, Hrolf chopped off the head of Soti's horse, and then both of them were on foot. Soti struck at Hrolf, but he dodged, and the spear plunged into the earth all the way up to Soti's hands. Hrolf struck at Soti's shoulder with both hands, and the sword broke apart at the hilt. Hrolf flew into a rage and rushed at Soti and drove the sword's studded hilt into his head so that it stuck in his brain. Soti couldn't do anything to stop that, and he fell to the ground dead. By then, King Eirek had killed Nordri. The Tartars panicked and fled, each man running as fast as he could. King Eirek and his men pursued the fleeing army and killed everyone they caught. They won a great booty of gold and silver, weapons, clothes and other costly treasures.

Hrolf didn't want to chase the fleeing army. He caught a horse for himself and jumped on its back and rode out into the forest to Vilhjalm and told him how it had gone. Hrolf asked him to take the horse and his weapons—"act bravely, and hurry now to the wedding."

Vilhjalm said, "We've done well, and my wit and wisdom are priceless, considering how much I've been able to bring about. I'll become a famous man."

Hrolf smiled at his words and said that he didn't think he was doing many good deeds to win fame.

Vilhjalm mounted the horse and rode to the king's sister Gyda in full armor, and told her a great deal about his courage and brave deeds. King Eirek had come home by then and had gone to drink in his hall. Vilhjalm came before the king and greeted him and said, "The day was almost lost for you, my lord, before I helped you. You don't need to guess who I am or what I could do, because I'm no weakling."

The king said, "I think, Vilhjalm, that the weapons and the armor were yours, but the hands were Hrolf's."

Hrolf said, "I think that I'd be quite willing to marry your sister and be able to claim Vilhjalm's brave deeds by right. But it would be petty of me to falsely claim honors which I didn't achieve and which I'm not entitled to."

Vilhjalm said, "My lord, the men must find it unbelievable when they hear that you're willing to sling mud at my fame and achievements. Or do you think it would do you more honor for a peasant born and bred, like Hrolf, to achieve them and marry your sister? For he must seem unlikely to be a ruler fit to govern a people or accomplish great deeds. But I am a jarl by rank, the son of a jarl and of royal blood in my own right, handsome in appearance and the most stout-hearted man, and excelling in all matters pertaining to noble men. Now if you don't want the betrothal or the wedding to go ahead as we agreed, I'll leave—and I'll spread word of your dishonor to every land, that you have acted shamefully towards me and broken your word and trust. It was said in my land that any princess would be fully honored by marriage to me."

King Eirek said, "It shall not be said that I've acted shamefully to you, and I will hold to all my agreements. But I wonder why Hrolf is constantly on my mind when I think about the way you two have behaved, because I don't think that's part of your arrangement."

They ended their conversation, and the king had the wedding celebrations prepared, and a splendid feast was laid on. Vilhjalm came to the feast to marry King Eirek's sister Gyda, and she had no objections. Vilhjalm got many men to serve him, and he bragged about himself a great deal.

CHAPTER XIX

Early one morning, Hrolf went into the bower where Vilhjalm was sleeping. He went up to the bed and said, "Now, Vilhjalm, it's come to this: you've become the king's son-in-law, and I have served you all this time. I now declare to you that my servitude is over and our agreement is completely dissolved. You may well say that you're pleased that we're parting in this way. I value my valor more than your foppishness."

Hrolf left at once, and Vilhjalm was quite vexed. Gyda asked why Hrolf had left so quickly, and why he had brought such a message.

Vilhjalm said, "That's his nature; he never wants to stay in the same place more than a month or two, if it's up to him. I've held him here for a long time by fear. It would be difficult for anyone who had him as a servant to be worse off, because he's a bad man in every way. He's a thief and a villain, but I don't know whether I care to have him killed here, in a strange land. Yet he will quickly reveal what sort of man he is, and he will poorly repay those who treat him best."

They ended their conversation. The feasting continued.

It's said that the men who escaped from Soti's host sailed home to Tartary, having suffered heavy losses. King Menelaus had thought that their expedition would end badly, and that's how it turned out.

Early in the spring, Sorkvir and Brynjolf came from Jotunheim, bringing King Eirek many rare treasures. They and Grim had fought many battles and always won victories. Hrolf stayed in the king's household, and there was coldness between him and Sorkvir, Brynjolf and Vilhjalm. But Hrolf was in favor with his benchmates, because he was always giving money away with both hands, but he'd done good to no one while he was serving Vilhjalm.

This was now the third winter that the princess had to find a man to joust against Sorkvir. King Eirek thought about it, and felt that the princess wouldn't find anyone.

CHAPTER XX

A little while later, the princess's messengers came to King Eirek, informing him that she requested that he summon a huge assembly. At that assembly she would choose a man to joust against Sorkvir—but if she couldn't get anyone who was willing, she would be engaged to the king, according to the previous stipulation and settlement between them. The king was greatly cheered by their message, and felt that the maiden was within his grasp. He summoned an assembly and invited a mob and a multitude to come from the towns and castles and nearby districts. The princess herself also summoned the best and most valiant men from her kingdom. And many people came there without an invitation, because many were curious as to how it would turn out. All the people of the land were heartsick for her.

The assembly was held a short distance from Princess Ingigerd's castle. King Eirek came to the assembly with a great throng. Sorkvir and Brynjolf were there with him, along with Vilhjalm his son-in-law, and they all boasted a great deal. Hrolf also traveled there, and he brought the spear Hreggvid's Gift with him. He seemed of no account. A vast multitude assembled. This is how they were arranged at the assembly: ranks of men were arranged in circles, with an aisle connecting them. Vilhjalm sat nearest to the king, with Sorkvir and Brynjolf next to him, and the other distinguished men seated themselves. Hrolf sat in the outermost circle and lay low.

Once the men were arranged, Princess Ingigerd entered the assembly, so fair and delightful that it was impossible to exaggerate her loveliness. All the men turned to watch her, except Hrolf; he didn't look at her and pulled his hood down over his face. The princess came before each man and looked into his eyes. She went around the second circle, and then the next one out. In the end, she came to where Hrolf sat, and gripped his hand, but he stayed where he was. She lifted up his hood and said, "There's not a good choice of men here, but I choose this man to joust on my behalf against Sorkvir, and this man shall wed me if he wishes."

Hrolf said, "You've made a completely stupid choice, because I don't know how to ride a horse by myself without falling down. Also, I get scared when people frown at me."

The princess said, "I've never seen you before—yet you shall not leave, if I have any say in the matter."

King Eirek said, "Young lady, I think you must choose a man from this country, not from other kingdoms. Hrolf is Vilhjalm's servant and my man. He should be released from this."

Hrolf said, "In this land, I am no man's servant. And I shall certainly grant the princess the first favor that she asks for, if she thinks she'll be any more free afterwards than before."

Hrolf stood up and went with the princess and all her men into her castle. She seated Hrolf in the high seat and offered him all honor and good cheer. King Eirek left the assembly and went to another castle, and he was very unhappy. Most people were astounded that the princess would choose this man, the likeliest to be defeated. The king deeply regretted making the agreement with the princess, and he ordered Sorkvir to put forth all his effort and not hold back any of the tricks up his sleeve. "This man has always weighed on my mind. Now you must guard the armor Hreggvid's Gift carefully, so that it can't harm us."

Hrolf stayed in the castle beside the princess and was given a warm welcome. He told her about his mission on behalf of the jarl, but she said that she already knew that. "So I have decided that I will escape from here with you. I believe you're the one who most deserves to enjoy me, if you can free me from the power of my enemies." That said, they parted.

In the morning, Hrolf got up early and put on the armor Hreggvid's Gift, and girded himself with the good sword. The princess fetched him the lance and shield that her father had owned. She asked him to go and take the stallion Dulcifal. He had been driven into a strong stockade with many horses; he bit and kicked and killed many of them. Hrolf went to the stockade and struck the lance on the shield. Dulcifal came to Hrolf, and the lance and shield rang out so loudly that all the bystanders were astonished. Hrolf saddled the horse and nimbly leaped up in full armor. Dulcifal sprang from his place and leaped over the fences without ever touching them, and then charged forth onto the field.

Sorkvir had also come to the jousting field, and the king with him, together with Vilhjalm and Brynjolf and a huge rabble.

CHAPTER XXI

Now each man couched his lance and rode at the other as fast as the horses could run. Each man stabbed at the other with great force. Sorkvir's spear hit Hrolf's shield and glanced off, but Hrolf knocked Sorkvir's helmet off. At that moment, Sorkvir had only ridden a third as far as Hrolf had. Dulcifal didn't want to hold still and turned back around, and Sorkvir hadn't ridden a fourth of the way before they met. Each stabbed at the other again, and it went as before: Sorkvir didn't accomplish anything and lost his shield. Then they rode at each other a third time. Dulcifal ran as fast as a bird flies until they met. Hrolf stabbed at Sorkvir so that the lance stuck in his mailcoat, and he lifted him out of the saddle. He galloped over the field with him until he flung him down headlong into a stinking cesspit, so that Sorkvir's neck broke. Then Dulcifal stood as still as if he had sunk down into the earth. The princess and all the people of her land were overjoyed.

When King Eirek saw that, he flew into a rage and ordered all his men to surround Hrolf and kill him as quickly as possible. He swore that Hrolf would do worse deeds later if he were to get free now. They did as the king commanded and attacked Hrolf on all sides. But when Dulcifal saw that, he reared up on his hind legs and kicked with his forelegs and bit with his teeth, bringing death to many men. His eyes were as red as blood clots, and it seemed if fire were blazing from his nose and mouth, and he charged so fast that he trampled men underfoot. Hrolf stayed on his back and didn't sit quietly. He put the sword Hreggvid's Gift to the test, striking and stabbing men and horses alike, left and right. There was certain death for everyone who faced him. Now everyone fled. Hrolf rode towards where the king had been, but he had run away. Hrolf killed more than a hundred men before he escaped into the forest, and he was weary but not wounded. King Eirek thought that he had suffered severe losses. He went home to his own castle that evening, quite dejected.

That same evening, the princess celebrated with her men, and rewarded them freely. She got all her chambermaids so drunk that they fell asleep, but when the night was almost through, Hrolf came to the castle and found the princess and told her to get ready to go with him. She said that she wasn't unprepared. Hrolf had brought two large chests with him, and the princess's treasures went inside. Then they mounted Dulcifal and rode on their way. It isn't said where they went or how long they were on the road, but they traveled for longer than a night and a day.

CHAPTER XXII

Now there is to say about King Eirek: he awoke in the morning and ordered his men to arm themselves and search for Hrolf. This was done, and they searched for three days, but didn't find him. Then the king had the princess's castle searched, but she had disappeared, so that no one knew what had become of her. All this together filled the king with terrible dread, and he was very angry. He said to Vilhjalm, "I see that you have lied to me about everything, both about yourself and about Hrolf. Now I understand that he is quite the opposite of what you have said. I see that Hrolf entered the mound, not you. He got the good suit of armor, but I got the useless one. I could tell that he was a mighty man, but you're a swindler who's accomplished nothing, a coward in every nerve. You knew everything he was planning and didn't dare tell me. I think you're some thrall-spawned peasant along with all your ancestors, not the owner of a kingdom or anything else of quality. You're fit for me to have hanged from a gallows for the fraud and deceit that you have played me and my sister. That death awaits you, though it won't happen just yet."

At these words from the king, Vilhjalm became very angry, and he said, "Even so, I shall soon reveal what sort of man I am. I stand on this stump and swear this oath:[46] that I shall not get into bed with your sister Gyda before I have taken Hrolf's life and brought you his head and that girl's. I shall make use of no man's strength or aid in this."

Vilhjalm took his weapons and horse and rode after Hrolf as fast as he could. King Eirek stayed behind in Russia, and he felt that matters were going badly.

CHAPTER XXIII

Now the saga returns to Denmark, to Jarl Thorgnyr and his men. That same autumn when Hrolf went to Russia, the jarl traveled through his kingdom holding feasts, as was his custom.

One day, a stranger came before the jarl and gave his name as Mondul, son of Patti.[47] He said that he had traveled far and wide in distant lands, and claimed that he could tell of many things and had done many great deeds. He was short in stature and very broad-shouldered, handsome in appearance, but quite wall-eyed. The jarl welcomed this man and invited him to live with him, and he accepted. He frequently entertained the jarl and spoke cleverly of many things. In the end, the jarl took him into such confidence that he called on him in every situation. Mondul was always conversing with him, night and day, so that the jarl neglected the governance of his own kingdom.

On one occasion, as often before, Bjorn the Counsellor came before Jarl Thorgnyr, and he rebuked him for having made a complete stranger his trusted adviser. He said that rumors that the jarl was neglecting his kingdom because of him were getting out of hand. The jarl grew angry at Bjorn's words and said that he would do as he thought best, whatever Bjorn said. Mondul heard Bjorn's words and didn't react to them. Bjorn spoke many truthful words, and then went away.

Bjorn had a house in the fortress near the jarl's residence, with another estate outside the fort, as was said earlier. One day, Mondul came to Bjorn's residence when he was not at home, and neither was anyone else, except for his wife Ingibjorg. He flirted with her cheerfully, and she took it well. He tried to seduce her with many fair words and offered her many fine treasures, but he spoke ill of Bjorn with every word, saying that he wasn't a real man. Ingibjorg became very angry at this and answered him scornfully, saying that she would never go with him. Mondul took a tankard out from under his overcoat and asked her to drink a peace-draught with him, but she struck the tankard from below with her hand, knocking it up into his face. This made him angry, and he said, "You and your husband Bjorn won't see the last of me until I have paid you back as you deserve for the dishonor that you have done me with both words and deeds."

Then he left and came before Jarl Thorgnyr and said, "My lord, I would like for you to be so kind as to accept a certain belt from me, which I inherited from my father." He laid it on the table before the jarl. It was wrought with gold and set with gemstones. The jarl thought that he had never seen a better treasure. The jarl thanked him and said that he had never received such a gift from a commoner. Mondul spent the winter there, still as a dear friend. Stefnir and Bjorn were rarely with him. The jarl took great care of the belt and always showed it to his friends when he held a feast.

Bjorn's wife Ingibjorg caught a strange illness over the winter. She turned blue-black all over, like a corpse, and she paid no attention to anything, as if she had lost her mind. This caused Bjorn great distress, because he loved her very much.

In the spring, at a certain feast, the belt that Mondul had given the jarl disappeared. It was searched for, far and wide, and not found. The jarl felt that this was a severe blow, and he had a wide region searched, but it wasn't found. The jarl asked Mondul what he thought had happened, and how they should search.

Mondul said, "It's hard for me to name the man who has taken it, though I think I can guess pretty closely. It's most likely that the one who has taken the belt has stolen more from you than just this. A powerful man must have done it, one who has always held a grudge against your honor. I advise you to search for the belt when everyone least expects it, and let no one avoid it, not even a prominent man. The man who has taken it will not let his treasure chest be opened of his own free will. Whoever has done this may justly hang on a gallows."

The jarl felt that this was good advice, and he said that it should be so. He summoned all his retainers and told them that he wanted to search every man's treasure-chest, his son Stefnir's first and then Bjorn's, so that the other men might be more content with it. They said that they were prepared. Stefnir showed his treasure-chests first, and the belt wasn't found. Then Bjorn's were searched, as well as the chests of everyone who lived in the fortress, and they couldn't find it.

Mondul said, "Bjorn must have more chests than those here. They haven't been searched."

Stefnir said, "Bjorn has lodgings outside the fortress, but I don't believe we should search there."

The jarl said that they had to go there, and so they did. Bjorn let the search proceed as before. Mondul came to an old chest and asked what was in it. Bjorn said that it was old ship's nails. The jarl ordered it to be opened. Bjorn searched for the key but couldn't find it. The jarl went over to the chest, broke it up and took out the contents—and at the very bottom, there lay the belt. Everyone was astonished at this, and Bjorn most of all, because he knew that he was innocent. The jarl was furious, and he ordered Bjorn to be seized. He said, "I shall hang you on the highest gallows as soon as morning comes, because you must have done this beforehand, though it's only now come to light."

Bjorn was captured and tied up tightly, because no one dared to speak for him, even though he didn't appear to deserve it. Bjorn asked to be tried by ordeal, as was the custom of the land, but the jarl wouldn't hear of it. Stefnir got his father to let him live for seven nights, in case anything should be found that might help him—but he had to be in Mondul's custody and not go home to his fortress. Many were grieved at this, because Bjorn had many friends. The jarl went home to his estate with his men, and they sat down to drinking. But as soon as the household had tasted the first dish and drunk the first cup, all of their friendship with Bjorn disappeared, and they all felt that the jarl had a just case.[48]

Mondul now stayed at Bjorn's estate and drove all his retainers away. He took Ingibjorg and lay in bed next to her every night, right before Bjorn's eyes. She had all her pleasure with him, and none with her husband Bjorn. Bjorn felt that things were going wretchedly, and these seven nights passed in the same way that we have told of.

The story now returns to where it had left off, because two events cannot be told of at once, even if both happened at the same time.

CHAPTER XXIV

Now it is time to tell of how, as Hrolf and the princess were leaving Russia, they saw a man riding after them one day. He was wearing linen underwear and was girded with a sword. He came after them quickly. Hrolf recognized that it was Vilhjalm. As soon as Vilhjalm saw Hrolf, he fell at his feet and begged for mercy for himself in many ways. "I've had hard times since we parted," said Vilhjalm, "because the king kept me in a dark room and wanted to have me killed. I was frozen and starving, but I figured out how to escape. And I am now at your mercy, my dear Hrolf, whatever you wish to do with me. I never wanted to do anything to displease you, and I want to be faithful and true to you every day from now on, if you will let me live and return to Denmark with you."

Hrolf was moved by Vilhjalm's tale of woe, and he said that he didn't have the heart to kill him, although he deserved it. The princess said that this was a bad idea, "because he has an evil look about him, and he will prove to be evil."

Vilhjalm now traveled with them and made himself very obliging—but it was always dangerous for him to come close to Dulcifal, because he bit and kicked at Vilhjalm if he came within reach.

They traveled until they were only one day's journey from Jarl Thorgnyr. They took shelter for the night in some woods and raised a brush shelter that evening. Hrolf and the princess had lain together every night, with a naked sword between them.[49] Vilhjalm stuck Hrolf with a sleep-thorn[50] that night. In the morning he got up early and took Dulcifal and saddled him, and Dulcifal would accept only this from Vilhjalm. Hrolf was lying in his armor, with the cloak Vefreyja's Gift on the outside. Ingigerd stood up. She pounded on Hrolf and couldn't manage to wake him, try as she might. She went out of the shelter and wept. Vilhjalm saw that and asked whether she might not be pleased with Hrolf in bed. She said, "I'm quite pleased with him, but he's sleeping so soundly that I can't manage to wake him."

"Then I'll wake him," said Vilhjalm.

He tore down the shelters, and then he chopped both of Hrolf's feet off and slipped them into his clothes. Hrolf kept on sleeping. The princess asked what had just broken. "Hrolf's lifespan," said Vilhjalm.

The princess said, "May you have the worst life of anyone. That was the vilest deed ever done. You must expect evil from evil."

Vilhjalm said, "You have two options: pick whichever one you prefer. One is for you to come with me to Jarl Thorgnyr and assent to what I say, because I think there'd be little honor for me in going back to Russia. The other is for me to kill you where you're standing."

She decided not to choose death while she had the option to live, but she felt that Vilhjalm was capable of any evil. She said that she would go with him and not speak out against what he said, as long as he didn't dishonor her with his words. She had to swear to this with an oath.

Vilhjalm wanted to take Dulcifal, but it wasn't possible, because he bit and kicked in all directions so that Vilhjalm could never get near him, and he couldn't get at Hrolf because of the horse. He couldn't travel with Hrolf's sword because of its weight. Hrolf was left behind, and they went on their way. The princess found it a heavy burden to leave, and a terrible thing to part with Hrolf in such a bad way.

There's nothing to say about their journey until they came to Jarl Thorgnyr. He came out to meet the princess with all honor and good cheer. He asked what sort of man Vilhjalm might be. Vilhjalm answered, "I am a farmer's son of good family here in Denmark, and I went on the journey with Hrolf when he went to Russia. We've accomplished many deeds. In the end, he beat King Eirek's champion Sorkvir and killed him. The king wouldn't stand for that, and he had Hrolf captured and killed. Here are his feet, which I've brought with me to show you. Then I took the princess and brought her here. I have placed myself in many mortal perils out of obligation to you, as did Hrolf and I together. And no one was bolder than he, because he never surrendered until he lost both feet. I believe it's time for me to marry your daughter Thora. It's no disgrace for you to have me as your son-in-law, on account of my lineage and prowess. There's no need to delay, now that both weddings can be held together."

Most people found Vilhjalm's story plausible. They all mourned the death of Hrolf, the jarl and his son Stefnir most of all. Ingigerd wept bitterly. The jarl comforted her and asked whether Vilhjalm had told him the truth. She said, "Vilhjalm will no more lie to you than to anyone else. But I want to ask you to delay the weddings for a month. Many things may happen that you would think impossible."

Thora was vexed, and she looked at Vilhjalm and asked for the same thing. When Vilhjalm heard that, he began babbling, "Whatever they say, don't let the weddings be delayed, for it's not worth paying attention to a woman's moods."

Stefnir said, "It's well established that the princess should decide this, and it's not a long wait."

Vilhjalm said, "You're not speaking as a ruler should, letting women decide their own intentions for themselves or their sons, if they make even worse decisions."

Stefnir was angered at his words and said that the women would decide, not Vilhjalm—"or else you'll have to kill me."

Vilhjalm said that it would be no great loss if he were killed. The jarl ordered them both not to argue, "yet Stefnir must decide this, since he has the right. But you, Vilhjalm, will be betrothed to my daughter, because you have earned it."

Stefnir took Ingigerd by the hand and led her to his sister's bower, locked her in, and hid the key himself. People say that Princess Ingigerd had cared for the feet and laid herbs beside them, so that they wouldn't die.[51] Vilhjalm hated Stefnir, but he had to let matters stand.

CHAPTER XXV

Now we must tell about Hrolf. He lay as if dead until the evening, because the sleep-thorn was stuck in his head. Vilhjalm hadn't taken it out. Dulcifal stood over him, saddled and bridled, until he walked up to Hrolf and rolled him around the field with his head, and that's when the sleep-thorn fell out. That woke Hrolf up, and he discovered that both his feet were gone, his shelter had been torn down, and Vilhjalm had left with the princess. The sword Hreggvid's Gift was lying there. Hrolf felt that matters had taken a terrible turn, but he roused himself and took the life-stone and scraped it over his stumps. That quickly took the burning out of the wounds. Hrolf dragged himself towards the horse, who lay down. Hrolf managed to roll himself into the saddle, and then Dulcifal stood up.

Hrolf rode until he came to the estate of his friend Bjorn, for he didn't want to ride to the fortress, and it seemed a long way to his own castle. Dulcifal lay down as soon as he came into the yard; Hrolf took off his bridle and dragged himself into the house, which he found quite opulent. Hrolf entered the kitchen and threw himself down on a seat in the shadows, and lay there for a while. Then he saw a woman walking and tending the fire. This woman appeared to be dark blue, as were her clothes, and severely swollen.[52] She poked up the fire.

A little later, a man came in, wearing a scarlet outfit and a gold band around his forehead. He was short and stout. He was leading a man behind him who was tied hand and foot. Hrolf recognized his friend Bjorn, who seemed to have been harshly treated. The man laid Bjorn down and sat down by the fire. He seated the woman next to him and kissed her.[53]

Bjorn said, "You do evil, Mondul, seducing my wife and slandering me to the jarl so badly that he will have me hanged three nights from now, without cause. This would not have happened if Sturlaug's son Hrolf had been in the land. He will avenge me, if he's fated to return."

Mondul answered, "From now on, he will never help you nor avenge you. I can tell you this much about him: both his feet are gone, and he's barely alive. He will never come back alive."

Hrolf forced himself up into the seat by his stumps and grabbed Mondul by the neck with both hands and said, "You'll find out that Hrolf's hands are still alive, even though his feet are missing." He pressed Mondul down under himself until he was gasping and gurgling.

Then Mondul said, "Be so kind as not to kill me, Hrolf. I shall make you whole, because I have these ointments, unlike any in the Northlands. I have such healing skill that within three nights, I can make anyone who's dying completely healthy. I will reveal to you that I am a dwarf, living in the earth, and I have natural dwarvish skill in healing and craftsmanship.[54] I came here because I intended to bewitch the jarl's daughter Thora, or Ingibjorg, and carry her off with me. But because Bjorn most clearly saw what I was, I wanted to overcome him. I took the belt and slipped it into his chest, but I took the key away so that it would seem more likely that he had stolen it, since he was unwilling to open the chest. I have turned every man's friendship against Bjorn. Now to save my life, I will gladly do anything you ask, because I will never betray the man who spares my life."

Hrolf said, "I'll take a chance on sparing your life, but first you must heal Ingibjorg and free Bjorn." He let Mondul stand up, and Mondul was swarthy and ugly, according to his true shape. He released Bjorn, and he got Ingibjorg out of her clothes and smeared her skin with fine ointments and gave her a memory-draught to drink. She quickly recovered her senses, her skin turned fair, and she regained her health—and she lost all love for the dwarf. She and Bjorn thanked Hrolf, as was fitting.

After that, Mondul left and returned only a moment later with Hrolf's feet and a large medicine box full of ointment. He said, "Now I must heal you, Hrolf—which I had never intended to do. You must lie down by the fire and warm the stumps." Hrolf did so. Then the dwarf smeared ointments on the wounds and fitted the feet to them and splinted them. He had Hrolf lie there for three nights, and then he untied the bandages and told Hrolf to stand up and test his legs. Hrolf did so. His feet were as painless and soft-skinned as if he had never been wounded.

Now although people find such accounts unreliable, still, everyone has to tell what he has seen and heard. It's difficult to contradict what the wise men of old have put together. They could well have said that it had happened in another way, had they wanted to. And there have been some sages who have very often spoken figuratively about some matters, such as Master Galterus in the saga of Alexander,[55] or the poet Homer in the saga of the Trojans, and the masters who have come after them have taken these things to be true, rather than denying that such things could be. There's no need to put any more faith in this story. All the same, may everyone enjoy it as long as he's listening.

Hrolf said to Mondul, "Now you've done well by healing me. You'll get some things that you ask for, if you stay with me. I'll ask you to come with me to Russia, if I go back there."

Mondul said that he would—"but now I must go home to my family. I've taken our dealings hard, and it's hardest for me to part with Ingibjorg. Still, that's how it has to be now."

Mondul the dwarf left, leaving matters as they stood, and Hrolf didn't know what became of him.

CHAPTER XXVI

The next morning, Hrolf stood up and armed himself. He said to Bjorn, "Now the two of us must go to the fortress and stand before the jarl."

Bjorn said, "I'm not willing to do this, because the agreed term for the truce has expired now, and it's certain death for me if I go there."

Hrolf said, "You have to risk it."

They went to the fortress and entered the hall, seating themselves on the edge. The jarl sat at his feasting-table and didn't recognize Hrolf and didn't see that he had entered. But as soon as the jarl's men saw Bjorn, they all shouted at him, "That thief Bjorn is a rash man to come before the jarl's eyes. Mondul hasn't watched him carefully, if he's broken free."

One man picked up a large ox bone and flung it at Bjorn, but Hrolf snatched it out of the air and sent it back at the one who threw it. The bone struck him in the chest and pierced him through and stuck fast in the timber wall. Everyone was dumbstruck, and terrified of the huge man who had come in.[56]

Hrolf said to Bjorn, "Go before Stefnir's seat and say this: 'Hrolf son of Sturlaug would invite you in, if he were here and you came to him.'"

Bjorn crept into the hall, for he was very frightened—until he came before Stefnir. Then he spoke the words that Hrolf had asked him to. When Stefnir heard his words, he jumped over the table and ran out to Hrolf and raised the hood of the cloak that was covering Hrolf's face. He recognized Hrolf and welcomed him heartily and brought him before his father. The jarl was happy at Hrolf's arrival and stood up to greet him in great happiness.

Vilhjalm couldn't bear to look when he saw Hrolf. Fear made his face change back and forth, from red to pale as birchbark.

Jarl Thorgnyr said, "I do believe that Hrolf is here, Vilhjalm, not dead."

Hrolf asked if Vilhjalm was there.

Vilhjalm said, "Here I am, my dear Hrolf, and all my affairs are in your power."

Hrolf said, "You didn't part with me as a friend, Vilhjalm. You must have been scheming evil in your heart for a long time, but it's all come out now. Now I wish that you'd tell your life story, even if it's no good, because your life must have been a dishonorable one up to now."

"I shall do as you wish, my dear Hrolf, because that will be most helpful," said Vilhjalm.

CHAPTER XXVII

"The beginning of my story is that my father lived by a forest, here in Denmark. His name was Ulf. He had a wife and eight children, and I was the oldest one. My father had many goats that were very unruly. It was my job to herd them, and I did every task that came to hand, but I didn't get fed much, and I was poorly dressed. When I didn't bring any of the goats home, I was whipped. I hated that more and more, until the night I came home and set fire to the buildings and burned my family inside. I lived at that farm for a long time, until I was fully grown.

"One night I dreamed that a huge man came to me. He gave his name as Grim. He said that I was a very promising man, and that an excellent marriage was in store for me if I could attain it. He said that he wanted to make a deal with me. I asked what sort of deal that would be. He said, 'I will give you more strength than you've ever had, along with weapons and fine clothes and many other things. You are to go and find Hrolf Sturlaugsson and betray him if you can, because he has gone on a journey, intending to come to Russia and take the princess away. He will cause much harm if he is not put to death. Your luck may end up making you King Eirek's son-in-law, but Hrolf may get his death.' I agreed to this. He took a horn from under his mantle and gave me a drink, and I felt strength surging within me. Having made that agreement, we parted, and when I awoke, both weapons and clothes were lying there. I traveled until I met my kinsman Olvir. Everything that happened after that was my idea, because I realized that you would keep your oath and I would have the chance to kill you when I wanted, once you'd accomplished those brave deeds for me. I now realize that it must have been Grim Aegir who appeared to me. I left Russia and came after you because I was afraid that he would take terrible vengeance on me if I didn't do what I'd promised. Now I'd meant to take Thora as my wife, and that's why I brought Ingigerd here, not to Russia. I'd never been free from anxiety there, if the truth be told about my state of mind, and I'd meant to kill Stefnir and then the jarl and take Ingigerd as my wife and rule the kingdom alone from then on. I would have severed your head from your shoulders in the forest, my dear Hrolf, if I hadn't been afraid of Dulcifal. And now my life story is over. Now, my dear Hrolf, I do hope that you'll spare my life, even though I'm not worthy, because the fact that I wanted to win the honors that were offered, along with such a marriage and a great kingdom, is rather excusable."

After that, Vilhjalm fell silent. Everyone who heard this story thought that he was the worst of traitors.

Then Hrolf began his story, starting with how he left his home in Denmark, and then with what happened afterwards. The people felt that he had great worth because of his boldness and brave deeds, and it seemed that the dwarf had been sent to him as a stroke of luck.

Bjorn now took back the rank and honors that he had formerly held. Vilhjalm was arrested, and a great assembly was summoned to judge him. They debated which manner of death was most fitting for him.[57] All agreed that he should die the most dreadful death. A gag was set in his jaws and he was hanged from the highest gallows. Vilhjalm lost his life in the way that we have told, and it was to be expected that a bad man would come to a bad end, since he was such a deceiver and murderer.

Princess Ingigerd was glad that Hrolf had returned and that he had been healed. The jarl talked with her and said that there was no need to wait for the wedding any longer. She said, "You should know, lord, that my father King Hreggvid hasn't been avenged. Besides, I will not enter any man's bed until this is done: King Eirek must be killed, along with Grim Aegir and all the men who have done us the most harm. I also do not want the men of Russia to serve under any other leader than the man whom I shall marry."

Hrolf said, "Since I brought the princess out of Russia, and she wanted wholeheartedly to go with me, then she may not be compelled by any man, if I have anything to say about it. But I will ask you, my lord, to let me go to Russia with our forces and accomplish there such deeds as I may do."

The jarl said, "I want to thank you, Hrolf, for the good will that you have shown me, in this matter and in all your service. Now I am eager for you and Stefnir to lead this expedition. I shall make ready for you all the forces of ships and men that I can muster for this expedition, because I want you to bring about such vengeance as pleases the princess. And the wedding shall not take place before you come back, if it's fated to happen."

The princess said that this pleased her well, and this agreement between them was fixed. Hrolf's men had waited for him in the castle while he was away, and they were glad to see him return home.

CHAPTER XXVIII

Now Jarl Thorgnyr had ships and weapons prepared throughout the summer, for as far as his kingdom extended. His kinsmen and allies sent him large forces from Sweden and Frisia, and he also got much aid from Normandy. Great preparations were made in Jutland for this expedition, and when the host was all assembled, it was a splendid host and well equipped. They had a hundred ships, most of them large. Hrolf and Stefnir were in command of this force. They spent several days waiting for a favorable wind.

One day, a man came up to board Hrolf's ship. He was short and stout and carried a large bag on his shoulders. He walked up the gangplank onto the ship. Hrolf recognized him: it was Mondul the dwarf who had arrived. Hrolf welcomed him warmly. Mondul put down his bag and said, "I've come here as you asked, Hrolf, and I will go with you if you want, on the condition that I have command over every plan that I make, and that no one will deviate from my plans. Yet it will all be necessary if it's to turn out well."

Hrolf replied, saying that they would all take his advice, and that he wanted very much to accept him into his following.

The dwarf said, "My first condition is that you, Hrolf, must be on the ship that leads the entire fleet, because you have the gold ring given to you by the elf-queen. You can't get lost. We must tie all our ships together, each one to the prow of the next. I shall be in the ship that goes last. We must not cast off before the sails are raised on all the ships, and if any ship breaks away from the fleet, then no one shall sail after it. You must steer straight ahead and not veer off, no matter what noises you hear or what sights you may see, and that will be a great help to us. We must never land, or delay for any reason, until we reach Russia. We must hoist sails now, because there will be no shortage of wind."

Everything was done as Mondul had said. Jarl Thorgnyr wished them well, and so did Ingigerd. Bjorn the Counsellor stayed behind with the jarl to keep watch over the kingdom.

Now a favorable wind blew, and Hrolf and his men sailed out to sea. Their journey started out comfortably, but they noticed that there must be different weather high in the sky. The sea was topsy-turvy all around them, and great rumblings were heard from above. Mondul sat at the tiller of the last ship. He took a large stick and bound it with a black thread and dragged it behind the ship, in the wake.

One night, a warship was seen advancing against Hrolf and pressing a fierce attack at him. Mondul called out and said that no one should pay it any attention, but the sailors said that he was so terrified that he didn't dare to defend Hrolf's forces. They released one ship from the fleet and wanted it to sail against the other ship, but they had no chance, because the wind turned against the ship and drove it behind all the others. The last Hrolf saw of them was a huge walrus attacking the ship and capsizing it, and every mother's son there was lost. The others were completely astonished, and men felt that their conflict wasn't an even fight. They lost twenty ships in all before they reached Russia.

They anchored in the Don River and raided both banks, burning farms and plundering the livestock they caught. Many people went over to their side, and this way they got a multitude of men. They soon found out where King Eirik was with his host of men. Then they laid their ships up in an anchorage. Mondul took a boat and rowed around all the ships in a ring. Then he landed and told the men to pitch their tents against a nearby cliff; "every tent must butt against the end of another." When this was done, he untied his bag and took out a black silk tent. He spread the tent over all the other tents, so broadly and firmly that no holes were ever found.

They had entered Russia before Winternights.[58] Mondul the dwarf said, "You must carry our stores from the ships into the tent, and finish the job in three days. Then you must go into the tent and not look outside before I tell you to." Everything was done according to his instructions. Finally, Mondul went inside, but before he did that, he walked all around the tent.

A little later they heard the wind beginning to rise, roaring outside the tent. They felt it was a wonder. One man was so curious that he loosened the tent and looked outside, but when he came back in, he had lost his mind and his speech, and in a short time he was dead. The wind kept up for three nights.

Mondul said, "We won't all come back to Denmark if Grim Aegir has anything to say about it, because he was the walrus that destroyed our ships.[59] He would have treated all our ships the same way if I had not gone last, because he couldn't come any closer than that stick which I was dragging behind me. He's sent an ice storm at you, so that all of you would have met your deaths if the tents hadn't saved you. Now twelve men have come down into the forest a short way from here, whom Grim has sent to King Eirek. They have come down from Ermland and are now working sorcery.[60] They must be intending to use sorcery against you, Hrolf and Stefnir, to make you kill each other yourselves. Seven of us must go out to face them together and see what happens."

They set out until they entered the forest, where they saw a single house. They could hear evil howls as the men worked their sorcery. They went into the house and saw a high platform there, held up by four pillars.[61] Mondul went underneath the platform and carved counterspells on the pillars, with a charm to trap the sorcerers themselves. They went right out into the forest and stayed there for a while. But the sorcerers were affected so powerfully that they smashed the platform down and charged out of the house shrieking, each in a different direction. Some leaped into swamps or the sea, and some over crags and cliffs, and all of them killed themselves in this fashion.[62]

Hrolf's men went right back to their ships, which were in good shape. They saw that the storm had reached no farther than a circle around the ships and tents.

Mondul said, "Hrolf, it's come to this. I won't go into battle, because I don't have the valor or bravery. But you'd be short of men if you had seen to this alone. You and Stefnir were meant to die as those sorcerers died, as you see now."

They thanked him for his stratagems, and prepared themselves to land.

CHAPTER XXIX

Soon after Hrolf and his men left Jutland and traveled to Russia, Tryggvi the berserk, whom we mentioned earlier in this saga, invaded the country. His great multitude of men gave him an overwhelming force. Since fleeing from Hrolf and Stefnir, he had most often been in Scotland and England, but now he had heard that they were out of the country and there would be little resistance.

As soon as Jarl Thorgnyr heard the news of war, he summoned his forces, but since Tryggvi had come quite unexpectedly, and also since all the best men were out of the country, the jarl got a small force against such a huge host. The two sides met a short distance from the fort, where the fiercest battle broke out at once. Both sides advanced boldly. Jarl Thorgnyr had his banner borne forward bravely and advanced beside it himself. He fought most bravely, killing many men. Bjorn the Counsellor followed him manfully and killed many men, because they were accustomed to warlike deeds and eager to advance. Tryggvi also came on fiercely, charging right through the jarl's ranks so that no one withstood him, and the battle turned against the jarl's men. The battle lasted all day. In the end Jarl Thorgnyr fell, winning great glory, and Tryggvi killed him. Bjorn the Counsellor fled to the fort with the survivors, where they held their position. But Tryggvi surrounded the fort.

Late that evening, men saw three ships sailing to land, all of them large and painted black on the sides. They laid up in an anchorage and set up awnings over their ships. By now the fort's defenders were sick at heart over their situation. But as soon as morning came, the men from the ships advanced towards the fort with their forces arrayed in ranks. Twelve men led them, and two of them had masks before their faces. Tryggvi also deployed his forces, and when they met, there weren't many greetings, because the masked men rushed into battle and attacked fiercely. When the fort's defenders saw that, they came out of the fort and attacked the enemy's left flank.[63] Tryggvi was penned in tightly, and many of his men fell. Men attacked Tryggvi fiercely, and in the end, he and the better part of his forces all fell. The defenders claimed much plunder. The masked men went straight to their ships without speaking with anyone else. The men of the land wondered what sort of men these might be that couldn't say anything.

Afterwards there was peace, and Jarl Thorgnyr was laid in a mound. Thorir keenly felt the death of his father, as did many other men of that land, for he had been a good and capable ruler and had governed the kingdom for a long time and kept it at peace. Everyone lamented his passing.

CHAPTER XXX

Now we pick up the story where we left off, telling how Hrolf summoned all his forces against King Eirek. They encountered each other a short distance from Ladoga. The king had a large force of stalwart men. Many were the great chieftains with King Eirek. One of them was a jarl named Imi. He was huge and strong and a great fighter, of Russian descent.

With him was his half-brother named Rondolf. He might well be called a troll on account of his size and strength. His mother's family came from Aluborg in Jotunheim, and there he had grown up. He had a club for a weapon, six ells long and very thick at the far end. Most iron couldn't cut the fur cloak that he wore. Rondolf went into a berserk rage and bellowed like a troll when he got angry. Brynjolf was with the king, but Thord and Grim hadn't arrived, because they had assembled their forces farther inland.

Both sides pitched their tents on a level plain, not far from the sea, and slept for the night. Early in the morning, they prepared for battle. The king arranged his forces on two wings, commanding one himself, with Brynjolf bearing the king's banner. In front of the banner the king set Rondolf and all the greatest champions. Jarl Imi commanded the other wing with more men of rank, although they aren't named. A man named Arnodd, a great champion, bore his banner.

Hrolf also arranged his forces on two wings. He placed himself opposite King Eirek, with the Swedes and Frisians under his command. Stefnir took the other wing with the Jutes. A man named Ali, the most valiant of men, bore his banner before him. Hrolf wore the mailcoat Hreggvid's Gift and rode Dulcifal. Both armies fielded huge forces of knights. Stefnir wore Hrolf's other cape. Mondul wasn't in the battle, because he wasn't used to bearing weapons.

Once both sides were drawn up, they screamed their battle cries, and the ranks closed together. At once there was hard fighting and terrible slaughter on both sides. Mounted knights made the first charge, but then there was a fierce battle with cuts and thrusts. Rondolf charged, striking right and left with the club and killing both men and horses. No knight was strong enough to endure one of his blows. Everyone retreated before him. Brynjolf bore the standard forward manfully, and there was unrest in Hrolf's army.

Hrolf rode forth on Dulcifal, and no one who faced him and his blows was strong enough to stay in the saddle. He struck both men and horses with the sword Hreggvid's Gift, and he killed many men, because the sword bit as if it were slashing through water and was never checked in its stroke. The battle was dreadful, with men falling one across the other.

Now we must tell how Stefnir charged forward into Jarl Imi's ranks, doing harm to many knights, until Jarl Imi came against him. Each rode at the other with great prowess, aiming at the other's shield. When they met, Imi's spear shaft broke in the middle, but Stefnir knocked the jarl backwards out of the saddle so that he landed far away, beneath the horses. He quickly sprang to his feet and drew his sword. Stefnir leaped from his horse's back and struck at Imi, but he brought up his sword to block the blow. Stefnir's sword struck Imi's spiked hilt and cut off his hand along with it. Then Stefnir ran him through with his sword, and thus the jarl lost his life. Stefnir charged ahead.

In another place, Ali and Arnodd encountered each other and attacked with great valor. They struck each other until all their armor was cut off. Both of them had thrown away their banners, and their encounter ended when Arnodd stabbed Ali in the belly with his sword, leaving it sticking out through his back. But Ali took the blow and struck a two-handed blow at Arnodd's head, leaving his sword sticking in his teeth. They both fell to the ground dead.

Now Hrolf saw the havoc that Rondolf had wreaked in his ranks, and he saw that this couldn't go on as it was. He leaped from Dulcifal's back and charged Rondolf. When they met, Rondolf swung his iron club at Hrolf, but he dodged it; he didn't believe he could withstand such a heavy blow. The club hit two men who had been standing right behind Hrolf and broke every bone in their bodies. Hrolf whipped his sword around at Rondolf's hand and cut it off at the wrist, and sliced off all the toes on his other foot. Rondolf brandished the cudgel with his other hand and swung at Hrolf with all his might. The club hit the ground and sank up to its middle, but Hrolf wasn't hurt. Hrolf cut off Rondolf's other hand so that it fell down. Rondolf turned and ran, waving his stumps and bellowing like a bull. At that moment, Hrolf sliced off both his buttocks so that they were left hanging from the backs of his knees.[64] Dragging a trail behind him, Rondolf charged howling into King Eirek's ranks so that everyone shrank away, and he killed many men.

Hrolf and Stefnir and their men made good use of this. They struck down and laid low every man who faced them. King Eirek's men fell in droves. Rondolf had no idea what was in front of him, and he charged Brynjolf, who fell on his back holding the banner. He staggered to his feet and ran away. But when King Eirek's men saw the banner fall, every one of them fled. And when Eirek saw that, he fled to the forts like the others. Hrolf and Stefnir pursued the fleeing host, killing everyone they caught. There was such a great slaughter that the dead could scarcely be numbered. Rondolf leaped out into the river and drowned himself, but King Eirek and the survivors barricaded themselves in the fort, and with that the battle ended.

By that time, evening had come on. Hrolf went to his tent and had his men's wounds bound. Many of his men had fallen. But as evening was passing, Hrolf's men saw three warships sailing towards land. They laid up at an anchorage and dropped anchor. Three hundred men came out of the ships, a most valiant and well-equipped host, led by the largest of the men. These men went to Hrolf's tent, and when they met, Hrolf realized that his father Sturlaug had come, along with Eirek his brother. There was a joyous reunion for them all together. Hrolf asked his father for news and inquired about his journey. At that time, Sturlaug was very old and hadn't been on any war expeditions for a long time. He said that he had heard about Hrolf's journey, and so he had come from Norway to Russia to offer Hrolf assistance. They drank through the evening and enjoyed much merriment. Sturlaug had his own mailcoat and the knife Vefreyja's Gift. Many champions and bold men from Ringerike were with him. One of them was named Torfi the Strong, another was Bard, the third was Gardi, the fourth was Atli, the fifth was Birgir, the sixth was Solvi, the seventh was Lodin, and the eighth was Knut Boil. All of them were the boldest of men, and Torfi and Knut were the best of them. They took their rest through the night, keeping a strong watch.

CHAPTER XXXI

Many men flocked to King Eirek that night, mustering from the surrounding district. Grim Aegir and Thord the Bald Man of Hlesey arrived in the evening with a countless host. There were many champions and berserks with them, and twelve are named:[65] Ein and Orn of Ermland, Ulf, Harr and Gellir, Sorli Longnose and Tjorfi, Tjosnir, Lodmund, Haki, Lifolf, Styr the Strong and Brusi Bonejack.[66] All of them were dangerous to meet, more like trolls than men, but four of them were the worst: Tjosnir and Gellir and the brothers Styr and Brusi.

King Eirik was cheered by their arrival. He told them that he had suffered heavy losses, and that Hrolf was unlike most men on account of his prowess and the armor that he owned. "It was terrible luck for us that Hrolf got the sword Hreggvid's Gift."

Grim said, "I'll help. In the morning, we'll make up for the slaughter that you suffered today."

The night passed, and day came. Both sides now prepared for battle. King Eirek came out of the fort with all his forces and drew up his ranks. Brynjolf bore his banner, and under the banner stood eight berserks: Orn of Ermland, Ulf, Harr, Sorli, Lifolf, Lodmund, Haki,[67] and Tjorfi, along with Grim Aegir. On the other wing stood Thord the Bald Man of Hlesey, with a standard carried before him. Tjosnir and Gellir were there, with Styr and Brusi and many other men.

Hrolf and Stefnir drew up their forces opposite King Eirek, with Knut Boil and Torfi the Strong with them. Sturlaug and Eirek his son were deployed against Thord, with their six champions: Hadd, Gardi, Atli, Birgir, Solvi and Lodinn. Aside from Brynjolf, we're not told who bore the banners. The forces were so greatly mismatched that the king had a three to one advantage.

A trumpet sounded, and then the ranks closed together, with battle-cries and shouts of encouragement and a great clashing of weapons. First there was a sharp volley of arrows, and then fighting at close quarters as each side charged towards the other. Many things and events happened at the same moment, yet must be told one by one.

Mondul the dwarf was not in the battle, but he was standing on a certain hill, shooting arrows from his bow and making a terrible slaughter.[68] Both sides charged so fiercely that there was no need to question their ferocity. Knut Boil and Torfi the Strong came against Grim Aegir. Both of them were strong and sorcerous, and they battled him all day long. Their fighting was so fierce that men had to watch out that they didn't get too close.

The king's berserks fought hard and broke through Hrolf's ranks, so that everyone retreated. Many a good warrior never returned to his own kingdom. There was no helm so stout, nor shield so thick, that it did not have to yield before their blows. Hrolf's army was on the verge of fleeing. Hrolf and Stefnir had advanced into King Eirek's ranks and done great damage there, before they saw the berserks charging. They turned to face them, and when they met, there was no question of the mighty blows that each had ready for the others. Hrolf struck at Orn, but he brought up his shield, which split in two—but the sword point ripped open his entire belly, so that his bowels fell out. After that, Hrolf ran Haki through and cut both feet out from under Lifolf. Stefnir stabbed at Ulf with a spear, but he brought up his shield to block the blow. The spear broke through the shield and pierced his thigh, making a terrible wound, but Ulf chopped the spearhead from the shaft. Har charged at Hrolf and struck him on the outside of his helm with a spiked club, so hard that Hrolf was on the verge of fainting—but he fell upon Ulf and stabbed him with his sword. Ulf's mailcoat was of no use, and the sword ran him through. Lodmund thrust his spear at Stefnir; it struck his calf and pierced it. Hrolf came at him, swinging his sword at Lodmund's head with both hands. He cleaved him completely in two, leaving his sword sticking in the ground. At that moment, Sorli and Tjorfi struck at Hrolf, and Har struck Hrolf's back with the club. That would have been the death of him if the cloak and armor hadn't saved him. He fell to his knees, but he quickly sprang up and struck at Har's leg, cutting it off at the knee. Hrolf also swung the sword into Tjorfi's side and chopped him apart in the middle. Sorli fled, and Har pulled himself up on the other leg and bashed anyone in front of him with his club. He killed eleven men before Stefnir struck him a deadly blow. He laid down his life in good honor.

Now there was a fierce battle. King Eirek and Brynjolf killed many men. Mondul shot King Eirek through the arm with a shaft. Hrolf and Stefnir renewed their fierce attacks, because the battle had turned against them badly. They came to the place where Grim and Torfi and Knut had fought each other, and the ground was torn up. Their encounter had ended with Knut dead and Torfi crippled by his wounds. Grim was exhausted, yet by then he had killed even more men. Hrolf and Stefnir both struck at him at the same time, but he escaped down into the earth, as if into water.

Now we must relate what was happening at the same time, as Sturlaug and Eirek were fighting on the other wing of the army. Each one broke through the opposing ranks with powerful blows and mighty spear-thrusts. There was a tremendous slaughter. Sturlaug struck and stabbed left and right with the knife Vefreyja's Gift. Anyone scratched by that weapon had no need to bind his wound. His son Eirek went with him and killed many men. Thord the Bald Man of Hlesey boldly went up against Sturlaug. He held his bald head in front of him; even if it were hewed with swords or axes, they wouldn't cut, and thus he could advance in safety. Forty of Sturlaug's men from Norway came against him, and they all attacked him, but he defended himself bravely.

Elsewhere, Styr the Strong met up with Brusi Bonejack, but Hadd, Gard, Birgir and Solvi came against them. Three of them attacked the pair, and they had all they could handle. Their attacks were both hard and fierce, and their blows and thrusts aren't described in detail, but in the end, Styr and Brusi perished from exhaustion. By then, they had killed Hadd and Gard and cut off both of Solvi's hands, and Birgir was badly wounded. Solvi rushed at one man and smashed his chest with his head, crushing his ribcage and killing him. After that, he knocked another man down and bit his windpipe in two. Then he was run through with a spear, laying down his life with great valor.

Lodin and Atli both attacked Gellir, and their encounter was savage, because he was the wickedest of men. They wounded him with many wounds. Gellir struck Atli with the blade of his thrusting spear, piercing and splitting his helmet so that the blade came to rest in his brain. Lodin wanted to avenge him and stabbed Gellir with his sword, through his mailcoat and into his thigh. That was a dreadful wound. Gellir struck at Lodin, and his blow landed on his collarbone, breaking it in two and slicing his heart, and he fell down dead. Then Sturlaug's son Eirek came at Gellir and struck him his deathblow.

Now Tjosnir and Sturlaug met. Each struck at the other, but neither was wounded. Sturlaug chopped away all of Tjosnir's shield, but had to retreat before Tjosnir's mighty blows. Mondul saw this. He nocked an arrow on his bowstring and shot a barbed arrow into Tjosnir's eye, so that it sank a long way up the shaft. Tjosnir gripped the shaft and tore out the arrow with his eye on it. Sturlaug was waiting for that, and at that moment he hewed Tjosnir apart in the middle, so that each half fell down. Now Sturlaug saw how Thord had done him such great damage that his forces were at the point of fleeing, and some were killed. He sought out where Thord was, but Thord turned to face him. Their combat was both fierce and long, until Sturlaug landed a direct hit on Thord. It landed on his bald head and failed no more than usual. The blow was so great that it split Thord's head and his whole torso all the way through, so that he fell to the ground in two pieces. Sturlaug had accomplished an incredible deed. He dropped his long knife, and it pierced down into the earth and was never found. The books are in great disagreement concerning this event, for it is said in the *Saga of Sturlaug* and many other sagas that Sturlaug died of an illness at home in Ringerike and was buried in a mound there. But here it is said that after Thord's fall, Grim Aegir came up out of the earth behind Sturlaug and struck him in the spine with a blade, chopping him in two at the middle. We don't know which is closer to the truth.

Eirek his son saw this, because he was standing nearby. In his fury, he struck at Grim with his sword. The sword hit him on the shoulder and crashed against it as if it had struck a rock, but it didn't cut. Grim turned to face Eirek and spewed such hot venom in his face that Eirik fell down dead at once. Everyone trembled at this sight, even though the battle was still raging and the slaughter was dreadful. When Hrolf heard the news, he flew into a rage, and he didn't hold back Hreggvid's Gift. He struck both hard and fast, so that everyone who had to face him shrank away. At times he killed two or three men at one blow, storming forward as if he were wading through a strong current.

This battle lasted all day, until it was so dark that there wasn't enough light for fighting. Then King Eirek had the peace-shields raised, and the battle ended. The king went into the fortress with his own men, and Hrolf went to his tents, and the wounds of the men who were expected to live were bandaged. So many of Hrolf and Stefnir's men had fallen than there were no more than two thousand men left out of all their host, and most of them were badly wounded. There was grumbling in the ranks. Men took their rest and fell asleep quickly after such dreadful exertion.

CHAPTER XXXII

As soon as the men were asleep, Hrolf stood up silently. He walked over to Dulcifal, got on his back and rode until he came to Hreggvid's burial mound. The moonlight was bright. Hrolf dismounted and walked up onto the mound. He saw King Hreggvid sitting outside by the mound, facing the moon and saying:

> Hreggvid is glad
> of the great journey
> of brave-hearted Hrolf
> here to this land.
> This valiant man
> will avenge the king
> upon Eirek
> and all his crew.
>
> Hreggvid is glad
> of Grim's death,
> of Thord's and his scoundrels'
> short time to live.
> This fearsome flock
> of foes of mine
> won't stand before Hrolf;
> they'll sink to earth.
>
> Hreggvid is glad
> that Hrolf will win
> Ingigerd,
> the girl so young.
> He'll have the rule
> in Russian lands:
> the son of Sturlaug.
> The song is ended."

Hrolf came before him and greeted him in a worthy manner. The king accepted his greeting and asked how matters were going for him.

Hrolf said, "You'll understand clearly even if I say nothing about it. The fighting has gone badly for us, on account of the huge losses that we have taken. Now you need to give us some good advice that can help us."

Hreggvid said, "I believe there's a good chance that you'll manage to avenge me. Victory will be destined for you, though it may seem unlikely. Here are two buckets that you should take. You should serve drink from one of them to all your men as soon as they wake in the morning. You and Stefnir should drink from the smaller bucket, and from then on you'll never have a falling-out. I can tell you this: Stefnir intended my daughter Ingigerd for himself as soon as he saw how beautiful she was, not for his own father Thorgnyr, nor for you. Now I grant her to you to enjoy. Stefnir will be well satisfied with what you want to do, once you two have drunk from the bucket. Here also are a knife and belt that I will give you. No treasures like these are to be found in all the Northlands. You are to give them to the one man whom you think deserves them best. But now we two must part and never see each other again. You must close up the mound, as I told you before. Bring my greetings to my daughter Ingigerd. My will is that all the valor and good fortune that once followed me should come to you. Fare hale and well now, and may everything go as you wish."

Then Hreggvid walked backwards inside the mound. Hrolf closed the mound back up as he was ordered. Then he mounted Dulcifal and turned homewards. When he had gone most of the way to the camp, Stefnir came towards him, fully armed and very angry. He said, "You've acted wrongly, Hrolf, entering Hreggvid's mound and wanting fame for yourself alone. You think you'll get Princess Ingigerd as well, but that isn't any more certain."

Hrolf said, "I haven't won any fame, even if I traveled farther than you all night long. I have no intention of marrying the princess. The one who is fated will enjoy her, which I never thought to do."

Then Hrolf told Stefnir about his journey to the mound and showed him the buckets. They sat down and drank from the bucket, and they felt themselves grow much stronger from that drink. Stefnir grew cheerful with Hrolf and said that he was the most deserving of Ingigerd—"and it's true that you'll win her, rather than my father, as old as he is." They went straight to their tents and slept for the remaining part of the night.

Early in the morning, Hrolf awakened his men and served them all from the bucket. As soon as each man had drunk, he didn't feel his wounds, even if he had been crippled as soon as he had been struck. Those who had once wanted most keenly to flee now encouraged each other most to fight. Mondul looked into the bucket and said that such a thing brought friendship—"but I don't want to drink this ale. All terrors may flee, so that good help to win this fight may come to us before this day is over. The men will have some stories to tell."

Everyone put on his armor and prepared for battle. Mondul said, "Now the day has come when you'll need your cloak, Hrolf. Here is a brown silk veil that you must tuck up under the cloak's hood. Never let it drop from in front of your face, even if it feels hot to you."[69]

Hrolf accepted the veil and arranged it as the dwarf had said. They went to the battlefield and deployed their forces, showing themselves ready to fight. They took up a different battlefield, since their previous one was unusable because of all the slain warriors. Mondul walked twice widdershins around the fallen. He blew and whistled in all directions and muttered ancient magic over them, and said that the fallen would come to no harm.

CHAPTER XXXIII

The evening after the battle, King Eirek had gone into the fort to bind the wounds of his men. He had suffered heavy casualties and had lost all his champions: of all of those who had come with Grim and Thord, Sorli Longnose alone had survived. Many men from the provinces came to the king, night and day. King Eirek and Grim thought that they had Hrolf and his men well in hand, thanks to their superior numbers. Grim prepared himself with many spells through the night, as did Brynjolf. The arm wound that King Eirek took from Mondul's arrow began to swell badly, and his hand was crippled.

Early in the morning, King Eirek rode out of the fort with all his host. He formed his ranks, and a shield-castle formed up around him. Brynjolf was to defend the shield-castle, but a man named Snak[70] carried the standard, with Grim Aegir and Sorli Longnose on the other flank. The forces were so unequally matched that Eirek had six men for each of Hrolf's.

When Hrolf saw that, he said to his men that they should not form ranks. "We will charge in detachments of thirty or forty in a group, so that we can't be surrounded by their superior numbers. I will face Grim Aegir, and Stefnir and Torfi will face King Eirik. Dwarf Mondul, I expect you to counter Grim's magic, so that he can't murder our men with his sorcery."

Mondul came forth. He'd come in a black cloak, and no part of him was exposed. Under one arm he had a large bag; the inside was made of animal skin, but the outside was gold cloth. He had a bow and a quiver in the other hand. Everyone found his outfit strange.

Grim went to where the slain men were lying, and rolled the dead men over and wanted them to rise up—but he couldn't do it.[71] His appearance grew so terrifying that most men didn't dare to look at him, because his eyes were like fire, and black smoke and the foulest stench billowed from his nostrils and mouth.

Soon after that, both sides screamed their battle cries and charged each other. Grim bellowed so loudly that his howling could be heard above all the battle cries. He rushed forward ahead of his ranks, shaking a sack and driving a black mist out of it at Hrolf's men. When Mondul saw that, he advanced and shook his bag, and strong winds blew out against the mist, driving the mist back into the eyes of Grim's men.[72] This struck them blind at once, and they fell on their faces and were trampled to death by their own men. Grim was enraged. He nocked an arrow on the string and shot at Mondul, but Mondul shot back, and their arrows hit each other, right on their points, and fell down. This happened three times.[73]

At the same moment, fierce fighting broke out, as each man encouraged another with crashes and shouts, because Hrolf's men were so bold that they held nothing back and acted as if victory was certain. Stefnir charged against King Eirek, and Torfi and Birgir went with him. They quickly cleared a path before them, and it would take a long time to recount their strikes and thrusts. They killed so many men that they could hardly be counted. Brynjolf also charged forward with Snak the standard-bearer, killing forty knights in the first onslaught.

Hrolf charged Grim Aegir and struck at him, but he turned into a flying dragon and escaped up into the air, spewing venom over Hrolf. Mondul was standing nearby and held the bag out underneath, so that it filled with the venom. He rushed at Sorli Longnose with the bag and poured it out in his face so that he fell dead. Grim turned into a man, even though he had killed nine men with the venom. He rushed at the dwarf and wanted to catch him, but Mondul didn't want to wait and plunged down into the earth right where he was standing. Grim went down after him, so that the earth closed over their heads together.

Hrolf now charged, striking to left and right. Resistance slackened before him as one man fell across another. He needed to give no one more than a single blow. Everyone whom he caught with his sword got death in exchange for life. Both his arms were bloody up to the shoulders. His charge struck fear into most men. The battle was a huge slaughter on both wings.

The next thing that happened was that some men in the battle saw fifteen ships rowing to land as fast as they could. They laid up at an anchorage. A huge and warlike force came from the ships. Two men were the tallest of them all, wearing masks in front of their faces. They went straight into battle alongside Hrolf and attacked King Eirek's left flank in force, and many in his ranks began to turn and flee. The masked men were the boldest, striking hard and fast. Now the battle was so fierce that there was never one like it before. There one might see many a shield cloven and many a strong helm shattered, mailcoats slashed and many men of high degree laid low. No one took warning from another's woe.[74] Spears, javelins, thong-spears, hand-axes and many other missile weapons were flung.

Hrolf now attacked the shield-castle and encountered fierce resistance. Grim Aegir returned to the battle, scowling horribly and killing everyone in his way. Birgir and Torfi came against him, along with both masked men, and they all attacked him with great valor, but they couldn't wound him. He dealt them many large blows. They grew both wounded and weary.

At the same moment, Stefnir encountered Sval and struck at him with his sword. The blow penetrated the shield, cutting off what it hit and chopping the banner-staff in two. Sval struck in return, splitting Stefnir's shield completely in two, but Stefnir wasn't wounded. He struck at Sval, and the blow struck his helm and glanced off his beard and plunged down onto his shoulder, splitting his shoulder blade in two and penetrating his chest. That was the death of him, and King Eirek's banner fell in the grass.

Brynjolf saw that and attacked Stefnir, with a grim expression: he was tusked like a wild boar. He struck at Stefnir, and each struck at the other, but Brynjolf's strike didn't cut Vefreyja's Gift, and Stefnir's sword didn't cut Brynjolf. They struck at each other for a long time, and Stefnir grew exhausted, until his sword shattered below the hilt. Stefnir ran in to grapple Brynjolf, but he countered powerfully. Brynjolf bit Stefnir's shoulder and ripped the flesh away from the bones, as much as he could get in his maw, because his teeth couldn't bite through the cloak. Stefnir defended himself manfully; he clutched Brynjolf's mouth with his hands and ripped off his face all the way to the ears. This left him quite unkissable.[75] They wrestled for so long that the bout went first one way and then another, until Brynjolf fell on his back next to Sval. He clasped Stefnir's back with both hands, so hard that Stefnir couldn't turn anywhere. He had to protect his face as best he could, so that Brynjolf wouldn't bite him.

Now we must tell about Hrolf. He attacked the shield-castle with great ferocity. He took many blows and thrusts and powerful attacks, because all of King Eirek's mightiest picked warriors were there. He would have suffered dreadful wounds and great hurt there, if the cloak and the armor had not protected him. Hrolf killed seventy knights single-handedly, and then he broke up the entire shield-castle. King Eirek defended himself well and skillfully, crying out to Grim Aegir in a loud voice and begging him to help him and spare no one. When Grim heard that, he hurried over. By then he had killed Torfi and Birgir, wounded one of the masked men, and wounded the other mortally. Sometimes he turned into a flying dragon, but sometimes a serpent, boar, or bull, or other harmful monstrosities that cause the most hurt to men.

When Hrolf saw him, he spoke. "You'll sink down in the earth again, as you did when we met yesterday. Come here, Aegir, and fight me if you dare, until one or the other of us falls."

Grim said, "You'll find out that I've come here," and he struck at Hrolf, and Hrolf struck in return. There one might see the mighty blows and fierce attacks that each gave the other, but they never struck so hard that any of them landed. Their attack was so fierce that everyone nearby jumped away. Such flames leaped from their clashing weapons that the land was ablaze on all sides.

The tall masked man encountered King Eirek, and their fight was quite fierce. King Eirek carried his shield on his wounded arm, but he struck with the other arm frequently and hard, because he was the greatest champion. Their exchange ended when the masked man chopped away the king's entire shield. After that he cut both feet out from under King Eirek and killed him. He laid down his life with great valor. The army took to its heels, and each man fled as best he could. Now the slaughter began anew, as the raiders boldly pursued the fleeing host.

Hrolf and Grim turned away from the ranks and fought with great boldness, until Hrolf split Grim's sword down the middle with Hreggvid's Gift. Grim made a mighty leap at Hrolf, who had to throw away his sword and grapple him. Grim raged so fiercely that he was wading through the earth up to his knees. Hrolf broke free, but had to save himself from falling. Sometimes Grim spewed venom at Hrolf, and sometimes flames. That would have meant death for him, if he hadn't had the cloak in front of him, or the veil that Mondul gave him. Grim's breath was so hot that it almost seemed to burn through Vefreyja's Gift and the armor. Grim squeezed the flesh from Hrolf's bones wherever he touched him. Hrolf thought that he had never been more sorely tested. He realized that he would die of exhaustion if they fought any longer. They stomped so hard that grass and turf were torn up wherever they went.

Hrolf saw Mondul come running. He seized a sword that lay on the field and swung at Grim's leg with both hands, but it didn't cut any more than if it had hit a stone. Mondul dashed back to the slain bodies and found Hreggvid's Gift. He smeared his spittle on the edge and dragged the sword to where they were wrestling, because he couldn't manage to carry or swing the sword on account of its weight. He managed to drag the sword onto Grim's calves from behind, severing the tendons in his legs, and Grim fell. The dwarf said, "Hold him, Hrolf, so that he can't get loose."

Grim struggled hard and forced his way down into the earth, but Hrolf used his strength and held him back. Then Grim said, "You've got great luck, Hrolf, and you'll become famous for killing me and for the mighty deeds that you've accomplished in Russia. A mound must be raised after me and set facing the sea, and all who dock there when they reach land will find certain death. I've set many deadly traps for you, because my heart warned me for a long time about what has happened now. I sent Vilhjalm to you to betray you, but you were destined to live longer. You wouldn't have beaten me if that wicked dwarf hadn't been there to guide you."

Mondul rushed up and stuck a thick stick into Grim's mouth so that it stuck fast. Then Mondul said, "If Grim had been able to talk longer, he would have cursed you and most of the others so badly that you would have rotted into pieces and become nothing but dust.[76] You must kill him quickly and run your sword through his chest. But don't dismember him, because everything that is cut from him will turn into poison. And no one must come before his eyes as he dies, because that's deadly."

Hrolf took Hreggvid's Gift and ran Grim through the chest, so that the sword stuck out from his back. The dwarf took a shield and laid it in front of Grim's face. And as unlikely as it might seem, it's said that the shield crumbled and melted like snow in a fire and turned completely to dust. Thus Grim laid down his life, with savage death-struggles and wild thrashings of his arms, and Hrolf lay on top of him until he was dead. Hrolf was on the brink of fainting from his struggles with Grim Aegir.

The tall masked man turned back to the battlefield once he had chased the fleeing host for a while. He came to where Stefnir and Brynjolf were lying, as we mentioned before. He wanted to help Stefnir, and he loosened Brynjolf's hand from him, but he wasn't able to do that until he had broken every one of his fingers. Then they bashed him into Hel with clubs. Stefnir had become so stiff from his grappling bout that he could hardly walk by himself with the other men.

Now this huge battle was over, and there had been such a huge slaughter that men had scarcely heard of the like. Headless bodies lay so thickly all over the field that it wasn't possible to walk on the ground, on account of the great slaughter. Most of King Eirek's men had fallen. Hrolf and Stefnir had lost all their men except for eight hundred survivors, most of them wounded. There was no shortage of weapons or treasures which the dead had owned. Hrolf and Stefnir went to their tents. Mondul the dwarf bandaged men's wounds, and they all praised his wisdom and helpfulness. Mondul said that if Grim had caught him when he plunged down into the earth, that would have been the death of him. "I benefited from the fact that my friends were more numerous than his," he said. The masked man went to his ships in the evening with his men, and they pitched their tents. Both sides now rested, and most felt it was high time to rest. King Eirek's men who had escaped fled to the fort and stayed there.

CHAPTER XXXIV

That night, as the men were sleeping, Hrolf and Stefnir went to the camp of the men from the ships. They were all asleep in their own armor. Hrolf took the knife and the belt that Hreggvid had given him, and tied them to the masked man's spear shaft. He said, "I give this treasure to the leader of this host, and with it I thank him for his brave service and assistance. I think I am obliged to do him all the good that I can offer him and that he will accept from me."

No one answered. They went to their own tents and slept through the night.

Early in the morning, Hrolf went to the fortress with his men. The masked man also came there with his own men. Hrolf held a parley with the men in the fortress and agreed to grant them a truce, if they would surrender the fortress. They accepted his offer. Hrolf and all his men entered the fort and summoned the household. Hrolf announced that they had come on behalf of Princess Ingigerd, to win back her kingdom from her enemies, and that she was in Denmark, safe and ready to travel. The people of the land were overjoyed at this news and felt willing to serve under her authority.

Now Hrolf went to the hall and sat down to feasting with great cheer. The unknown man then took off his mask. Hrolf and Stefnir recognized that it was Hrafn, who had once stayed in Jutland, and to whom Hrolf had given the clothing. He told them about events in Denmark, the fall of Jarl Thorgnyr and what he had accomplished there. Hrolf and Stefnir were saddened at this news, and they thanked him very much for his aid.

Hrafn said that he had thought they must have been too late, reaching them only the day before. "My help was a fitting exchange for the gift of life and the clothes that you gave me a long time ago. But my brother Krak fell yesterday before Grim Aegir, and I feel that is the worst loss, though I have to accept it for now."

Now they ended their conversation. They stayed there that night and were well treated.

The next morning, Hrolf had the battlefield cleared and divided the plunder with his men. Three huge burial mounds were raised there. Hrolf laid his father Sturlaug in one, along with Hrafn's brother Krak, and all the greatest champions who had fallen in their ranks. King Eirek, Brynjolf and Thord and their best men were laid in the second mound. In the third, where it seemed least likely that a ship would land, Grim Aegir was laid facing the sea, and the fallen commoners were buried there.

Hrolf appointed governors over all the kingdom until the princess could come. The dwarf took his leave of Hrolf, and he thanked him for his help and gave him whatever he wanted. King Eirek's sister Gyda vanished from Russia, and some people think that Mondul must have carried her off.[77]

After that, Hrolf and his men prepared to return home. They set out from Russia and didn't stop until they came to Denmark, landing at Aarhus. Thorgnyr had fortified that place the most. Bjorn and all the inhabitants came to meet them with a great welcome. The maidens were glad that they had come back. Ingigerd thanked them for their exploits. Bjorn had protected the ladies in an underground house ever since the jarl fell. Ingigerd now said firmly that she would marry no man but Hrolf Sturlaugsson, because he had paid the greatest price to avenge her father—"now he has lost his own father and brother and other friends and kinsmen, and placed himself in the greatest dangers."

No one spoke out against it. Bjorn prepared a worthy feast for them, and they drank the inheritance-ale for Jarl Thorgnyr.

CHAPTER XXXV

One day at the feast, Hrafn stood up and asked for a hearing and said, "I want to thank you, Hrolf and Stefnir, for the honor and the good turns that you have done me, both now and when I was here before. I want to reveal my name and my lineage to you. There was a king named Edgar who ruled over a kingdom in England and who had his royal seat in the town named Winchester. He had two sons and one daughter. His older son was named Harald, and the younger was named Sigurd. Alfhild was the name of his daughter. I am that same Harald, but my brother Sigurd fell in Russia, as you saw. Our mother's kin live here in Denmark. But when I was fifteen years old and my brother was thirteen, my father was betrayed by his kinsman Heinrek, a great champion and an unruly man. He had himself raised to the kingship and has held the kingdom ever since, and we two brothers escaped with difficulty. We got Alfhild to safety in the fortress called Brentford,[78] and she has been there ever since. We two brothers traveled in disguise through various lands, giving our names as Krak and Hrafn. We have gotten these men and ships by serving alongside various chieftains, along with the support of our kinfolk. Heinrek has much support from Scotland, because he married the daughter of Jarl Melans of Moray, and he is a great friend of the High King, who is named Duncan. Duncansby is named for him because he had that place fortified.[79] Now I want to ask you, Hrolf and Stefnir, to grant me aid and support in avenging my father and winning back my inheritance."

Hrolf said, "I shall grant you all the strength and support that I can. I shall not part from you until you have won back your kingdom and driven away your sorrow—or else I shall lay down my life."

Stefnir said the same. Harald thanked them for their words and their goodwill.

After the feast, they prepared themselves for the journey and chose all the bravest men that they could get. They left Bjorn the Counsellor and other mighty men to look after the land. Before they left, Harald put forth his suit and asked for the hand of Stefnir's sister Thora. Hrolf supported his case, as did many other honored men. In the end, Harald was betrothed to her, and she had to stay there betrothed until they came back.

After that, they sailed from Jutland in thirty ships, all well equipped. They didn't break their journey until they had sailed westward to England, to the island called Lindsey.[80] They laid up there in an anchorage and stayed there for several days and waited for a favorable wind, because they didn't want to raid there.

CHAPTER XXXVI

It's said that a man named Annis was with King Heinrek. He was old, but he knew both the newest and the most ancient wickedness and sorcery. He had fostered Heinrek and had always been his adviser.

A month in advance, Annis had told the king that Harald and Hrolf would arrive with a great host, and what they meant to do. Annis spoke of the great valor of Hrolf and Stefnir and said that Heinrek would need some counsel. "My advice is to send word to Scotland for your father-in-law Jarl Melans to come to aid you. You should also send a message to King Duncan asking him to send you help. As soon as Hrolf comes to this land, you should send a man to him to mark out the battlefield with hazel stakes[81] and summon them to battle. Under the provisions of Viking law, they cannot raid.[82] You must set the battlefield by Ashingdon, north of the Danes' forest.[83] The lay of the land there is worst for a fleeing host. Leave half of your forces in the forest until they can attack from behind and take them on the flank. Then we shall surround them and let none escape alive."

The king found this a good plan, and he went ahead with it as Annis had said. Jarl Melans came from Scotland with a large force. There was also the fine force that King Duncan sent to King Heinrek. Leading the force were two berserks, one named Amon and the other named Hjalmar, outstanding in strength and hardiness. Heinrek now had an overwhelming host. His messengers came to Lindsey and told Hrolf and his men that a field was marked with hazel stakes and prepared for battle next to Ashingdon. Some found it ill-advised to land such a small force on the mainland, since there was a great multitude facing them. They sailed for the place called Sherston,[84] and there they left their ships behind and prepared to go ashore. They didn't break their journey until they came to Ashingdon. King Heinrek and Jarl Melans were there ahead of time with an overwhelming force, and in the forest were Amon and Hjalmar with a great force. Hrolf was not aware of this.

Now the armies were arranged in formation. King Heinrek deployed three ranks. He himself was in the center, and Jarl Melans was on one side. On his other side was the count named Engilbert, the greatest champion. With him was a man named Raudam, both tall and strong, the most fearless of men. Banners were borne before them all. Annis was not in the battle. Harald wanted to deploy facing King Heinrek, and Stefnir facing Jarl Melans. Hrolf drew up his forces facing Raudam and Engilbert.

There was a blast on trumpets, and both sides pressed the attack with battle-cries and shouts of encouragement. First a storm of arrows broke out, and then the fiercest fight at close quarters, as both sides charged forward. At first the Scots and Englishmen were very fierce, but the Danes met them well and sharply. Engilbert and Raudam encountered Hrolf at the beginning, as the ranks were closing up, and they both attacked him at the same time, but he defended himself well and bravely. He was in his armor, and wearing Vefreyja's Gift on the outside. Raudam and Englibert were both agile and strong, and Hrolf never landed a blow on them, but he chopped off all their armor. Hrolf grew weary, but no weapon landed on him, on account of his protection. He was terribly exhausted. He was forced to throw away his sword, and he rushed headlong under Count Engilbert, heaving the count up over his head and flinging him down on his head, breaking his neck. At that moment Raudam struck Hrolf in the back with both hands, shattering his sword below the hilt. He wanted to own the treasure Hreggvid's Gift. Hrolf leaped at him and let him feel the difference in their strength, and pinned him under himself and forced his knee down onto his breast, so hard that his ribs were smashed in. Raudam and Engilbert laid down their lives. They seemed the boldest of men.

Now Hrolf took up Hreggvid's Gift and struck right and left. The Scots found it a most keen edge, and they recoiled from it. Hrolf could not pursue them at the time, but he killed everyone that stood before him. The Danes suddenly realized that their weapons wouldn't bite. Although they struck doggedly, as if there was no armor before them, it was as if they were striking with cudgels—except for Hreggvid's Gift, which cut as if it were plunging into water. That had not been able to be blunted except by Grim Aegir, as men had seen. Now more Danes fell than Englishmen.

Just then they heard a trumpet blast and a battle cry. The berserks charged out of the forest in full force and attacked Hrolf's men on the flank. They made a fierce attack, and the Danes fell in heaps. Hrolf ordered his men to turn to face them and stand back to back, and he advancedagainst the berserks with his own banner. Now the battle was at its fiercest.

Stefnir traded blows with Jarl Melans, and that was a difficult encounter, because he was a great champion and Stefnir's sword didn't bite. Amon and Hjalmar now came against Hrolf. They both struck at him, but he held his shield before him and bore up bravely. Hrolf swept his sword at Hjalmar and hit him on the thigh, above the hip, cutting his leg off. He died shortly afterwards. Then Annis came forward, holding a shield as big as a door before him, but carrying a little knife in the other hand. He stabbed Hrolf's standard-bearer in the midriff, running him through, and the banner fell to the earth. As soon as Annis had advanced, the Danes' weapons bit. Now everyone fought as best he could. Many fell on both sides, yet more fell on the Danes' side.

Hrolf wanted to avenge his standard-bearer, and he struck at Annis. The blow went down to the center of the shield, cleaving it down to the handle. The sword stuck fast, but Annis held his shield so strongly that it never quaked. Hrolf wanted to let the sword slip, but this was impossible, because both his hands were stuck to the hilt. Annis ordered the Scots to punish Hrolf—"because the wolf's been caught in a trap." They did so: a great many of them crowded around Hrolf. Others struck or beat him. He was pelted with stones and hewed with axes and bashed with cudgels. Hrolf grimaced horribly and struggled fiercely with hard kicks. He still couldn't get free.

Now we must tell how Stefnir fought with Jarl Melans. His sword began to bite. He struck the jarl on the helmet with all his strength. That blow was so great that it cleaved the helmet and head and all his armored body completely through, so that the sword stuck fast in the earth. They had fought for a long time.

Stefnir was amazed that he couldn't see Hrolf's banner, nor Hrolf himself. He searched for him until he saw the fix he was in: they were trying to cut his feet out from under him. He rushed to help him and attacked Annis by surprise, striking the rim of his helmet with his sword and splitting it, along with his entire face and both arms at the elbow-joints. He butchered Annis crudely. Hrolf got free, and it wasn't a good idea to stand in front of him. He turned on Amon and swung his sword at him with both hands. The sword landed on his shield and split it in two, and the point of the sword sliced his chest and belly so that his intestines fell out, and Amon fell dead to the ground. Hrolf was so enraged that he spared no one. He struck boldly wherever he could reach quickly with his drawn sword, and three or four men fell before each of his strokes. The slaughter could best be compared to chips flying furiously from a stump that men are making into charcoal. Stefnir did the same. The Englishmen now fell so quickly that they amounted to many hundreds.

King Heinrek and Harald had encountered each other early in the battle and had been fighting all day. They were both wounded and weary, but Harald was getting the worst of it. Hrolf saw their encounter. By then he had gone through King Heinrek's ranks and back again four times. He charged the king and struck him from behind, so that he fell dead to the ground in two pieces. When the Scots and Englishmen saw that their king had fallen, everyone fled who had feet to run with. The other side pursued the fleeing host, killing everyone they caught and offering no quarter. Hrolf pursued the host for a long time. Whoever he caught with his sword had no need for a truce, and a multitude of the fleeing warriors fell.

Then the Danes turned back and stripped the dead, taking a great plunder. Annis was captured in the battle. Hrolf had him torn to pieces by cattle, and thus his life ended. Hrolf was badly wounded on his arms and legs, and he was bruised and sore from mighty blows all over his body, although they hadn't cut.

Harald and his men went to the town of Winchester, which surrendered to them. All the inhabitants gladly submitted to Harald. Now he was raised to kingship over all the kingdom which his father had had. He thanked Hrolf and Stefnir for their support and valor, as was right.

The Scots who escaped went to find Duncan and told him of their misfortune and losses. They said that Hrolf was more like a troll than a man, on account of his strength and size. Duncan wasn't at all pleased with the losses he had suffered, but he had to put up with them.

CHAPTER XXXVII

Hrolf and Steinir now stayed quietly with Harald until the winter was over. Harald had his sister Alfhild fetched from the fort of Brentford, and she went with a goodly retinue and following, as befitted her. Harald and his sister were glad to see each other. She was the loveliest young maiden, skilled in the arts that were seemly for a king's child. Stefnir soon fell in love with her and went to speak with her, and he found her both wise and well-mannered. Stefnir proposed marriage to her, and she responded favorably but turned to her brother. Harald readily gave his consent, because Stefnir's great bravery and valor were well known to him. In the end, Stefnir betrothed himself to Alfhild, and Harald provided her with a dowry of gold and fine treasures.

As soon as spring came, they all prepared to return to Denmark. They loaded their ships with malt, mead, wine, and costly clothes, and all the wares that were most treasured in Denmark and that could be bought in England. Then they set sail back to Denmark, and Alfhild went with them. All the folk in Jutland were glad that they had come back. The young maidens welcomed them warmly, and so did Bjorn the Counsellor. Alfhild came to Ingigerd and Thora, and there was much rejoicing among them all together. They had their ship unloaded, and they arranged for a noble feast with all the best provisions that could be had in Denmark or nearby lands. No expense was spared for the halls and tapestries and everything that was to be found in the Northlands. To this feast there were invited burgesses and retainers, counts and jarls, along with dukes and kings and all other men of high degree. Most of the nobles in Denmark attended this feast. All the men who had come there were arranged in their seats, and courteous squires and well-mannered courtiers served there. All sorts of dishes were brought out, with the costliest spices: the flesh of beasts and birds of all kinds, reindeer and stags and excellent wild boar, geese and ptarmigans, with peppered peacocks. There was no lack of the costliest drink: ale and English mead, together with the finest of wines, and also spiced and honeyed wines.[85] And with the wedding appointed and the feast arranged, one might hear all manner of stringed instruments: harps and viols, hurdy-gurdies and psalteries. Drums were beaten and pipes were blown, and there were all manner of delightful games that one's body might enjoy. After that, the young maidens were led in with their splendid coiffures and delightful throng of ladies. Two noblemen led each lady whom the bridegrooms were to marry. Over them was borne a cloth canopy on painted posts, intended to shade their bright raiment and fair procession until they had reached their seats. Then the canopy was taken away, and no color surpassed the color of their skin and hair shining, and their gold glowing, set with gemstones gleaming. Everyone found that even Alfhild and Thora seemed pallid next to Ingigerd.

Now the feast was at the height of its splendor, and at this feast Hrolf married Ingigerd, Stefnir married Alfhild, and Harald married Thora. For seven nights continued the feasting, being appointed and arranged in the manner that I am now describing, and in glory and splendor concluding, with the bridegrooms bestowing fine gifts upon all noble men and thanking them for coming. Each fared to his own household, praising their lordliness as much as their magnificence, with everyone in friendship parting.[86] Great love began to grow between the wedded couples.

King Harald did not stay for long in Denmark before preparing to go home to England. He parted with his brother-in-law Stefnir and with Hrolf in friendship and went straight to his kingdom. Thora was his queen, and they settled down peacefully. They had children together, though they aren't named.

England is said to be the richest of all the western lands, because all metals are smelted there, and wheat and grapes are produced there, and all sorts of crops may be had there. Also, clothes and many sorts of fabrics are made there, more than in other places. London is the principal city there, along with Canterbury. Scarborough and Hastings[87] are there, along with Winchester and many other cities and towns which will not be named here.[88]

The title of jarl over all Jutland was given to Stefnir. He usually stayed in Ribe.

Denmark is divided into many parts, but Jutland makes up the greater part of the kingdom; it lies to the south along the ocean. It is called Jutlandside along the west coast from Skagen southwards to Ribe. There are many important cities in Jutland. The southernmost is Hedeby; next is Ribe, a third is Aarhus, and a fourth is Viborg, which is where the Danes choose their king. The Limfjord cuts through Jutland and runs from north to south. In the interior of the fjord, Harald's Neck leads west to the sea; that's where King Harald Sigurdsson had his ships dragged, when he escaped the enmity of the King of Sweden.[89] To the west of the Limfjord lies Skagen, which curves northwards. The principal town is Hjorring. Between Jutland and Fyn lies the Little Belt. The principal town on Fyn is Odense. The Great Belt runs between Fyn and Zealand; the principal town on Zealand is Roskilde. The Oresund runs to the north of Zealand, and north of that is Skane; there the principal town is Lund. Many great islands lie between Jutland and Skane; there are Samso, Als, Lolland, and Langeland. Bornholm lies in the sea to the east. The Skjoldung kings held this kingdom at this time. Although other kings and jarls had kingdoms to rule, no smaller than the kings in Denmark had, the Skjoldungs bore greater distinction on account of their name and descent.[90]

CHAPTER XXXVIII

It's said that Jarl Stefnir must not have lived long, and he had no children that survived infancy. Hrolf and Stefnir parted in great friendship, and maintained their fellowship for as long as they both lived. It's not said that Hrolf ever came to Ringerike again—but it's said that Harald traveled westward to England that summer. Hrolf sailed east from Denmark to Novgorod with ten ships, and Ingigerd went with him. There, Hrolf was raised to the kingship over all Russia, on the advice of the princess and other powerful personages.

One third of Russia is called Kiev. It lies along the mountain range that separates Russia from Jotunheim. There are also Ermland and many other small realms.

Hrolf ruled his kingdom and was highly respected. He was both wise and a good ruler. No chieftains dared to invade his lands, on account of his fame and his boldness. Hrolf and Ingigerd loved each other very much and had many children. One son of theirs was named Hreggvid, an outstanding man; he went raiding in the Eastern realms and never came back. Wise men say that another son of Hrolf's was King Olaf, who was attacked by Helgi the Bold. Hromund Gripsson aided Olaf and killed Helgi, as is told in his saga.[91] Hrolf's daughters were Dagny and Dagbjort, who healed Hromund, but it isn't recorded whether they were Ingigerd's children or not.[92] Hrolf's third son was named Hord, the father of Kari, father of Horda-Knut.[93] It's said that Hrolf lived to be old, but it's not clear whether he died of illness or was slain with weapons.

Now, even though this saga may not seem to agree with other sagas which treat this matter, concerning people's names and events, or what each one achieved or did by means of bravery or wisdom or sorcery or treachery, or where the chieftains ruled—it's quite likely that those who have written and compiled these events must have had something in front of them, either old lays or the accounts of learned men. And there must be few or no stories of ancient heroes that are so truthful that men would swear oaths that events happened as described, because most stories become filled out with words, and not all words and details are recorded in every place, because most things are quicker in the telling. Thus it's best not to blame the stories of learned men or call them lies, unless someone can tell them in a more plausible way, or express them more eloquently. Old lays and tales have been created more for momentary enjoyment than everlasting faith. Few things are told that are so implausible that a true example cannot be found of something else that happened in that way. And truly is it written that God has given wit and discernment in earthly affairs to heathens, in the same way as Christians, along with surpassing valor, wealth, and splendid form.

Now this tale of Hrolf the son of Sturlaug and his mighty deeds, comes to an end here. Thanks to everyone who listened and was entertained, but grief to those who were annoyed by it and can't enjoy anything. *Amen.*

THE SAGA OF HROMUND GRIPSSON

Hrómundar saga Gripssonar

CHAPTER I

A king named Olaf ruled over Russia.[1] He was the son of Gnod-Asmund,[2] and a renowned man. Two brothers, Kari and Ornulf, were in charge of defending the king's lands. They were mighty warriors.

A powerful farmer named Grip lived there. He was married to a woman named Gunnlod, the daughter of Hrok the Black.[3] They had nine sons, and these are their names: Hrolf, Haki, Gaut, Throst, Angantyr, Logi, Hromund, Helgi, and Hrok. They were all promising men, but Hromund was ahead of them all. He didn't know how to be afraid. He had light eyes, bright hair and broad shoulders, and he was tall and strong, most like his mother's father Hrok.

There were two men in the king's retinue, one named Bild and the other named Vali. They were wicked and deceitful. The king valued them highly.

Once, King Olaf sailed eastward off the coast of Norway with his forces, and they headed for the Elfar Skerries.[4] They raided and anchored along an island. The king ordered Kari and Ornulf to go up onto the island and find out whether they could see any warships. They went up onto the land and noticed six warships anchored along a certain cliff, including one splendidly ornamented dragon-ship. Kari called out to them and asked who was in command of the ships.

An ogre stood up on the dragon-ship and said that his name was Hrongvid—"but what's your name?"

Kari gave his name and his brother's, and said, "I don't know anyone worse than you, and therefore I'll chop you into little pieces."

Hrongvid said, "I have been raiding for thirty-three years, summer and winter, and I have fought sixty battles and always won victory. My sword is called Mail-Piercer[5], and it has never been blunted. Come here in the morning, Kari. I'll sheathe it in your breast."

Kari said that he wouldn't fail.

Hrongvid could choose one man to be stabbed by his sword's point each day.

CHAPTER II

The brothers returned to the king and told him what had happened. The king ordered his men to give battle, and it was done. The two sides met, and a fierce battle broke out. The brothers advanced boldly. Kari always killed eight or twelve men with every stroke. Hrongvid saw that. He leaped up onto the king's ship and charged at Kari and ran him through with his sword. As soon as Kari had received the wound, he said to the king, "Farewell, my lord. I must lodge with Odin."

Hrongvid impaled Ornulf on his spear and heaved him up. After the brothers fell, Hrongvid shouted that they should surrender. There was an angry uproar among the king's men. No iron bit Hrongvid.

It's said that Hromund Gripsson was in the king's retinue. He picked up a club, tied a long gray goat's beard onto his face, and set a hat on his head.[6] He charged forward, and found both the brothers dead. He picked up the king's banner and beat the black men[7] to death with his club.

Hrongvid asked who that might be. "Could that be the father of that wicked Kari?"

Hromund said his name, and he said that he wanted to avenge the brothers—"but Kari was no relation to me. All the same, I shall kill you."

With that, he gave Hrongvid such a mighty blow with his club that Hrongvid's head was knocked askew, and he said, "I've been in battle far and wide, and never received such a blow." Hromund struck Hrongvid another blow, so that his skull broke. At the third blow, he lost his life. After that, everyone who was left alive submitted to the king, and so the battle ended.

CHAPTER III

Now Hromund searched the ship and found one man leaning up against the prow. He asked the man his name. He said he was called Helgi the Bold, Hrongvid's brother—"and I have no intention of asking for peace."

Hromund had Helgi the Bold healed. Helgi later sailed back to Sweden and took charge of the kingdom's defenses.

Afterwards, King Olaf led his forces westwards to the Hebrides. They landed there and pillaged. An old man lived nearby. The king's men had taken his cattle and driven them away. He felt very wretched over this loss. Hromund came and asked who he was. The old man said that his home was a very short distance from there, and said there was greater honor to be gained by breaking into mounds and plundering riches from the dead. This old man said that his name was Mani.

Hromund ordered him to tell him if he knew of any such mounds.

Mani said that he certainly did know. He said, "Thrain, who conquered Normandy and was king there, a huge and strong berserk, full of magic spells—he was set in a mound with his sword, armor, and great riches. But few people have any desire to go there."

Hromund asked him what course they should sail to get there. He said that he could sail directly south for six days. Hromund thanked the old man for this information, gave him money, and let him take his own cattle. They sailed away in that direction that the old man had shown them, and after six days they saw the burial mound, right in front of the prow.

CHAPTER IV

They came to Normandy from the west and found the mound and broke into it. After six days had passed, they had made an opening into the mound. They saw a huge ogre sitting there on a throne, black and bloated, dressed all in gold so that he sparkled. He roared a great deal and blew on a fire.

Hromund asked who wanted to go into the mound now, and said that that man could choose three treasures for himself.

Vali said, "No one would want to give his own life for this. There are sixty men here now, and this troll will bring death to them all."

Hromund said, "Kari would have dared this, if he were alive"—and he said it would be most fitting for him to be let down on the rope, even though it might be preferable to have to deal with any other eight men. So Hromund went down on the rope. The stench was almost overwhelming.[8] And when he came down, he heaped up a great deal of wealth and tied it up with the end of the rope.

Thrain had been king over Normandy in olden days, and gained everything by means of magic spells. He became very wicked. When he was so old that he couldn't do any more harm, he had himself placed alive in the mound, and a great deal of wealth with him.

Now Hromund saw where the sword was hanging up on a post. He pulled it down, buckled it at his side, and went up to the throne and said, "It must be time for me to leave this mound, since no one's resisting. Say, how's it going for you, old man? Don't you see that I've piled up your wealth as you were quietly limping along, you mangy dog? What had you turned to look at when I took the sword and necklace and so many of your other treasures?"

Thrain said that he felt it was no great matter if he should stay quietly on his throne. "I knew how to fight once. I must have become rather a weakling if you plunder my wealth by yourself. I want to keep the treasures from you. You should beware of me, since I'm dead."

Hromund said, "Haul yourself up on your feet, you weak little sissy, and take the sword back from me, if you dare."

The dead man said, "It does you no honor to bear a sword against me when I'm unarmed. I'd rather test my strength against you in wrestling."

Hromund threw down the sword, trusting his own strength. Thrain saw that and let down his cauldron, which had been hanging up. He was scowling, and he blew on the fire so that he was ready to eat from the cauldron.[9] There was a great flame between the cauldron's legs, and it was filled with human corpses.[10] He was wearing a tunic embroidered with gold. Both his hands were twisted, and his nails curved down over his fingertips.

Hromund said, "Get off your throne, you cowardly wretch, stripped of all your wealth."

The dead man said, "Now it must be time to get on my feet, since you're questioning my courage."

The day had passed and evening was coming on, and it grew dark inside the mound. Thrain went to wrestle with Hromund, throwing down his cauldron. Hromund put forth his strength, and they went at it so fiercely that pebbles and stones flew into the air. The dead man dropped to one knee and said, "You've staggered me, and you're certainly a strong man."

Hromund said "Get back on your feet, and no propping yourself up. You're far weaker than old man Mani said."

Then Thrain began to turn into a troll, and the mound was filled with a vile stench. He sank his claws into the back of Hromund's neck and tore the flesh from his bones, all the way down to his loins. He said, "You can't complain, even though this game's turned rough and your back's gone sore, because now I shall tear you in two alive."

"I don't know how a pack of cats got into this mound," said Hromund.[11]

The dead man said, "You must have been raised by Gunnlod. There are few like you."

"It'll be bad for you to claw me any longer," said Hromund.

They wrestled so fiercely and so long that everything around them shook—until, in the end, Hromund brought Thrain down with a leg-throw. By then it had grown very dim. The dead man said, "Now you've beaten me by your skill, and my sword is captured. That puts an end to our game.

I have lived a long time in my mound and hung onto my wealth, but it's no good putting too much trust in your own treasures, even if they seem fine. And I never supposed that you, Mistletoe, my good sword, would do me harm."

Hromund got free and picked up the sword and said, "Tell me now how many men you vanquished in duels with Mistletoe."

"A hundred and twenty-four," said the dead man, "and I never got a scratch. King Seming,[12] who ruled in Sweden, and I put our skills to the test, and he thought it would be a long time before I could be beaten."

"You've done harm to men for a long time," said Hromund, "and it will be a fortunate deed to let you die as soon as possible."

He chopped off the dead man's head and burned him up completely on a pyre, and went out of the mound. The men asked how he and Thrain had parted. He said that it had gone as he wanted it to—"because I cut off his head."

Hromund took possession of three treasures that he fetched out of the mound: a ring, a necklace, and Mistletoe. Everyone got plenty of riches. King Olaf sailed away from there, northward to his own kingdom, and settled down quietly on his lands.

CHAPTER V

After that, Hromund was very famous, popular and generous. He once gave a good gold ring, which weighed an ounce, to a man named Hrok.[13] Vali managed to find out, and he killed Hrok during the night and took the ring. When Hromund found out, he said that he would pay Vali back some day for his dirty trick.[14]

The king had two sisters. One of them was named Dagny, and the other was Svanhvit. Svanhvit was foremost in every way, and there was no one like her between Sweden and Halogaland. Hromund Gripsson now stayed at home and enjoyed himself with Svanhvit, and never tried to avoid Vali or Bild.[15] She spoke with Hromund once and said that Vali and Bild would slander him to the king. He said, "I'm not afraid of any filthy cowards. As long as you're willing to grant me an audience, I'll converse with you."

But this slander became so strong that Hromund and his brothers had to leave the king's household, and they went home to their father. A little while later, Svanhvit spoke with King Olaf and said, "Now Hromund, who most increased our honor, has been exiled from the king's household. In his place, you have those two with you, who never care about their reputation or deeds."

The king answered, "I found out that he might seduce you. The sword shall sever your love."

"Little do you remember," she said, "when he went into the mound alone, and no one else dared. Vali and Bild will be hanged first," she said, and then she turned and went away.

CHAPTER VI

A little while later, two kings came from Sweden. They were both named Hadding.[16] Hrongvid's brother Helgi was with them. They summoned King Olaf to battle, on frozen Lake Vanern in the west. He preferred to meet them, rather than fleeing his ancestral lands. He sent word to Hromund and his brothers to come with him. Hromund didn't want to go anywhere, and he said that Bild and Vali would be quite helpful and accomplish everything with the king.

The king left home with his forces. Svanhvit was broken-hearted over this, and she went to Hromund's home. He welcomed her warmly.

"Pay more attention to this favor I'm begging you for than to my brother's demands," she said, "and offer the king your help. I will give you a shield and this ribbon that goes with it. You won't be harmed as long as you have that."

Hromund thanked her for this gift, and then she cheered up. He and his eight brothers prepared to travel.

Now the king came to frozen Lake Vanern with his forces. The Swedish forces were there ahead of him. In the morning, as soon as there was enough light for fighting, they armed themselves on the ice, and the Swedes attacked fiercely. Bild was killed as soon as the battle began, and Vali wasn't there. King Olaf and King Hadding were wounded.[17]

Hromund had set up his tent on that side of the lake. His brothers put on their armor early in the morning. Hromund said, "I had a bad dream last night, and everything won't go as we wish. I won't go to the battle today."

His brothers said that it would be a great disgrace to come on this mission but not dare to offer the king assistance. They went to the battle and pressed forward fiercely, and when they met the Haddings' forces, one foe fell across another.

A sorceress had come there in the form of a swan. She shrieked such powerful magic spells that none of Olaf's men remembered to defend himself. She flew over the sons of Grip and sang out loud. Her name was Kara. Helgi the Bold encountered the brothers all at once, and killed all eight of them together.

CHAPTER VII

At that moment, Hromund entered the battle. Helgi the Bold noticed him and said, "Now the man who killed my brother Hrongvid has arrived. You may beware of his sword, which he retrieved from the mound. You were far away when I killed your brothers."

Hromund said, "You don't need to question my courage, Helgi, because either I or you must now fall."

Helgi said, "Mistletoe is such a heavy weapon that you can't manage to wield it. I want to lend you this other sword that you'll be able to wield."

Hromund said, "You don't need to accuse me of being timid. You must remember the blow that I gave Hrongvid, when his skull shattered."

Helgi said, "Hromund, you've tied a certain maiden's garter around your arm. Put away that shield that you bear. You won't be wounded as long as you carry it, and I believe it's true that you believe in that maiden."

Hromund couldn't stand these taunts, and flung down his shield. Helgi the Bold had always won victory, and accomplished it by means of sorcery. His lover was named Kara, the one who was there in the likeness of a swan. Helgi swung his sword up so high over himself that it cut through the swan's leg, and he plunged the sword downwards into the earth up to the hilt. He said, "Now my luck is gone, and it went badly when I missed you."

Hromund said, "You've suffered the worst mishap, Helgi, since you killed your lover yourself. Your luck must be gone."

Kara dropped down dead. But as Helgi struck that blow at Hromund, when the sword plunged down to the hilt, the swordpoint touched Hromund's belly and sliced it downwards. Helgi bent over from the blow. Hromund lost no time and struck Helgi's head with Mistletoe, splitting his helmet and his head, so that the sword came to rest in his shoulders. The blade suffered a notch.

After that, Hromund took his knife, which hung from a thong on his belt, and stuck it into the edges of the wound ripped in his belly. He pushed his intestines back inside, which were hanging out, wrapped up his belly with the ribbon and bound it firmly with a cloth. He fought fiercely and felled one man across another, and fought on until the middle of the night. What was left of the Haddings' forces fled, and with that the battle ended.

Hromund then saw one man standing there on the ice. He knew that the same man must have made the lake freeze over with spells. He recognized that it was Vali. He said that he wasn't free of the obligation to pay him back, and he rushed at him, brandishing Mistletoe and meaning to strike him. Vali blew the sword out of his hand, and it landed in a hole in the ice and sank down to the bottom. Then Vali laughed and said, "Now you're doomed to die, since you let Mistletoe slip out of your hand."

Hromund said, "You'll die before I do." He leaped at Vali and heaved him up and slammed him down against the ice, so that his neck broke. That sorceror lay there dead.

Hromund sat down on the ice. He said, "I didn't take the maiden's advice. For that, I have now suffered fourteen wounds, and still my eight brothers have fallen, and my good sword Mistletoe fell into the lake, and I'll never get compensation for having lost the sword."

He went away from there and went back to his tent, and rested a little.

CHAPTER VIII

Now the king's sisters were sent for. Svanhvit examined Hromund's wounds and sewed his belly together and tried to find relief for him. She had him brought to an old man for healing; his name was Hagal. His wife was clever. They accepted him and nursed him back to health. Hromund found that this couple was skilled in many things.[18]

The old man customarily went fishing, and on one occasion when he was fishing, he hauled in a pike. When he came home and gutted it, he found Hromund's sword Mistletoe in its stomach, and he brought it to him. Hromund was happy and kissed the sword's hilt, and rewarded the old man well.[19]

There was one man in King Hadding's host who was named Blind the Evil. He told the king that Hromund was alive and well, in hiding with the old man Hagal and his wife. The king said that it was unbelievable that they would dare to conceal him. The king ordered a search for him. Blind went with some men to the house of Hagal and his wife, and asked if Hromund was being kept there. The old woman said that he wouldn't be found there. Blind searched carefully and didn't find him, because the old woman had hidden Hromund under her stew-kettle.

Blind and his fellows went away, and when they had gone on their way, Blind said, "Our trip has accomplished nothing, and we should go back."

They did so, and came to the house and found the old woman. Blind said that she was crafty and she had kept Hromund under her kettle. "Search and take him then," she said. She said that because as soon as she saw them turn back, she put Hromund in women's clothing and had him grind grain and turn the grindstone. They searched the buildings, and as soon as they came to where the woman was turning the grindstone, they went peering all around. She likewise stared at the king's men, scowling. They turned and left and didn't find her.

When they had gone on their way, Blind said that the old woman must have deceived their sight, and said that he suspected that Hromund must have been the one who was turning the grindstone in women's clothes. "I see that we have been outdone. It did us no good to contend with the old woman, because she's cleverer than we are." They wished her ill and went back home to the king, leaving matters as they stood.[20]

CHAPTER IX

The winter afterwards, many things appeared to Blind in his sleep, and he told the king one of his dreams. He said, "A lone wolf appeared to me, running from the east. He bit you, king, and gave you a wound."

The king said that he interpreted the dream in this way: "A king from some place will come here. The meeting will be hostile at first, but end in a settlement."

Again Blind said that he had dreamed that many hawks were sitting in one house—"and I noticed your falcon there, lord. It was completely featherless and skinned."

The king said, "Wind shall come from the clouds and shake our fortress."

Blind told a third dream in this way: "I saw many swine running from the south to the king's hall. They rooted up the earth with their snouts."

The king said, "That means swells on the sea, wet weather, and the growth of plants that grow on moisture from the lake, when the sun shines on the heath."

Blind told a fourth dream. "A horrible giant appeared to me, coming from the east. He bit you and made a great wound."

The king said, "Messengers from some kings will come into my hall. They will stab upwards with all their weapons, and that will make me angry."

"I had a fifth dream," said Blind, "that a savage serpent appeared to be lying around Sweden."

"A splendid dragon-ship will land here," said the king, "laden with treasures."

"I dreamed a sixth time," said Blind, "that dark clouds with talons and wings appeared to be coming from the land, and they flew away with you, king. Then I had another dream that a lone serpent was with the old man Hagal. He bit men fiercely, and devoured both you and me and all the king's men. What can this mean?"

The king said, "I have heard that a certain bear lies in his den a short way from Hagal's home. I will go and defeat the bear, and then he will bristle a great deal."

"Next I dreamed that a dragon's skin was dragged around the king's hall, and it hung there next to Hromund's belt."

The king said, "Don't you know that Hromund lost his sword and shield in the lake? Or are you scared of Hromund now?"

Blind dreamed more dreams, every one of which he told the king, but the king interpreted all of them in his favor, but none as a sign of any importance.[21]

Now Blind told one more of his dreams that concerned himself, and he said, "It seemed to me that an iron ring was set on my neck."

The king said, "The interpretation of that dream is that you will be hanged, and besides, that both of us are doomed to die."

CHAPTER X

After that, King Olaf summoned his forces and set his course for Sweden at once. Hromund went with him. They came to King Hadding's hall by surprise. He was lying in an outbuilding. He didn't become aware of anything until the building's doors were broken down. Hadding shouted to his men and asked who was attacking in the night. Hromund said that it was he.

The king said, "You must want to avenge your brothers."

Hromund said that he shouldn't say anything about the fall of his brothers. "Now you'll pay for that, and lose your life here."

A champion of King Hadding's rushed up, as huge as a giant. Hromund killed him. King Hadding defended himself in his bed and suffered no wounds, because every time Hromund struck at him, the flat of the sword struck the king. Then Hromund took a club and bashed King Hadding down to Hel.[22] Hromund said, "Here I have felled King Hadding, and I have never seen a more renowned man."

The old man Blind, whose real name was Bolvis, was tied up and hanged, and so his dream came true.[23] They took a great deal of gold and other wealth and then headed for home.

King Olaf betrothed Svanhvit to Hromund. They loved each other well, and had sons and daughters together, and were more excellent than others. Kingly lineages and great champions are descended from them.

Here ends the saga of Hromund Gripsson.

APPENDIX:

THE TALE OF GIFT-REF AND THE FOOLS OF THE VALLEY

Sögupáttr af Gjafa-Ref ok Dala-Fíflum

CHAPTER I

There was a king named Gauti who ruled over Gautland; he was a wise and well-mannered man, generous and outspoken. He often went out during the day to hunt with his hounds and hawks. And one day, when the king and his retainers had gone hunting animals, the king flung a spear at a stag, and the spear stuck in the wound. The king felt it would be shameful not to get his spear, and he rode following the fresh blood and became separated from his men. The weather turned cloudy, and the king lost the way. Then the king flung off his mantle and tunic and other clothes, so that he was left in nothing but his shirt and linen drawers.

Just then he heard a dog barking, and then he came to a farm. A man stood outside, in front of the gate. Right before the king's eyes, he beat the dog to death. Then the king meant to go inside, but the other man stepped in front of the gate. The king charged him and they wrestled for a while, and so the king managed to get in against the will of the man who stood outside. The buildings were well built, and the people were handsome and tall in proportion. They were afraid of the king. The man who the king felt must be the farmer spoke: "What action did you take when the hound howled?"

"I killed him," said the thrall.

"That was the right thing to do," said the farmer. "I will give you your freedom, and you shall go with me."

The king went to the table and sat down to eat with the farmer, but the farmer didn't speak. No one spoke to anyone else. Then the people went off to sleep, and everything was still. The king felt that this was a fine piece of work. Just then, a woman came to the king and said, "Wouldn't it be a better idea for you to accept a favor from me?"

The king said, "Things are looking up, now that you want to talk with me. Your way of life is strange here. But what's your name?"

She said, "I'm called Snotra. I'm the daughter of old man Gilling and old lady Totra, and my sisters are called Hjotra and Fjotra. My brothers are called Skafnaurtung, Heimsigull, and Fjolmod. Here on our farm are

Gilling's Cliff and Family Crag, and it's called that because people fall off it as soon as something extraordinary happens which has never happened before in our memory. And my older siblings will perish because you've come here, because it's not to be expected that guests would come here, and they have to go over Family Crag."

The king said, "You're the most well-spoken of the people here, and you must want to have my trust, because I see that you're a virgin. And you must sleep with me tonight and see how matters turn out."

"It's all the same," she said, and she did as the king wished.

Early in the morning, the king got up and said, "I have to ask you for a favor, Skafnortung. I came to your farm without shoes, so I'd like to get shoes from you."

He didn't answer, but he gave him shoes and pulled out the laces. Then the king left, and Snotra showed him the road. He invited her to come with him, "because I suspect that something will come of our meeting; and if it's the case that you're pregnant and it's a boy, you must name him Gautrek."

She said that it would be so—"but I have to go back home, because I don't want to let my inheritance slip away, after my brothers and sisters, because they're all going over Family Crag." Then she turned away.

CHAPTER II

When she came home, her father Gilling was sitting over his store of wealth, and he said, "A great wonder has come about here, that a man's had lodging from me, and so I must go over Family Crag today. Before that, I want to divide my wealth among my children. First, Skafnaurtung shall have the finr ox, and Fjolmod shall have my bars of gold, and Heimsigull all the grain. Fjolmod must marry his sister Fjotra, and Heimsigull must marry Hjotra, and Skafnaurtung must marry Snotra. But I'll go to Gilling's Cliff and over Family Crag with Totra and our thrall; we can't live any longer with this incredible portent, and I can't reward the thrall any better for killing the dog. See to it that you don't allow your numbers to increase such that you can't manage to keep your inheritances, on account of too many people in the house."

They led their father and mother and the thrall over Family Crag, and they settled there afterwards. They pinned homespun cloth around themselves so that none of them could touch another's bare skin, and that's how they slept. Then Snotra suspected that she was pregnant. It so happened that she shifted the pins in the homespun cloth and took Skafnaurtung's hand and laid it on her cheek and acted as if she were sleeping.

He woke up and said, "Now matters have taken a most unexpected turn. Have I hurt you at all?"

She said, "It's no use hiding it, but keep quiet about this: I'm pregnant."

"A dreadful calamity has happened now," he said, "and I must tell my brothers."

Soon afterwards, a boy child was born there. Her brothers came and said, "Now all our plans will collapse, and this is a serious violation of the rules." Skafnaurtung replied,

> I've stumbled upon
> a stupid thing,
> feeling that woman's face.
> Siring sons
> is a small matter,
> and that's how Gautrek was begotten.

They said that he wasn't to blame, since he said that he hadn't wanted it to happen. But he said that he didn't want to wait to go over Family Cliff, since it would be counted less of a portent, and so he went on his way.

On one occasion, Fjolmod was brooding over his wealth and had his bars of gold with him, and he fell asleep. When he woke up, two snails had crawled up onto his gold bars. It seemed to him that there were dents where they'd crawled, and that the gold was diminished. He thought that they would eat it up right before his eyes. He then said, "I won't wait for more wonders. It won't be good to come poor and penniless to Valhall to King Odin, and it's best to go before all my wealth slips out of my hands." He went to his brother and told him that snails[1] had tried to eat his gold bars. They felt that this was terrible, and Fjolmod went on his way.

It's said that Heimsigull walked through his fields every morning. He saw that a bird called a sparrow took a grain out of an ear. He said, "That was spoilage that the sparrow did; that will bring trouble to me and my girlfriend Hjotra."[2] At once they went over Family Crag.

Gautrek was seven years old, and he saw the fine ox that Skafnaurtung had owned. As it happened, he stabbed it with a spear and killed it. Snotra went with her son to King Gauti, and he received him well. This Gautrek has been called the most excellent of all ancient kings, and people have great sagas of his generosity. King Gauti died, and Gautrek took over the rulership of Gautland after him, and he was the most generous with his wealth, this King Gautrek, to rich and poor alike.

CHAPTER III

Neri was the name of a jarl in Gautland. He was such a powerful and wise man that no one like him could be found. Everyone came to him and asked for some advice in their affairs, and everything he set his mind to turned out well. He never wanted to accept riches, because he didn't want to repay anything, on account of his greed.

Reimir was the name of a farmer who lived on Reimsey. He had a wife and a son who was named Ref. Ref was young, and he lay in the cookhouse and bit twigs and bark and kindled the fire; he was very tall and never washed the filth from himself. Yet he was well-known, but not for any cleverness or achievement. The farmer had little love for his son.

Farmer Reimir had one fine possession, and it was an ox; there was none like it in the land, both in size and all its beauty. The horns were carved, and gold was inlaid into the carvings and on the tips. A great silver chain ran between the horns, with three large gold rings on it.

One day, when farmer Reimir went to the cookhouse, he tripped over Ref where he was lying flat, up against the ash-pit. Reimir said, "It's a terrible misfortune to have such a son. Get out of here as fast as you can."

Ref said, "You'll find it the most fitting for both possessions to leave your ownership: the ox, which you think the best, and I, whom you think the worst."

Reimir agreed to this. Then Ref stood up and shook his head. He took the good ox and led it behind him, and he went away, wearing a short cloak and ankle-length breeches. Men had never seen a more handsome cow, nor a better decorated one. He approached the hall of King Gautrek; men were outside and saw him going, and they said, "Here comes Ref, Reimir's fool, with the good ox, and he must want to give it to the king." Men dashed into the hall and told the king. The king ordered them not to mock him on his way. Ref came to the king's hall, but he didn't come before the king, and he stayed there for one night.

Early in the morning he prepared to go—the men had misjudged Ref's gift. Then Ref took the path that he knew ran to the hall of Jarl Neri, who was in charge of the defense of the king's lands. There were men outside on the playing field. They said, "There goes Ref the fool with the precious ox." Then Ref came to the hall doors and said, "Ask the jarl to come out!"

They said, "You're not giving up your foolishness at all. The jarl's not in the habit of jumping up to speak with every peasant."

"Take him my message," said Ref, "and let him decide on an answer."

They went and told the jarl that Ref had arrived: "he's asking you to come out."

The jarl said, "I shall certainly meet him, because you never know what luck each person may bring."

The jarl went outside and greeted Ref, and he accepted the greeting. The jarl said, "What's the meaning of you coming here?"

Ref said, "I want to give you this ox that I've led here."

The jarl said, "Haven't you heard before that I don't want to accept gifts, because I'm not willing to repay anyone?"

Ref said, "That will go as it may."

"Why didn't you give him to King Gautrek?" said the jarl. "For he is a generous man. Didn't you go there?"

"I certainly went there," said Ref. "This is everything I own, and I don't suppose that anyone's better suited to enjoy it than you, however stingy you're said to be."

"I won't reward you much," said the jarl, "but I'll still give you clothes, so that you're not shameful." Then his tattered rags were taken off him, and respectable clothing was brought in, and Ref looked like the most excellent man. He stayed there for a while, and then the jarl said, "I don't let men stay here for so long who don't busy themselves with something. You should go to King Gautrek, and you shall bring him this whetstone to trade."

Ref said, "I'm not used to going between men, because I don't see what use it will be."

The jarl said, "My cleverness wouldn't be of much use if I couldn't see farther forward than you. But the only trial for you will be to find the king, because you mustn't talk to him. I'm told that the king sits on a burial mound for a long time and hunts with his hawk, and when day is passing, the hawk droops. Then the king fumbles around his chair with his hands. Stand behind the king's back. And if it so happens that the king doesn't get anything to throw at the hawk, put the stone in the king's hand, and if something is laid in your hand, accept it."

Ref went at once and came to the king's mound. It went as the jarl had guessed: the king flung everything that he picked up at the hawk. Ref sat down behind the king's back. The king reached out his hand behind him. Ref stuck the stone into the king's hand, and the king threw the stone and the king threw it right at the hawk's back. The hawk flew up sharply. The king felt that he had done well, and he didn't want the one who had given him the stone to be left in want. He passed a gold ring behind his back, without looking at Ref. Ref took the ring and went home to meet the jarl. He asked how it had gone.

Ref said, "Sitting there wasn't useless."

"I see that this is a fine treasure," said the jarl.

Ref stayed there over the winter. When spring came, the jarl said, "What will you accomplish now, Ref?"

Ref said, "Wouldn't it be best to sell the ring for cash?"

The jarl said, "I'll give you some more help. There is a king named Ælle who rules over England. You must give the ring to him, and you won't lose money from it. But come to me in the autumn, because I won't withhold food or advice from you, though it won't amount to payment for the ox."

Ref said, "I wish you wouldn't mention that."

CHAPTER IV

Then he traveled to England and came before King Ælle and greeted him. Ref was suitably dressed. The king asked who this man might be. "My name is Ref, my lord," said he, "and I want you to accept this gold ring from me," and he laid it on the table before the king.

The king said, "This is a great treasure. But who gave it to you?"

"King Gautrek," said Ref.

"What did you give him?"

"A whetstone," said Ref.

"Great is King Gautrek's generosity," said King Ælle, "since he gave gold in exchange for pebbles. I will accept the ring, and I invite you to stay here."

Ref said, "I want to return to Jarl Neri, my foster-father."

"Then you must stay here for a while," said King Ælle. And when men readied his own ship to travel, King Ælle said, "A ship is readied here to sail to Gautland with the most suitable cargo, and I will give you that ship, Ref, with all its cargo and crew. Yet this is a little thing, compared to what King Gautrek gave you for one whetstone."

"Such rewards are magnificent," said Ref. Then Ref boarded his ship with plenty provisions, and he thanked the king well.

The king said, "Accept these two dogs. They're quite small and pretty." Ref had never seen anything like them. They had on golden harnesses, and a gold ring was around the neck of each one, with seven little rings on the leash. No one thought he'd ever seen such treasures.

Then he left for Jarl Neri's realm. The jarl went to meet him and welcomed him—"and come visit us."

Ref said, "I have enough to pay our way."

"That is well," said Jarl Neri, "but you mustn't diminish those goods of yours. You shall bring yourself and your men to our property, though it's not a great reward for the ox."

Now Ref stayed with the jarl for the winter, with all his men. When spring came, the jarl spoke with Ref: "What will you do now?"

Ref said, "Now everything's easy; there's no lack of money if the men want to set out raiding or trading."

The jarl said, "I have to lend you a hand again. You must go to Denmark, to meet King Hrolf Kraki, and bring him the dogs, because they aren't possessions for a commoner. Once again, you won't lose money from it, if he will accept them."

Ref said, "It's up to you, but I'm not short of money."

Then he made ready and put out to sea and sailed to Denmark. He met King Hrolf and greeted him. The king asked who he might be. "I'm called Ref," he said.

The king said, "Are you Gift-Ref?"

"I've accepted gifts from chieftains," said Ref, "yet I've also given them now and again. I want to give you these little dogs, my lord, along with their harness."

The king looked at them and said, "Such things are treasures. But who gave them to you?"

Ref said, "King Ælle."

"What did you give him?"

"A gold ring."

King Hrolf asked, "But who gave you that?"

Ref said, "King Gautrek."

The king said, "Great is the generosity of such men. But what did you give him?"

"A whetstone."

The king said, "Such graciousness is a grand thing, to give gold for peddles. I will accept the dogs. Stay with us."

Ref answered, "I have to return in the fall to Jarl Neri, my foster-father."

King Hrolf answered, "So be it."

Ref stayed with the king for a while. Then he readied his ship. The king said, "I've decided on a reward for you. You shall accept a ship from me, just like the one from the king of England, and the finest cargo and men shall go with it."

Ref said, "Thank you very much, my lord, for a noble gift," and then he got ready to leave.

King Hrolf said, "Here are two things that you should accept from me: a helmet and a mailcoat."

Ref accepted the treasures. They were both made of red gold. After that, Ref went home to Jarl Neri, captaining two ships. The jarl welcomed him and said, "Come to us as before. I must seem meddlesome to you, but it wouldn't be seemly for me to withhold my advice, since it's helpful for you."

Ref said, "I benefit from you and your guidance in all these affairs." Ref stayed there for another winter.

CHAPTER V

Now there is to say, concerning King Gautrek, that he ruled his kingdom well. He had many counsellors. There was a man named Hrosskel, a friend of the king. The king owned a splendid stallion; he was gray in color. There was a mare with the stallion, pale as silk and so lovely that a finer one was not to be found. One autumn, the king invited Hrosskel to his estate and gave him the stallion, and they parted as good friends.

There was a king named Harald who ruled over the southern Baltic lands. He was wise, but not much of a warrior. He had a queen and a daughter named Alfhild, the loveliest of women, but not wise. King Gautrek set out once on a journey to the Baltic shore and asked to marry King Harald's daughter. His proposal received a favorable answer, and he married her and brought her home to Gautland. They had a daughter named Helga. She was wise and well mannered and the loveliest of women. King Gautrek ruled his kingdom well, in glory and honor and truth.

Now we return to Ref, who stayed with Jarl Neri. When he had been there for a while, the jarl asked what he wanted to accomplish. Ref said, "There's no lack of money now."

"I think that's true," said the jarl, "but there is just one expedition that I want to propose to you. There's a king named Olaf, who goes out raiding and has eighty ships. He sails out to sea in winter and in summer. You must bring him the helmet and the mailcoat, and if he accepts, I expect that he will ask you to choose a reward for it. You must choose to command his ships and men for a month, and take them wherever you want. But there's a man named Refnef with the king. He is a fierce and hateful man, and he is the king's counsellor. I can scarcely tell whether our luck or his sorcery might be greater, but you'll have to risk it, however it turns out. You must lead all the men into my stables, and then I'll have to see again whether I get you rewarded for the fine ox."

Ref said, "I think you mention that often. The ox was paid for a long time ago."

Then Ref set out to seek Olaf the sea-king, and in the end he found him with all his fleet. He sailed up to the king's ship and greeted the king. The king asked who he might be. "I'm called Ref."

"Are you called Gift-Ref?"

"My lord," said Ref, "certainly I have both accepted gifts and given then. I want to give two gifts to you, a helmet and a mailcoat, if you find these treasures befitting your rank."

"Who gave you such treasures? For I've never seen any others as good, and I've never heard of these, although I have traveled through most lands."

Ref said, "King Hrolf gave them to me."

"What did you give him?"

"Two dogs."

"Who gave you those?"

"King Ælle."

"What did you give him?"

Ref said, "A gold ring."

The king said, "Who gave it to you?"

"King Gautrek."

"What did you give him?"

Ref said, "A whetstone."

The king said, "Great is the generosity of such kings. But should I accept these gifts, Refnef?"

Refnef said, "I don't think it's a good idea for you to accept the treasures, if you don't have the sense to give something in return." And with that, he seized the treasures and jumped overboard with them. Ref saw that he'd soon be badly played if Refnef got away. Ref went after him, and they had the fiercest fight, but in the end Ref got the mailcoat. Refnef kept the helmet and turned into a troll down on the bottom. When Ref came up, he was exhausted. Then this was said:

> I must reckon
> that Refnef's advice
> was not at all like
> what Neri counseled;
> he didn't fling
> far out to sea
> the gold ring which Gautrek
> gave to Ref.

King Olaf said, "You are an excellent man."

Ref said, "I'd like you to accept the remaining treasure."

The king said that he was certainly willing to accept, and he was just as thankful as if he'd accepted both. "It was because of trickery that I didn't accept both right away. It's surprising that I listened to the counsel of a wicked man. Choose your reward for it."

"I want to command your ships and men for half a month, and you must send them wherever I want."

"A strange reward," said the king, "but they'll be at your disposal."

At once they headed for Gautland and entered Jarl Neri's kingdom. They arrived late in the day. The jarl had heard of his coming and went to meet Ref and said, "Now things have come to the point, foster-son, that there's a chance, however it comes about. You're a very lucky man."

Ref told him the story.

"I thought as much," said the jarl. "The next time we meet, you must not show surprise at what I say, and respond according to what I hand you."

The jarl went away and came to the king of Gautland around midnight, and went straight into the king's lodging; he was allowed to do that. The king jumped up and welcomed the jarl and asked what could have happened, that he was on his feet at night. The jarl said, "A host has come into your kingdom and intended to lay the land waste."

The king asked, "Who is the leader?"

The jarl said, "Ref, our friend, who's not at all likely to be peaceful."

The king said, "Wouldn't it be a good idea to summon our forces?"

The jarl said, "There's no chance, because they must have already conquered a great kingdom, for they have countless numbers and are sailing in eighty ships and two boats. I would rather go with a suitable message and find out whether we can reach a settlement, because my realm is the first in their path."

The king answered, "We've heeded your counsel for a long time."

Then they went out and approached the ships. The jarl said, "Is Ref leading these ships?"

"He is," he said.

The jarl said, "Can something be found to show that there will be peace in this land and that a suitable offer be made to you?"

"I shall accept that," said Ref.

The jarl said, "I know that you'll demand much, and that isn't surprising, because your mother's father was a mighty jarl. I can tell what you must have in mind; you must want to have my realm and become the king's kinsman and marry his daughter. You must admit that pleases you."

Ref said, "I'll see to it. I will say yes to what you're offering."

Then the jarl said to the king, "My lord, it seems to me that only this can bring peace and quiet: to betroth your daughter to him, a man descended from jarls and of the best family. Let him be the overseer of your kingdom."

The king said, "Why shouldn't you decide this? For you have often given me helpful advice."

Then this was confirmed with oaths, and the king went away.

Ref said, "You've granted me good help, King Olaf. You shall now go on your way."

King Olaf said, "Wiser men than you have taken part in this." Then King Olaf sailed away. And when the fleet had left, King Gautrek said, "I've had to deal with tricks and cunning, and that will be remembered, but that's how it has to be now."

The jarl said to Ref, "I suppose that that huge force was useful to you, and now only your men are left. And I think we need to decide that I have repaid you for the ox, but I haven't rewarded you as much as you did me, because you gave me all you had, while I have plenty of possessions left."

Ref claimed the jarldom and married the king's daughter, and was thought to be the most renowned man in all respects; his family was descended from nobly-born men. Ref ruled this kingdom, but he didn't live to be old. Jarl Neri died suddenly, and so did King Gautrek's queen, and a funeral feast was held for them.

King Gautrek was a famous man for his generosity, but he wasn't a wise man. He was the most well-liked and generous of all men. By this time he was bowed down by old age. After the death of his queen, his men encouraged him to marry a queen. King Gautrek accepted this advice and set out from home with eighty men, well equipped.

CHAPTER VI

There was a powerful man named Thorir; he was a hersir[3] and had a large estate in Sogn. He was an outstanding man, the mightiest of men. He was married and had one daughter named Ingibjorg; she was both wise and lovely. Many men had asked for her hand, and she had shown them all the door.

It so happened that King Gautrek arrived. He was warmly welcomed and given a fine feast. A certain prince had also come there, who was named Olaf, with a hundred men. He had asked for Ingibjorg's hand, and she had responded favorably, for he was young and the most handsome of men. Gautrek heard about this but paid no attention, and he brought forth his proposal and asked for Ingibjorg's hand.

Thorir said, "The matter has come to this, as you know, that a prince named Olaf has come here; he is the most handsome man, and he has asked for Ingibjorg's hand. We have been informed about you, King Gautrek, that you are the most excellent of kings, and have ruled your kingdom long and well. Thus she herself shall choose the man that she wants."

They were pleased with this answer, and they went directly to Ingibjorg's bower. Her father told her how matters stood and asked her to decide whom she wished to marry.

"It seems to me," she said, "that these are both excellent men and more than an equal match for me, whichever one I choose. Olaf seems to me to have promise as a ruler, although he is little tested. But King Gautrek is known to us. He has the acclamation of his entire nation, both the mighty and the wretched. And I would rather choose King Gautrek, although he is old. We know neither the good points nor the bad ones of the other man, although he is handsome to look at. I would rather be betrothed to an excellent king, even though he may live a short while, rather than to a young and unsteady one, even if he were to grow as old as a stone bridge. I may have fine sons with him, and I would be content with that for a very long time, after the king has passed on."

And when they heard her words, King Gautrek leaped up and betrothed himself to Ingibjorg. Olaf grew very angry and said that he would take revenge on King Gautrek himself, and on his men. King Gautrek said that he would just have to put up with a misfortune that he couldn't stand. Olaf went away with his men, extremely angry.

King Gautrek stayed there for several nights. After that, he prepared to take his leave. Ingibjorg went on the journey with the king; he wanted to celebrate his wedding to her at home. Thorir was very rich, and bestowed a great deal of wealth in gold and silver. Gautrek rode home with his retinue, and as they were riding close to a certain forest, a large fighting force suddenly appeared beside them. Olaf had come there with all his men, and he ordered King Gautrek to do one of two things: fight him, or give up Ingibjorg and her dowry. King Gautrek said, "It is wicked for you to take the maiden from me, and then I would have lived far too long." And he ordered his men to cut down the warriors and draw their weapons. The fiercest battle broke out. King Gautrek advanced with the greatest vigor into the ranks of Olaf and all his men, who fell one across another. Nothing could stop him. Olaf and all his men fell there, so that not one of them was left standing. King Gautrek wasn't wounded, and few of his men had died. He traveled home then, and his journeying was thought to be the most splendid. He celebrated his wedding with a great crowd of men. Warm love began to grow between them. Not much time passed before the queen bore a boy-child. He was brought to the king, who had him named Ketil . He grew up there and was rather short in stature. The queen bore another son, and he was named Hrolf. These boys were brought up carefully. Hrolf grew strong at an early age.

And here now ends the tale of Gift-Ref and the Fools of the Valley.

BIBLIOGRAPHY

Icelandic authors have been alphabetized by first name, as is common practice. All "sagas of Icelanders" whose publication information is not specifically cited may be found in translation in *Complete Sagas of Icelanders*, edited by Viðar Hreinsson. All *fornaldarsögur* whose publication information is not otherwise specified may be found in Guðni Jónsson and Bjarni Vilhjálmson's 1943-44 edition of *Fornaldarsögur Norðurlanda*.

Aarne, Antti (ed. transl. Stith Thompson). *The Types of the Folktale: A Classification and Bibliography*. Helsinki: Suomalainen Tiedeakatemia, 1981.

Adam of Bremen (Francis J. Tschan, transl.) *History of the Archbishops of Hamburg-Bremen*. New York: Columbia University Press, 2002.

Adamson, Melitta Weiss. *Food in Medieval Times*. Westport, Conn.: Greenwood Press, 2004.

Anderson, Andrew Runni. "Bucephalas and His Legend." *American Journal of Philology*, vol. 51 (1930), pp. 1-21.

Andersson, Theodore M. "'Helgakviða Hjǫrvarðssonar' and European Bridal-Quest Narrative." *Journal of English and Germanic Philology*, vol. 84, no. 1 (1985), pp. 51-75.

Andrews, A. LeRoy. "Studies in the Fornaldarsǫgur Norðrlanda. I: The Hrómundar saga Gripssonar." *Modern Philology*, vol. 8, no. 4 (1911), pp. 527-544.

——. "Studies in the Fornaldarsǫgur Norðrlanda [continued]. I: The Hrómundar saga Gripssonar." *Modern Philology*, vol. 9, no. 3 (1912), pp. 371-397.

Bachman, W. Bryant, trans. *Forty Old Icelandic Tales*. Lanham, Md.: University Press of America, 1992.

Bachman, W. Bryant, and Guðmundur Erlingsson. *Six Old Icelandic Sagas*. Lanham, Md.: University Press of America, 1993.

Bampi, Massimiliano. "What's in a Variant? On Editing the Longer Redaction of *Gautreks saga*." *On Editing Old Scandinavian Texts: Problems and Perspectives*. Fulvio Ferrari and Massimiliano Bampi, eds. Trento: Universitá degli Studi di Trento, 2006, pp. 57-67.

—. "Between Tradition and Innovation: The Story of Starkaðr in *Gautreks saga*." *The Fantastic in Old Norse/Icelandic Literature: Sagas and the British Isles*, John McKinnell, David Ashurst, and Donata Kick, eds. Durham: Centre for Medieval and Renaissance Studies, 2006. Vol. 2, pp. 88-96.

Barnes, Geraldine. "Romance in Iceland." *Old Icelandic Literature and Society*. Margaret Clunies Ross, ed. Cambridge: Cambridge University Press, 2000, pp. 266-286.

Bately, Janet and Englert, Anton. *Ohthere's Voyages*. Roskilde: Viking Ship Museum, 2007.

Battles, Paul. "Dwarfs in Germanic Literature: *Deutsche Mythologie* or Grimm's Myths?" *The Shadow-Walkers: Jacob Grimm's Mythology of the Monstrous*. Tom Shippey, ed. Tempe, Ariz.: Arizona Center for Medieval and Renaissance Studies, 2005, pp. 29-82.

Beard, D. J. "Á Þá Bitu Engi Járn: A Brief Note on the Concept of Invulnerability in the Old Norse Sagas." *Studies in English Language and Early Literature in Honour of Paul Christophersen. Occasional Papers in Linguistics and Language Teaching*, no. 8. P. M. Tilling, ed. Belfast: New University of Ulster, 1981, pp. 13-31.

Benati, Chiara. "Ásmund *á austrvega*: The Faroese Oral Tradition on Ásmund and its Relation to the Icelandic Saga." *Á austrvega: Saga and East Scandinavia. Preprint Papers of the 14th International Saga Conference*. Volume 1. Agneta Ney, Henrik Williams, and Fredrik Charpentier Ljungqvist, eds. Gävle: Gävle University Press, 2009. pp. 110-118.

Bibire, Paul. "On Reading the Icelandic Sagas: Approaches to Old Icelandic Texts." *West Over Sea: Studies in Scandinavian Sea-Borne Expansion and Settlement Before 1300.* Beverley Ballin Smith, Simon Taylor, and Gareth Williams, eds. Leiden: Brill, 2007. pp. 3-18.

Bjarni Guðnason, ed. *Danakonunga Sögur. Íslenzk Fornrit* vol. XXXV. Reykjavík: Hið Íslenzka Fornritafélag, 1982.

Blake, N. F. (ed. transl.) *The Saga of the Jomsvikings.* London: Thomas Nelson, 1962.

Borovsky, Zoe. "Folk Dramas, Farce, and the *Fornaldarsögur.*" Presented at the 9th Colloquium of the Société Internationale pour l'Étude du Théâtre Médiéval (SITM), Odense, Denmark, 1998. http://www.sitm.info/history/1998-2001/SITM_files/SummariesIII.html#ZoeBorovsky

Boyer, Régis. *Les Sagas Légendaires.* Paris: Les Belles Lettres, 1998.

Brodeur, Arthur Gilchrist. *The Art of* Beowulf. Berkeley and Los Angeles: University of California Press, 1959.

Brown, Ursula [Dronke]. "The Saga of Hrómund Gripsson and Þorgilssaga." *Saga-Book of the Viking Society* , vol. 13 (1947-48), pp. 51-77.

Byock, Jesse L., trans. *The Saga of King Hrolf Kraki.* London: Penguin, 1998.

—. *The Saga of the Volsungs.* London: Penguin, 1999.

Chesnutt, Michael. "The Content and Meaning of *Gjafa-Refs saga.*" *Fornaldarsagaerne: Myter og Virkilighed.* Agneta Ney, Ármann Jakobsson, and Annette Lassen, eds. Copenhagen: Museum Tusculanums Forlag, 2009. pp. 93-106.

Clover, Carol. "Maiden Warriors and Other Sons." *Journal of English and Germanic Philology*, vol. 85, no. 1 (1986), pp. 35-49.

Clunies-Ross, Margaret. "Poet into Myth: Starkaðr and Bragi." *Viking and Medieval Scandinavia*, vol. 2 (2006), pp. 31-43.

Cronan, Dennis. "The Thematic Unity of the Younger 'Gautreks saga'." *Journal of English and Germanic Philology* vol. 106, no. 1 (2007), pp. 81-123.

Davidson, Hilda Ellis. *The Sword in Anglo-Saxon England: Its Archaeology and Literature.* Corrected ed. Woodbridge: Boydell, 1994.

DeAngelo, Jeremy. "The North and the Depiction of the *Finnar* in the Icelandic Sagas." *Scandinavian Studies* vol. 82, no. 3 (2010), pp. 257-286.

Donecker, Stefan. "The Werewolves of Livonia: Lycanthropy and Shape-Changing in Scholarly Texts, 1550–1720." *Preternature: Critical and Historical Studies on the Preternatural,* vol. 1, no. 2, pp. 289-322.

Driscoll, Matthew. "*Nitida Saga.*" *Medieval Scandinavia.* Ed. Phillip Pulsiano and Kirsten Wolf. London: Routledge, 1993. p. 432.

—. *The Unwashed Children of Eve: The Production, Dissemination and Reception of Popular Literature in Post-Reformation Iceland.* Enfiedl Lock: Hisarlik Press, 1997.

—. "Fornaldarsögur Norðurlanda: The Stories That Wouldn't Die." *Fornaldarsagornas Sturuktur och Ideologi: Handlingar Från ett Symposium i Uppsala 31.8–2.9 2001.* Ármann Jakobsson, Annette Lassen, and Agneta Ney, eds. Uppsala: Uppsala Universitet, 2003. pp. 257-267.

—. "Late Prose Fiction (*lygisögur*)." *A Companion to Old Norse-Icelandic Literature and Culture.* Rory McTurk, ed. Malden, Mass.: Blackwell, 2005. pp. 190-204.

—. "A New Edition of the *Fornaldarsögur Norðurlanda*: Some Basic Questions." *On Editing Old Scandinavian Texts: Problems and Perspectives.* M. Bampi and F. Ferrari, eds. Trento: Universitá da Trento, 2009. pp. 71-84.

—. "The Long and Winding Road: Manuscript Culture in Late Pre-Modern Iceland." *White Field, Black Seeds: Nordic Literacy Practices in the Long Nineteenth Century.* Anna Kuismin and M. J. Driscoll, eds. Helsinki: Finnish Literature Society, 2013. pp. 50-63.

Driscoll, Matthew, and Silvia Hufnagel. "*Fornaldarsögur norðurlanda*: A Bibliography of Manuscripts, Editions, Translations and Secondary Literature." Arnamagnæan Institute, Copenhagen. http://nfi.ku.dk/fornaldarsogur/

Einar Ólafur Sveinsson, ed. *Íslenzk Fornrit* XII. *Brennu-Njáls Saga*. Reykjavík: Hið Íslenzka Fornritafélag, 1954.

— (Einar G. Pétursson, rev.; Benedikt Benedikz, transl.; Anthony Faulkes, ed.) *The Folk-Stories of Iceland*. London: Viking Society for Northern Research, 2003.

Ewing, Thor. *Viking Clothing*. Stroud, Gloucestershire: The History Press, 2009.

Finlay, Alison. "Monstrous Allegations: An Exchange of *ýki* in *Bjarnar saga Hítdœlakappa*." *Alvíssmál*, vol. 10 (2001), pp. 21-44.

Finnur Jónsson. *Fernir Forníslenskir Rímnaflokkar*. Kaupmannahöfn [Copenhagen]: S. L. Møller, 1896.

Fjalldal, Magnús. *The Long Arm of Coincidence: The Frustrated Connection Between* Beowulf *and* Grettis saga. Toronto: University of Toronto Press, 1998.

—. *Anglo-Saxon England in Icelandic Medieval Texts*. Toronto: University of Toronto Press, 2005.

Foote, Peter G. "Sagnaskemtan: Reykjahólar 1119." *Saga-Book of the Viking Society*, vol. 14 (1953-57), pp. 226-239.

Gade, Kari Ellen. "Penile Puns: Personal Names and Phallic Symbols in Skaldic Poetry." *Essays in Medieval Studies*, vol. 6 (1989), pp. 57-67.

—. "Northern Lights on the Battle of Hastings." *Viator*, vol. 28 (1997), pp. 65-81.

Gallo, Lorenzo Lozzi. "Persistent Motifs of Cursing from Old Norse Literature in *Buslubœn*." *Linguistica e Filologia*, vol 18 (2004), pp. 119-146.

Gilliam, Terry, and Terry Jones (dir.) *Monty Python and the Holy Grail.* Graham Chapman, John Cleese, Eric Idle, Terry Gilliam, Terry Jones, Michael Palin, perf. London: Python (Monty) Pictures, 1975.

Grimm, Jacob (James Steven Stallybrass, transl.) *Teutonic Mythology.* 4th ed. London: W. Swan Sonnenschein & Allen, 1880.

Gould, Chester Nathan. "Dwarf-Names: A Study in Old Icelandic Religion." *PMLA*, vol. 44, no. 4 (1929), pp. 939-967.

Guðni Jónsson and Bjarni Vilhjálmson, eds. *Fornaldarsögur Norðurlanda.* 3 vols. Reykjavík: Bókaútgáfan Forni, 1943.

Gunnell, Terry. *The Origins of Drama in Scandinavia.* Woodbridge: Boydell and Brewer, 1995.

—. "The Relationship Between Icelandic *Knattleikur* and Early Irish Hurling." *Béaloideas*, vol. 80 (2012), pp. 52-69.

Harris, Joseph. "The Prosimetrum of Icelandic Saga and Some Relatives." Joseph Harris and Karl Reichl, eds. *Prosimetrum: Cross-Cultural Perspectives on Narrative in Prose and Verse.* Cambridge: D. S. Brewer, 1997.

Hartmann, Jacob Wittmer. *The Gǫngu-Hrólfssaga: A Study in Old Norse Philology.* New York: Columbia University Press, 1912.

Haymes, Edward. *The Saga of Thidrek of Bern.* New York: Garland, 1988.

Heide, Eldar. "Spinning *Seiðr*". *Old Norse Religion in Long-Term Perspectives: Origins, Changes, and Interactions.* Ed. Anders Andrén, Kristina Jennbert, and Catharina Raudvere. Lund: Nordic Academic Press, 2006. pp. 164-170.

Hofstra, Tette and Kees Samplonius. "Viking Expansion Northwards: Mediæval Sources." *Arctic*, vol. 48, no. 3 (1995), pp. 235-247.

Hollander, Lee M. "The Gautland Cycle of Sagas: I. The Source of the Polyphemos Episode of the Hrólfssaga Gautrekssonar." *Journal of English and Germanic Philology*, vol. 11, no. 1 (1912), pp. 61-81.

—. "The Gautland Cycle of Sagas: II. Evidences of the Cycle." *Journal of English and Germanic Philology*, vol. 11, no. 2 (1912), pp. 209-217.

—. "The 'Faithless Wife' Motif in Old Norse Literature." *Modern Language Notes*, vol. 27, no. 3 (1912), pp. 71-73.

—, transl. *The Poetic Edda*. 2nd ed. Austin: University of Texas Press, 1962.

Hooper, A. G. "*Hrómundar saga Gripssonar* and the *Griplur.*" *Leeds Studies in English*, vol. 3 (1934), pp. 51-56.

Íslendinga Sögur, Udgivne efter Gamle Haandskrifter af det Kongelike Nordiske Oldskrift-Selskab. Kjöbenhavn [Copenhagen]: S. L. Möllers Bogtrykkeri, 1843.

Jackson, Tatjana N. "On the Possible Sources of the Textual Map of Denmark in *Göngu-Hrólfs saga.*" *Skemmtiligastar Lygisögur: Studies in Honour of Galina Glazyrina*. Ed. Tatjana N. Jackson and Elena A. Melnikova. Moscow: Dmitriy Pozharsky University, 2012. Pp. 62-70.

Jakob Benediktsson, ed. *Íslendingabók. Landnámabók. Íslenzk Fornrit* vol. 1. Reykjavík: Hið Íslenzka Fornritafélag, 1986.

Jesch, Judith. "Hrómundr Gripsson Revisited." *Skandinavistik* 14 (1984), pp. 89–105.

Jiriczek, Otto Luitpold. *Die Bósa-Saga in Zwei Fassungen*. Strassburg (Strasbourg): Karl J. Trübner, 1893.

Jochens, Jenny. "Before the Male Gaze: The Absence of the Female Body in Old Norse." *Sex in the Middle Ages: A Book of Essays*. Joyce E. Salisbury, ed. New York: Garland Publishing, 1991. Pp. 3-29.

—. *Women in Old Norse Society*. Ithaca, N. Y.: Cornell University Press, 1995.

Jóhanna Katrín Friðriksdóttir. "From Heroic Legend to 'Medieval Screwball Comedy'? The Origins, Development, and Interpretation of the Maiden-King Narrative." *The Legendary Sagas: Origins and Development*. Annette Lassen, Agneta Ney, and Ármann Jakobsson, eds. Reykjavík: University of Iceland Press, 2012. Pp. 229-250.

—. *Women in Old Norse Literature: Bodies, Words, and Power.* New York: Palgrave Macmillan, 2013.

Jón Árnason. *Íslenzkar Þjóðsögur og Æfintýri.* 2 vols. Leipzig: J. C. Hinrich, 1862.

Jón Hnefill Aðalsteinsson (Joan Turville-Petre, transl.). "Wrestling with a Ghost in Icelandic Popular Belief." *A Piece of Horse Liver: Myth, Ritual and Folklore in Old Icelandic Sources.* Reykjavík: Háskólaútgáfan, 1998. pp. 143-162.

— (Terry Gunnell, transl.). "The Ghost that Wrestled with Guðmundur." *A Piece of Horse Liver: Myth, Ritual and Folklore in Old Icelandic Sources.* Reykjavík: Háskólaútgáfan, 1998. pp. 163-174.

Jón Karl Helgason. "Continuity? The Icelandic Sagas in Post-Medieval Times." *A Companion to Old Norse-Icelandic Literature and Culture.* Rory McTurk, ed. Malden, Mass.: Blackwell, 2005. pp. 64-81.

Jón Viðar Sigurðsson. "Changing Layers of Jurisdiction and the Reshaping of Icelandic Society c. 1220–1350." *Communities in European History: Representations, Jurisdictions, Conflicts.* Juan Pan-Montojo and Frederik Petersen, eds. Pisa: Edizioni Plus / Pisa University Press, 2007. pp. 173-187.

Jorgensen, Peter A. "The Neglected Genre of *Rímur*-Derived Prose and Post-Reformation *Jónatas saga.*" *Gripla,* vol. 7 (1990), pp. 187-201.

Kahle, Bernhard (ed.) *Kristnisaga; Þáttr Þorvalds ens víðforla; Þáttr Ísleifs biskups Gizurarsonar; Hungrvaka.* Altnordische Saga-Bibliothek, no. 11. Halle: Niemeyer, 1905.

Kalinke, Marianne E. *Bridal-Quest Romance in Medieval Iceland.* Ithaca, N.Y. and London: Cornell University Press, 1990.

—. "Endogamy as the Crux of the Dalafífla þáttr." *Fornaldarsagaerne: Myter og Virkilighed.* Agneta Ney, Ármann Jakobsson, and Annette Lassen, eds. Copenhagen: Museum Tusculanums Forlag, 2009. pp. 107-121.

—. "Textual Instability, Generic Hybridity, and the Development of Some *Fornaldarsögur.*" *The Legendary Sagas: Origins and Development.* Annette Lassen, Agneta Ney, and Ármann Jakobsson, eds. Reykjavík: University of Iceland Press, 2012. Pp. 201-227.

Kålund, K., ed. *Alfræði Íslenzk: Islandsk Encyclopædisk Litteratur.* Vol. 1. Copenhagen: S. L. Møllers Bogtrykkeri, 1908.

Kershaw, Nora. *Stories and Ballads of the Far Past.* Cambridge: Cambridge University Press, 1921.

Krapp, George Philip and Elliott van Kirk Dobbie. *The Anglo-Saxon Poetic Records. Vol. III: The Exeter Book.* New York: Columbia University Press, 1938.

Kunin, Devra (transl.), Carl Phelpstead (ed.) *A History of Norway and the Passion and Miracles of the Blessed Óláfr.* London: Viking Society for Northern Research, 2001.

Kvideland, Reimund and Henning K. Sehmsdorf (eds.) *Scandinavian Folk Belief and Legend.* Minneapolis: University of Minnesota Press, 1988.

Larrington, Carolyne. "Diet, Defecation, and the Devil: Disgust and the Pagan Past." *Medieval Obscenities*, ed. Nicola McDonald. Woodbridge: York Medieval Press / Boydell, 2006. pp. 138-155.

Larson, Laurence M. (transl.). *The Earliest Norwegian Laws: Being the Gulathing Law and the Frostathing Law.* New York: Columbia University Press, 1935.

LeMire, Eugene D., ed. *The Unpublished Lectures of William Morris.* Detroit: Wayne State University Press, 1969.

Lens, M. "Huon of Bordeaux". *A Dictionary of Medieval Heroes*, ed. Willem P. Gerritsen and Anthony G. van Melle. Woodbridge: Boydell, 1998. pp. 149-151.

Liestol, Aslak. "The Runes of Bergen: Voices from the Middle Ages." *Minnesota History*, vol. 40, no. 2 (1968), pp. 49-58.

Lincoln, Bruce. *"Gautrek's Saga* and the Gift Fox." *Theorizing Myth: Narrative, Ideology, and Scholarship.* Chicago: University of Chicago Press, 2000. pp. 171-182.

Lindow, John. "Supernatural and Ethnic Others: A Millennium of World View." *Scandinavian Studies*, vol. 67 (1995), pp. 8-31.

Loth, Agnete. *Late Medieval Icelandic Romances. Vol. IV. Editiones Arnamagnæanæ* Series B, no. 23. Copenhagen: Munksgaard, 1964.

Lövkrona, Inger. "The Pregnant Frog and the Farmer's Wife: Childbirth in the Middle Ages as Shown Through a Legend." *Arv: Nordic Yearbook of Folklore*, vol. 45 (1989), pp. 73-124.

MacGregor, Jessie. "Scandinavian Mythology from the Picturesque Side." *Proceedings of the Literary and Philosophical Society of Liverpool*, vol. 38 (1884), pp. 129-153.

MacLeod, Mindy, and Bernard Mees. *Runic Amulets and Magic Objects.* Woodbridge: Boydell, 2006.

Magnús Már Lárusson. "On the So-Called 'Armenian' Bishops." *Studia Islandica*, vol. 18 (1960), pp. 23-38.

Magoun, Francis Peabody. "Whence 'Dúlcifal' in *Göngu-Hrólfs saga?*" *Studia Germanica Tillägnade Ernst Albin Kock den 6 December 1934.* Lund: Gleerup, 1934. pp. 176-191.

Martin, John D. "Hreggviðr's Revenge: Supernatural Forces in *Göngu-Hrólfs saga.*" *Scandinavian Studies*, vol. 70, no. 3 (1998), pp. 313-324.

Matyushina, Inna. "Magic Mirrors, Monsters, Maiden-Kings (the Fantastic in *Riddarasögur*)." *The Fantastic in Old Norse/Icelandic Literature: Sagas and the British Isles*, John McKinnell, David Ashurst, and Donata Kick, eds. Durham: Centre for Medieval and Renaissance Studies, 2006. Vol. 2, pp. 660-670.

McDonald, Sheryl. "*Nítíða saga*: A Normalised Icelandic Text and Translation." *Leeds Studies in English*, vol. 40, pp. 119-145.

McKay, J. G. "The Deer-Cult and the Deer-Goddess Cult of the Ancient Caledonians." *Folklore*, vol. 43, no. 2 (1932), pp. 144-174.

McKinnell, John. *Meeting the Other in Norse Myth and Legend.* Cambridge: D. S. Brewer, 2005.

Meulengracht Sørensen, Preben (Joan Turville-Petre, transl.) *The Unmanly Man: Concepts of Sexual Defamation in Early Northern Society.* Odense: Odense University Press, 1983.

Miller, Clarence H. "Fragments of Danish History". *ANQ*, vol. 20, no. 3 (2007), pp. 9-22.

Miller, William I. *The Anatomy of Disgust.* Cambridge, Mass.: Harvard University Press, 1997.

Millroy, James. "The Story of *Ætternisstapi* in *Gautreks Saga.*" *Saga-Book of the Viking Society*, vol. 17 (1966-1969), pp. 206-223.

Mitchell, Stephen A. "The Whetstone as Symbol of Authority in Old Norse and Old English." *Scandinavian Studies*, vol. 57, no. 1 (1985), pp. 1-31.

—. *Heroic Sagas and Ballads.* Ithaca, N.Y.: Cornell University Press, 1991.

—. "Anaphrodisiac Charms in the Nordic Middle Ages: Impotence, Infertility, and Magic." *Norveg: The Norwegian Journal of Folklore*, vol. 38 (1998), pp. 19-42.

Murray, Alexander S. *Manual of Mythology: Greek and Roman, Norse and Old German, Hindoo and Egyptian Mythology.* Philadelphia: Henry Altemus, 1898.

Nitzsche, Jane C. "The Structural Unity of *Beowulf*: The Problem of Grendel's Mother." *Texas Studies in Literature and Language*, vol. 22 (1980), pp. 287-303.

O'Connor, Ralph. "History or Fiction? Truth-Claims and Defensive Narrators in Icelandic Romance-Sagas." *Medieval Scandinavia*, vol. 15 (2005), 101-169.

—, ed. trans. *Icelandic Histories and Romances.* 2ⁿᵈ ed. Stroud, Gloucestershire: Tempus, 2006.

Ogle, M. B. "The Stag-Messenger Episode." *American Journal of Philology,* vol. 37, no. 4 (1916), pp. 387-416.

Orchard, Andy (transl.) *The Elder Edda: A Book of Viking Lore.* London: Penguin, 2011.

Page, R. I. *Gibbons Saga. Editiones Arnamagnæanæ Series B,* no. 2. Copenhagen: Munksgaard, 1960.

Pálsson, Hermann and Paul Edwards, trans. *Göngu-Hrolfs Saga: A Viking Romance.* Edinburgh: Canongate, 1980.

—. *Orkneyinga Saga: The History of the Earls of Orkney.* Harmondsworth: Penguin, 1981.

—. *Seven Viking Romances.* London: Penguin, 1985.

Pizarro, Joaquín Martínez. "Transformations of the Bear's Son Tale in the Sagas of the Hrafnistumenn." *Arv,* vol. 32-33 (1976-77), pp. 263-281.

Pliny the Elder (H. Rackham, transl.) *Natural History.* 10 vols. Loeb Classical Library. Cambridge, Mass.: Harvard University Press, 1969/

Power, Rosemary. "Journeys to the North in the Icelandic Fornaldarsögur." *Arv,* vol. 40 (1984), pp. 7-25.

Quinn, Judy. "Interrogating Genre in the *Fornaldarsögur:* Round-Table Discussion." *Viking and Medieval Studies,* vol. 1 2 (2007), pp. 275-96.

Radzin, Hilda. "The Name 'Gǫngu-Hrólf' in the Old Norse 'Gǫngu-Hrólfs Saga'." *Literary Onomastics Studies,* vol. 1 (1974), pp. 47-52.

Ranisch, Wilhelm. *Die Gautrekssaga in Zwei Fassungen. Palaestra,* vol. 11. Berlin: Mayer and Müller, 1900.

Renaud, Jean, "Eroticism in the *Saga of Bósi and Herrauðr*". *Litteratur og Kjønn i Norden: Fordrag på den XX Studiekonferanse i International Association for Scandinavian Studies (IASS)*. Ed. Helga Kress. Reykjavík: Háskólaútgáfan, 1996. pp. 67–74.

Righter-Gould, Ruth. "The *Fornaldar Sögur Norðurlanda*: A Structural Analysis." *Scandinavian Studies*, vol. 52, no. 4 (1980), pp. 423-441.

Ross, Alan S. C. *The Terfinnas and Beormas of Ohthere*. Reprinted edition. London: Viking Society for Northern Research, 1981.

Rowe, Elizabeth Ashliman. "Folktale and Parable: The Unity of *Gautreks saga*." *Gripla*, vol. 10 (1998), pp. 155-166.

Russom, Geoffrey R. "A Germanic Concept of Nobility in The Gifts of Men and Beowulf." *Speculum*, vol. 53, no. 1 (1978), pp. 1-15.

Sanders, Christopher. "*Sturlaugs saga starfsama*: Humour and Textual Archaeology." *The Fantastic in Old Norse/Icelandic Literature: Sagas and the British Isles*, John McKinnell, David Ashurst, and Donata Kick, eds. Durham: Centre for Medieval and Renaissance Studies, 2006. Vol. 2, pp. 876-885.

Saxo Grammaticus. *The History of the Danes: Books I-IX*. Ed. Hilda R. Ellis-Davidson, trans. Peter Fisher. Rochester, N.Y.: D.S. Brewer, 1996.

Schach, Paul, trans. *The Saga of Tristram and Ísönd*. Lincoln: University of Nebraska Press, 1973.

Schier, Kurt. *Sagaliteratur*. Stuttgart: J. B. Metzler, 1970.

Schlauch, Margaret. *Romance in Iceland*. Princeton: Princeton University Press, 1934.

Schramm, Ken. *The Compleat Meadmaker*. Boulder, Colo.: Brewers Publications, 2003.

Sigurður Gylfi Magnússon. *Wasteland with Words: A Social History of Iceland*. London: Reaktion Books, 2010.

Simek, Rudolf. *Altnordische Kosmographie: Studien und Quellen zu Weltbild und Weltbescreibung in Norwegen und Island vom 12. bis zum 14. Jahrhundert.* Berlin and New York: Walter de Gruyter, 1990.

Snorri Sturluson (ed. Anthony Faulkes). *Edda.* Vol. 1: *Prologue and Gylfaginning.* Vol. 2a: *Skaldskaparmál: Introduction, Text, and Notes.* Vol. 2b: *Skáldskaparmál: Glossary and Index of Names.* London: Viking Society for Northern Research, 2005-2008.

— (transl. Lee M. Hollander). *Heimskringla: History of the Kings of Norway.* Austin: University of Texas Press, 1991.

Stitt, J. Michael. *Beowulf and the Bear's Son: Epic, Saga, and Fairytale in Northern Germanic Tradition.* New York and London: Garland, 1992.

Sverrir Tómasson (ed.) *Bósa saga og Herrauðs.* Reykjavík: Mál og Menning, 1996.

Tacitus, Cornelius. *Germania. Tacitus I: Agricola, Germania, Dialogus.* Transl. M. Hutton, rev. E. H. Warrington. Loeb Classical Library. Cambridge, Mass.: Harvard University Press, 1970.

Thomas, J. W. and Carolyn Dussére, transl. *The Legend of Duke Ernst.* Lincoln: University of Nebraska Press, 1979.

Thompson, Claiborne W. "The Runes in *Bósa saga ok Herrauðs.*" *Scandinavian Studies,* vol. 50 (1978), pp. 50–56.

Thompson, Stith. *Motif-Index of Folk Literature.* 5 vols. Rev. ed. Bloomington: Indiana University Press, 1973.

Tolkien, Christopher. *The Saga of Heidrek the Wise.* London: Thomas Nelson and Sons, 1960.

Tulinius, Torfi. *The Matter of the North: The Rise of Literary Fiction in Thirteenth-Century Iceland.* Odense: Odense University Press, 2002.

—. "Sagas of Icelandic Prehistory (*fornaldarsögur*)." *A Companion to Old Norse–Icelandic Literature and Culture.* Ed. Rory McTurk. Oxford; Malden, Mass.: Blackwell Publications, 2005. pp. 447-461.

Turville-Petre, Gabriel. *Myth and Religion of the North: The Religion of Ancient Scandinavia.* New York: Holt, Rinehart and Winston, 1964.

—. "Dreams in Icelandic Tradition." *Nine Norse Studies.* London: Viking Society for Northern Research, 1972. pp. 30-51.

Vésteinn Ólason. "The Marvellous North and Authorial Presence in the Icelandic Fornaldarsaga." *Contexts of Pre-Novel Narrative: The European Tradition.* Roy Eriksen, ed. Berlin: Mouton de Gruyter, 1994. pp. 101-134.

Viðar Hreinsson, ed. *Complete Sagas of the Icelanders.* 5 vols. Reykjavík: Leifur Eiriksson Publishing, 1997.

Waggoner, Ben. *The Sagas of Fridthjof the Bold.* Troth Publications, 2009.

Webster, Kenneth G. T. *Guinevere: A Study of her Abductions.* Milton, Mass.: The Turtle Press, 1951.

Whitelock, Dorothy, ed. *The Anglo-Saxon Chronicle: A Revised Translation.* New Brunswick, N.J.: Rutgers University Press, 1961.

Wikander, Stig. "Från Indisk Djurfabel till Isländsk Saga." *Vetenskaps-Societeten i Lund, Årsbok* (1964), pp. 87-114.

Wittkower, Rudolf. "Marvels of the East: A Study in the History of Monsters." *Journal of the Wartburg and Courtauld Institutes,* vol. 5 (1942), pp. 159-197.

Wolf, Kirsten. "*Alexanders saga.*" *Medieval Scandinavia.* Ed. Phillip Pulsiano and Kirsten Wolf. London: Routledge, 1993. pp. 7-8.

Zitzelberger, Otto J. *The Two Versions of* Sturlaugs saga starfsama: *A Decipherment, Edition, and Translation of a Fourteenth-Century Icelandic Mythical-Heroic Saga.* Düsseldorf: Michael Triltsch Verlag, 1969.

—. "*Sturlaugs saga starfsama.*" *Medieval Scandinavia.* Ed. Phillip Pulsiano and Kirsten Wolf. London: Routledge, 1993. pp. 614-615.

Þórir Óskarson. "Rhetoric and Style." *A Companion to Old Norse-Icelandic Literature and Culture.* Rory McTurk, ed. Malden, Mass.: Blackwell, 2005. pp. 354-371.

ENDNOTES

1. transl. Stallybrass, *Teutonic Mythology*, vol. 1, p. 10.
2. Murray, *Manual of Mythology*, p. 356.
3. MacGregor, "Scandinavian Mythology from the Picturesque Side", p. 136-137.
4. "The Early Literature of the North—Iceland"; ed. LeMire, *The Unpublished Lectures of William Morris*, p. 181.
5. Driscoll, "The Long and Winding Road," pp. 50-53, *Unwashed Children of Eve*, pp. 13-25, 38-46; Sigurður Gylfi Magnússon, *Wasteland with Words*, pp. 85-87, 147-160.
6. Kalinké, *Bridal-Quest Romance*, pp. 1-5, gives an overview.
7. See Quinn, "Interrogating Genre", for a recent discussion of the controversy.
8. Mitchell, *Heroic Sagas and Ballads*, p. 27.
9. Schier, *Sagaliteratur*, pp. 72-91.
10. Harris, "The Prosimetrum of Icelandic Saga", pp. 131-135; Tulinius, *The Matter of the North*, pp. 55-63.
11. Righter-Gould, "The *Fornaldar Sögur Norðurlanda*," pp. 423-435; Tulinius, "Sagas of Icelandic Prehistory", pp. 447-449.
12. Elizabeth Ashliman Rowe, quoted in Quinn, *Interrogating Genre*, pp. 284-286.
13. Quoted in Driscoll, "Late Prose Fiction", p. 197; see also Kalinké, *Bridal-Quest Romance*, pp. 18-19.
14. Driscoll, "Late Prose Fiction," p. 198.
15. Tulinius, *The Matter of the North*, pp. 290-295.
16. Driscoll, "Fornaldarsögur Norðurlanda," pp. 258-261; "A New Edition of the *Fornaldarsögur Norðurlanda*," pp. 9-11. As Driscoll points out, uncatalogued manuscripts continue to be discovered; his 2003 article lists only 68 manuscripts of *Göngu-Hrólfs saga*, and his 2009 article lists 69. I have updated his figures using the online database "Stories For All Time".
17. Vésteinn Ólason, "The Marvellous North," p. 117.
18. O'Connor, "History or Fiction?", pp. 130-133.
19. For example, the ending of the shorter recension of *Friðþjófs saga* (transl. Waggoner, *Sagas of Fridthjof the Bold*, p. 128), or the end of *Mírmanns saga* (transl. O'Connor, *Icelandic Histories and Romances*, p. 296).
20. Thompson, *Motif-Index of Folk Literature*, F159.1, "Otherworld reached by

hunting animal" (vol. 3, p. 27); N774, "Adventures from pursuing enchanted animal" (vol. 5, pp. 130-131). There are over two dozen episodes in Arthurian romances in which a hero is led to otherworldly adventure while hunting a mysterious white stag, or sometimes another beast (Webster, *Guinevere*, pp. 89-104). Other parallels appear in the Welsh *Mabinogion* (e.g. Pwyll's hunt leading him to Annwn; Goronwy's hunt leading him to Blodeuedd; Pryderi and Manawyddan's pursuit of the boar). As Webster writes, ""The office of the white stag in these romances is to toll the hero to the other world, to get him into the power of a supernatural being. He who succeeded with the stag crossed into fairyland, won a fairy queen for his bride, or released her from a spell, and so on, with innumerable variations of the theme." (*Guinevere*, p. 90) The ultimate origin of the motif may be Celtic, but Ogle argues for Classical origins, comparing it with the myth of Hercules hunting the Ceryneian hind ("The Stag-Messenger Episode"), and Littleton points out close parallels in Scythian legend (*From Scythia to Camelot*, pp. 101-103).

21. Five Breton *lais* feature variations on the motif of a hunted beast leading the hero to an otherworldly encounter, and three of these are known to have been translated into Norse: *Graelent* (*Grelents saga*, whose hunting episode is probably the closest to the native sagas, although the hunting scene has not survived in the fragmentary Norse manuscript), *Guigemar* (*Guiamars ljóð*), *Desiré* (*Desire ljóð*), *Tyolet*, and *Guingemor* (not known in Norse translation). Grimm's tale "The Six Swans" also opens with such a hunt. The French romance of Parténopeus de Blois begins with a similar hunt, and this was translated into Norse as *Partálopa saga*. Ogle ("The Stag-Messenger Episode", pp. 410-412) points out that the Roman pagan Placidus was said to have hunted an uncatchable stag that revealed itself to be Christ, resulting in Placidus converting to Christianity and taking the name of Eustace. Placidus's life was well known in Norse literature from the prose *Plácitus saga* and the long poem *Plácitusdrápa*.

22. Aside from *Göngu-Hrólfs saga* in this book (ch. 15), hunts leading to otherworldly encounters appear in the *fornaldarsögur Hervarar saga ok Heiðreks* [U-redaction; Tolkien, *The Saga of King Heiðrek*, p. 68] and *Egils saga einhenda ok Ásmundar kappabana* (ch. 6), and in the indigenous romance *Gibbons saga* (ch. 1; ed. Page, pp. 3-4). In *Göngu-Hrólfs saga* and *Gibbons saga*, the hero is led to a beautiful and supernaturally powerful lady. Although he is not actually hunting an animal, the hero of *Helga þáttr Þórissonar* (ch. 1) also meets a beautiful lady after getting lost in the woods.

23. Gauti's dealings with the family resemble Aarne-Thompson tale type AT 1544, "The Man Who Got a Night's Lodging", although Gauti does not cheat his hosts outright, as is usual in folktales of this type. (Aarne, *The Types of the Folktale*, p. 446). Marianne Kalinke has argued that Gauti's hunt is simply an example of the folk motif, without any parodistic intent ("Endogamy and the Crux of the "Dalafifla Táttr", pp. 109-111); but I think that Rowe, "Folktale and Parable," p. 157 n7 makes a stronger counterargument in favor of parody.

24. e.g. Turville-Petre, *Myth and Religion of the North*, p. 254.

25. Milroy, "The Story of *Ætternisstapi*", pp. 206-212.
26. Rowe, "Folktale and Parable," pp. 159-160.
27. Mitchell, *Heroic Sagas and Ballads*, pp. 55-58. Ref's constant "trading up" resembles what Aarne calls "cumulative tales" (AT 2000-2047, *The Types of the Folktale*, pp. 522-535), although none of his specific tale types match exactly.
28. *History of the Danes* VIII:296-298; transl. Davidson and Fisher, pp. 270-273.
29. Chesnutt, "The Content and Meaning of *Gjafa-Refs saga*", pp. 101-102; Wikander, "Från Indisk Djurfabel till Isländsk Saga," pp. 101-107.
30. Chesnutt, "The Content and Meaning of *Gjafa-Refs saga*", pp. 102-104. See also Lincoln, "*Gautrek's Saga* and the Gift Fox," pp. 179-182.
31. For example, Arrow-Odd's death song at the end of *Örvar-Odds saga*; Hjalmar's death-song in the same saga and in *Hervarar saga ok Heiðreks* (ch. 3); and the *Krákumál*, associated with *Ragnars saga loðbrókar* although not formally a part of it. See also *Grettis saga*, not part of the *fornaldarsögur* corpus as such, but with many fantastic elements and other points of similarity.
32. e.g. *Hervarar saga ok Heiðreks* (U-redaction); ed. transl. Tolkien, *The Saga of Heidrek the Wise*, pp. 66-67.
33. Saxo, *History of the Danes* VI:183; transl. Davidson and Fisher, p. 170.
34. Brodeur, *The Art of Beowulf*, pp. 174-175.
35. *Hávamál* 138-139; Orchard, *The Elder Edda*, p. 35.
36. Snorri Sturluson (Anthony Faulkes, ed.) *Edda*, vol. 1, p. 21; vol. 2a, pp. 5, 7, 67, 68, 71; vol. 2b, p. 471.
37. quoted in Cronan, "The Thematic Unity of the Younger *Gautreks saga*", p. 81, n2.
38. For a discussion of how *Víkars þáttr* was probably reshaped from an earlier form of the Starkaðr legend, see Bampi, "Between Tradition and Innovation," pp. 88-96.
39. See also Jón Viðar Sigurðsson, "Changing Layers of Jurisdiction," pp. 175-178. Jón Viðar Sigurðsson also points out that in the old Icelandic economy, marked by reciprocal gift-exchanges and redistribution of wealth through traditional avenues such as gifting and feasting, chieftains could not accumulate large amounts of wealth. Once Iceland had come under royal control and the old social networks had faded, chieftains could accumulate much more property in the market-dominated economy that replaced the old mixed economy. (pp. 182-184.) *Gautreks saga* may be seen as a comment, and not a favorable one, on the new market economy in Iceland.
40. Durrenberger, "Reciprocity in Gautrek's Saga", pp. 25-32. Chesnutt, "The Content and Meaning of *Gjafa-Refs saga*", p. 103, critiques Durrenberger's analysis, but the general conclusion that the saga is "all about" generosity and exchange seem widely accepted.
41. Rowe, "Folktale and Parable," pp. 162-164.
42. Rowe, "Folktale and Parable," pp. 155-157.
43. Cronan, "The Thematic Unity of the Younger *Gautreks saga*", pp. 85-89.
44. Driscoll and Hufnagel, "Stories for All Time", http://nfi.ku.dk/fornaldarsogur/

45. *Fornaldarsögur Norðurlanda* vol. 2, pp. 309-355.

46. Ranisch, *Die Gautrekssaga*, p. cx.

47. For a general overview see Bampi, "What's in a Variant?", pp. 57-67.

48. Ranisch, *Die Gautrekssaga*, pp. cx-cxi.

49. Anderson, "'Helgakviða Hjǫrvarðssonar' and European Bridal-Quest Narrative," pp. 70-74.

50. Kalinké, *Bridal-Quest Romance*, pp. 59-60.

51. *Germania* ch. 8; transl. Hutton, p. 143.

52. e.g. *Maxims I*, 81-92, in which a lord's wife must *rune healdan*, "keep secrets", and *ræd witan. . . þæm ætsomne*, "formulate advice. . . for both of them." (Krapp and Dobbie, *The Exeter Book*, p. 160). See also Wealhtheow's speeches to Beowulf in *Beowulf*.

53. Jóhanna Katrín Friðriksdóttir, *Women in Old Norse Literature*, pp. 25-45.

54. Clover, "Maiden Warriors and Other Sons," pp. 35-43.

55. Jóhanna Katrín Friðriksdóttir, "From Heroic Legend to 'Medieval Screwball Comedy'?", pp. 229-238.

56. Jóhanna Katrín Friðriksdóttir, *Women in Old Norse Literature*, pp. 131-133.

57. Jóhanna Katrín Friðriksdóttir, "From Heroic Legend to 'Medieval Screwball Comedy'?", pp. 240-243; see also *Women in Old Norse Literature*, pp. 112-116. In her willingness to resume her discarded shield-maiden role to help her husband, Thornbjorg resembles Lathgertha, the first wife of Ragnar Lodbrok, in Saxo's *Danish History* (IX.303-304, transl. Ellis Davidson and Fisher, pp. 282-283). See also Clover, "Maiden Warriors and Other Sons," pp. 40-41. Jóhanna Friðriksdóttir speculates that the character of Thornbjorg could be a reflection of Margaret Valdemarsdatter, the de facto ruler of Scandinavia from 1375 to 1412 (*Women in Old Norse Literature*, p. 116). The saga itself is known to be older than Margaret, but perhaps she had an influence on later redactions.

58. At least he is portrayed as wise and courteous in the later recension of the saga. Marianne Kalinke points out that in the older recension, he's quite rude and aggressive in his wooing of Thornbjorg / Thorberg. ("Textual Instability," pp. 204-209)

59. Kalinké, *Bridal-Quest Romance*, pp. 56-57.

60. Tulinius, *The Matter of the North*, pp. 169-173.

61. Driscoll and Hufnagel, "Stories for All Time", http://nfi.ku.dk/fornaldarsogur/

62. *Fornaldarsögur Norðurlanda* vol. 2, pp. 309-355.

63. Hollander, "The Gautland Cycle of Sagas II," pp. 209-217.

64. Vésteinn Ólason, "The Marvellous North," pp. 116-117.

65. Barnes, "Romance in Iceland," pp. 279-283.

66. Jóhanna Katrín Friðriksdóttir, *Women in Old Norse Literature*, p. 68.

67. Jochens, *Women in Old Norse Society*, pp. 68-73; Miller, *Anatomy of Disgust*, pp. 145-146.

68. Gade, "Penile Puns," pp. 58-65.

69. Sverrir Tómasson, ed. *Bósa saga og Herrauðs*, pp. 60-62.

70. Renaud, "Eroticism in the *Saga of Bósi and Herrauðr*," pp. 70-72.

71. Schlauch, *Romance in Iceland*, p. 82.
72. Renaud, "Eroticism in the *Saga of Bósi and Herrauðr*," p. 67. See Thomas and Dussére, transl. *The Legend of Duke Ernst*; for a summary of Huon de Bordeaux, see Lens, "Huon of Bordeaux", *Dictionary of Medieval Heroes*, pp. 149-151.
73. Power, "Journeys to the North," pp. 22-24.
74. The name of Jómali is borrowed from a Finnic language (cf. modern Finnish *jumala*, "God").
75. See the text, translation, and articles in Bately and Englert, *Ohthere's Voyages*.
76. Reviewed in Hofstra and Samplonius, "Viking Expansion Northwards," pp. 240-244.
77. See, e.g., DeAngelo, "The North and the Description of the *Finnar*," pp. 257-281.
78. Power, "Journeys to the North," pp. 8-16.
79. McKinnell, *Meeting the Other*, pp. 101-104.
80. McKinnell, pp. 126-138.
81. Driscoll and Hufnagel, "Stories for All Time", http://nfi.ku.dk/fornaldarsogur/
82. *Fornaldarsögur Norðurlanda* vol. 2, pp. 309-355.
83. Jiriczek, *Die Bósa-Saga*, pp. ix-xxvi.
84. Jiriczek, *Die Bósa-Saga*, pp. xxxv-xxxvi.
85. Sverrir Tómasson, ed. *Bósa saga og Herrauðs*.
86. Pálsson and Edwards, *Seven Viking Romances*, pp. 199-227.
87. Tulinius, quoted in "Interrogating Genre", pp. 279-280.
88. Sanders, "*Sturlaugs saga starfsama*: Humour and Textual Archaeology", p. 881.
89. Kalinké, *Bridal-Quest Romance*, p. 33.
90. Driscoll, "*Nitida saga*," p. 432.
91. *Nítíða saga* ch. 2; McDonald, "*Nítíða saga*", pp. 128-131.
92. *Nítíða saga* ch. 5; McDonald, "*Nítíða saga*", pp. 138-141.
93. See McDonald, "*Nítíða saga*", pp. 124-145.
94. *Historia Naturalis* VII.ii.23; Rackham, ed. transl., vol. 2, pp. 520-521.
95. See Wittkower, "Marvels of the East", pp. 159-, for a handy overview.
96. The primary sources are *Hauksbók*, written in the early 1300s (AM 544; Text 15 of Simek, *Altnordische Kosmographie*, pp. 465-467) and the manuscript AM 194, dated to 1387 (Text 16 of Simek, pp. 470-471; see also Kålund, ed., *Alfræði Íslenzk*, vol 1, p. 36). These describe the *Hundingjar* in almost identical terms.
97. Donecker, "The Werewolves of Livonia", pp. 294-295
98. *History of the Archbishops of Hamburg-Bremen* IV.xix; transl. Tschan, p. 200. Note that "having their heads on their breasts" (*in pectore caput habent*) sounds like Pliny's race of Blemmyae, headless men with faces on their chests; Adam of Bremen may have mixed up two of the "Plinian races."
99. Zitzelberger, *The Two Versions of* Sturlaugs saga starfsama, p. 307.
100. Driscoll and Hufnagel, "Stories for All Time", http://nfi.ku.dk/fornaldarsogur/
101. *Fornaldarsögur Norðurlanda* vol. 2, pp. 309-355.
102. Zitzelberger, *The Two Versions of* Sturlaugs saga starfsama, pp. 7-29. Zitzelberger also gives an exhaustive textual filiation and list of variants.

103. Zitzelberger, *The Two Versions of* Sturlaugs saga starfsama, pp. 395-398; "Sturlaugs saga starfsama" p. 615.

104. Radzin, "The Name 'Gǫngu-Hrólf'," pp. 49-52; for the historical Gǫngu-Hrólf see Kunin, *A History of Norway*, p. 9; *Orkneyinga saga* ch. 4.

105. Jón Viðar Sigurðsson, "Changing Layers of Jurisdiction," pp. 175-178.

106. Martin, "Hreggviðr's Revenge," pp. 314-321.

107. Martin, "Hreggviðr's Revenge," p. 319.

108. King Sverrir was not at the wedding—in fact, he was born over thirty years after the wedding. He evidently heard or read this saga at a later date, and the author of *Þorgils saga* interpolated his reaction into his account of the feast. The comment that "men are able to reckon their ancestry from Hromund Gripsson" may be meant ironically; since Sverrir had probably fabricated his own genealogy to support his claim to the throne of Norway, he had little right to dismiss others' genealogies as "lying sagas." (Bibire, "On Reading the Icelandic Sagas," p. 8)

109. My translation from the text in Guðni Jónsson, ed. *Sturlunga Saga*, vol. 1.

110. Jesch, "Hrómundr Gripsson Revisited," pp. 95-96. For a discussion of the *Þorgils saga* passage and its authenticity and textual history, see Foote, "Sagnaskemtan."

111. *Landnámabók* SH6-9; Jakob Benediktsson, ed. *Íslenzk Fornrit* vol. 1, pp. 38-46. See also *Flóamanna saga* ch. 1.

112. Pizarro, "Transformations of the Bear's Son Tale," pp. 278-280.

113. Jesch, pp. 97-98.

114. Early manuscripts of this saga contain a scribal note to the effect that it has been copied from a saga manuscript that was almost illegible. Hooper, "Hrómundar Saga Gripssonar," took this statement as truth and argued that the saga in its current form was copied from a much older saga manuscript, with defects filled in by reference to *Griplur*. Most recent scholars have rejected this scenario, arguing that the saga was derived directly from *Griplur*, while concurring that the scribe's copy of *Griplur* must have been illegible at several points. (Brown, "Saga of Hrómund Gripsson", pp. 71-77; Jesch, "Hrómundr Gripsson Revisited", pp. 89-91; however, see Bibire, "On Reading the Icelandic Sagas", p. 7)

115. Jorgensen, "The Neglected Genre of *Rímur*-Derived Prose", pp. 187-192.

116. *Grettis saga Ásmundarsonar* ch. 66; *Harðar saga ok Hólmverja* chs. 14-15; *Bárðar saga Snæfellsáss* chs. 20-21; *Gull-Þóris saga* chs. 3-5. The episode at the cave of Dollzhellir in *Orkneyinga saga* (ch. 61) draws on this motif, as do a number of legendary sagas. See excerpts and discussion in Stitt, *Beowulf and the Bear's Son*, pp. 129-156; Jón Hnefill Aðalsteinsson, "Wrestling with a Ghost," pp. 143-150.

117. Stitt, *Beowulf and the Bear's Son*, pp. 167-169, 200-204. Stitt argues that the "Gravemound Battle" is primarily a literary motif, not one from the folk tradition; but see Jón Hnefill Aðalsteinsson, "Wrestling with a Ghost," pp. 151-161, and "The Ghost that Wrestled with Guðmundur," pp. 163-173, for examples of this motif in Icelandic folklore.

118. Orchard, *The Elder Edda*, pp. 116-145.
119. Chadwick notes parallels between the three reborn heroes named Helgi in Norse tradition and the three reborn women named Étaín in Irish tradition. Especially noteworthy is the fact that both Kara and Étaín take the form of swans. ("Literary Tradition in the Old Norse and Celtic World," pp. 178-182.)
120. Andrews, "Studies in the Fornaldarsǫgur Norðrlanda," p. 537.
121. Andrews, "Studies in the Fornaldarsǫgur Norðrlanda," pp. 540-544; Stitt, *Beowulf and the Bear's Son*, pp. 171-182.
122. Driscoll and Hufnagel, "Stories for All Time", http://nfi.ku.dk/fornaldarsogur/
123. Driscoll, The Unwashed Children of Eve, pp. 13-25.
124. Jón Karl Helgason, "Continuity?", pp. 64-69; Sigurður Gylfi Magnússon, *Wasteland with Words*, pp. 85-87; Driscoll, *The Unwashed Children of Eve*, pp. 38-46.
125. Driscoll, "Late Prose Fiction", pp. 202-203.

Gautrek's Saga

1. As discussed in the Introduction, the motif of an uncanny beast leading a hunter to an otherworldly encounter is widespread in medieval romances, and there are many avenues by which it could have entered the Norse sagas. Whatever the source, the episode in *Gautreks saga* is clearly a burlesque.
2. *Skafnortungr* is related to *skafa*, "to shave; to scrape." Ranisch states that *skaf* refers to bark scraped from trees, while *nortungr* comes from *narta*, "to pinch" (*Die Gautrekssaga*, p. lxxx). The point is that bark shaved from trees was fed to cattle in times of scarcity; to be frugal with such starvation rations implies extreme stinginess. Pálsson and Edwards render the name as "Skinflint."
3. *Tötra* means "tatters."
4. *Fjölmóðr* is the name of the purple sandpiper (*Calidris maritima*). In Icelandic folklore it is considered the most insignificant of all birds; the word *fjölmóðarvíl*, "sandpiper's misery," refers to making a big fuss over nothing. (Ranisch, *Die Gautrekssaga*, p. lxxx; Jón Árnarson, *Íslenzkar Þjóðsögur og Æfintýri*, vol. 1, p. xi)
5. *Imsigull* is hard to interpret. The name might mean something like "various gold items", if divided as "Imsi-Gull", from *ýmiss* or *ímiss*, "various; alternating" and *gull*, "gold". Ranisch, however, divides the name as *Íms-igull*, "dirty hedgehog", from *ím*, "dust; ashes" and *igull*, "hedgehog" (or possibly "sea urchin").
6. *Gillingr* might mean "valued at full worth." Note that in the older redaction, Gilling is the name of the father.
7. *Snotra* means "wise"; the name appears in the *Prose Edda* as one of the handmaidens of the goddess Frigg. (Snorri Sturluson, *Gylfaginning* 35, ed. Faulkes, *Edda*, vol. 1, p. 30)
8. *Fjötra* is related to a Norwegian dialect verb *fjatra*, "to falter, stumble; to speak foolishly," and *Hjötra* may be related to another Norwegian verb *hotta*, "to bounce around". (Ranisch, *Die Gautrekssaga*, p. lxxx-lxxxi)
9. In the shorter redaction of this saga, Gilling is the father of the family and Skafnaurtung is one of Snotra's brothers. This was presumably the original

arrangement; Gilling's Crag was named for the head of the family.

10. Valhalla (Norse *Valhöll*, "Hall of the Slain") is Odin's home and the home of slain warriors, who fight each other all day and feast together all night. In the recorded myths, the only way to reach it was by a heroic death in battle. (Snorri Sturluson, *Gylfaginning* 38-41, ed. Faulkes, *Edda*, vol. 1, pp. 32-34) The family's attempt to reach it by committing suicide out of an outrageous sense of violated greed would have been ridiculous to an audience who knew the myths.

11. There has been some controversy over whether this description of suicide by leaping from a cliff has any basis in authentic pagan practice. There are a few historical references to old and helpless people being thrown from cliffs during famines in Iceland (*Viðrauki Skarðsarbókar*, published in *Islendinga sögur*, vol. 1, p. 323); claims that pagans sacrificed "the worst men" to the gods by pushing them over cliffs (*Kristni saga* ch. 12, ed. Kahle, p. 40); and recent Swedish folk traditions of *ättestupor*, "family cliffs," over which old people were once thrown. However, the references to starvation and old age, and to meeting Odin, are not found in the older and shorter redaction of this saga, and were probably added to give antiquarian "pagan flavor". While people may indeed have gone over cliffs, willingly or not, as punishment or in times of famine, *Gautreks saga* probably does not preserve a genuine memory of pre-Christian religious practices. (Millroy, "The Story of Ætternisstapi", pp. 206-223)

12. Saxo tells the same story about the stingy King Huglek, who gave away a pair of shoes but kept the laces (*History of the Danes* VI.185-186; transl. Davidson and Fisher, pp. 172-173).

13. The Norse text puns on Gauti's name combined with *rekstri*, "chase"—i.e. the stag hunt that brought Gauti to Snotra's home. I had to deviate slightly from the literal meaning to convey the pun.

14. In the older version of this tale, the father explicitly tells his children to marry each other to keep the family's wealth intact, while also warning them against having children at all (which of course undermines his purpose, because it will lead the family to extinction; this might be an oversight by the saga composer, but is probably a deliberate sign of how stupid the family is). The younger version deletes the father's command of incestuous marriage, while retaining the children's odd method of birth control, which now seems rather pointless. (Kalinke, "Endogamy as the Crux of the Dalafífla þáttr," pp. 113-117)

15. A number of sagas deal with human male heroes who travel to the realm of giants and impregnate female giants; the half-giant sons that they sire may come to live with their fathers and become mighty heroes (e.g. Jokul in *Kjálnesinga saga*; Vignir in *Örvar-Odds saga*). Although Snotra is not actually a giantess, the first part of *Gautreks saga* is a humanized parody of an encounter with the Otherworld, and Gautrek fits the narrative pattern.

16. Their story is told in *Friðþjófs saga en frækna*. The main plot of *Friðþjófs saga* seems to be derived from an Arabian tale, which means that it is not a *fornaldarsaga* according to Mitchell's definition (*Heroic Sagas and Ballads*, pp. 27-29), but the

names and family history of Fridthjof and Ingibjorg might come from native Scandinavian tradition, even if their famous romance does not.

17. *Hálfs saga ok Hálfsrekka* (ch. 1) tells of Vikar's birth and the way in which Odin fated him to be sacrificed. Note, however, that Vikar in *Hálfs saga* has a different father (Alrek, king of Hordaland), and the details of his life do not correspond to *Gautreks saga.*

18. In other sagas, Alfheim is more or less equal to the modern Swedish province of Bohuslän, between the rivers Gautelfr and Raumelfr, the Göta älv and the Glomma River. (*Ynglinga saga* ch. 48; *Heimskringla*, transl. Hollander, p. 48; *Hversu Nóregr byggðist* ch. 1; *Sögubrot* ch. 6). However, a few sagas seem to conflate the "mundane" Alfheim with the mythological realm of the *álfar* or elves, mentioning that its inhabitants are more beautiful than other men (*Sögubrot* ch. 10, see Waggoner, *Sagas of Ragnar Lodbrok*, pp. 106-107 n20; *Hervarar saga* U-redaction, transl. Tolkien, *Saga of Heidrek the Wise*, p. 67; *Þorsteins saga Víkingssonar* ch. 1), and it may be that this episode derives from a myth of a giant carrying off a goddess.

19. Much the same tale of Starkad Ala-Warrior (*Áludreng*) and his kidnapping of Alfhild appears in the U-redaction of *Hervarar saga* (ed. transl. Tolkien, p. 67), although in *Hervarar saga* Storvirk is the father of Starkad Ala-Warrior, whose only child with Alfhild is a daughter, Bauggerd.

20. This is the present-day island of Tromøy, a large island just across from the city of Arendal.

21. Possibly present-day Stadlandet, in the Nordfjord district of Norway, although this seems a little too far north to be reached in two days' sailing.

22. Now the settlement of Ask on the island Askøy, off the present-day city of Bergen. In *Egils saga* (ch. 37), a man named Thorgeir Thornfoot is said to live at Ask on Fenhring; he is described as a devout pagan worshipper and a sorceror.

23. "Coal-biter" (*kolbítr*) is the usual epithet for an unpromising young man who does nothing but sit idly by the fire, but who may be revealed as a great hero when the right challenge comes along (like Ref in chapter VI of this saga). The *kolbítr* is similar to the *askeladden* ("ash-lad") or *askefisen* ("ash-fart") of Norwegian folktales.

24. The traditional province of Närke in south-central Sweden.

25. The *svínfylking*, literally "swine-formation", is the wedge formation, named from its supposed resemblance to a pig's head. Odin teaches it to kings whom he favors (Saxo, *History of the Danes* I.32, ed. Davidson and Fisher, p. 31; VII.248-249, Davidson and Fisher, pp. 226-227; *Sögubrot* ch. 8; *Reginsmál* 23, trans. Orchard, *Elder Edda*, p. 159). Although this is not explicitly stated, the fact that Vikar is using the wedge is probably meant to suggest his close relationship with Odin.

26. Now Rennesøy, north of Stavanger.

27. "To cast wood-chips" (*falla spán*) refers to a rite of divination. In other texts the expression is *falla blótspán*, "to cast sacrificial wood-chips," suggesting that the rite was associated with religious sacrifices.

28. *Skáldatal,* a list of ancient poets preserved in some manuscripts of the *Prose Edda*, lists Starkad first, and calls his poems "the most ancient of those which people now know". (Clunies-Ross, "Poet into Myth", p. 31).

29. Agni was a legendary Swedish king of the Yngling dynasty. He married the "Finn" (Saami) woman Skjalf ("shiver") after killing her father King Frosti. Skjalf took revenge by hanging Agni by surprise, hauling him up by the neck into a tree while he was asleep (*Ynglinga saga* ch. 19; transl. Hollander, *Heimskringla*, p. 22). Thus Eirek and Alrek's father's death mirrors Vikar's death.

30. A *thul* is an official of the king, whose role included giving advice, remembering and reciting old lore, and mediating between gods and men. Russel Poole has pointed out that Starkad's poem *Víkarsbálkr*, along with other poems and acts of Starkad preserved in Saxo's *History of the Danes*, contain very much the sort of knowledge and counsel that a thul would be expected to provide (cited in Clunies-Ross, "Poet into Myth", pp. 34-36). It's ironic that Starkad calls himself a "silent thul", since the word seems to be related to Old Norse *þylja*, "to utter".

31. Eirek and Alrek's fight over their horses is also told in *Ynglinga saga* ch. 20 (*Heimskringla*, transl. Hollander, p. 23), although here the two brothers kill each other. Hel is the land of the dead, and also the name of the goddess who rules the land of the dead and its inhabitants.

32. See ch. 20 of *Hrólfs saga Gautrekssonar* for the bizarre consequences of this gift.

33. Ankle-length breeches (*ökulbrokar*) may have been lower-class garments. A few other sagas mention them specifically as being worn by bumpkins or coal-biters, and artistic depictions of upper-class men often show them wearing short, wide, full breeches, rather than long trousers. (Ewing, *Viking Clothing*, pp. 98-99)

34. This is a more significant gift than it appears. In the sagas and other sources, including archaeological finds, whetstones are associated with rulership—both with a ruler's literal ability to grant his followers good sharp swords, and with his metaphorical ability to "whet" his men—to incite and encourage them. The jarl's gift of a whetstone thus foreshadows Ref's earning the right of rulership. (Mitchell, "The Whetstone as Symbol of Authority," pp. 1-22).

35. Hrolf Kraki ("Hrolf Pole") is a legendary ruler of Denmark; versions of his legend are told in *Hrólfs saga kraka* and in a number of other texts, including a brief appearance in *Beowulf.*

36. *Refr*'s name means "fox"; *Refnef* means "fox nose."

The Saga of Hrolf Gautreksson

1. A hersir was a local military leader who owed allegiance to a jarl or king.

2. Kalinké (*Bridal-Quest Romance*, p. 74, n10) suggests that a similar apple-tree motif in a different saga is derived from the Biblical *Song of Solomon* 2:3: "As the apple tree among the trees of the wood, so is my beloved among the sons." (KJV) But comparing men to trees is a common metaphor in Eddic poetry (e.g. *brynþings apaldr*, "mailcoat-assembly's apple tree", i.e. "apple tree of battle",

applied to Sigurðr in *Sigrdrífumál*, or *rógapaldr*, "apple tree of strife", applied to Helgi in *Helgakviða Hjörvarðssonar*).

3. As discussed in the Introduction, the theme of the maiden who chooses an older but more accomplished suitor over a younger man was probably based on *Völsunga saga* ch. 11, in which Hjordis chooses the aged but famous Sigmund over the young but less accomplished Lyngvi. In both sagas, the rejected younger king returns with an army and attacks his older rival; however, Hrolf kills Olaf in *Hrólfs saga Gautrekssonar*, while Lyngvi vanquishes Sigurd and takes Hjordis (thanks to the god Odin's intervention) in *Völsunga saga*. (Kalinké, *Bridal-Quest Romance*, pp. 26-29)

4. In the old Norse rite of naming a child, a baby was brought to its father, who acknowledged his paternity, sprinkled the baby with water, and gave it its name. The entire rite was called *ausa vatni*, "to sprinkle water." Despite outward similarity with the rite of Christian baptism (which is never called *ausa vatni* in the sagas, but always *skírn*, literally "cleansing; purification"), the rite seems to go back to pre-Christian times; it is well attested in sagas and Eddic poems.

5. *Ullarakr* (modern Swedish Ulleråker) is a district near Uppsala. The name probably means "Field of Wool"—it appears in Saxo's Latin *Danish History* as Campus Laneus—but it could also mean "Field of Ullr," referring to the Norse god of hunting and archery. Jóhanna Friðriksdóttir points out that in *Heimskringla* (*Óláfs saga helga* ch. 78, transl. Hollander, pp. 316-317), Princess Ingigerd of Sweden has an estate in her own right at Ullarakr, where she negotiates whether she should be betrothed to King Olaf of Norway to make peace between Norway and Sweden (*Women in Old Norse Literature*, p. 87, p. 161 n43).

6. The rule of primogeniture, under which the oldest son of a king is automatically heir to the throne, did not become established until the late 13th century (Jochens, *Women in Old Norse Society*, pp. 94-97). This "law" is an anachronism in the saga's setting, but it probably reflects the royal ideology that had been introduced to Iceland after its union with Norway.

7. This is also said of both the legendary Hrolf Sturlaugson, known as *Göngu-Hrólfr* or "Hrolf the Walker", in *Göngu-Hrólfs saga* (ch. 4), and also the historical Hrolf who conquered Normandy, also known as Rollo or Rolf the Ganger (*Historia Norvegiae*, transl. Kunin, *History of Norway*, pp. 8-9).

8. The fetch (*fylgja*, etymologically "follower" or "one that accompanies") is a spirit being that accompanies a person; it is usually invisible, but often appears in dreams. It usually takes the form of an animal whose assumed nature is like its person's: kings have "noble beasts" like lions or stags, warriors have bears or wolves or other fierce beasts, treacherous sorcerors have foxes, and so on. (Turville-Petre, "Dreams in Icelandic Tradition," pp. 36-39)

9. Noble antagonists in the legendary sagas often hold some of their ships back in battle, in order to even the odds; e.g. *Þorsteins saga Víkingssonar* ch. 7, *Örvar-Odds saga* ch. 9.

10. White "peace-shields" were used to signal peaceful intent, while red "war-shields" signaled hostile intentions; see *Eiríks saga rauða* (chs. 10-11).

11. The word *klámhögg*, "foul blow" or "shaming-stroke", was the legal term for a strike on the buttocks. It was disgraceful for a man to receive one, because it symbolically "womanized" him; law codes ranked it alongside castration (Meulengracht Sørensen, *The Unmanly Man*, pp. 68-70). *Lendaklái̇̇̇ði*, literally "loin-itching", implies sexual wantonness, and the sword may be understood as a metaphorical penis (Heide, "Spinning *Seiðr*", p. 168). Ketil is thus simultaneously insulting Thorberg's masculinity and femininity.

12. The text just says that she struck him with the axe, but since Ketil survives, she presumably struck with the hammer-like back of the axehead. In the sagas, striking with the back of the axehead is sometimes done to humiliate opponents; the implication is they are not worth killing with the blade (*Völsunga saga* 35; *Þórðar saga hreðu* ch. 9; see *Viking Weapons and Combat Techniques*, p. 84).

13. Eating raw meat is typical of berserks, trolls, and other not-wholly-human villains (e.g. Grim Ægir in *Göngu-Hrólfs saga* ch. 2) It is specifically forbidden in *Örvar-odds saga* ch. 9, as *líkari. . . vörgum en mönnum*, "more suitable for wolves than for men."

14. In the legendary sagas, huge clubs are "standard operating procedure" for dealing with berserks or enchanted enemies that cannot be harmed with bladed weapons. (Beard, "Á Þá Bitu Engi Járn," pp. 16-17; see note 22 to *Hrómundar saga Gripssonar*)

15. A similar brilliantly colored ship, which the hero sees and instantly desires to own regardless of the cost, appears in *Sörla saga sterka* ch. 11.

16. Basins and towels for washing the hands were traditionally offered to guests at feasts; e.g. *Hávamál* 4 (transl. Orchard, *The Elder Edda*, p. 15).

17. In a number of sagas, the sword used to kill a giant or other monster—sometimes the only sword that can kill it—is kept in the monster's own lair (e.g. *Hjálmþers saga ok Ölvis* ch. 9; *Egils saga einhenda ok Ásmundar berserkjabana* ch. 15; *Fljótsdæla saga* ch. 5; *Þorsteins saga uxafóts* ch. 9; cf. G519.2, "Ogre killed with his own iron bar"; Thompson, *Motif-Index of Folk Loterature*, vol. 3, p. 360). The same motif appears in folktales such as the Norwegian tale "Soria Moria Castle," but its oldest appearance seems to be Beowulf's encounter with Grendel's mother (*Beowulf* 1557-1569).

18. This is a reworking of the "Polyphemus motif" familiar from the *Odyssey*; the same motif turns up in the legendary *Egils saga einhenda ok Ásmundar berserkjabani* (ch. 10). Hollander points out a number of similarities with an episode in chapter 5 of *Vatnsdælasaga*, a "saga of Icelanders," in which Thorstein kills a robber named Jokul in his hut ("The Gautland Cycle of Sagas I", pp. 65-72). He also points out links with the *fornaldarsaga Þórsteins saga Víkingssonar*, in which, for example, the evil giant Harek is also armed with a forked iron poker and skewers two men at a time. ("The Gautland Cycle of Sagas I", pp. 72-77)

19. Hollander points out that in both *Beowulf* and *Hrólfs saga Gautrekssonar*, the monster-slaying sword is said to be so heavy that only the hero can wield it. ("The Gautland Cycle of Sagas I", pp. 70-71)

20. This type of insult was defined in law as *ýki*, "exaggeration"; the old Norwegian

law code *Gulaþingslög* defines *ýki* as "if a man says about another that which cannot be nor come to be, and has not been." Insults equating a man with a mare itself, implying that the man has sought out sexual penetration, are more common in the sagas; accusations of bestiality with a passive animal partner are rarer (Meulengracht Sørensen, *The Unmanly Man*, pp. 15-17; Finlay, "Monstrous Allegations," pp. 38-42).

21. All the names in this story are derived from horses: *Hrosskell* "horse-kettle" (short for *Hross-ketill*); *Hrossþjóf* "horse-thief"; *Hesthöfði* "horse-head". Boyer (*Les Sagas Légendaires*, pp. 143-145) suggests that a distant remembrance of totemism may be behind this story, pointing out that a number of legendary families are named for animals (*Ylfingar* from wolves, *Hundingjar* from dogs, and so on).

22. The Eddic poem *Hyndluljóð* 22 (Orchard, *The Elder Edda*, p. 253) mentions Thorir Ironshield. He is associated with "Hrolf the Old", who is presumably Hrolf Gautreksson (who is said to have lived to an old age in ch. 37 of this saga).

23. "Ring Horn". The god Baldr is said to have owned a ship by that name (Snorri Sturluson, *Gylfaginning* 49, ed. Faulkes, *Edda*, vol. 1, p. 46); the connection, if any, is not clear. Drinking horns that can provide omens appear in *Þorsteins saga bæjarmagns* (chs. 8-9), while weapons that give omens by making loud noises appear in *Göngu-Hrólfs saga* (ch. 1, note 8).

24. In *Ragnarssona þáttr* (ch. 2), Ragnar Lodbrok gets much the same warning from his wife Aslaug when he plans to invade England: large ships are inadvisable because the island is surrounded by treacherous currents and sandbars.

25. Kalinké (*Bridal-Guest Romance*, p. 58 n26) suggests that Thomas of Cantimpré's *Liber de natura rerum* was the source for this beast-lore. Thomas states that elephants can be overcome by the grunting of pigs, and also that they are fond of wine. The saga author may have substituted a lion for the elephant, inspired by the "grateful lion" first found in *Ívens saga* (the Norse translation of Chrétien de Troyes's *Yvain*) and appearing in several later sagas.

26. "Grim the Hardy" is mentioned in *Hyndluljóð* alongside Thorir Ironshield (Orchard, *The Elder Edda*, p. 253), and may have been intended as a retainer of "Hrolf the Old", probably Hrolf Gautreksson (see note 22 above).

27. This is a possible reference to the "Loathly Lady" motif, in which a hero sleeps with (or just sleeps next to) an elderly and/or hideous woman, discovering the next morning that she has transformed into a young and beautiful woman. (D732 in Thompson, *Motif-Index*, vol. 2, p. 84; Z116 in Thompson, vol. 5, p. 560. For examples in the legendary sagas see *Hrólfs saga kraka* ch. 15, *Þorsteins saga Víkingssonar* ch. 19, and *Gríms saga loðinkinna* ch. 2)

28. *Friðþjófs saga* (ch. 12) also features a king testing the hero's loyalty by falling asleep, or pretending to fall asleep, to see whether the hero will try to kill him or not. The ultimate source might be the Biblical story of David, who has an opportunity to kill Saul but spares him (1 Samuel 24:1-22). See Kalinké, *Bridal-Quest Romance*, pp. 59-60, 117-118.

29. Berserks are often depicted going around in groups of twelve in the sagas (this

saga chs. 16, 20; also *Egils saga* ch. 9; *Örvar-Odds saga* ch. 14; *Hrólfs saga kraka* ch. 16, 37; *Gautreks saga* ch. 7). Harek's eleven companions have no role in the story here; the saga writer may have included them solely to follow tradition.

30. In formal legal duels (*holmganga*), the combatants stood on a cow hide or on a cloak; a man who stepped off the cloak or out of bounds had forfeited the duel. Each man's "second" held a shield before him. (e.g. *Kormaks saga* ch. 10)

31. Kalinké (*Bridal-Quest Romance*, pp. 61-62) suggests that the direct inspiration for this episode is an episode of *Egils saga* (ch. 64) in which Egil fights the berserk Ljot the Pale, who has challenged the unwarlike Fridgeir to a duel in order to take Fridgeir's sister. Fridgeir's mother and Thord's sister both share the name Gyda. The *Egils saga* episode in turn may derive from an episode in Chrétien de Troyes's *Yvain* (known in Norse translation as *Ívens saga*), in which Yvain saves a girl from the giant Harpin de la Montaigne, who has killed two of her brothers and is threatening to kill the other four.

32. This is a widespread folk motif; in Saxo's *Danish History* (IX.321; transl. Davidson and Fisher, p. 297), King Gorm of Denmark makes a similar promise to kill whoever tells him that his son is dead. Usually, the point is that the messenger has to come up with a creative way to make the king blurt out the bad news himself (J1675.2.1, "Tidings brought to the king"; Thompson, *Motif-Index of Folk Literature*, vol. 4, p. 136).

33. The realm of the dead in Norse mythology, but by the date of composition probably not sharply distinguished from the Christian Hell.

34. This episode seems to draw on the imprisonment of Sigmund and Sinfjotli in a mound in *Völsunga saga* ch. 8; in both sagas, the imprisoned men are aided by a woman of their enemy's family dropping a sword into their underground prison. (See also *Sturlaugs saga* ch. 17, note 40)

35. The saga text is *býsn skal til batnaðar*—"there must be a disaster for recovery," i.e. "things must get worse before they get better."

36. See K781, "Castle captured with assistance of owner's daughter. She loves the attacker", in Thompson, *Motif-Index of Folk Literature*, vol. 4, p. 339; R162, "Rescue by captor's daughter", in Thompson, vol. 5, p. 285.

37. Although this is not explicitly stated, the implication is probably that the king and his men are being forced to defecate inside their own hall—which was considered not just disgusting, but shameful. The episode may be based on a famous episode in *Laxdæla saga* (ch. 47): when Kjartan single-handedly blocks the residents of the farmhouse at Laugar from coming out for three days, forcing them to defecate indoors, the residents found it more disgraceful than if Kjartan had killed some of them outright. (Miller, *Anatomy of Disgust*, pp. 144-148; Larrington, "Diet, Defecation, and the Devil," p. 146)

38. In *Örvar-Odds saga* (ch. 27), the hero has been concealing his identity by wearing bark, but his true identity is revealed when a tear in his costume reveals a red sleeve and a thick gold ring on his arm. In both legendary and historical sagas, red clothing is an especially strong token of wealth and luxury (Ewing, *Viking Clothing*, pp. 154-156); Thorir's red sleeve and heavy gold ring are strong

indicators, not just of his humanity, but of his noble rank.

The Saga of Bosi and Herraud

1. This prologue is not in Guðni Jónsson's text, and is taken from Sverrir Tómasson's edition (*Bósa saga og Herrauðs*, p. 5). The tone seems quite tongue-in-cheek (Vésteinn Ólason, "The Marvellous North," p. 117), although O'Connor has argued that prologues like this may well have been intended seriously ("Truth and Lies in the Fornaldarsögur", pp. 363-367).

2. This is the so-called Learned Prehistory, in which the gods were euhemerized as human leaders who had migrated from Asia (from which the name of the main clan of gods, the *Æsir*, was supposedly derived). Snorri Sturluson's *Edda* presents the Learned Prehistory in detail, connecting various pagan deities with the heroes of the Trojan War (*Prologue* 4-11 and *Skáldskaparmál*, Epilogue; trans. Faulkes, *Edda*, pp. 3-5, 64-66; see also *Ynglinga saga* chs. 1-5 in *Heimskringla*, trans. Hollander, p. 6-10). The Learned Prehistory has no historical validity at all; reasoning like this was common in medieval scholarship, and it was a popular way to neutralize the old myths and make it acceptable for Christians to discuss and record them. See note 1 to *Sturlaugs saga*.

3. *Dagfari* and *Náttfari* mean "day-traveler" and "night-traveler"; their father's name *Sæfari* means "seafarer".

4. Harald Wartooth's story is told in the *Sögubrot* and in Saxo Grammaticus's *History of the Danes* (VII.246-255, transl. Ellis Davidson and Fisher, pp. 225-233).

5. *Sjóðr* means "purse". Several puns on this name follow; I've left them untranslated.

6. The word *brynþvari*, literally "chainmail-piercer", means a type of thrusting spear; *Egils saga* (ch. 53) uses the word for a spear with a swordlike blade. Thvari's name complements that of his wife, *Brynhildr* ("chainmail-Hildr"), and may allude to his victory in their fight. Alternatively, his name could be a sexual pun, in keeping with the escapades described later.

7. This king is not mentioned in other sagas, but *Nóatún*, "ships' enclosure", is the mythological home of Njörðr, the god of the sea, shipping, and wealth.

8. *Smiðr* means "smith; craftsman."

9. Old Norse *soppleikr*, "ball game." The description is not precise enough to identify how the game was played, but it could be the same or similar to *knáttleikr*, a team sport played with a ball and sticks. *Knáttleikr* seems to have resembled the Irish game of hurling (Gunnell, "Icelandic *Knattleikur* and Early Irish Hurling," pp. 68-69, and sources therein). Like this game of *soppleikr*, *knáttleikr* matches had a way of turning violent. See *Göngu-Hrólfs saga* ch. 9, notes 30-31.

10. An ell is roughly two feet (61 cm), although the precise definition varied from place to place. The motif of the traveller who stands on cliffs and asks for passage from a ship is probably borrowed from the Volsung tradition, in which the traveler is Odin (*Völsunga saga* ch. 17; *Norna-Gests þáttr* ch. 6; *Reginsmál* 16-25, transl. Orchard, *The Elder Edda*, pp. 158-159); Odin or a very Odin-like man also appears on a cliff asking for passage on his protegé's ship in Saxo's *Danish*

History (I.32; transl. Ellis-Davidson and Fisher, p. 31). Inserting Bosi into this scene is probably meant as parody.

11. The small rocky islands at the mouth of the Göta alv, on the present-day border between Norway and Sweden.

12. The southern Baltic coast east of Denmark, home in the early Middle Ages to the Wends, a Slavic people.

13. Gallo ("Persistent Motifs of Cursing", pp. 121-128) has noted that these stanzas that threaten disaster if the king sails or rides are structurally similar to oaths of truce, and specifically to the lists of disasters that are to befall the breakers of such oaths. He concludes that "Buslubæn" is not an authentic pre-Christian curse, but is "a sort of *potpourri* of ancient curse-formulas" (p. 135); as such, it is still informative about pre-Christian practices.

14. The name *Syrpa* is related to words for "rubbish" and probably means "dirty woman." It appears as the name of an ogress in a few sources (e.g. *Jökuls þáttr Búasonar* chs. 1-2; the *Allra flagða þula* in *Vilhjálms saga sjóðs*—see Loth, *Late Medieval Icelandic Romances* vol. IV, p. 67). In the Icelandic saga *Finnboga saga ramma* it is the name of a poor old (human) woman. *Ljósvetninga saga* refers to a "party game" called *Syrpuþingslög*, "Law of Syrpa's Assembly", apparently some kind of mock court involving harassment of women.

15. These runes are to be read by taking the first letters of each group of six, then the second letters, then the third letters, and so on. Thus unscrambled, they spell **ristil aistil þistil kistil mistil uistil**. This is a version of a magic formula known as "thistle, mistletoe" or "*thistill–mistill–kistill*." Examples appear on several memorial runestones and other Viking-era and post-Viking inscriptions, usually scrambled in the same way as in this saga. Not all of the words have a clear meaning, and some might be "nonsense rhymes," but a possible interpretation would be "ploughshare?–testicle?–thistle–casket–mistletoe–*uistil*'. (MacLeod and Mees, *Runic Amulets and Magical Objects*, pp. 145-148; Thompson, "The Runes in *Bósa saga ok Herrauðs*", pp. 50-56) Boyer points out that a slight rearrangement of the first letters of these words spell **raþumk**, i.e. *ráðumk*, "I decide; I order; I counsel" (*Les Sagas Légendaires*, p. 290) Note that Busla isn't reciting this part of the spell orally, since she could not have pronounced the "bound" rune letters, but would have had to show them written down to King Hring. The formula's meaning and intent have also shifted—it originally seems to have been protective—and on these grounds, her "prayer" has been interpreted as a late literary creation. (Thompson, pp. 55-56) On the other hand, the Eddic poem *Fôr Skírnis* and several inscriptions use the thistle or the word **þistil** in curses against virility or fertility (Mitchell, "Anaphrodisiac Charms," pp. 26-31), so the "prayer" may still reflect older traditions.

16. Bjarmaland is the coast of the White Sea, inhabited at the time by the *Bjarmar*, a Finnic-speaking people. There were several historical Norse voyages to Bjarmaland; these inspired a number of legendary sagas, in which Bjarmaland figures as a land of sorcery and monsters (see Introduction).

17. The wordplay here is hard to translate fully. When applied to a person, *herða*, "to harden", means "to encourage", and I've rendered it as "battle-harden" or "test in battle"—but it also means to harden steel by heating and quenching. "Put to the test" is my rendering of *komit í aflinn*, literally "brought into strength" or "brought into violence"—but *afl*, "strength, is a homonym of *afl*, "a forge." Finally, Sverrir Tómasson suggests that *jarl* here means an iron bar (*Bósa saga og Herrauðs*, p. 75). The wordplay compares Bósi's penis to both a young warrior and a bar of iron, and the woman's vagina is both the warrior's battleground and the forge where steel is tempered (and where it softens after being inside for a while).

18. Norse *Jómali* is derived from Finnish *Jumala*, "god," or a cognate in a closely related language (Ross, "The Terfinnas and Beormas of Ohthere," pp. 48-50). Several legendary sagas contain accounts of heroes looting Jómali's idol or temple; these seem to go back to an account in *Óláfs saga helga* (ch. 133) in *Heimskringla* (transl. Hollander, p. 403-408), in which Thorir Hund and his companions travel to Bjarmaland, trade peacefully, and then raid Jómali's sacred place before making their escape.

19. The rare Norse word *dangandi* is derived from *danga*, "to thrash", and has an obvious sexual meaning in context (Jiriczek, *Die Bósa-Saga*, pp. xxxvi). The English slang expression "banging" seemed to fit especially well.

20. The phrase *ýmsi váru undir* ("by turns they were underneath") echoes Bosi's later sexual encounter in ch. 11, in which his partner *var ýmist ofan á eða undir* ("she was by turns on top or underneath"). Similar sexual innuendo appears in Beowulf's fight with Grendel's mother, who also manages to get on top of Beowulf as they grapple (Nitzsche, "The Structural Unity of Beowulf," pp. 293-296).

21. In *Grettis saga* (ch. 65), Grettir also has a wrestling bout with a female troll which ends when he chops off her arm at the shoulder. The *Grettis saga* episode has long been considered a relative of the same story found in *Beowulf*, although the relationship has been questioned (see Fjalldal, *The Long Arm of Coincidence*).

22. In *Óláfs saga helga* (ch. 133; transl. Hollander, *Heimskringla*, p. 405), the idol of Jómali also holds a large silver bowl and wears a heavy necklace.

23. Literally *þeir sögðu, at mörgu svaraði frestin*—"they said that a delay answered for much". Sverrir Tómasson interprets this to mean that Bosi and Herraud are admitting that their delay in rescuing Hleid shows the limitations of their strength (*Bósa saga og Herrauðs*, p. 76), but this just seems an odd thing to say.

24. Literally, *vit Bósi höfum sungit yfir hausamótum hennar*, "Bosi and I have sung over her skull-sutures." This is anachronistic for a tale that supposedly takes place in distant heathen times, but such lapses in historical accuracy are not uncommon in legendary sagas, and don't seem to have bothered the saga authors.

25. In the later version of this saga, the vulture has two eggs. One is golden and precious (and is not broken when it's given to King Hring), and the other is a *fjöregg* or "life-egg" containing the soul or the life force of the troll-priestess, who can only be killed if her *fjöregg* is broken. (Jiriczek, *Die Bósa-Saga*, p. 108;

Einar Ólafur Sveinsson, *The Folk-Stories of Iceland*, pp. 59-61). Although this is not spelled out, it's possible that the golden egg in this earlier recension was understood to be the priestess's *fjöregg*, and it cracked when she died. The motif is widespread in European folktales (AT 302, "The Ogre's Heart in the Egg," Aarne, *Types of the Folktale*, pp. 93-94)

26. The Battle of Brávellir was a colossal battle between the forces of Harald Wartooth and Sigurd Hring, involving virtually every hero and warrior in northern Europe. The battle is described in the saga fragment *Sögubrot* (chs. 7-9) and in Saxo's *History of the Danes* (VIII.257-265, transl. Ellis Davidson and Fisher, pp. 238-244). While there just might be a distantly remembered and distorted historical basis for the battle, it is primarily a matter of legend.

27. The ability to get a favorable wind at will is a personal magical "knack" mentioned in the legendary *Örvar-Odds saga* and the other "Hrafnista sagas".

28. As mentioned in the introduction, this scene almost certainly borrowed from a French *fabliau* called "*La damoisele qui ne pooit oïr parler de foutre*" ("The girl who could not bear to hear talk of fucking"). As the young woman in the fabliau is being felt up by her seducer, he lays his hand between her legs and asks what he's touching. She tells him it's her pasture, with her well just below. When she does the same to him and asks what she has hold of, he tells her it's his foal. She invites him to graze his foal in her pasture and water it in her well. (Sverrir Tómasson, ed. *Bósa saga og Herrauðs*, pp. 60-62)

29. The idea of specific tunes or poems with the magical effect of forcing people to dance and/or making objects move also appears in *Þorsteins þáttr jarlaskálds*.

30. *Faldafeykir*, "Headdress Blower", is given as the name of one of the Jólasveinar, "Yule-Swains", the sons of the hideous ogress Grýla in Icelandic folklore (Jón Árnason, *Íslenzkar þjóðsögur og æfintýri*, vol. 1, p. 219). It's not clear to me what the connection is, if any.

31. This is presumably a drone string, not directly plucked by the musician but tuned to vibrate sympathetically with the melody strings, adding richness to the tone. Drone strings were not used on known Viking-era harps, but they are used in later Scandinavian folk instruments, notably the Icelandic *langspil*, which has a large hollow body that looks like something that could conceal a person.

32. A harp large enough to conceal a girl also turns up in *Ragnars saga loðbrokar* ch. 1.

33. The obscure word translated "wineskin" here is *traus*. This seems to be a borrowing from medieval French *trousse*, meaning a small purse or bag but also a euphemism for the vulva. The word was probably borrowed from one of the *fabliaux*. (Sverrir Tómasson, *Bósa saga og Herrauðs*, p. 62) "To put a stopper in," *sponsa*, is a borrowing from Middle High German *Spond*.

34. *Skálkr* originally meant "servant," but in Norse had come to mean something more like "rascal."

35. A similar feat is described in the Faroese *Hildibrands táttur*, a section of the ballad *Sniolvs kvæði*: *Hildibrand gav so stórt eitt hogg / av so miklum móði, / klývur brynju av Ásmundi, / han nakin eftir stóð*. ("Hildibrand gave so great a blow / from such great wrath, / he cleaved the mailcoat from Asmund, / he was left standing

naked." Quoted in Benati, "Ásmund *á austrvega*", pp. 114.) The ballad parallels a completely different saga, *Ásmundar saga kappabana*; how this brief motif came to be shared is not clear.

36. Svidi Bold-Attacker appears in *Hálfdanar saga Eysteinssonar*, and is said to be the father of the hero of *Illuga saga Gríðarfóstra*. Svidi's son Vilmund has his own saga, *Vilmundar saga viðutan*, usually considered one of the indigenous *riddarasögur* or "sagas of chivalry" but approaching the *fornaldarsögur* in style and setting. (Loth, *Late Medieval Icelandic Romances*, vol. 4, pp. 137-201)

37. The full story of Ragnar winning Thora is found in *Ragnars saga lóðbrokar* chs. 2-4, and in Saxo's *History of the Danes* (IX.302, transl. Ellis Davidson and Fisher, pp. 281-282).

38. This invocation to "Saint Busla" is not in Guðni Jónsson's edition, but appears in both AM 586 4to and AM 510 4to. Sverrir Tómasson points out a similar tongue-in-cheek invocation at the end of *Vilhjálms sögu sjóðs* to two of its female villains, "Holy" Balbumba and "Saint" Sisigambr. (*Bósa saga og Herrauðs*, p. 79; Loth, *Late Medieval Icelandic Romances*, p. 136)

The Saga of Sturlaug the Hard-Working

1. This is a brief summary of the Learned Prehistory, a euhemerization of old Norse mythology in which the gods were seen as humans who had migrated from Asia and ruled Scandinavia. (See Note 1 to *Bósa saga*.) This opening paragraph of the saga is suspected of being a later addition to the text (Sanders, "*Sturlaugs saga*", p. 2, p. 6).

2. *Kaupangr* is Norse for "market"; the word is fairly common in place names. In manuscript AM 335 4to, Jarl Hring is said to live at Hamarkaupangr ("cliff market" or "rocky hill market"), which is the modern town of Hamar in Hedmark, in southeastern Norway near the Swedish border (Zitzelberger, *The Two Versions of* Sturlaugs saga starfsama, p. 8.6). However, Trondheim is on the North Sea, a long distance north and west of Hamar—and it was originally named Kaupangr. Since the other locations in this chapter seem to be near Trondheim, presumably this is meant here. That said, Icelandic sagas are not always reliable guides to geography; recensions of this saga were composed at a time when Icelanders' contacts with Norway were growing rarer.

3. *Naumudælafylki*, "the shire of Namdalen," is just north of modern Trondheim.

4. The modern form of the name is Skarstad. There are several Skarstads in Norway; the one meant here may be the one northeast of Trondheim and Namsos, near the village of Høylandet in Nord-Trøndelag county.

5. *Njarðey* means "island of Njörðr", the god of ships and the sea. Presumably present-day Nærøy, north of Trondheim.

6. *Tunglaheimr* means "heavenly-body home", possibly "moon home." It is probably the present-day Tinglem, north of the Trondheimsfjord, between the present-day towns of Malm and Namsos.

7. Loka may be the modern Lokøy or Lokøyna, an island west of Bergen, although

this is some distance south of the Trondheim region. The island of Urga has not been located.

8. A woman named Vefreyja is briefly introduced at the end of *Þorsteins saga Víkingssonar*. Like Vefreyja in this saga, she is said to be wise and slightly uncanny (her mother is a princess transformed into an ogre), but it's not certain whether the two sagas refer to the same person.

9. *Vé* can mean "estate; mansion", but more usually means "temple". *Freyja* means "lady", and Vefreyja's name could be interpreted as "lady of the estate." Freyja is also the name of a goddess, and so Vefreyja could mean "lady of the temple" or "goddess of the temple". It might be tempting to interpret Vefreyja as a euhemerized goddess.

10. Expressions in the sagas like "knowledgeable about many things" (*margvíss, margfróðr*) are often euphemisms for having magical knowledge.

11. It's a commonplace in the legendary sagas that the "good guys" only raid and plunder robbers and other "bad guys," leaving innocent farmers and merchants in peace. See *Göngu-Hrólfs saga* ch. 6; other examples include *Þorsteins saga Víkingssonar* ch. 22; *Friðþjófs saga inn frækna* ch. 11; *Örvar-Odds saga* ch. 9.

12. Kalinké (*Bridal-Quest Romance*, pp. 25-33) points out that the same plot device appears in *Völsunga saga* (ch. 11, trans. Byock, p. 52) and in *Hrólfs saga Gautrekssonar* (ch. 1): An elderly widower king (Sigmund/Gautrek) seeks to marry a young woman (Hjordis/Ingibjorg). In the other two sagas, a young king (Lyngvi/Olaf) also seeks the woman's hand, and when her father (Eylimi/Thorir) allows her to make her own choice, she chooses the older man for his fame and renown, while the rejected younger man prepares to attack his rival. Here, Harald's villainous actions break the expected pattern—probably another example of the writer burlesquing the expected conventions of the romantic sagas.

13. The betrothed bride who has to wait for three years for her marriage appears in several sagas of Icelanders (*Gunnlaugs saga ormstungu* ch. 5, *Bjarnar saga hítdælakappa* ch. 2). In these sagas there is generally a narrative reason for the three-year wait; here, the wait seems to be arbitrary, except perhaps as a send-up of the convention.

14. "Hewing-spear" (*höggspjót*) was one of several names for weapons that were probably polearms with long blades, something like the glaive later medieval Europe. The word is usually, if not quite accurately, translated as "halberd."

15. The name *Kolr krappi* is literally "Kol the Crafty". However, other sagas have very similar troll-like villains named Kolr ("Swarthy") with a nickname derived from *kroppi*, "hunchbacked". Kolr *kroppinbakr* (Crooked-Back) appears in *Þorsteins saga Víkingssonar*, Kolr *kryppa* (Hunch), appears in *Vilmunds saga viðútan* (Loth, *Late Medieval Icelandic Romances*, vol. 4). Thus it's possible that *krappi* was originally *kroppi*; I hedged my bets by translating the name with a word which could mean either.

16. Hall suggests that the story told in chapters 6-13 in *Sturlaugs saga* shares ancestry with the story of chapters 2-3 of the R recension of *Heiðreks saga*. In *Sturlaugs*

saga, Kol demands to marry Asa, whom Harald has already claimed, but Sturlaug becomes Harald's champion, gains a magic sword, and defeats Kol. In *Heiðreks saga*, Hjalmar demands to marry Ingjald's daughter, whom Hjorvard has already claimed, but Angantyr becomes Hjorvard's champion, gains a magic sword and defeats Hjalmar.

17. A proverb. Literally, *er eigi í hættu um gamlan mann*, "there's nothing at stake for an old man."

18. The word for a judicial combat is *hólmganga*, literally "going to the island." Such duels did not necessarily take place on a literal island, although they often did. It's not clear exactly where the duel is taking place in this saga, but since the setting is on the banks of a river, I have assumed that a literal island is meant here.

19. Judicial duels in Icelandic society were governed by a legal code (the *hólmgöngulög*). The dueling ground was circumscribed by a spread-out cloak or hide, and/or a ring of stakes; anyone who stepped out of bounds was judged to have lost. Formal combats in the sagas of Icelanders usually end at first blood. See *Kormaks saga* ch. 10 for a description.

20. The chivalric saga *Hrings saga ok Tryggva* has a somewhat similar plot: the heroine Brynhild is betrothed to Hring, but when a raider tries to win her hand by attacking her father's kingdom, her father is forced to betroth her to Tryggvi as a condition for his help (Kalinké, *Bridal-Quest Romance*, pp. 199-201).

21. In *Hauks þáttr Hábrokar* in *Flateyjarbók* (trans. Bachman, *Forty Old Icelandic Tales*, p. 14), a giantess undresses and feels the hero and declares him "lucky", implying that he will survive an upcoming battle and possibly giving him magical protection. "Wise women" do the same for their favored heroes, usually their foster-sons, in several sagas of Icelanders (*Kormaks saga* ch. 1; *Heiðarvíga saga* ch. 23; *Reykdæla saga* ch. 5).

22. A parody of *Völsunga saga* ch. 29, in which Sigurd (disguised as Gunnar) lies next to Brynhild with a naked sword between them; and/or a parody of the Tristan legend (known in Norse translation as *Tristrams saga og Ísöndar*, chs. 65-66, trans. Schach, pp. 102-103), in which Tristan and Isolde place a sword between them when they sleep together in the woods. See also *Göngu-Hrólfs saga* ch. 24, note 49.

23. This cape plays no role in the saga, but capes made by Vefreyja appear in the "sequel" *Göngu-Hrolfs saga* (ch. 4; trans. Pálsson and Edwards, p. 37). They are impervious to both weapons and venom.

24. Though it's not expressly stated here, Kol probably has the ability to blunt weapons with his gaze. Several villains in Saxo's *History of the Danes* have this ability: Visinn (VI.187, p. 173); Grimmi (VII.223, p. 207); and Hildiger (VII.244, p. 223). So does Thororm in *Gunnlaugs saga* (ch. 7) and Thorgrim in *Vatnsdæla saga* (ch. 29). In *Hávamál* in the *Poetic Edda* (148; transl. Orchard, p. 37), and in *Ynglinga saga* (ch. 6, transl. Hollander, *Heimskringla*, p. 10), Odin has the ability to blunt his enemies' weapons by magic, as do the berserks Sorkvir and Brynjolf in *Göngu-Hrólfs saga* (ch. 2)

25. The Norse reads *herjans syni*, "to [the mind of] a rascal's son." *Herjan* was once a name of the god Odin, but by the time this saga was written, *herjan* had become an epithet, meaning something like "fiend".

26. An expression meaning "I shall never accept money as compensation for my brother's death, but will always seek vengeance." See also *Grettis saga* ch. 22.

27. *Blámenn*, "black men", is the name used for black Africans in historical sagas (e.g. *Orkneyinga saga* ch. 88, trans. Pálsson and Edwards, p. 172). However, the "black men" of the legendary sagas are stock villains, hideous and supernaturally powerful, whose primary narrative function is to be killed by the hero after an exciting battle scene. They appear in geographically incongruous places— Snorri Sturluson places them in Siberia (*Ynglinga saga* ch. 1 in *Heimskringla*, trans. Hollander, p. 6)—but still belong to a tradition in Norse literature of attributing uncanny powers to ethnic outsiders. See Lindow, "Supernatural and Ethnic Others".

28. The name *Jökull* means "glacier"; *Frosti*, of course, means "frost." As noted in footnote 17 to *Bósa saga*, the word for "to harden" (*herða*) also means "to encourage; to test in battle" when applied to a person; this wordplay is not quite translatable. Two men named Jökull and Frosti are paired up in *Þorsteins þáttr bæjarmagns* (ch. 6).

29. *Finnr* in Norse sagas usually means a Saami ("Lapp"). "Finns" often appear in the sagas as wielders of powerful magic.

30. There are a number of instances of fights between humans who have shapeshifted into animal form (*Hrólfs saga kraka* ch. 33; *Hjálmþés saga ok Ölvis* ch. 11; *Landnámabók* S350/H309, Jakob Benediktsson, ed. *Íslenzk Fornrit* vol. 1, pp. 355-356; *Svarfdæla saga* ch. 19). In most accounts, however, a shapeshifter (*hamrammr*) is asleep or unconscious, as his or her consciousness leaves the body and takes animal form; in the *Landnámabók* account, the battle is only visible to someone with second sight. Usually, a person takes on only one animal form (although the god Odin was said to be able to take on many forms; see *Ynglinga saga* ch. 7). This saga's account is unusual in depicting shape-shifting of the total body in broad daylight, while the fighters are awake, each into more than one animal form.

31. The author of the saga has a kite-shaped shield in mind, rather than the round shields of the historical Viking era.

32. *Austrvík* means "eastern bay". Presumably this is the White Sea, which is more usually called *Gandvík*, "Magic Bay". Like Austrvik, Gandvík is often described as the haunt of giantesses and sorcery.

33. *Hornnefja* means "horn nose." Several giantesses in the *fornaldarsögur* have names that imply that their noses are bizarre: *Járnnef* ("iron nose"), *Arinnefja* ("eagle nose"), *Skinnnefja* ("leather nose"), *Skellinefja* ("rattle nose").

34. Giants and giantesses are often depicted wearing hides, instead of more "civilized" clothing of woven cloth; Saxo's *Danish History* mentions one man who dresses entirely in hides and is taken for a giant (I.13-17; Ellis Davidson and Fisher, transl., pp. 16-19). Zoe Borovsky has pointed out that Hrolf's

costume resembles the costume of men who dressed in hides and skins and impersonated giantesses in medieval folk dramas and guising, such as the *Grýla* tradition in Iceland. ("Folk Dramas, Farce, and the *Fornaldarsögur*"; see also Gunnell, *The Origins of Drama in Medieval Scandinavia*, pp. 160-178)

35. Giantesses are rarely said to be able to change their size in the sagas, but Harthgrepa in Saxo's *Danish History* can do this (I.20-22; Ellis Davidson and Fisher, transl., pp. 22-23). Giantesses are frequently depicted as lustful for human men (Jóhanna Friðriksdóttir, *Women in Old Norse Literature*, pp. 67-69).

36. This is a twist on the motif of the hero finding the only weapon that will kill the monster in the monster's own lair (K818.2, "Giantess killed with the spear she herself has given hero", in Thompson, *Motif-Index of Folk Literature*, vol. 4, p. 342). See note 17 to *Hrólfs saga Gautrekssonar*.

37. As discussed in the Introduction, the Hundings ("dog people") are probably derived from medieval European traditions concerning the monstrous races at the far ends of the world, dating back to the Cynocephali of the Roman author Pliny the Elder but possibly also drawing on an independent northern European tradition.

38. As discussed in the Introduction, Bjarmaland is the land on the shores of the White Sea; There are historical accounts of Norse voyages to Bjarmaland, but in the legendary sagas, Bjarmaland is always a place of sorcery, monsters, and exotic treasures. This episode may be compared with the Bjarmaland temple in *Bósa saga ok Herrauds* (ch. 8), which also holds amazing treasures and monstrous guardians.

39. Zitzelberger suggests that both the Hundings and the temple are borrowed from Adam of Bremen's *History of the Archbishops of Hamburg–Bremen*, which mentions both the Hundings (Cynocephali) living on the north Baltic coast, and the pagan temple at Uppsala. (*The Two Versions of* Sturlaugs saga starfsama, p. 307)

40. This scene references a scene in *Völsunga saga* (ch. 8), in which Sigmund and Sinfjotli are imprisoned in a barrow with stone-walled chambers. Unlike *Völsunga saga* and a similar scene in *Hrólfs saga Gautrekssonar* (ch. 29), a friendly woman does not smuggle food and weapons into the hero's prison. However, Sturlaug is like Sigmund in that he saws through the stone with his weapon. Since *Völsunga saga* is thought to have reached its present form around 1300, this places a limit on the date of *Sturlaugs saga* (Zitzelberger, *The Two Versions of* Sturlaugs saga starfsama, pp. 5-6).

41. A common way of asking for help from a helper in folktales and legendary sagas; see Einar Ólafur Sveinsson, *The Folk-Stories of Iceland*, p. 257)

42. The god *Freyr*, also known as *Yngvi* and *Yngvi-Freyr*, was said to be the founder of the Yngling dynasty that ruled Sweden in legendary times (*Ynglinga saga* ch. 10, trans. Hollander, *Heimskringla*, pp. 13-14). Presumably this is who is meant here, although the saga author gives no sign that he understood Ingvi-Frey to be a deity.

43. Another Rondolf from Bjarmaland appears in *Göngu-Hrolfs saga* (ch. 30); this

Rondolf is part giant, prone to battle-frenzy, and armed with a huge club.

44. *Sturlaugs rímur*, a retelling of the saga, concludes with this victory over the Hundings (transl. Zitzelberger, *The Two Version of* Sturlaugs saga starfsama, pp. 412-40), as does the later "version B" of the saga. Both the *rímur* and version B of the saga may be derived from an earlier version of the saga that lacked the story of the Yule oaths. (Sanders, "*Sturlaugs saga starfsamá*", p. 2)

45. Oaths sworn at Yule feasts seem to have been especially binding and significant; they appear in several *fornaldarsögur* (e.g. *Hervarar saga ok Heiðreks* ch. 2; *Ketils saga hængs* ch. 4) and other sources (e.g. *Harðar saga ok Hólmverja* ch. 14; *Helgakviða Hjörvarðssonar* in the *Poetic Edda*).

46. This is a *heitstrenging* or "oath contest" in which each man must swear an oath no less worthy than those that have already been sworn. This particular episode may be based on the story of the Jómsvíkings' oaths (*Jómsvíkinga saga* ch. 26, transl. Blake, *The Saga of the Jomsvikings*, pp. 28-29; *Óláfs saga Tryggvasonar* ch. 35, trans. Hollander, *Heimskringla*, pp. 175-176). But similar oaths to accomplish great feats—including oaths to get into bed with unattainable women—are also found in medieval romances and in a number of Icelandic *riddarasögur*. See Schlauch, *Romance in Iceland*, pp. 102-103.

47. This could be an ordinary message, but other sagas mention rune-inscribed objects used as magical charms to affect a woman's mind or emotions (e.g. *Egils saga* chs. 73, 77; *History of the Danes* III.79, p. 77). Rune-carved sticks have been excavated and dated to the 13th and 14th centuries; they include both mundane letters and apparent love charms (Liestol, "Runes of Bergen").

48. The texts *Hversu Nóregr byggðist* [How Norway Was Settled] and *Fundinn Nóregr* [The Finding of Norway; usually included as the opening chapters of *Orkneyinga saga*] give the genealogy of the legendary King Snær the Old, "Snow", who lived in the far north. His daughters are Fönn, "Snowdrift"; Drífa, "Snowfall"; and Mjöll, "Snow Powder". Drífa was said to have married Vanlandi, the Yngling king of Sweden (*Ynglinga saga* ch. 13, *Heimskringla*, trans. Hollander, pp. 16-17). In *Bárðar saga snæfellsáss* (ch. 1), Mjöll is said to have been abducted by the giant king Dumbr and become the mother of the legendary Icelander Bard Snæfellsass.

49. In the sagas, *Gestr*—"guest" in Old Norse—or a variant of the name, is a common pseudonym used by wanderers who are seeking lodging. (e.g. this saga ch. 25; *Norna-Gests þáttr* ch. 1; *Hervarar saga* ch. 10)

50. Sanders ("*Sturlaugs saga starfsamá*" p. 6) suggests that the substitution of Frosti for Sturlaug on the wedding night might be yet another takeoff on *Völsunga saga*—this time on the episode in which Sigurd wins Brynhild while disguised as Gunnar (ch. 29, trans. Byock, pp. 80-82).

51. "To turn toward" (*snúast at*) someone is a common euphemism for sexual intercourse (Jochens, *Women in Old Norse Society*, pp. 72-73); we should probably assume that Frosti and Mjoll are *in copula* as the conversation is going on.

52. Several legendary sagas mention cows or bulls that have been turned monstrous and savage by being worshipped (*Ragnars saga loðbrókar* chs. 8-9, 12; *Hjálmpés saga*

ok Ölvis ch. 10; *Þorsteins þáttr uxafóts* ch. 13). *Ynglinga saga* (ch. 26; *Heimskringla,* trans. Hollander, p. 30) mentions that King Egil Aunsson was killed by a bull which had turned savage while being kept for sacrifice.

53. Guðni Jónsson's text based on AM 173 has *þat mun hneppa mik á kaf undir sik ok halda niðri,* "it will hold me in the sea under itself and keep [me] down," which seems odd. I've emended the text using manuscript AM 335 4to, which has *briota dyrit i kaf undir sig ok hallda nidri,* "[he] will force it into the sea under himself and hold it down." (Zitzelberger, *The Two Versions of* Sturlaugs saga starfsama, pp. 25.46-26.1) Also noteworthy is that in AM 173, Godrid speaks of herself in the third person as the auroch's killer; in AM 335, she says that someone named Geirreydr will kill the aurochs. Assuming that *Geirreydr* is the same name as the normalized form *Geirröðr,* then Geirreydr would presumably be male, since a male giant by that name is attested elsewhere in Norse myth.

54. Saxo's *History of the Danes* mentions other instances of supernatural women associated with cows or cow-like beasts from the sea: one killed by Hadding (I.29-30; transl. Ellis-Davidson and Fisher, pp. 29-30) and one that kills Frothi (V.171-172, transl. Ellis-Davidson and Fisher, pp. 157-158). There is also the uncanny four-horned bull who is the son of a supernatural woman in *Laxdœla saga* ch. 31. The saga does not parallel Saxo's accounts closely, but it may be referring to (or parodying) these or similar tales. Thompson lists a folk motif from the Baltic that the Devil's cows have only one horn (A2286.2.3; *Motif-Index of Folk Literature,* vol. 1, p. 282).

55. Several other sagas make it clear that women from the Finnic peoples of the far North have powerful magic and are dangerous to take as wives. Examples include Snæfrid in *Haralds saga hárfagra* (ch. 25, trans. Hollander, *Heimskringla,* pp. 80-81), Drífa in *Ynglinga saga* (ch. 13, trans. Hollander, p. 16), and Gunnhild in *Egils saga* and several others.

56. Guðni Jónsson's text based on AM 173 says that they go *vestr til Gautlands,* "westward to Götland," which makes no sense; I've emended the text from AM 335, which has *austr til Gardalandz,* "eastward to Russia." (Zitzelberger, *The Two Versions of* Sturlaugs saga starfsama, p. 26.26)

57. Norse *Aldeigjuborg,* the present-day Staraya Ladoga.

58. Several historical sagas list female healers who treat wounds and illness, and Ellis-Davidson (*Roles of the Northern Goddess,* p. 161-163) suggests that the Norse may have seen women as especially gifted in healing. But the gentle princess who heals anyone in need probably derives from the *riddarasögur;* compare Ingigerd with Ísodd in *Tristrams saga* (ch. 29; trans. Schach, pp. 46-47), or with princesses in the native *riddarasögur* such as Cecilia in *Mírmanns saga* (chs. 14-15; trans. O'Connor, *Icelandic Histories,* pp. 268-269) or Nítíða and Sýjalín in *Nítíða saga* (chs. 1, 5; transl. McDonald, "*Nítíða saga,*" pp. 124-127, 142-143), or with healer-princesses in several other romances (Schlauch, *Romance in Iceland,* p. 153)

59. Although she is not depicted as a ruler, Ingigerd resembles the "maiden king" (*meykongr*) figures of Icelandic romances; however, the typical *meykongr* disdains

the very idea of marriage and sends her suitors packing with harsh words and mockery. (Kalinké, *Bridal-Quest Romance*, pp. 99-100) Framar's failed attempts to woo her may be parodies of "maiden king" episodes in other sagas.

60. *Snækollr* means "snow-peak" or "snow-head". If the name means that Framar is old, or pretending to be old, this episode may be a parody of the old king who courts a young bride, seen in *Hrólfs saga Gautrekssonar* chs. 1-2 and *Völsunga saga* ch. 11 (see this book, p. XX). Oddly enough, a Viking named Snækollr appears in the saga later and seemingly turns out to be one of King Ingvar's allies; this seems rather awkwardly tacked on.

61. The Old Norse word translated "sorcerers" is *seiðmenn*, i.e. men who practice *seiðr*. *Seiðr* is a type of magic, sometimes used to foretell the future or to protect someone in battle, but often used to create illusions and confuse enemies. According to Snorri Sturluson (*Ynglinga saga* ch. 7; *Heimskringla*, trans. Hollander, p. 11), its use was considered unmanly. There are instances in historical sagas of kings putting *seiðmenn* to death (e.g. *Haralds saga hárfagra* ch. 34; *Heimskringla*, trans. Hollander, pp. 88-89).

62. Persons who magically shape-shift may be recognized by their eyes; see, for example, *Kormaks saga* ch. 18, or the legendary *Ketils saga hængs* ch. 3; or *Ála flekks saga* ch. 10 (transl. Bachmann and Erlingson, *Six Old Icelandic Sagas*, p. 51).

63. This is probably a parody of episodes in other sagas in which a wounded man has to keep his internal organs from falling out, such as Bolli in *Laxdæla saga* (ch. 60), Starkad the Old in *Sögubrót* (ch. 9), and Hromund Gripsson in *Hrómundar saga Gripssonar* (ch. 7).

64. The author evidently forgot to explain who Hvitserk is. The name ("White Shirt") is fairly common in legendary sagas for princes of foreign lands, so presumably he is Ingvar's son or kinsman.

65. Heinrek and Ingolf aren't mentioned in other *fornaldarsögur*. *Göngu-Hrólfs saga* lists four sons of Sturlaug and Asa: Rögnvaldr, Fraðmarr, Eirekr, and the saga's protagonist Hrólfr (ch. 4). Presumably this version of *Sturlaugs saga* pre-dates *Göngu-Hrólfs saga* (Zitzelberger, *The Two Version of* Sturlaugs saga starfsama, p. 6).

66. Peace-Frodi (*Frið-Fróði*) is mentioned in the *Poetic Edda* (*Gróttasöngr*, Introductory Prose, transl. Orchard, *The Elder Edda*, p. 257), the *Skjöldunga saga* (trans. Miller, "Fragments of Danish History", ch. 3, p. 10), and Saxo's *Danish History* (V.170, transl. Ellis-Davidson and Fisher, pp. 156-157) as a legendary king of Denmark, whose reign was marked by surpassing peace and fruitfulness. Christian writers thought of him as living at the time of Christ, dying some time after the Crucifixion.

The Saga of Hrolf the Walker

1. The Norse text has *fornskræðum*, "old manuscripts", but this misses the point that author is contasting oral and written sources. The same prologue appears in *Sigurðar saga þögla* with *fornkvæðum*, "old poems", and this makes more sense;

fornskræðum is probably a scribal error. (O'Connor, "Truth and Lies in the *Fornaldarsögur*," p. 368, n6)

2. Eyvindr *kinnrifi* (Split-Cheek) is a sorceror tortured to death by King Óláfr Tryggvason; before he dies, he claims to be a spirit magically brought into human form. (*Óláfs saga Tryggvasonar* ch. 76; transl. Hollander, *Heimskringla*, p. 211) Gunnar Half-and-Half destroyed an animated idol of the god Frey that was possessed by a "devil" in *Ögmundar þáttr dytts*, a tale embedded in *Óláfs saga Tryggvasonar* as found in *Flateyjarbók*. I have been unable to track down Einarr *skarfr* (Cormorant); Pálsson and Edwards state that he appears in *Heimskringla*, but I have been unable to locate him in the standard editions.

3. A version of this same prologue also begins the romance *Sigurðar saga þögla* (Loth, *Late Medieval Icelandic Romances*, vol. 2, pp. 95-96).

4. Several "sagas of Icelanders" describe beautiful women as having exceptionally long, blonde hair (e.g. Hallgerd in *Njáls saga* ch. 9 and Helga in *Gunnars saga ormstungu* ch. 4, whose hair is described almost identically with this passage). Usually this is the woman's only physical feature to be described in any detail. Since unmarried women wore their hair loose while married women kept theirs covered with a headdress, a display of long hair carried connotations of sexuality and marriageability (Jochens, "Before the Male Gaze," pp. 12-14).

5. Norse *Dýna* means the Danube (Simek, *Altnordische Kosmographie*, p. 203), but since the Danube doesn't flow close to Russia, the geography is a bit confused. *Yngvars saga viðförla* (see next note) claims that this river that Yngvar explored was the largest of three rivers that flowed through Russia; the Don River might fit this description.

6. *Yngvars saga viðförla* tells his story. This saga is thought to be loosely based on an actual Viking excursion in the year 1041.

7. Dúlcifal is derived from *Bucephalus*, the legendary horse of Alexander the Great. The saga name might be derived from Balkan versions of the Alexander legend, in which the horse's name has become Douchipal, but how the name was transmitted to Iceland is not clear. In any case, Dúlcifal's immense strength and speed, and its viciousness to everyone but its fated master, are clearly based on classical and medieval legends of Bucephalus. (Magoun, "Whence 'Dúlcifal'?")

8. This is reminiscent of the famous thrusting-spear in *Njáls saga* (ch. 30, 54, 78, etc.), which rang out loudly if it was about to be used to kill someone.

9. Some medieval French versions of the legend of Alexander claim that Bucephalus was a cross between an elephant and a dromedary (Anderson, "Bucephalas and His Legend", p. 10).

10. One Sigurd Wool-String (*ullstrengr*) appears as one of King Magnús's retainers in Norse historical sources (e.g. *Morkinskinna* ch. 56; transl. Andersson and Gade, pp. 288-294; *Mágnúss saga berfætts* ch. 5-6; transl. Hollander, *Heimskringla*, pp. 671-672). In a scene in *Morkinskinna* (p. 293, n5), one of Sigurd's adversaries mocks him and compares him to an imaginary bandit named Sigurd Wool-Yarn (*ullband*); the name is meant to be an insulting variant of "Wool-String," but it's not clear what's so insulting about it. The compiler of *Göngu-Hrólfs saga*

might have borrowed the name without understanding its intent. It's tempting to speculate that a saga compiler or one of his sources might have borrowed *ullband* from the Gothic *ulbandus*, "camel," and thus that this very legendary saga set in eastern Europe might actually preserve a small fragment of accurate information about peoples in Eastern Europe. Given that the Norse cognate of *ulbandus*, *úlfaldi*, does appear as a man's by-name (e.g. *Óláfs saga helga* chs. 61-62; transl. Hollander, *Heimskringla*, pp. 294-296), and that sagas like *Hervarar saga* do preserve Gothic names, the name "Sigurd Camel" might make a little more sense than "Sigurd Wool-Yarn." In the absence of better evidence, this speculation must remain wool-gathering.

11. The ability to blunt an enemy's blades is a common magical skill in the sagas, especially among villains; see note 24 to *Sturlaugs saga*, ch. 9.

12. *Hlésey* (modern Danish *Læsø*) is a large island in the Kattegat, between Jutland and Norway; it features in several sagas as a setting for strange doings.

13. In Norse mythology, Ægir is the god of the sea; he is also known as Hlér, and the island of Hlésey was named for him. Gróa is the name of a seeress in Snorri's *Edda* (*Skáldskaparmál*, ed. Faulkes, vol. 2a, p. 22) and in the Eddic poem *Svípdagsmál*. It's not clear if Gróa in this saga should be identified with either of these; nonetheless, a few fragments of older myth seem to have been incorporated into the narrative here. The name may be Celtic in origin; cf. Irish and Scots Gaelic *gruach*, "woman."

14. The war-arrow (*herör*) was an arrow or arrow-shaped token that was sent from farm to farm as a summons to arms; whoever received it was obliged to pass it on to his neighbor and then muster into service. It is mentioned in several historical sagas (e.g. *Hákonar saga góða* ch. 23; *Óláfs sags Tryggvasonar* chs. 17, 40, 53, 65; in *Heimskringla*) and in the Norwegian law codes (e.g. *Gulaþingslög* 151, 312, transl. Larson, *The Earliest Norwegian Laws*, pp. 128, 197).

15. The sorcerous Harek Ironskull in *Þorsteins saga Víkingssonar* (ch. 3) also has a bald head that cannot be hurt by normal weapons.

16. "Life-stones" that go with famous swords are mentioned in the "sagas of Icelanders" *Kormáks saga* (chs. 12, 13) and *Laxdæla saga* (ch. 57). These were not permanently fastened to the sword, but were kept in small bags. At least in *Laxdæla saga*, the life-stone is said to be the only thing that can heal wounds inflicted by its sword. Davidson translates the text of *Göngu-Hrólfs saga* to mean that the life-stones were "shut into the pommel", and mentions continental descriptions of Christian relics kept in sword hilts (*The Sword in Anglo-Saxon England*, pp. 181-184). Guðni Jónsson's text has *leystir lífsteinar*, "loose life-stones"; Davidson emends *leystir* to *læstir*, "shut in," but given that life-stones in the other sagas are not permanently mounted on or in the sword, *leystir* seems reasonable. Crystal, amber, and meerschaum beads, kept close to a sword's hilt but not permanently fastened to it, have been found in several early medieval graves in England and Germany; these probably had an amuletic function and may have been the basis for the *lífsteinar* of the sagas. (Davidson, pp. 82-85)

17. The word translated "spell" and "sorcery" here is *seiðr*, which could encompass

several types of magical effect, including clairvoyance, divination, protection, and creating illusions or altering mental states. (See notes 60-61.)

18. Ermland is probably the province of Warmia, which lies along the Baltic Coast, mostly within the borders of present-day Poland. However, Norse geographical texts refer to Armenia as *Ermland* or *Ermland hit mikla* ("Greater Ermland"), and it's just possible, if not likely, that this is what the saga author meant. (Simek, *Altnordische Kosmographie*, pp. 203-204; Magnús Már Lárusson, "On the So-Called 'Armenian' Bishops," pp. 23-28)

19. In Norse mythology, Jotunheim is the realm of the giants. In the legendary sagas, it frequently appears as a land on Earth, rather nebulously defined as lying in the Arctic and/or Siberia. Aluborg or Alaborg also appears in *Hálfdans saga Eysteinssonar*; it seems to have been located east of Aldeigjuborg (Staraja Ladoga), not far from present-day St. Petersburg.

20. The word *kastala* and the idea of castles are both borrowed from the sagas of chivalry; the historical Viking-age Norse did not build castles as such.

21. Yes, this is a discrepancy: in *Sturlaugs saga* the temple is located in Bjarmaland, probably on the White Sea coast.

22. Located in southeastern Norway on the Swedish border, due east of Ringerike.

23. Atli's father's name is derived from *ótryggr*, "faithless; untrustworthy".

24. The realm of the dead in Norse mythology.

25. Värmland is to the north of Götland, and rather far off Hrolf's actual line of march.

26. *Stigandi* means "stepping", a fitting alias for Hrolf the Walker.

27. As noted in *Sturlaugs saga starfsama* ch. 4 (note 11), it's common in legendary sagas to "whitewash" a hero's Viking career by claiming that he only robbed villains who deserved it, while leaving farmers and merchants in peace. Jolgeir directly inverts this rule of the "Viking Code."

28. Courland (*Kúrland*) is a region on the Baltic coast, part of present-day Latvia.

29. *Hrafn* means "raven"; *Krákr* means "crow".

30. The ball game is *knáttleikr*, mentioned in both legendary and historical sagas as a popular and potentially violent sport involving a ball that was hit with sticks. The rules are not precisely laid out in the saga accounts, but it resembled the Irish game of hurling (Gunnell, "Icelandic *Knattleikur* and Early Irish Hurling," pp. 68-69, and sources therein). See *Bósa saga* chs. 2-3, note 9.

31. Saga accounts of *knáttleikr* state that opposing players normally played one-on-one and were supposed to be matched in strength and size (e.g. *Gisla saga surssonar* ch. 15, 18; *Grettis saga* ch. 15). *Eyrbyggja saga* (ch. 43) implies that a man can be barred from the games for being too strong; the account also mentions two brothers who are so big and strong that they are only allowed to play against each other. Some variants of hurling, notably Cornish hurling, had the same rule that players had to be matched by pairs (Gunnell, "Icelandic *Knattleikur* and Early Irish Hurling," pp. 68-69)

32. For a scholarly study of the abilities of European swallows to carry various loads, see Gilliam and Jones, *Monty Python and the Holy Grail* (scene 1).

33. This motif derives from the Tristan legend, in which King Mark sees a bird carrying a woman's beautiful hair, and vows to marry the woman whose hair it is, sending Tristan on the quest for his bride. (Kalinké, *Bridal-Quest Romance*, p. 147 n54)

34. The motif of the uncatchable stag which leads the hunter to a supernatural woman has been discussed in the Introduction and in *Gautreks saga* (note 1). The decoration on the stag's horns is very similar to the decoration on the cow's horns in *Gautreks saga* (ch. 6); see Thompson, *Motif-Index of Folk Literature* B101, "Animals with members of precious metal" (vol. 1, pp. 374-375).

35. The seeress in *Eiríks saga rauða* wears an identical garment, a *blár tuglamöttull* or "blue-black mantle fastened with straps." The color *blár* can encompass shades ranging from deep blue to pitch black. It seems to be associated with death and the uncanny; men who are setting out to kill often wear *blár*, while women often put on *blár* clothing to work magic or confront a magic-worker (e.g. Geirrid's *blá skikkja* in *Eyrbyggja saga* ch. 20). See Wolf, "The Color Blue in Old Norse–Icelandic Literature," for an overview.

36. It's worth noting the similarity of this encounter to Scottish folklore about a giant female being (*sídhe*) known as the *Cailleach* (Old Woman) who keeps the deer as her herds, and may or may not release them for a hunter to take (McKay, "The Deer-Cult", p. 147-151).

37. An Icelandic folk tale concerns an elf-woman who cannot give birth without a human to assist ("Álfkona í Barnsnauð", in Jón Árnason, *Íslenzkar Þjóðsögur og Æfintýri*, vol. 1, pp. 15-16; see also Einar Ólafur Sveinsson, *The Folk-Stories of Iceland*, p. 172). Similar tales are widespread in Scandinavia and found all over Europe (F372.1, "Fairies take human midwife to attend fairy woman," in Thompson, *Motif-Index of Folk Literature*, vol. 3, p. 75; see Lövkrona, "The Pregnant Frog and the Farmer's Wife", pp. 79-89, and Kvideland and Sehmsdorf, *Scandinavian Folk Belief and Legend*, pp. 227-228, for more Scandinavian examples).

38. The motif of two weapons that are outwardly identical, with the inferior copy given to a king who demands it and the genuine one concealed by the man who will need it, appears in the tale of Velent in *Þiðreks saga af Bern* (ch. 67; transl. Haymes, *The Saga of Thidrek of Bern*, p. 47)

39. The encounter with Hreggvid is a clever inversion of the *haugbrot* or "Gravemound Battle" seen in *Hrómundar saga Gripssonar* (ch. 4) and in several other sagas. Instead of selfishly fighting to keep his treasure, Hreggvid generously gives it to the man whom he wants to make his heir. A foul stench is usual in encounters with the undead, but in this case it's not the fault of the undead man. And in *Hrómundar saga* and several other "Gravemound Battle" episodes, a necklace is specifically mentioned as an item whose attempted theft causes the dead man to attack (Stitt, *Beowulf and the Bear's Son*, pp. 149, 155, 168)—whereas here, the undead man makes a special point of giving it freely. This episode especially resembles the first *haugbrot* in *Gull-Þóris saga* (ch. 3), in which the mound-breakers also face a storm, and one of them has a vision of

the mound-dweller, who turns out to be his kinsman and who offers him gifts.

40. Several sagas mention kings who are discerning judges of craftsmanship; Olaf Haraldsson, for example, is described as skilled at judging handicrafts, "whether he himself had made them or others." (*Óláfs saga helga* ch. 3; see Russom, "A Germanic Concept of Nobility," pp. 7-9)

41. In "Gravemound Battle" episodes, retainers are often charged with holding the rope that the hero descends on. When the fighting begins, the helpers are terrified by the noise, or else they assume that the hero has been killed, and they abandon their posts, leaving the hero to climb out on his own. (Stitt, *Beowulf and the Bear's Son*, pp. 129-156) Icelandic audiences, who presumably knew very well how such episodes were "supposed to go", no doubt found Vilhjalm's bold brazenfaced lie amusing.

42. The story of Hedin the son of Hjarrandi is told in full in *Sörla þáttr*, a story preserved in *Flateyjarbók*, which makes Hjarrandi the king of Arabia. The story is also told or alluded to in several other Norse sources and even Old English and Middle German texts. Hedinsey is probably the Baltic island of Hiddensee, off the coast of present-day eastern Germany.

43. The name *Sóti* means "soot-colored." Berserks and other sorcerous villains in the legendary sagas sometimes sport black skin or other unusual color schemes. Villains named Soti also appear in the legendary *Ketils saga hœngs* (ch. 5) and *Hálfdans saga Brönufóstra* (ch. 1), and in the nominal "saga of Icelanders" *Harðar saga ok Hólmverja* (chs. 14-15), although the name appears neutrally in *Sturlaugs saga starfsama* (ch. 1). See the comments on *blámenn* in *Sturlaugs saga*, note 27.

44. The resemblance to the story of Achilles is striking, but it's not uncommon in legendary sagas for a warrior, usually a sorcerous and villainous one, to be enchanted so that blades cannot cut him. (Beard, "*Á Þá Bitu Engi Járn*," pp. 13-16)

45. In the mythology, *Norðri* ("northern") is the name of a dwarf, one of the four who are said to hold up the sky (*Gylfaginning* 8; Snorri Sturluson, *Edda*, ed. Faulkes, vol. 1, p. 12). The connection between the mythological dwarf and Soti's standard bearer is unclear, if indeed there is one.

46. Sagas and poems refer to swearing an oath by a stone, sometimes while standing on a stone. In *Guðrúnarkviða III*, 3, Gudrun swears her innocence on or by a sacred white stone (transl. Orchard, *The Elder Edda*, p. 203); *Helgakviða Hundingsbana* II 31 mentions oaths sworn *at úrsvölum Unnarsteini*, "on the ice-cold Unnar-stone" (transl. Orchard, p. 141); and *Atlakviða* 30 mentions an oath *at Sigtýs bergi*, "on Sigtyr's (Odin's) rock." (transl. Orchard, p. 213). Men swear oaths at a feast while placing their feet on a stone in *Hœnsa-Þóris saga* ch. 12. Saxo Grammaticus claims that the ancients stood on a stone to choose their kings, "as though to augur the durability of their action through the firmness of the rocks beneath them" (*History of the Danes* I.11, transl. Ellis Davidson and Fisher, p. 14, n5). The fact that Vilhjalm swears his oath while standing on a stump—which unlike stone is subject to fire and decay—may have connoted to readers and listeners that his oath is not trustworthy.

47. *Möndull* means the handle or axle of a hand-mill (in modern Icelandic it means "axis"). Why a dwarf should be named this isn't clear; the name may be a joke, implying that dwarves, like hand-mill axles, are thick and stumpy. Given Mondul's sexual appetite, the name could also be a phallic joke—something like "Shaft" or "Johnson" in modern colloquial English. That said, several other attested dwarf-names relate to various tools (*Fíli*, "file"; *Heptifíli*, "file with a haft"; *Kíli*, "wedge"; *Dóri*, "auger"; *Viggr*, "axe-bit"; etc.), and all are probably connected with dwarves' reputation as skilled craftsmen. *Patti* is a pet name for a baby boy, derived from a word meaning "teat" (cf. Danish *pattekarl*, "baby at the breast"), but figuratively meaning something like "little shaver." Presumably this is a joke based on dwarves' short and stout build. (Gould, "Dwarf-Names," pp. 951, 953, 962-963)

48. The implication is that the food and drink have been enchanted by Mondul to cause friendships to be forgotten. This motif may have come from the Volsung legend (e.g. *Völsunga saga* ch. 25), as may the drink that Mondul offered Bjorn's wife, and the "memory-draught" that he will give her in the next chapter.

49. The motif of a couple maintaining chastity by sleeping with a naked sword between them was probably borrowed from *Tristrams saga og Ísöndar* and/or *Völsunga saga*. It's parodied in *Sturlaugs saga starfsama* (ch. 9, see note 22).

50. The sleep-thorn (*svefnþorn*) is mentioned in *Sigrdrífumál* in the *Poetic Edda* (transl. Orchard, *The Elder Edda*, p. 170) and *Völsunga saga* (ch. 20), in *Hrólfs saga kraka* (ch. 8), in as well as in later Icelandic folklore—and, of course, in "Sleeping Beauty" and allied tales (Grimm, *Teutonic Mythology*, vol. 1, p. 419).

51. This method of keping severed body parts alive appears in several sagas. In *Ynglingasaga* ch. 4, Odin preserves Mimir's head with herbs to keep it alive; in *Egils saga ok Asmundar*, a troll-woman keeps the hero's severed hand alive in a linen cloth with herbs; and in *Völsa þáttr*, a severed horse penis is preserved in the same way.

52. The combination of blue color and a swollen body is typical of decaying corpses, and several undead in the sagas show this combination of features (Þórólfr bægifótr in *Eyrbyggja saga* ch. 63; Glámr in *Grettis saga* ch. 32). Ingibjorg is not merely sick and deranged; she is essentially a *draugr*, an undead corpse.

53. Hollander ("The 'Faithless Wife' Motif," pp. 71-73) points out similarities of this episode with medieval German stories of Salman and Morolf, and German and Slavic references to the hero Walther—all of these contain the "Faithless Wife" motif, in which a man is forced to witness his own wife's infidelity. In the stories of Salman and Morolf the seducer uses herbs to put the wife into a swoon. See also AT 1511, "The Faithless Queen," in Aarne, *The Types of the Folktale*, p. 430.

54. The ability to both heal and cause illness is universal for Germanic dwarves, even more so than their skill as smiths; it appears in Old English medical texts, in medieval German romances, and in Norse sagas. (Battles, "Dwarfs in Germanic Literature," pp. 74-75)

55. "Master Galterus" is Walter of Châtillon, or Galterus de Castillione, author

315

of the 12th-century Latin epic *Alexandreis*. The poem was known in Iceland in a prose translation, *Alexanders saga*, made in 1262–3. (Wolf, *"Alexanders saga"*, pp. 7-8)

56. A similar incident appears in *Hrólfs saga kraka* ch. 34, in which the hero Böðvarr-Bjarki defends the timid Höttr from a flung bone by catching it and throwing it right through the man who flung it, terrifying everyone in the hall. Some of the legendary material in *Hrólfs saga* is very old, but the surviving saga text dates from the 17th century, and it's not clear which saga might have borrowed this episode, assuming that it was borrowed at all.

57. Literally *hvern dauðadag hann skyldi helzt hafa*, "what death-day he should have most," but the sense seems clear from the following sentence.

58. The Winternights (*Vetrnætr*) were several days in mid-October marking the start of the winter season. An important holiday in pagan times, they continued to be marked as secular holidays after Christianization of Iceland.

59. An evil sorceror takes the form of a huge walrus in *Hjálmþes saga* ch. 11, while a witch appears as a walrus and attacks a ship while her body lies on land in *Kormáks saga* ch. 18.

60. *Seiðr* (translated as "sorcery" here) could encompass several kinds of magical effect, but often it involved altering others' mental states, creating illusions or desires. *Seiðr* usually has a wicked reputation in the sagas, and it is said to be especially degrading for men to use (*Ynglinga saga* ch. 7 in Hollander, *Heimskringla*, pp. 10-11). Thus the presence of no fewer than twelve male *seiðmenn* in this episode is especially outrageous.

61. *Seiðr* is commonly worked from a high place, sometimes a roof, but often a specially-built platform or scaffolding, the *seiðhjallr* or *hásæti* (e.g. *Eiríks saga rauða* ch. 4; *Friðþjófs saga* ch. 5). See Heide, "Spinning *Seiðr*," p. 166.

62. In the Eddic poem *Hávamál* (stanza 151; transl. Orchard, *The Elder Edda*, p. 37), the god Odin states that if someone tries to cast a harmful spell on him, he can turn the spell to strike its caster. The poem implies that Odin carves rune letters to work this and other magic spells that he knows; evidently Mondul is doing much the same thing.

63. The Norse is *kómu í opna skjöldu*, literally "they came into open (hollow) shields". An attack from behind and to the left would be directed against the rear of a shield held by a right-handed opponent, and would be especially dangerous.

64. A similar buttock amputation appears in *Örvar-Odds saga* ch. 23. Aside from the gross humor of the situation, a blow on the buttocks (*klámhögg*) was considered shameful; it was symbolically equated with forcing the recipient to submit to sexual penetration and loss of manhood. See Meulengracht Sørensen, *The Unmanly Man*, pp. 68-70, and note 11 to *Hrólfs saga Gautrekssonar*.

65. Legendary and historical sagas usually depict berserks in groups of twelve, especially when they form part of a royal household (e.g. *Hervarar saga* chs. 1-3; *Hrólfs saga kraka* chs. 16, 37; *Grettis saga* ch. 19; *Egils saga* ch. 9).

66. According to Cleasby and Vigfusson's dictionary, a "bonejack" (*beinserkr*, literally "bone shirt") is an abnormal bone growth between the lower ribs and the

spine.

67. The text has *Herkir* here, presumably an error for Haki.

68. *Þorsteins saga Víkingssonar* (ch. 23) also depicts dwarves helping a hero in battle by shooting arrows from a distance.

69. At least three *riddarasögur* mention a coat or other garment that is impervious to poison (see Matyushina, "Magic Mirrors, Monsters, Maiden-Kings", for an overview).

70. *Snákr* means "snake"; unlike its English cognate, it's a poetic term not used in ordinary speech.

71. A sorceress raises those killed in battle to fight in *Hrólfs saga kraka* (ch. 51) and in *Sörla þáttr*; this is evidnetly what Grim has in mind.

72. The motif of a magic bag of winds or gases is common in folklore, best known from the *Odyssey*. Magic bags with various properties appear in the *riddarasögur*, see Matyushina, "Magic Mirrors, Monsters, Maiden-Kings", for an overview.

73. A similar archery duel in which the arrows hit each other in midair appears in *Ketils saga hœngs* (ch. 3).

74. A proverb; see *Njáls saga* ch. 37; *Þorsteins þáttr stangarhöggs*.

75. This seems a rather strange thing to say, but a similar comment turns up in some manuscripts of *Jómsvíkinga saga*; when the Jómsvíking leader Bui gets his lips and chin chopped off, he wryly comments that the Danish girls on Bornholm won't much care for kissing him now (ch. 33; ed. Blake, *The Saga of the Jomsvikings*, p. 37). Tearing off the face of a trollish or sorcerous opponent appears in *Örvar-Odds saga* (ch. 23) and *Orms þáttr Stórólfssonar* (ch. 8).

76. The idea that a dying man can put a curse on his adversary with his last words is a common trope in Norse romances (Schauch, *Romance in Iceland*, pp. 129-130). Thorstein stops the dying ogre Faxi from speaking his last words in *Þorsteins saga Víkingssonar* ch. 23, probably to stop him from speaking a curse.

77. Note that Mondul's first and last appearances in this saga both show him lusting after human women, a trait also shown by the dwarves in the Eddic poem *Alvíssmál* (Orchard, *The Elder Edda*, pp. 108-113) and the tale *Sörla þáttr* (although in these two the women are in fact goddesses), and in several Middle High German romances, notably *König Laurin*. (Battles, "Dwarfs in Germanic Literature," pp. 47, 57-65, 79).

78. Most of the English place names in this part of the saga can be found mentioned by name in the section of *Knýtlinga saga* that deals with Knut's invasion of England in 1016 (chs. 8-12). *Knýtlinga saga* is the probable source of two later passages in this saga (see note 90 below), and it's likely that the author of *Göngu-Hrólfs saga* inserted place names from this source, or a related one— possibly Óttarr the Black's praise-poem on Knutr, which is quoted in *Knýtlinga saga* and includes every English place name seen here. The names don't make geographical sense and cannot be based on any first-hand knowledge. The phrase "the fortress called Brentford" *(borg þá, er Brandfurða heitir)* is identical with a phrase in *Knýtlinga saga* ch. 12 (ed. Bjarni Guðnason, *Danakonunga Sögur*, p. 112).

79. The saga gives his name as *Dungall* and the place as *Dungalsbær*, in other manuscripts it appears as *Dungansbær* or *Dungaðsbær*. Located at the northeastern tip of Scotland, Duncansby appears in *Orkneyinga saga* and *Njáls saga*. The name *Melans* may be a variant of *Moldan* (original Gaelic possibly *Modudhan*), a Scot from Duncansby who is also mentioned in *Njáls saga*. (*Brennu-Njáls saga* ch. 83; ed. Einar Ól. Sveinsson, p. 202 n5)

80. Lindsey (*Lindisey*) is not technically an island, although it was surrounded by fenlands at the time; it is now the northern part of Lincolnshire. It is also referred to in *Knýtlinga saga* (ch. 8) because this is where Knut fights his first battle (ch. 8; ed. Bjarni Guðnason, *Danakonunga Sögur*, p. 106)

81. Marking a field with hazel stakes was traditionally done before *hólmganga*, judicial single combat (e.g. *Kormaks saga* ch. 10), but there are some references to marking an entire battlefield with hazel stakes (*Hervarar saga* ch. 10; *Egils saga* ch. 52; *Hákonar saga góða* ch. 24 and *Óláfs saga Tryggvasonar* ch. 18, in *Heimskringla*). Possibly this was done to indicate ritually that the battle's outcome was meant to be the final and just resolution of the conflict.

82. The same legal provision that invaders may not raid once they have been formally challenged and their battlefield marked with hazel stakes, also appears in *Hervarar saga* ch. 10 (ed. Tolkien, p. 55).

83. This place is *Asatún* in the saga, presumably the same as *Assatún* in *Knýtlinga saga* (ch. 12), the site of the final battle between Knut and Edmund Ironsides in 1016; probably modern Ashingdon, Essex. The forest nearby is called Kanaskógr in the saga, but *Knýtlinga saga* has *Danaskógr*, "Danes' forest". (ed. Bjarni Guðnason, *Danakonunga Sögur*, p. 112-113)

84. *Skorsteinn* appears as the site of yet another battle in 1016 between Knut and Edmund II Ironsides (*Knýtlinga saga* chs. 10; ed. Bjarni Guðnason, *Danakonunga Sögur*, pp. 108-109). The *Anglo-Saxon Chronicle* names this site *Sceorstan*, the present-day Sherston in Wiltshire (ed. Whitelock, p. 95). Since Sherston is landlocked, no Vikings ever sailed there.

85. Norse *pímet ok klaret*, "pyment and claret". *Pyment* is used today for mead brewed with grapes or grape juice (Schramm, *The Compleat Meadmaker*, pp. 121-128) but in the Middle Ages, *pyment* usually meant a sweetened wine. *Claret* or *clary* in the Middle Ages referred to wine (not necessarily red) poured through a bag of spices, flavoring and also clarifying it. (Adamson, *Food in Medieval Times*, pp. 50-51)

86. The preceding two sentences are essentially a long, rhythmic, half-rhyming string of dependent clauses, with all the verbs as present participles ending in *–andi* (equivalent to English *–ing*). This device, known as *homoeoteleuton* (words with similar endings), is typical of the elevated rhetorical style found in translated "sagas of chivalry" and also in saints' lives and other religious texts. The entire description of the wedding feast resembles the "sagas of chivalry," with a heavy use of foreign words (*kurteisir, klaret, salteríum*, etc.), parallel clauses and synonyms, and assorted flourishes. (Þórir Óskarson, "Rhetoric and Style," p. 366-369)

87. The text reads *Helsingjaborg*, which is the Norse name for Helsingborg in Sweden. No town in England is known to have had that name; it's presumably a mistake for *Helsingjaport*, used in *Heimskringla* for Hastings, but itself probably a scribal error for Old English *Hæstinga port*. (Gade, "Northern Lights on the Battle of Hastings", p. 65 n1)

88. The source of this geographic digression is uncertain; it might be a highly abridged version of the opening of Bede's *History*, which also mentions crops, cloth, and metals. In any case, it agrees well with most descriptions of England in both historical and legendary sagas, as a rich country with excellent trading prospects. See Fjalldal, *Anglo-Saxon England*, pp. 25-26.

89. Harald Sigurdsson is better known as Harald Hardrada. His sailing up the Limfjord and having his ships dragged over a narrow isthmus and into the North Sea is described in *Haralds saga Sigurðarsson* in *Heimskringla*, ch. 60, where "Harald's Neck" (*Haraldseið* in this saga) is called *Lúsbreið* ("broad as a louse"). In *Heimskringla*, Harald is said to have been escaping the Danes, not the Swedish king.

90. This digression closely parallels a description of Denmark in *Knýtlinga saga*, ch. 32 (ed. Guðnason, *Danakonunga Sögur*, pp. 150-152). *Knýtlinga saga* lists the "important cities" as diocesan seats and includes information on their bishops and churches. The author of *Göngu-Hrólfs saga* did not mention the churches, possibly because it would have clashed with the pagan atmosphere he was trying to create (Hartmann, *The Gǫngu-Hrólfssaga*, pp. 72-75). On the other hand, he may have used a lost source that was also used by the author of *Knýtlinga saga*, who added the church-related material (Jackson, "On the Possible Sources of the Textual Map," pp. 62-70).

91. The second part of *Hrómunds saga Gripssonar* (chs. 6-8) tells how King Olaf was attacked by Helgi Haddingjaskati ("Champion of the Haddings") but defended by Hromund Gripsson.

92. In the surviving version of *Hrómunds saga Gripssonar*, Olaf's sisters are called Dagny and Svanhvit. After a battle, Svanhvit helps Hromund, but she takes him to an old man named Hagal and his wife, who nurse him back to health (ch. 8). As discussed in the Introduction, this difference is evidence of how the story of Hromund Gripsson grew and accreted material; the author of *Göngu-Hrólfs saga* may have been working from an older version of the story in which Hagal and his wife had not been interpolated. (Andrews, "Studies in the Fornaldarsǫgur Norðrlanda I", pp. 39-40; Jesch, "Hrómundr Gripsson Revisited," pp. 94-95)

93. Several persons named Hörða-Knútr are mentioned in various sources, but only the youngest—King Hardecanute of England—is well attested historically. The name might have been borrowed from *Knýtlinga saga*.

The Saga of Hromund Gripsson

1. The text as printed by Guðni Jónsson, ultimately from manuscript AM 587b,

has *Görðum í Danmörk*, "Gardar in Denmark." As a common noun, *garðar* means "towns; fortresses", and the author of AM 587b may have meant that Olaf ruled over towns in Denmark. But other manuscripts just have *Görðum*, "Gardar" (Andrews, "Studies in the Fornaldarsǫgur Norðrlanda," p. 529), which usually refers to Russia (often called *Garðaríki*, "realm of towns"). This reading makes more sense, since both *Göngu-Hrólfs saga* and *Egils saga einhenda ok Ásmundar berserkjabana* place Olaf's father in Russia (although they disagree as to who Olaf's father actually is; see footnote 2). However, Andrews (p. 543 n1) read *Görðum* as a mistake for *Hörðum*, Hordaland in Norway.

2. Asmund is one of the heroes of *Egils saga einhenda ok Ásmundar berserkjabana*. The *Gnóð* was his legendary ship. Note that *Göngu-Hrólfs saga* makes Olaf the son of Hrólf, not Asmund.

3. Hrok the Black appears in *Hálfs saga ok Hálfsrekka*.

4. The text has *Úlfasker*, "Wolf Skerries," which don't seem to exist. Andrews considers this an error for *Elfasker*, the Elfar Skerries, at the mouth of the Göta alv river ("Studies in the Fornaldarsǫgur Norðrlanda," p. 543).

5. Old Norse *Brynþvari*; the word *brynþvari* is used in *Egils saga* ch. 53 for a spear with a swordlike blade. See note 6 to *Bósa saga*.

6. The reason for the goat's beard and hat isn't clear. Brown ("Saga of Hrómund Gripsson," p. 63) considered it simply comedy, but Hromund may be concealing his identity from Hrongvid, since a dying enemy might cast a deadly curse on his foe if he knew his name (e.g. *Fáfnismál* 1-2; transl. Orchard, *The Elder Edda*, pp. 160-161). Uncanny villains who can't be cut by iron weapons are fairly common in legendary sagas (e.g. Sóti in *Göngu-Hrólfs saga* chs. 17-18), and it is more or less standard operating procedure for heroes to dispatch them with clubs—as Hromund does again at the very end of the saga.

7. *Blámenn*, "black men", are stock villains in the legendary sagas. The word is occasionally used for Africans, but *blámenn* in the legendary sagas have nothing to do with actual Africans. Hideous and trollish, their main function is to be killed entertainingly by heroes.

8. The text reads *Var þat á nóttu*, "That was at night"—but the point of Hromund's dealings with Thrain seems to be that Thrain is weak by day and strong at night. If it is night when Hromund enters the mound, the point is lost and the timing of the scene is confused. Brown suggests that the saga writer misread *Griplur*, which at this point in the narrative reads *nógt um þókti nadda lesti, nær sem væri frykrinn mesti*, "the shield-breaker felt that he was nearly overcome by the greatest stench" (II.60; Finnur Jónsson, *Fernir Forníslenskir Rímnaflokkar*, p. 26). If the manuscript was partly illegible here, the saga writer may have read *nótt*, "night", for *nógt*, "almost". ("Saga of Hrómund Gripsson," p. 76) I've taken the liberty of emending my translation to something closer to the sense of *Griplur*.

9. The implication seems to be that Thrain must consume special food from the cauldron in order to have his full strength—a motif that appears in Saxo's *History of the Danes* III.76-77 (ed. Ellis-Davidson and Fisher, pp. 74-75).

10. The text reads that the cauldron is *fullr í búki*, "full in body" or "full in torso;

full in belly," which is ambiguous. Kershaw interprets *búkr* as the cauldron's own rounded shape (*Stories and Ballads*, p. 67), while Bachman and Erlingsson read the phrase to mean that the cauldron is right up against Thrain's belly (*Six Old Icelandic Sagas*, p. 6). I've followed Stitt (*Beowulf and the Bear's Son*, p. 230 n20), who noted that a later manuscript of the saga reads *fullr af búkum*, "full of bodies." *Griplur* also reads *fullur ketill af búkum* (III.4; Finnur Jónsson, *Fernir Forníslenskir Rímnaflokkar*, p. 27). Several sagas depict trolls and giants as cannibals, and some specifically depict them feeding on human flesh cooked in a cauldron, e.g. *Hálfdanar saga Brönufóstra* ch. 4.

11. Stitt points out that flesh-tearing nails are more typical of giants and trolls than of the undead (*Beowulf and the Bear's Son*, p. 142). The comparison with a cat may be more than simple metaphor, since trolls sometimes appear as cats; *Orms þáttr Stórólfssonar* (ch. 8) includes a troll in cat-shape who claws the hero, and in *Vatnsdæla saga* (ch. 28) the sorcerous villain Thorolf Sledge has a herd of twenty huge black cats that are *mjök tryllitr*, "very trollish".

12. Possibly the same as the legendary King Sæmingr. Snorri Sturluson calls Sæmingr a legendary king of Norway who was the son of the god Odin (*Edda*, Prologue 11, ed. Faulkes, vol. 1, p. 6; *Ynglinga saga* 8, transl. Hollander, *Heimskringla*, pp. 12-13), but also cites a now-lost poem that states that he was the son of the god Yngvi-Freyr, who was especially worshipped in Sweden. (*Hemiskringla*, Prologue, transl. Hollander, p. 3).

13. In *Griplur* (IV.4-7; Finnur Jónsson, *Fernir Forníslenskir Rímnaflokkar*, p. 31), Hromund gives a ring to a man named Grundi, in return for Grundi's gift of an excellent dog named Hrok, and Vali (or Vóli, as his name appears in *Griplur*) kills the dog. The saga-writer may have misread or misremembered the text of *Griplur*, or worked from a defective manuscript (Brown, "Saga of Hrómund Gripsson," p. 74).

14. The saga actually states that the king makes this threat, but according to *Griplur*, it is Hromund who promises to pay Vali back. This makes more dramatic sense, given that the king will soon be accepting Vali's slander of Hromund. This is probably an error in the sags resulting from the writer misreading a manuscript of *Griplur*. (Brown, "Saga of Hrómund Gripsson," p. 76) I have emended the saga accordingly.

15. Some authors (e.g. Kershaw, *Stories and Ballads*, p. 59) have seen a reflection of the myth of Balder's death in the characters Bildr and Vali, and in the name of Hromund's sword Mistletoe (since in Saxo Grammaticus's version of the myth of Balder, he is killed with a sword named Mistletoe, not a sprig of the plant mistletoe). The relationship, if any, seems very distant.

16. In the saga text as printed, the kings are named Halding, and Helgi's valkyrie lover is named Lara. The names are Hadding and Kára in *Griplur*, as well as in *Helgakviða Hundingsbana II* and other sources, and I've emended them here; Lara may be Rafn's misreading of the name *Cara* in manuscript (Andrews, "Studies in the Fornaldarsǫgur Norðrlanda," p. 528). The tradition of a pair of kings both named Hadding seems to be a very old one (Turville-Petre, *Myth and*

Religion of the North, pp. 216-220).

17. Jesch points out that this battle is modeled on a more famous battle on the ice of Lake Vanern—the battle between Aðils and Áli, told in the lost *Skjöldunga saga* (see Miller, "Fragments of Danish History", p. 18), described by Snorri Sturluson in *Ynglinga saga* (ch. 29; in *Heimskringla*, transl. Hollander, p. 33) and the *Prose Edda* (*Skáldskaparmál* 44, ed. Faulkes, pp. 58-59), and even alluded to in *Beowulf* (2392-2396). Hromund and his eleven brothers correspond to Hrólfr kraki's twelve berserks who fight on Aðils's side. ("Hrómundr Gripsson Revisited," p. 93)

18. "Skilled in many things" (*margkunnigr*) is a common saga euphemism for knowing magic or having second sight.

19. This is a variant of a folklore motif found throughout Europe and Asia (N211.1.4, "Lost sword found in fish", a version of N211.1, "Lost ring found in fish"; Thompson, *Motif-Index of Folk Literature*, vol. 5, pp. 87-88). But the immediate source for the episode was probably *Hervarar saga ok Heiðreks*, in which the hero Angantýr Heiðreksson finds the sword Tyrfing inside a pike.

20. This episode seems to have been borrowed from *Helgakviða Hundingsbana II* 1-4 (transl. Orchard, *The Elder Edda*, pp. 135-136). In these verses, Helgi is sheltered by a man named Hagal, who dresses him as a bondmaid and sets him to grinding grain in order to hide him from the king's wicked counsellor Blind.

21. Episodes in which one character has many foreboding dreams, all of which are foolishly rationalized away, appear in *Völsunga saga* (chs. 36-37) and in *Atlamál* 14-26 (transl. Orchard, *The Elder Edda*, pp. 217-219), one of the Völsung cycle of poems in the *Poetic Edda*. They also appear in the legendary *Hálfs saga* (ch. 11).

22. Again, we have the widespread motif of bashing an enemy to death with clubs because he cannot be killed with edged weapons thanks to some sorcery or monstrous nature. (e.g. *Hrólfs saga Gautrekssonar* note 14)

23. In the printed saga, the old man's name is Bavis, but this is probably a mistake for *Bölvís*, which is how his name appears in *Griplur* (VI.51; Finnur Jónsson, *Fernir Forníslenskir Rímnaflokkar*, p. 42). *Bölvísi* means "malicious" or "baleful"; in *Helgakviða Hundingsbana II*, the king's counsellor Blind is called *Blindr inn bölvísi*. Saxo Grammaticus also mentions a blind kings' counsellor named Bolwisus who delights in stirring up enmity (*History of the Danes* VII.232-236, ed. Ellis-Davidson and Fisher, pp. 213-216).

The Tale of Gift-Ref and the Valley-Fools

1. The L text actually says that his gold was eaten by *strútfuglar*, "ostriches," and the verse that would be expected here seems to be missing. Manuscript M is also missing the verse and has the nonsensical *strútflugur*, "ostrich-flies;" manuscript E has a verse with *slíkir fuglar*, "such birds"; and manuscript K has a verse with *stór sniglar*, "large snails." The younger saga begins Fjolmod's verse with *stuttir sniglar*, "stumpy snails," which is probably the original wording, and I've emended the text accordingly. Presumably L was copied from a manuscript in

which the verse was unclear, and the scribe of L made the best sense he could out of something like *st...t...glar.*

2. The words are similar to the verse preserved in the younger saga and in manuscripts E and K of the older saga, but much of the verse is missing in L, and the words are not indicated as poetry. Again, it seems likely that L was copied from a manuscript with missing or faded words.

3. A hersir was a local military leader who owed allegiance to a jarl or king.